FRACTURED VERDICT

AN ALEX HAYES LEGAL THRILLER
BOOK 1

L.T. RYAN

WITH
LAURA CHASE

LIQUID MIND MEDIA

ONE

THE GAVEL POUNDED, an empty sound swallowed by the cavernous courtroom. Another win for the defense, another monster back on the streets. The sharp sting of injustice settled like a weight on my chest. The defense attorney smirked as he shook the defendant's hand, a snake congratulating a rat on a job well done.

I gripped my pen tightly, resisting the urge to roll my eyes. Barely. Judge Campbell offered nothing more than a bland smile as he gathered his papers, either oblivious or indifferent to the travesty of justice that had just played out in his courtroom. Just another day at the office. For him, anyway. For me, it felt like another tiny piece of my soul had been chipped away.

The defense attorney—Jameson, smug as always—began making his way over to me, his expensive loafers clicking on the wood floor with a confidence that made me sick. "Better luck next time, Hayes." His voice dripped with condescension.

I snapped my briefcase shut with more force than necessary. The metallic click echoed through the emptying gallery like a gunshot. "Spare me," I muttered back, already on my way to the exit. I couldn't stomach the sight of his self-satisfied grin for another second.

Outside, the courthouse bustled with predators and prey. Lawyers

1

in two-thousand-dollar suits stalked the halls, their eyes gleaming with the thrill of their next paycheck. Deputies shuffled along with handcuffed defendants in tow, their eyes vacant, destined for the revolving door of the criminal justice system. It was all routine. A machine that churned on, uncaring and unfeeling.

My heels clicked sharply on the cold tile floor, keeping time with the tap-tap-tap of my frustration. Another slam-dunk case lost to the sly defense antics of people like Jameson. Facts warped by rhetorical tricks. Justice stymied by legal loopholes. No one cared about truth anymore, just who could put on the best show.

I rounded the corner and nearly collided with Lisa Cooper. She'd only been with the Harris County district attorney's office for two years now, but she was sharp. Most kids her age were still working the habeas circuit, buried in paperwork and writing replies to bullshit habeas corpus petitions from prisoners. Lisa, though, had proven herself early on and was already running support on bigger cases like mine.

"Alex, hi!" she greeted, her voice too chipper, her bright smile entirely out of place given our surroundings. "Heard you knocked it out of the park in there."

I snorted. "Oh yeah. Grand slam. Guy got probation for assault."

Lisa faltered. She was one of the few who still believed in the system. Not jaded yet. She hadn't been around long enough to know how broken it really was. I envied her, even as I pitied her naivety.

"You did your best." She placed her hand gently on my arm. Her touch was warm but it did nothing to ease the cold creeping inside me. "That's all any of us can do."

"My best doesn't seem to be good enough anymore." I tried to force my lips into a smile, but they could only manage a grimace. "I'm just so tired of the games these defense attorneys play. And the judges eat it up."

Lisa squeezed my arm. "It'll get better. Focus on the next case. We'll get through this, one day at a time."

Her optimism used to give me hope. Now, it just felt like another reminder of how far I'd fallen. But I pressed my lips together and thanked her. No need to spread my bitterness.

"I'll catch you later," I said, stepping away from her comforting hand. "I need to check in at the office."

"Right. I'm headed to a first appearance."

"Good luck."

The heat hit me like a wall as I exited the courthouse, the Houston sun beating down mercilessly. I started the two block walk to the DA's office, where my little cubicle of heaven resided. I'd been working this racket for the past five years since graduating from Texas A&M. Sometimes it felt like five decades. Most of my classmates had taken the blood money and gone to work for the oil companies.

Maybe I should have, too. I'd be making a lot more than seventy-five grand a year with the promise of a pension. But this was where I'd ended up. I had been more like Lisa at that point in my life, thinking I could make a difference by putting criminals behind bars.

But the truth was, the system didn't care. It chewed you up, spit you out, and asked for more. I'd learned that the hard way. Most days, it felt like a never-ending cycle of plea deals and red tape, the real criminals slipping through the cracks while we locked up the ones who couldn't afford a decent lawyer. I wasn't changing the world; I was just keeping it spinning in the same broken orbit. The idealism I had back then? It had worn thin, like the soles of my shoes after years of walking the courthouse halls.

My phone vibrated in my pocket, shaking me out of my thoughts. The caller ID flashed USP Beaumont, a high-security level federal prison located in Beaumont, Texas. I pressed the red button, rejecting the call. The walk in the brutal Houston summer sun was hot enough. I didn't need my criminal father to make my temper flare hotter.

I twisted my blonde hair up into a bun to get it off my neck for the walk. Most blonde women you see in Texas weren't born that way. I remember one time at a courthouse mixer, this woman with bottle-blonde curls kept eyeing me across the room. When I walked by, she leaned in and asked, "Honey, who does your color? It's perfect." I had to bite back a laugh when I told her it was natural. Apparently, I'd inherited it from my mother.

The AC was a wave of icy relief, cooling the sweat on my skin as I entered the DA's office. This was probably the only thing I enjoyed about walking from the courthouse to the office.

Before I got the chance to put my things down, Janice was hailing me. She always looked like she was out of breath, her face flushed, her hands shaking slightly. Maybe it was because she was old enough to be my grandmother. Maybe it was because her daily walk to the donut shop a block over was her idea of sufficient exercise. I'd asked her about her plans to retire, but she said she liked working. But I knew as well as anyone that a lot of people lied. I'd seen it time and time again —in my job and in my family. People clung to things because they were too scared to admit it was time to let go, too proud to show weakness, even when they were drowning. The victim in all this? The truth.

Janice didn't like working. She just couldn't admit that without it, she'd have nothing left.

"Tom wants to see you," she said, panting like she'd just run a marathon. I glanced at her, feeling a twinge of guilt. Maybe I was being too harsh. She was Tom's assistant, after all, and Tom was not known for being a patient man. It wasn't really her fault he made her run around like a maniac.

I took a deep breath as I entered Tom's office, bracing myself for whatever was coming next. The air in here felt different—heavier, like it had been soaked in too many tense conversations over the years. Tom Matthews, District Attorney for Harris County, sat behind his mahogany desk, papers strewn about in organized chaos. The smell of stale coffee lingered in the air, and the hum of the air conditioner droned in the background. His office was always a little too cold, and it didn't help the nervous knot forming in my stomach.

Perhaps he had already heard about my loss today. Unfortunately for my career, I'd been taking a lot of losses as of late. I was still trying to figure out why. After all, I was a prosecutor. I was supposed to be tough on crime, but it seemed like all I was doing was rolling over for it like a submissive puppy.

It wasn't that the cases were weak, or that I wasn't prepared. It was the judges, the politics, the endless bureaucracy. The defense always seemed to find a way to manipulate the system, to twist the law in their favor, while I was left playing by the rules.

Tom leaned back in his leather chair, his fingers steepled over his chest. His brow was furrowed and a slight scowl was pulling at the corners of his mouth. In my experience, this was never a good sign. He was only in his mid-forties, but the job had given him a gray temple, only on the left side of his head. Other than that, he was pretty unremarkable to look at—just another overworked lawyer beaten down by the system, much like the rest of us.

"Have a seat, Alex." His voice carried a weight that matched the tension in the room.

I sat in the armchair across the table from him, smoothing my pantsuit. It was a reflex, a way to ground myself when things felt uncertain. I was pretty sure this was how I got fired.

Tom sighed and removed his glasses. His eyes, usually sharp and calculating, were grave.

Yep, I was definitely getting fired.

"There's been a murder," he said. "High-profile case."

"I'll get my things—wait, what?" I blinked, caught off guard.

"A murder, Alex." He rubbed his gray temple, like the stress of the job was a permanent fixture there. Maybe that's why only the left side had changed color. "Are you listening?"

My stomach dropped, the room spinning just slightly. "Sorry, yes, but what's that got to do with me?"

He looked at me with wild eyes, as if he expected me to read his mind. "Everything. I'm promoting you to the capital crimes division."

The words hung there, and for a moment, I wasn't sure if I was awake. I closed my eyes, trying to shake off the absurdity of it. When I reopened them, Tom was still sitting there, staring at me with that serious expression, his fingers now tapping lightly on his desk.

"You're promoting me?" I was incredulous.

"Issue?" He raised an eyebrow.

I shook my head, still trying to process what was happening. "I just don't understand why."

He sighed. Tom was always sighing. "Look, I'm going to be straight with you, Alex. You're a woman."

"Thanks for noticing."

"You're also the only female prosecutor we have that's got enough experience in the crimes division. For some reason, most female assistant DAs end up in the civil transactional side."

"I hear they sync their menses over there, too," I muttered. Tom had never been one for political correctness, as this conversation demonstrated. But then again, most men in Texas weren't.

"Edward Martin. Multimillionaire business tycoon. He's accused of killing his wife."

Edward Martin. His name was familiar, I'd seen it in the papers. Rich, powerful, and now a murder suspect. Great. My mind was already racing, trying to piece together the case that was about to consume my life.

"Media's all over this," Tom continued. "The mayor's feeling the heat. It's gonna be a circus."

I rubbed my temples, the familiar throb of an impending headache building behind my eyes. "Wonderful. Just what I need—a media frenzy on top of everything else."

"I know it's not ideal. But a female prosecutor is going to present better to the jury given the nature of the crime."

"Is it a slam dunk?"

His face told me everything, but he still replied aloud. "No."

"And we're going for what crime?"

"First-degree."

I scoffed, leaning back in my chair. The first rule of prosecution: don't bring a case to trial if you have no chance of winning. When you have that chance, you, the prosecutor, are in control of what to charge a defendant with. If you can't get him on first degree murder, drop it down to voluntary manslaughter. If you can't get him on that, well, there's a host of charges underneath that will be easier to prove to a jury.

"Can you explain why?" I asked. "Why take this case when the defendant is already attracting media attention?"

"Political pressure," Tom admitted. At least he had the decency to be honest about it.

District attorneys were elected officials in Texas, and Tom was coming up on an election year. He needed a big win. If he didn't bring Ed in for first-degree, his opponent would have a field day. And in the game of politics, perception was everything.

People thought justice was blind, but that was just in the movies. If Lady Justice really existed, she'd be holding a wad of dollar bills in one hand, an election campaign banner in the other. And she definitely wouldn't be wearing a blindfold.

Part of me wanted to refuse, to tell Tom to shove this case where the sun didn't shine. I was greener than green when it came to capital crimes. If I lost this case, my reputation might never recover. But the other part—the part still clinging to some shred of idealism—couldn't back down. However broken the system was, turning away would make me complicit in its failures.

I met Tom's gaze, determination settling in my gut. "Tell me about the case."

He exhaled, a hint of tension easing from his shoulders. "Caroline Martin was found dead in the couple's Houston home. Blunt force trauma to the head. Bruise marks all around her neck. Edward claims he was with his mistress at the time."

"I guess he's not worried about the missus finding out anymore," I said dryly. "Is there a schedule yet?"

"Defendant refused to waive the Speedy Trial Act."

I squinted my eyes at Tom, suspicion prickling at the back of my mind. "What aren't you telling me?"

"Trial starts in two weeks. July twenty-second."

"Two *weeks*?" I all but yelled. By refusing to waive his Speedy Trial Act rights, the defendant had forced the court's hand to start the trial within seventy days of the indictment, leaving us with barely any time to prepare.

"And Michael Donovan is defending."

Just one blow after another. Michael Donovan. The shark of defense attorneys. Silver-tongued and ruthless. Just the sound of his name made my blood boil. Even if I hadn't made the mistake of sleeping with the man, I'd still hate him.

I clenched my jaw, trying to rein in the surge of anger. "So Martin's got himself the best dirty lawyer money can buy. Let me guess, you assumed they'd plea out or eventually waive speedy trial and now they're trying to pull the timecard on us."

Tom nodded, frustration evident in his eyes. "Exactly. Tess was handling the case, but she left on medical leave. This bombshell just landed on me. I thought we'd have more time to work out a deal or prepare a solid case."

Tessa Caldwell was the only senior prosecutor in the Capital Crimes Division who was female, and her sudden absence had clearly thrown Tom off balance.

"But now we're staring down the barrel of a gun."

"It appears so." Tom leveled me with a dour look. "Donovan will pull out all the stops on this one. The evidence against Martin is solid. But with Donovan involved..."

Donovan had a reputation for playing dirty—skirting right along the edge of what was legal, and sometimes taking a step or two beyond. I'd seen him twist witness testimonies so hard, they snapped in half. And then there was the time he'd managed to get crucial evidence thrown out on a technicality, letting a guilty man walk free. He wasn't just good; he was dangerous. And the worst part? I knew that better than anyone.

"Things just got a lot more complicated." I met Tom's gaze. "I'll do what I can, but I can't make any guarantees." The words tasted bitter on my tongue. "But you already know that. Don't you, Tom?"

Tom studied me for a moment, then nodded. "I know you'll do your best. That's all we can ask for."

I resisted the urge to laugh. Caroline Martin deserved justice, but that ideal had died long ago. Now, there was only the law. And often, the two were not the same.

TWO

THE HARSH FLUORESCENT lights of the precinct stung my eyes as I strode to Detective Daniel Andrews' desk. His dark hair balanced out his somewhat graying beard and piercing blue eyes. He was in his late forties, but his beard aged him.

"Afternoon, counselor." He glanced up when I tapped a finger on his desk. "Heard you're the lucky one to get the Martin case."

"So lucky I should have bought a lottery ticket today instead."

I took a seat in one of the empty chairs. I had worked with Andrews before. He was good at what he did. That made my job easier. Prosecutors and detectives didn't always work closely together on every case, but when it came to complex or high-profile crimes—especially homicides—the partnership became crucial. Detectives gathered the evidence and put the pieces together at the crime scene, while prosecutors built the case in court, making sure everything held up legally. We relied on each other to ensure that no stone was left unturned. A weak investigation made for a weak case, and as the prosecutor, I needed to be on the same page with Andrews from the start to make sure we were covering every angle before Donovan's team started picking things apart.

"Can you give me the quick and dirty?" I asked. "Let's start with the crime scene. I want fresh eyes on it before Donovan's team sweeps in."

"Donovan's on the case?" Andrews had spent enough time developing cases only for Donovan to blow them up in his face, too.

"Yeah. Lucky us, right?"

Andrews shuffled through photos of the stately Houston mansion and plopped them on the table. "Lucky us."

I pulled a few of the photos over. One of the mansion, one of the bedroom with blood stains on the carpet, and one of a very dead Caroline Martin hanging off the edge of the bed.

The image was jarring. Her face was a mask of pain, frozen in her final moments. Her neck was mottled with deep, dark bruises, the clear marks of strangulation. Her eyes were half-open, staring vacantly into the distance, as if they had seen the abyss and were now forever trapped in that horror. A large, gruesome gash marred her forehead, a jagged line of torn flesh and dried blood from where her head had struck the nightstand.

My stomach churned. I had seen dead bodies before, but nothing like this. Caroline's death was violent, personal. The brutality of it was palpable, seeping through the photo and into my bones. I swallowed hard, forcing down the bile rising in my throat.

"She was found like this?" I asked, my voice steady despite the turmoil churning inside.

Andrews nodded. "Edward reported the murder himself. Called 911 when he arrived at the house in the morning. Claims he spent the night with his mistress, only to return to find his number one as dead as a doorknob."

I gave him a weird look. "Nail."

"What?"

"Door-nail. The phrase is 'as dead as a doornail.'"

He shrugged. "You're the lawyer."

I glanced at the photo again, the brutal marks of the attack clear as day. "Seems like more of an execution than a murder. What evidence do we have on a potential killer besides Ed?"

"No signs of forced entry. No fingerprints recovered at the scene other than Ed's."

I rolled my eyes and held back a groan. "Are you serious? The hell is Tom thinking, putting me up for a case like this? First-degree and we've basically got nothing?"

"We'll dig some stuff up."

"Since when did you become Mr. Optimistic?" I gave him a sideways look. "Because I don't like it."

My phone buzzed. It was a text from Tom.

Head to the office. Holding a press conference in 30 minutes to announce you on the case.

Glorious.

"The media circus awaits," I said to Andrews as I stood. "Can you put together a timeline for me?"

"Already working on that, plus a potential witness list."

"You know just how I like it," I said with a hint of a smile.

"Any thought to who'll be second on this?"

"Not yet," I said, but that was not entirely true. "After I handle the media."

"Try not to let them get under your skin."

I smiled tightly. "I make no promises."

I UNLOCKED MY FRONT DOOR, the click of the lock echoing in the empty entryway. The house was modest, tucked into a quiet suburban neighborhood where the streets were lined with trimmed hedges and two-story homes that looked eerily similar. The familiar sight of home greeted me—dim lighting, the faint scent of lavender from the candle I'd lit last night, and the silence that seemed heavier tonight than usual. It was the kind of house that felt empty, despite being well-kept. The living room was minimalist: neutral tones, modern furniture, but no personal touches. No family photos hung on the walls, no mementos cluttered the shelves. Just clean, impersonal order. After the press conference, I thought coming home would offer some relief. Instead, the weight of the day followed me inside.

I set my leather satchel on the kitchen island and grabbed a glass of wine before sinking onto the couch. The cushions, though soft, felt suffocating, like they were pulling me deeper into the memories I was trying to escape. The wine tasted faintly bitter—a poor choice for tonight.

The voicemail icon blinked accusingly on my phone screen. I didn't need to check to know who it was from. My father. The absence of family photos seemed to mock me now, the gaps where memories should have been displayed as if the house itself was void of warmth. I had to give the old man credit. He had been leaving messages since the day he got taken away, as if each one could undo the damage of the past. Asking to meet. Attempting to explain away his betrayal. But there were no explanations that could fix what he'd done.

With a sharp exhale, I deleted it without even listening, just as I had done with all the others. The familiar sense of bitterness settled in my gut, twisting and churning. Some wounds just couldn't be mended. The damage had been done long ago, and no amount of words would ever make it right.

I took a sip of the wine. The liquid felt cold, but it didn't cool the heat building behind my eyes. I wasn't going to cry. I never cried anymore. Tears wouldn't change anything.

With a heavy sigh, I sank deeper into the couch and closed my eyes, but the darkness behind my eyelids only brought unwanted memories flooding back. I could still see the courtroom, the sterile, cold walls closing in around me. I was in my final year of law school. Except, I wasn't there for education. I was there, watching from the back, trying to disappear into the shadows, as my father pleaded guilty.

I had finals that week—classes I was barely keeping up with as my world crumbled around me. While my classmates were cramming for exams, I was watching my father's life fall apart. I should've been focusing on school, on my future. But how could I? Having a felon for a father was bad enough. Having one while I was in law school, the place where I was supposed to be shaping my career, was worse. It felt like a cosmic joke—one I wasn't in on.

The bailiffs cuffed his wrists without remorse, letting my father squirm and grunt against the cold metal restraints. His once-strong frame seemed smaller, weaker. As they led him away, his eyes met mine. The naked anguish there was seared into my memory, a permanent scar that I could never erase. In that moment, the last traces of my childhood innocence shattered, leaving jagged pieces behind.

I had always wanted to be a lawyer. It wasn't just a career choice—it was in my blood. My mother had been a lawyer and I used to watch Perry Mason reruns on public television when other kids were glued to the Disney Channel.

I had dreamed of following in her footsteps, of standing in courtrooms and fighting for justice. But the irony wasn't lost on me. The system that had taken my mother had now claimed my father, too. The system I had so desperately wanted to be a part of had ripped my family apart, piece by piece.

Maybe that's when the jadedness started to set in. After my father was taken away, I withdrew from my friends. What was I supposed to say? That my dad was a criminal, and I was still trying to make sense of it? I pushed everyone away, one by one, convinced that no one could understand. They all had normal families, normal lives. Mine had been turned into a spectacle, a cautionary tale.

The years that followed were a blur of sleepless nights and strained smiles. The tight knot of anger, frustration, and guilt wrapped itself around me and never let go. It fueled me, drove me to finish law school and pass the bar, but it also left me hollow. I threw myself into my work, hoping that somewhere in the fight for justice, I could find redemption—not for my father, but for me.

But every case, every guilty verdict, felt like a drop in the ocean. Nothing could fill the void left by the legal system, by the way it had taken everything from me—first my mother, and then my father. And yet, here I was, still a part of it. Still trying to make it work. Trying to prove that not everyone was corrupted by greed like my father had been.

I hated him for that. For proving that no one was immune to the lure of money. For betraying the ideals I had built my life around. He wasn't the man I thought he was. And maybe, in some way, I wasn't the person I had hoped to be either.

With one hand holding my glass of wine, and the other clutching my emotional security throw pillow, I opened my eyes and blinked back tears. It had been over five years, yet the rawness remained. I couldn't handle this. Not right now. Throwing myself into work had staved off the pain before, and it would again.

Which was what I was going to do tonight. I got up and pulled the Martin folder out of my briefcase. The files spilled out onto my kitchen table. Photographs, grand jury testimony, criminal records, all of it landing in a heap.

I wasn't the type of person to let anyone else organize a case file for me. Lots of attorneys let their paralegals or even legal assistants handle this sort of work, seeing it as beneath them. I, however, wanted to see all of it. Process all of it. Make sense of all of it. Then, I would organize it.

I grabbed the persons of interest list first. Most were familiar names—wealthy socialites, politicians, CEOs who always seemed to evade consequences. Rachel Adams was at the top of the list, noted as Ed's alibi. The mistress.

I started digging through the papers to find anything else on Rachel. Female, late twenties, executive assistant to Edward Martin at Martin Corp. I rolled my eyes. How cliché.

I grabbed Ed's interrogation transcript, stating his claim to have been with Rachel the morning Caroline was murdered. That's a pretty good alibi, if it proved to be true. I made a note to dig deeper into Rachel's background.

Character evidence wasn't usually admissible in criminal cases. However, if the defense brought up Rachel's character—intentionally or not—it would "open the door" for me to attack it in court. Normally, Donovan was too seasoned to make a rookie mistake like that. He knew better than to let character evidence slip in. But, with the whole mistress angle, he might not have much of a choice. If Donovan's back was up against the wall, he might have to tread into dangerous territory to salvage Ed's defense, and I'd be ready if he did.

Even after combing through the file again and again, doubt started creeping in. Something wasn't adding up. Usually, in cases like this, the motive jumps off the page—clear, simple. But not this time.

Why would Ed want his wife dead? From what I gathered, she knew about the affair. Hell, it seemed like half the office did. So why kill her now? What had changed?

There was a piece missing, or we were looking at the wrong man.

Maybe I needed to look at this with fresh eyes. I definitely needed someone to talk it through with. More than that, I needed to choose my second chair.

There were plenty of senior prosecutors I could choose at the office. Ones who had far more experience in major crimes than I did. But as I thought about each one of them, I found myself dismissing them for various reasons.

Mark was just too old. His last case, he got himself confused about who the defendant was when questioning a witness.

Bobby was too full of himself. I didn't even know that he would agree to serve as second chair. If he did, he'd probably be trying to oust me every second he got.

Philip? I couldn't. The man was from Virginia and he was damn proud of it. Talked with an accent and wore a different colored bow tie every day. Not that either of those things would be problematic. What was problematic about Philip was that he didn't believe women should be lawyers.

Tom was right. There weren't many of my kind at the office. Right now, it was just me and Lisa.

I sat up straighter and swirled my wine.

What about Lisa?

It was a crazy idea, but I'd rather have her than some washed-up senior prosecutor who would only get in the way. Besides, Lisa might look at things differently. That was always an asset on a case like this.

The doorbell rang. I jolted from my seat on the floor in front of the coffee table to answer it.

Opening the door, I grabbed the brown paper bag on the ground and headed back to the kitchen table. I took my carton of lo mein out and put it on top of the folder of victim photos. I didn't suppose Caroline would mind much. And, if she did, I doubted she would tell me.

THREE

I PUSHED through the heavy glass doors of the office, welcoming the cool air that instantly wrapped around me—a much-needed escape from the sweltering Texas heat. The courtroom had felt like a pressure cooker, and today I was thankful for the relative calm of a desk day. No juries, no cross-examinations, just paperwork.

My footsteps echoed softly against the polished floors, blending with the low murmur of voices and the clatter of keyboards from nearby desks. The office was alive with its own hum—phones ringing, colleagues debating cases in hushed tones, the occasional laugh breaking through the routine. Despite the activity, everything felt muted here compared to the courtroom, less urgent but still focused.

I passed a few familiar faces—some hunched over their desks, brows furrowed in concentration, others chatting quietly as they sipped coffee. The smell of stale takeout hung in the air, mixing with the faint scent of printer toner. It was the smell of work. My desk came into view, a mess of case files and notes that had piled up over the week, waiting for my attention. Just as I reached it, Janice appeared, scurrying over like she was late for a fire drill.

"Seriously, Janice, no need to run," I told her as she skidded to a stop in front of me.

"Tom wants to see you," she said between gasps.

Great, more drama on a desk day. Just what I needed.

I made my way down to Tom's office, pushing the door open without bothering to knock. Tom glanced up from his paperwork, looking haggard. It was possible he hadn't left the office since I'd seen him yesterday. Why anyone would actually want his job was beyond me.

His tone was serious but not unkind. "You handled the press conference well yesterday."

I shrugged, brushing off the praise. Lawyers weren't built for compliments, which was ironic considering our egos.

"Why am I here, Tom?"

"I'm pulling you off your other cases so you can focus on Martin."

I froze, disbelief coursing through me. For a moment, I didn't even know how to respond. I was glad I hadn't sat down, because if I had, I'd have shot back to my feet anyway. My heart pounded in my chest, and I stared at him, my jaw slack, the words catching in my throat. "I've poured countless hours into those cases." The frustration bubbled up, hot and fierce, anger lacing every syllable. "You can't just pull me off like they mean nothing."

"And you'll need to pour the rest of them into Martin. I'm not going to risk such a high-profile case over a few misdemeanors."

"Geez, guess my day-to-day is even less important when you put it like that."

His expression exuded exasperation. He clearly didn't appreciate my argument. "I need all your focus on Martin. Did you figure out who is going to be second?"

I folded my arms. "Lisa Cooper."

Tom's eyebrows shot up. "Cooper? She's barely out of law school. I can't have a forest of green on this case. Choose someone else."

"She's who I want, Tom. It's non-negotiable. You played your hand too soon. If you want me on this case, then Lisa will be my second."

Tom threw up his hands. "Fine."

I'd like to think he was proud of my negotiation skills, but he was probably just annoyed.

"Who's taking over my cases then?" What I was really asking was how good of a turnover I needed to prepare. If it was someone I liked, I'd try a little harder.

"I was going to give them to Lisa, but now you've created another problem for me."

"I'll solve it now then. Give the cases to Lisa. It will be good for her development. I can help her with them while we're working on Martin." I could also make sure the cases that had my name attached to them didn't go completely sideways. Reputation was everything in this business.

"Are you sure you can handle the extra workload?"

I gave him a confused look. "I'm honestly surprised that you care, Tom."

He blinked a few times. "You're right. I don't. Have it your way."

"Good. Anything else?"

"Free to go, Burger King."

I furrowed my eyebrows at him. "Excuse me?"

"Have it your way. It's their slogan."

"Stress is your thing, Tom, not jokes."

I was already out of his office before he responded. I was probably a little too casual with the way I talked to Tom, but that had always been my problem. I'd always hated hierarchy. It's why being a lawyer was a terrible career choice.

I made my way through the maze of desks, each cluttered with case files and half-empty coffee cups. Lisa was walking the other direction, which was perfect.

"Hey, where are you off to?" I asked. If she had an actual court appearance, then I'd have to respect it.

Lisa blinked. "Oh, just heading over to the library to do some research."

"Good. Nothing important. You're with me. I made you second on Martin."

She fell into line behind me without a single follow-up question. We'd have to work on that. Trust was a liability in this place. Luckily for her, I needed the help and I wasn't looking to throw her under any buses.

I grabbed a chair from the next cubicle over and dragged it in front of my desk. "Have a seat." I pointed at the chair and sat down on the other side of the desk. "What do you know about the Martin case?"

"Just what's been in the news."

"That's all?"

She hesitated. "I did briefly read through the transcript from the grand jury proceedings, plus the indictment."

A sense of satisfaction settled over me. This was exactly why I wanted Lisa as my second. She had a natural curiosity, diving into details even when they didn't directly involve her. It was a rare quality —one that made her invaluable, especially when it came to cases like this. She didn't need prompting; she took the initiative. I could rely on her. "And what do you think?"

"I think it should be a pretty easy win if we've brought him up on first-degree murder." She leaned forward at seeing my wince. "Please tell me the evidence is there."

"I wish I could. We've got our work cut out for us."

She chewed her bottom lip. She was holding something back.

"You're not saying something. What is it?" I prodded.

"It's just that if we lose this case, my record will look pretty bad."

She wasn't wrong. Litigators loved reporting what percentage of cases they'd won, assuming they'd won the majority.

"Don't worry about that. What's more important is the experience you'll gain from working on the case." I was lying. It wouldn't be good for either of us if we lost this case.

"Okay." She really needed to trust people less.

"You're also going to be sitting first chair on all my current cases so I can prioritize Martin."

Her eyes widened and she took in a breath. "Oh, wow."

"Wow, indeed. I'll help you as much or as little as you need. They're pretty straightforward."

I turned to my computer and clicked a few times. The printer behind me spat out the report and I grabbed it and handed it to her.

"That's my docket report. You'll see on it there's a trial tomorrow for a domestic."

"Is the judge really going to let you off the case on such short notice?"

"Maybe you haven't noticed, but us minor crimes ADAs are all pretty interchangeable."

She looked a little crestfallen at my words. I sighed. Maybe I shouldn't poison her too much.

"I'll be there with you, sitting second. There's too much to turn over in one afternoon."

She perked up at that.

"But I want you to take the opening and closing. I'll handle the witnesses."

"Sounds fair," she said.

Fair wasn't the word I would have chosen, but I bit back a comment, my expression saying more than I would have out loud. "Alright, grab your things. We're heading over to see Andrews. He's already working on the evidence for me."

I grabbed my bag and followed her to her cubicle. As she was grabbing her things, I found myself looking at a picture thumbtacked to the felt divider.

"Who's this?" I asked, touching the photograph.

She smiled. "That's my dad."

"He's a cop?" I already knew the answer based on his choice of wardrobe in the photo.

She nodded, her pride evident. "He just made Major last year, actually."

"You don't say."

I was sure there was a photo like this in existence with my dad somewhere. I hoped it stayed hidden.

"Ready?" she asked, oblivious to the internal turmoil the picture had sparked in me.

I nodded.

The drive over to the precinct wasn't long, and I was stuck in my head the whole way there. I should have been thinking about the

Martin case, but seeing that photo really did a number on me. My friend Sarah thought I needed therapy, but I didn't want to go. Mainly because I was terrified of what a therapist might say—that I needed to change careers, that this job was eating away at me, and that I was losing pieces of myself with every case. And I wasn't ready to hear that. I wasn't ready to start over.

Starting over wasn't an option. I'd poured years into this career, and it was more than just a job—it was tied to everything I'd built my life around. The idea of walking away from it now felt like admitting failure. Besides, what would I even do if I quit? The thought of trying to reinvent myself was paralyzing. This was who I was, who I had committed to being, and starting over would mean questioning everything I'd worked for.

We pulled up to the building and headed inside. Everyone there knew me, so I never had to waste time signing in or explaining myself.

"Andrews," I said, rounding his desk. "This is Lisa Cooper. She'll be second chair on this case with us."

"Nice to meet you, Coop," Andrews said. They shook hands.

"He's a nickname guy," I explained when Lisa gave me a sideways glance. "Although, ironically not for me. I'm hurt."

"Wow, I didn't know you had such a crush," he teased. "Did you want my autograph?"

"Actually, yes," I said. I grabbed a photo off his desk and pulled it out of the frame. It was him and a few other officers at some sort of barbecue. I handed it to him.

"Really?" he deadpanned.

I handed him a Sharpie and he wrote something flavorful on the photo and handed it back to me. I laughed and tucked it into my jacket.

"Now, as I was saying, before I was so rudely interrupted," he glanced at me, a hint of amusement in his voice, "I found something that's gonna make your day."

"Pretty hard to make my day, but try me."

The detective's smile turned into a grin. "The Martin residence has security cameras."

FOUR

"IS THAT SO?" I slid into the seat across from Andrews.

Andrews nodded. "The whole property is wired with cameras. State-of-the-art system."

"Is there any footage we can look at in evidence?" I didn't know why I asked the question. I had a feeling I already knew the answer.

"No, but shouldn't we be able to get it?"

I scoffed. "Yes, in theory. Discovery is the process where both sides have to exchange evidence before trial. It's supposed to ensure that no one is blindsided by new information in court. But Donovan—" I paused, shaking my head. "He's notorious for playing games with discovery. If that footage helps his case, we'll get it handed to us on a silver platter. If it doesn't, he'll pretend it doesn't exist unless we specifically ask for it. And even then, it might take a court order." "He can't do that!" Lisa exclaimed. "He could be disbarred for withholding evidence. That's highly prejudicial."

"And what you just said is highly idealistic," I said. "You'd have to prove that he intentionally withheld evidence. He's going to argue all day long that he forgot or thought it was irrelevant or his team just made a goof. Judges also hate discovery arguments. The way things are and the way things should be are two very different things."

Lisa tapped her fingers lightly against the table, her brow furrowed. "So then what do we do?"

"Make a note to look for the footage when we receive their discovery, which should be any day now. Better yet, let's get a motion to compel ready. I can almost guarantee that we'll need it."

Lisa nodded. I focused back on Andrews. "Any other juicy tidbits?"

Andrews handed me a heavy cardboard box. "I pulled together everything we've got so far." He leaned back, folding his arms. "But I'm real interested to hear what the witnesses have to say. Especially his alibi, Rachel Adams."

I rifled through the contents of the box—police reports, crime scene photographs, financial records. We'd need to comb through it all.

"We all want to know what Rachel Adams knows," I said. "Whether she's covering for him or not."

I suspected she held important information about Martin's dealings. In my experience, men often got chatty with their mistresses. A lot of high profile men had been undone because they'd opened their mouths to the women opening their legs for them. Rachel was going to be a crucial witness. Whether for the defense or prosecution was the question.

"If there's nothing else," I said, hoisting the box up further, "we'll be going."

"Let me know when you start the interviews."

"I always do."

I nodded at Lisa, and she helped me cart the heavy box of evidence out to my car. The late afternoon sun beat down on us as we loaded up the trunk.

"I need caffeine," I said, wiping sweat from my brow. "Let's grab a coffee."

We drove the few blocks to a Starbucks and got in line. The frothy whir of blenders helped drown out our conversation from passersby.

"So what do you make of Martin's motive?" I turned to Lisa as we waited for our drinks. "If he did kill Caroline, why?"

Lisa pursed her lips. "The affair seems too obvious. Caroline likely knew about it already. We can't hang our case on that."

The line moved forward and I studied the menu board, considering Lisa's perspective. She had a point—the affair motive was flimsy at best. We needed something more substantial.

"There must be another reason," Lisa continued. "Maybe Caroline found out something about Martin's business dealings. Something illegal. If she threatened to expose it..."

I nodded slowly. It wasn't a bad theory. Caroline had access to Martin's financial records through their joint accounts. If she'd stumbled onto something sinister, it could explain Martin's drastic actions.

I just hoped we could find the evidence to prove it because my gut told me this case ran deeper than an ordinary crime of passion.

Our drinks arrived, and we found a quiet table in the back corner. I sipped my black coffee, considering Lisa's theory about Martin's business dealings. It was a plausible explanation, but questions lingered.

"Even if Caroline found something sketchy in Martin's finances, what could she really do about it?" I asked. "They were married. She'd be implicating herself too if she went to the authorities."

Lisa nodded slowly. "You're right. It would have to be something pretty massive for her to take that risk."

I sighed, massaging my temples. This case was giving me a headache. "I just can't shake the feeling that Martin isn't our killer. But if not him, then who? I really don't want to be blindsided by Donovan."

Lisa gave me a sympathetic look. "Maybe we're overthinking it. What if it really is just jealousy? But Ed's, not Caroline's."

"I'm not following."

"I don't think the evidence points to Ed murdering Caroline because she found out about the affair. There was nothing to indicate she was filing for divorce or about to go public with the information. My understanding is that the affair was sort of a well-known thing." Lisa shook her head. "No, I mean, what if Caroline was the one having an affair, and Ed found out about it."

I sipped my coffee. "It's possible. It does give a better motive.

When we start to go through Andrews' box, we can see what the evidence tells us."

Lisa sat up straighter, her expression still hopeful, as if she hadn't lost faith in the case. The more I thought about it, the more I couldn't make sense of Tom's decision to let me run solo with this case. The capital crimes division had prosecuted plenty of first-degree murders during Tom's tenure, including a few cases of husbands killing their wives, and there hadn't always been a female lead prosecutor.

As we headed back to the parking lot, my phone rang. I glanced at the caller ID—it was Erin Rogers, an old law school friend. We didn't talk often, maybe once every few months, but we'd been close back in the day. I paused, a little surprised she was calling now.

I answered, curiosity piqued. "Hey Erin, what's up?"

"Alex, hi," she said briskly. "Listen, I heard through the grapevine you're working the Martin murder case. I might be able to help."

I raised my eyebrows in surprise. Erin was an assistant attorney general now, working for the federal government out of the Austin office. What could she know about a local homicide investigation? "Oh yeah?" I asked, trying not to sound too eager.

"I can't discuss it over the phone," Erin replied. "But we should meet up. I'm driving out your way tonight for a morning appointment. Are you free in the afternoon?"

I nodded before realizing she couldn't see me. "Yeah. I've got a morning trial, but I'll be around after. I'll text you when I'm done."

"I'll be at the Hyatt downtown. Come there after." I ended the call. Lisa gave me a curious look. I explained this was an old friend who was now a federal DA and she wanted to talk to me about the Martin case.

Lisa's eyes widened. "The Feds are involved?"

"Not sure yet." Which was the truth. I'd not personally worked with the Feds on a case, but I'd been around the rumor mill long enough. Sometimes they liked to get involved if one of our cases could help one of their cases. It was rarely the other way around.

I took a deep breath as I started the car, my mind racing. Lisa turned to me, her expression serious.

"What could the Feds have on Martin?" she asked. "This was supposed to be a straightforward domestic homicide."

My thoughts drifted to the crime scene photos, the expensive furnishings in the Martin home. Edward Martin was wealthy, supposedly successful. He was a real estate developer. Self-made man. Built from the ground up. All that stuff they say.

"Maybe it has something to do with Martin's business," I speculated. "Some financial crime. Insider trading, money laundering. Something Caroline found out about before she died."

Lisa nodded. "Could be. Or drugs, racketeering. The Feds don't get involved for nothing."

I sighed, switching off the ignition. "Well, we'll find out more soon. But right now, we need to prep for tomorrow's domestic."

FIVE

THE LAST OF our witnesses stepped down. Lisa leaned back, a small nod of satisfaction on her face. "The prosecution rests, Your Honor," she announced with measured confidence.

Lisa did a good job of following the script I'd given her. Litigating was eighty percent showmanship and twenty percent lawyering. The people who excelled at both were generally successful. Unfortunately, most only excelled at one or the other. It was possible Lisa might be one of the rare few who excelled at both. I was still trying to figure out where I fell on the spectrum.

I scribbled a few notes—information that might be helpful for cross-examination.

"Defense may call its first witness," Judge Reynolds declared, his voice flat.

"Thank you, Your Honor." The defense attorney, Greg Mitchell, rose from his seat with an oily grace that set my teeth on edge. Greg was a forgettable-looking man in his mid-fifties who had made his living working the misdemeanor circuit. An assault charge was almost punching outside his weight class. "The defense calls Mr. Fred Keller to the stand."

Keller shuffled forward, a wiry man with nervous eyes that darted around the courtroom. Sworn in, he took his place like a bird perched on a wire, ready to take flight.

Mitchell began to question his witness, his voice smooth. "Mr. Keller, where do you live?"

"In the townhome adjacent to the defendant's."

"Can you tell me a little bit about the townhomes?"

Keller's gaze flitted toward the jury. "Y-yes, sir. These are older townhomes, built close together, and you can hear just about everything through the walls. People don't get much privacy in places like that. You can hear arguments, TVs, even footsteps sometimes."

"And on the night in question, you were home?" Mitchell prodded, guiding the narrative. I was itching to object on the grounds that he was leading the witness, but I knew Mitchell was going to get what he wanted out of the witness regardless of how he asked the questions. Objecting this early in the defense's case might make me look petty to the jury.

"Home all evening," Keller confirmed, his fingers fidgeting with the edge of his jacket.

"Thank you, Mr. Keller." Mitchell backed away to look at his notepad.

I tapped my pen against the legal pad. My eyes locked onto Keller, searching for any telltale flicker of doubt. I would find it. I always did.

Mitchell stepped forward again and continued. "Can you recount the details of that night, Mr. Keller?"

I leaned forward, elbows on the table, as Keller's voice filled the courtroom. "Heard them yelling, clear as day. She was screaming about him coming home late again."

"Objection," I snapped, rising to my feet. "Hearsay, Your Honor."

Mitchell turned, feigning surprise. "Your Honor, we're not offering it for the truth of the matter asserted. We aim to show that the prosecution's narrative is flawed."

Judge Reynolds peered down through his spectacles, lips pursed in thought. "Overruled."

My jaw clenched. I should have trusted my gut and waited to object. I could feel some of the jurors looking at me.

Keller rambled on, recounting the shouts that pierced through the walls that night. I jotted notes, each word stoking the fire of my skepticism. He hadn't seen anything—only heard. Sounds could be deceiving. The defense spun a threadbare story, and threads can snap.

"And then what happened?" Mitchell asked.

"Then a thud. Loud one. Like someone hitting the floor."

"Did you often hear Mrs. Harper yelling at her husband?"

"Sure did."

"Thank you, Mr. Keller," Mitchell concluded, confidence oozing from every syllable. I tightened my grip on the pen in my hand, forcing myself to stay composed.

"Ms. Hayes," Judge Reynolds announced. "Your witness."

I stood up, smoothing my skirt. "Mr. Keller, you didn't actually see any of the altercation between the couple, did you?"

"No, ma'am, just heard it."

"And you can't testify with certainty who hit whom first, or even if what you heard was indeed a hit?"

He hesitated, licking his lips. "Well, no, can't say for sure."

"Thank you, Mr. Keller. No further questions." I retreated, knowing I'd chipped away at the credibility of his account.

The judge dismissed Keller and Mitchell called his next witness. "The defense calls Jenna Black to the stand."

Black took the oath, her gaze darting around the room, before settling into the witness chair. She looked too eager. Honest people were never eager to testify. People with motives, on the other hand, often enjoyed the chore.

"Ms. Black, you know Mrs. Harper, the defendant's wife?"

"Known her for years," she replied, almost smug.

"Can you describe her temperament?"

I was on my feet fast. "Objection. Character evidence, Your Honor."

"Your Honor, it goes to—"

"Sustained." Judge Reynolds cut in with finality. "Stricken from the record. The jury will disregard Mr. Mitchell's last question."

31

I sat down, eyes narrowed. Mitchell dismissed the witness without any further questions. I watched Black slink off the stand. Clearly, someone with a grudge against the defendant's wife. It was ballsy of Mitchell to even try and put her on. But that was defense attorneys for you.

"Defense calls Mr. Elijah Harper to the stand."

Lisa leaned toward me, confusion in her eyes. I whispered, low and steady, "Rookie move." A smile tugged at the corner of my mouth. "I'll have him for breakfast."

Harper squared his shoulders as he took the oath. His suit was pressed, but his eyes betrayed him—darting, searching.

"Mr. Harper, you said you were late coming home on the night in question?"

"That's right," Harper said. "Work had been picking up. I had a new client. The Martins. Good pay. Needed to impress them."

The moment the name "Martin" hit the air, my fingers twitched. I flipped through the file, my eyes scanning feverishly for any prior mention of the Martins. Nothing.

"Did your late hours cause tension at home?"

"Caused the argument," Harper admitted. "My wife didn't understand. Thought I cared more about work."

"Who was the aggressor in the altercation?"

"Her." Harper's voice was firm. "Always quick to anger. Things had been going downhill between us for a while."

I scribbled notes. His story unfolded, neat and rehearsed. To be expected. If Mitchell had agreed to let him take the stand, he'd coached him on what to say.

"Did you hit your wife, Mr. Harper?"

"No, sir."

"Did your wife hit you?"

"Yes, sir."

"No further questions." Mitchell sauntered back to the counsel table as if he'd just won some great victory.

Mitchell was neither good at showmanship nor lawyering, but he was one of the many who *thought* he was good at both.

"Ms. Hayes, your witness for cross," Judge Reynolds announced.

I rose, my gaze fixed on Harper. I never looked at the jury except during opening and closing. This was my tactic even before Amber Heard proved how pandering to a jury wasn't a good look.

"Mr. Harper, can you elaborate on the nature of your work at the Martin residence?"

"Electrical systems," he said, his voice steady but his eyes flicking away for just an instant. "Mr. Martin claimed he had some outages. Kept calling me back."

"Outages," I echoed, tasting the word. "Why did you have to keep going back?"

"I wasn't able to duplicate the problem. Every time I went, everything seemed to be working just fine."

"So, you weren't able to find the problem?"

"Objection, Your Honor." Mitchell was up now. "Relevance?"

"Ms. Hayes?" The judge looked at me, eyebrows raised in silent query.

"Your Honor, establishing the veracity of the defendant's whereabouts and activities is relevant to his state of mind and therefore to the events leading to the incident."

"Overruled," said the judge. "Let's get on with it, shall we, Ms. Hayes?"

A tight smile pulled at my lips. I turned back to Harper. "So, you were frustrated, weren't you? Called out multiple times, unable to fix an issue."

"Not really. It's all just part of the job."

"Sure, part of the job. But then when you came home from working extra hours to provide for your wife, she starts yelling at you. That must have been irritating."

Harper's back seemed to stiffen. "I guess, a little."

"So irritating that you just couldn't take it anymore and you lost your temper at her, didn't you?"

"Objection, Your Honor. Counsel is speculating."

"Ms. Hayes, watch your line of questioning," the judge warned, and with a slight nod of his head, sustained the objection.

"No further questions, Your Honor."

"Redirect?"

Mitchell stood. "Did you hit your wife, Mr. Harper?"

"No, sir."

"Nothing further, Your Honor. The defense rests their case."

Judge Reynolds removed his glasses. "I'm going to call a recess for lunch and then we'll reconvene to hear closing arguments."

"All rise!" the bailiff shouted. I never understood why they felt the need to shout it. We all knew the drill. The jury filed out of the courtroom. The judge struck the gavel and followed the jury out. "Court is now in recess."

I didn't stick around. I grabbed Lisa by the cuff of her jacket and pulled her out of the courtroom.

"Whoa!" she exclaimed. "What's the rush?"

"I don't want to talk to Mitchell and I've got an arraignment I need to handle quickly."

"Don't you think we should ask him about what the defendant knows about the Martins?" Lisa was doing her best to match my pace.

"No," was my blunt response. "We'll just subpoena Mr. Harper ourselves. Besides, if the jury gives us a guilty verdict, we can leverage a sentence recommendation for cooperation."

"Do you really think we're going to make it back in time for closing?"

I stopped my mad dash to the other side of the courthouse to look at my watch. Lisa had a point. Normally, I wouldn't try and cut it so close, but this arraignment was worth the risk.

"Good point," I said. "You go back and handle closing and I'll head to the arraignment. I'll catch up with you later."

I watched Lisa's face contort with anxiety, but I knew she was more than capable. Besides, I needed to lose my shadow for when I met with Erin. If she really was passing me information under the table, she wasn't going to do it with someone else in the room, no matter how much I vouched for them.

"Okay," Lisa conceded, turning around.

In five minutes, a judge would ask Officer Luis Ramirez if he was pleading guilty to a variety of crimes. Normally, I wouldn't rush to see the arraignment of a random police officer. But this wasn't just any officer—this was my father's former partner, being brought up on the same charges that had ruined my life.

SIX

I LOOKED at the text on my phone and then up at the door. 427. The numbers matched. I knocked, and the door opened almost immediately. Erin broke into a wide, warm smile.

"Alex! Good to see you," she said, her voice energetic as always. We exchanged a brief hug before she led me further into the room. Her hotel suite was neat and businesslike. I welcomed the calmness after the chaos of my day.

I sank onto the plush sofa while Erin perched on the edge of the adjacent armchair. She looked at me with that keen, inquisitive gaze she had perfected back in law school.

"How've you been?" she asked, genuine interest lacing her tone.

"Busy," I answered honestly. "Tired," I added for good measure, rubbing my temples.

Erin's eyes sparkled with a familiar mischief. "There's still a spot for you in my office, you know."

"You know my answer." The response was so automatic I didn't even need to think about it.

Erin laughed, the sound infectious. "Alright. I won't push it." She paused, amusement dancing in her eyes. "Yet."

I shook my head, fighting back a grin of my own. I had missed this easy camaraderie between us. Ever since law school, she had persistently tried to get me to join her at the federal level, and I had persistently declined. Our back-and-forth over it had become a comforting constant in our friendship.

Erin leaned forward, her expression becoming more serious. "So, how did the trial go? Did you get the verdict you wanted?"

I shifted on the sofa, the weight of the day's events pressing down on me. "I don't know yet. My colleague, Lisa Cooper, is handling closing arguments so I could come here. She's going to be my second on the Martin case, but I had a sense you might want to talk privately."

She nodded slowly. "You sensed right. I want you to take a look at something."

Erin stood and walked to the desk by the window. She rifled through a drawer before extracting a slim file folder. Turning back to me, she held it out, her expression serious.

I reached for it, but Erin pulled it back at the last moment. "Don't open it here. Wait until you're alone." She offered the folder in my direction again, her gaze boring into me. "And this stays between us. Nothing in that folder goes into evidence."

I raised an eyebrow, curiosity piqued. "Not much to go on."

"I know it's not ideal," Erin conceded, her voice softening. "But it may help provide some... clarity."

I studied her for a moment. There was something in her eyes— hesitation, maybe even a flicker of concern. It was unlike Erin to be this cautious, and that set off alarm bells in my mind. Still, I gave a small nod, acknowledging the unspoken weight of what she was handing over. Message received.

I slipped the file into my bag, tucking it carefully between a few case folders, ensuring it was buried deep. I exhaled slowly, my expression hardening as I closed the bag. Erin's eyes flicked to me, her brow creasing.

"You okay?" she asked, a trace of concern in her voice. I met her gaze, feeling a familiar mix of frustration and resignation. "I just came from Officer Luis Ramirez's arraignment."

Her eyes widened in surprise. "Your father's partner? He testified against your father, didn't he?"

"Yes," I said, my voice tight. "And now he's being brought up on the same charges."

"I remember. What does that mean for your father's case?"

I froze for a moment, the question hitting harder than expected. My chest tightened, and an old familiar ache began to throb beneath my ribs. It was like the scars had never fully healed, and now they were splitting open again. I swallowed, forcing myself to stay composed as I shook my head.

"No idea," I said, my voice barely above a whisper. "I don't speak to him anymore."

"Are you sure that's a good idea? Maybe you should—"

"It's the path I've chosen." My tone came out harsher than intended. I tried to soften it, but my emotions betrayed me. "Too far down the road to change course now."

I knew Erin meant well. She'd seen firsthand what I went through during law school, back when my father's arrest tore my world apart. She wasn't just a colleague, she was a friend who had watched me put myself back together, piece by piece.

Erin held my gaze for a moment, then nodded, understanding in her eyes.

An uneasy silence settled between us. I fingered the file in my bag, possibilities swirling in my mind. How far was I willing to go for answers? How much of myself had I already lost to this?

"Do you have any leads on the Martin case?" Erin asked, her tone gentle as she steered the conversation to safer ground.

I shook my head. "I only just got word I'd be working on it yesterday. I haven't even had a chance to look through the evidence Detective Andrews compiled."

Erin nodded. "When you do, if you find anything you think might be useful on my end, I hope you'll let me know."

I studied her for a moment. "How will I know?"

"When you read what I've given you, you should have a sense of what I'm investigating."

I nodded again, the slim file in my bag suddenly weighing it down. "I should go. Thank you, Erin."

We stood and hugged briefly, the warmth of our friendship dispelling the heaviness of the day's revelations. I left her hotel room with my mind racing. As I walked to my car, I mulled over the possibilities of what Erin's file could contain.

I slid into the driver's seat and tossed my bag onto the passenger seat, the temptation to open the file immediately almost overwhelming. But no—I needed privacy to pore over its contents properly.

Starting up the engine, I began driving back to the office. As I navigated the familiar streets, my thoughts drifted to Erin's question about my father. Was cutting off contact the smartest decision? Doubt flickered through me, but I pushed it away. As I said to her, I was too far down this road now to turn back. The damage had been done.

The traffic was light, and without the usual stop-and-go chaos to distract me, my mind began to drift. Memories crept in, uninvited. My father had always been a looming figure in my life, his fall from grace casting a long shadow that I still couldn't shake. With each empty stretch of road, the thought of him behind bars resurfaced—like a dull ache that never really went away.

I tightened my grip on the wheel, realizing how much time I spent trying to bury that pain. I'd built walls around it, thrown myself into my work, convinced myself that my cases, my pursuit of justice, were all that mattered. But in these quiet moments, I couldn't help but wonder if that was just an excuse to keep from dealing with the truth. I pulled into the office's parking garage and gathered my bag, tucking it under my arm. Riding up the elevator, anticipation flooded my veins. What secrets did this file hold?

The elevator doors opened with a ding, and I stepped out into the quiet hallway of the DA's office. It was late, and most of my colleagues had already gone home. I made my way to my desk, looking around to make sure no one would sneak up on me.

I dropped my bag on the desk and took a deep breath. This was it. I opened the bag and pulled out the file, my fingers trembling. I sat down, the worn leather chair creaking underneath me, and spread the contents of the file on my desk.

On the first page were various notes, written in Erin's neat handwriting. There was no particular order to the page. It looked like scratch paper. Names with question marks next to them and a few dates.

Behind that, receipts were paperclipped to bank statements, unusual transactions highlighted. Erin had marked certain dates and amounts, drawing lines between them. I flipped through the pages to find more of the same.

Three photographs slipped out of the pages as I continued flipping, landing face up on my desk. I stopped to pick them up, my breath catching in my throat as my fingers landed on one of Officer Louis Ramirez. He was standing with the mayor at what looked like a fundraiser, all smiles and handshakes. I picked up another photo of Ed Martin with the mayor and another man who looked vaguely familiar. They were in a park, locked in conversation, their heads bent close together. The tension between them was palpable, and they seemed unaware of the camera, but I got the feeling they didn't want to be seen. The third photograph was of Ramirez, not in uniform, and Ed in Ed's driveway.

The back of the first photo read, "Charity Gala, January 15, 2019." The worst year of my life. My father had pled guilty just the month after. On the back of the second photo was written, "June 14, 2023." On the back of the third, "July 20, 2024." The day before Caroline was found dead.

I leaned back in my chair and stared at the ceiling. Erin's caution echoed in my mind: *Nothing in that folder goes into evidence.* But why? She said this would clear things up for me, but I was more lost than before I'd gone to visit her. I still wasn't sure what all this was supposed to lead me to, and how I could use this information to help her. What was she really investigating?

A knock on the outside wall of my cubicle startled me out of my thoughts, causing me to jerk up from my slouch and my heart to race. I quickly gathered the papers and stuffed them back into the file, then shoved the whole thing into my desk drawer. "Come in," I called, trying to sound composed.

Lisa poked her head in. "Hey. Just wanted to update you on the Harper trial. Closing went fine and the jury's still out."

"Thanks," I said, forcing a smile. "I appreciate the update."

She nodded, glancing around. "You okay? You look... tense."

"I'm fine," I replied, a bit too quickly. "Just a lot on my mind."

"Alright," she said slowly, clearly not convinced. "If you need anything, you know where to find me."

"Thanks."

She left with a friendly goodbye. I exhaled slowly. The Martin case was bigger than I had realized, and now that I knew Ramirez was involved somehow, it was starting to feel personal.

I turned back to my desk drawer, pulling the handle slowly as the old hinges protested with a creak. The drawer slid open, revealing the stack of files. I reached in to pull out the one Erin had given me. There was still so much to unravel, and I needed to be methodical. But first, I had to understand exactly what Erin was trying to tell me.

SEVEN

THE PHOTOGRAPH FLASHED in my mind as I turned the key in the desk drawer, locking the file safe and sound for the night—or morning, depending on perspective. I had lost track of time hours ago, and the first light of dawn was just beginning to filter through the blinds. Despite how long I'd been at it, thoughts about the photos still swirled in my head.

Ramirez, a low-level beat cop with no more stripes on his sleeve than my father ever had, talking to the mayor. Their expressions indicated they were old pals. Even though Ramirez had been my father's partner, they hadn't exactly been close. They barely tolerated each other—something about clashing personalities or different views on how to handle the streets. I rarely saw Ramirez when I was younger, and when I did, he never bothered to engage. There was always a tension in the air between him and my dad, so I kept my distance. Now, seeing him cozying up to the mayor made even less sense. Wrong. All wrong. Mayors shook hands with politicians at these galas, not the foot soldiers. Then, within a year, Ramirez had been promoted from sergeant to assistant chief. Quite a jump.

I shook my head and slipped on my jacket. I needed more information on Ramirez's case. He'd been pictured with Martin, on multiple occasions. Martin had to be involved. But I refused to think his case had anything to do with my father. My heels echoed down the empty hallway as I made for the exit. I wanted to know who was prosecuting Ramirez. The arraigning attorney was a revolving door around here. But Janice would know who would be seeing the case through to trial. She just needed a little incentive to sing.

I blinked against the harsh sunlight as I stepped outside. Janice's coffee shop of choice was just across the street. The line inside stretched nearly to the entrance.

My heels clacked against the pavement as I walked across the open street, opened the glass door to the shop and took my place in line, not needing to look at the menu. Janice's usual was a large, iced latte and a croissant. I needed a lot of information, so better make it two croissants.

The line trickled forward at a snail's pace. Only one employee manned the register today, apparently thinking it would be slow. I tapped my foot impatiently and tried not to implode from impatience. I'd already been here for ten minutes and still needed to go through the evidence box Andrews had given to me.

Finally, I reached the counter and placed the order, my nerves easing at the simple, familiar routine. The promise of caffeine hung in the air, offering a brief but welcome respite from the chaos of my mind.

I drummed my fingers on the counter as I waited in the pickup area, my mind wandering back to the Harper case. How long would the jury take to deliberate? A few hours? A day? I had done all I could in court, but still, the uncertainty gnawed at me. The outcome was out of my hands now, and the waiting was always the worst part. A tap on my shoulder had me whirling around.

Donovan. My expression curdled like old milk. His grin resembled the Joker's; it was infuriating and stretched from ear to ear, eyebrows sharpened as if with a colored pencil.

"Shouldn't you be working?"

"I could say the same to you."

He put his hands up in mock surrender, not taking his eyes off me. "Touché."

I glared at him. He was the last person I wanted to deal with right now.

"Unless you have that discovery for me, I have no interest in talking to you." I spun back around to face the pickup counter.

He chuckled. "My office is working on it."

"More like working on what to omit."

He made sure to walk into my peripheral, feigning a wounded look with his hand over his heart. "Come on, Hayes. You know we're all about transparency."

I scoffed. "Right."

The barista called out my order. I glanced over my shoulder, eager to get back to Janice with her croissants—and to the mountain of work sitting on my desk. Between the case files and everything I'd tucked away in my drawer, there were plenty of things still needing my attention.

Donovan leaned closer, his voice a whisper meant only for me. "How about we go over the case tonight? For old time's sake?"

I kept my expression unreadable, but my blood began to boil, and I could almost feel the heat rising to my face. One year ago, after a tense motions hearing, we had crossed paths outside the courtroom. What started as an exchange of barbs quickly escalated—sharp words, personal jabs, both of us too stubborn to back down. The argument crackled with intensity, and somewhere between the adrenaline and the palpable tension, things shifted. I hadn't expected to feel it—that pull—but there it was, undeniable. Instead of walking away, I found myself drawn into something that went too far. The next thing I knew, we were wrapped in a mistake, a lapse in judgment that shouldn't have happened but did. A one-time thing, driven by rivalry and emotions neither of us could control. "Let's not rehash old history," I shot back, my voice steady despite the churning inside. "Especially not here."

It was frowned upon for opposing counsel to have a relationship, past or present. However, if every attorney had to recuse themselves from a case because they'd slept with opposing counsel, no one would have representation.

"Aw, c'mon." His grating laughter followed me to the door. "You're no fun."

"Fun's not part of the job description." The edge in my voice was sharp and I stopped before opening the door. " I'm not going to let you get me disqualified. That's what you're trying to do, isn't it?"

He didn't respond, but I could feel his smirk from yards away.

"Discovery by Friday morning, or I file a motion to compel. Your choice."

"Always such a pleasure, Alex," he called out behind me as I bolted through the doorway, his words dripping with sarcasm.

I strode back into the office, two iced lattes and Janice's croissants in hand. My heart still raced, Donovan's words lingering in my mind. Worse, his touch lingering on my skin. I pushed away the unease as I balanced the coffee tray. I needed to focus.

She eyed me expectantly as I placed the latte on her desk. This was an old game between us at this point. She knew when I wanted something.

"Thank you, dear," she said sweetly, and picked up the cup to take a long, luxurious sip. Then she leaned forward, resting her elbows on the table and asked, "What can I do for you?"

I leaned in close, lowering my voice. "I need to know who's handling the Ramirez case. The trial attorney, not his arraignment lawyer."

Not surprisingly, Ramirez had pled "not guilty."

Janice pursed her lips. I handed her the two croissants. She liked to make me work for it.

The brown paper bag crinkled under her grasp as she took it, peeking inside and grabbing one pastry for a bite. "Well, since you were so kind with the treats... I believe that case was assigned to Shaun Stevens."

I nodded, mentally filing away the information. Shaun was tough but fair. I didn't have much of a relationship with him, but I hoped he'd share information with me if I told him Ramirez might be connected to Martin.

As I turned to leave, Janice called out, "Say, I heard Donovan is going to be defense on Martin." She leveled me with a mischievous look. "How do you feel about that?"

I froze. Of course she knew. Janice knew everything.

I squared my shoulders and straightened my blazer. "Just fine."

Janice raised an eyebrow but didn't push further. We had an unspoken understanding—I got intel, she got gossip.

I quickened my pace down the hall, eager to be away from prying eyes. Donovan was firmly in my past. Now it was time to focus on digging up dirt on Ramirez. I tried to tell myself it was because he was in the photos Erin had given to me and not because his testimony had been what led to my father's conviction.

I could see Lisa pacing in front of my desk. She started to open her mouth in the hallway, but I shook my head. Not that my cubicle provided much privacy, but it was better than the open space.

When she was settled behind my desk, I nodded. "What's up?"

"Jury reached a verdict on the Harper case."

I looked at her with a brow raised, a silent request to go on.

"Guilty."

Relief washed over me. The tension in my shoulders relaxed.

"Good. We can work with this." I picked up the phone and dialed Mitchell's number. The receptionist picked up after one ring. "Alex Hayes for Greg Mitchell."

"Hold please."

"Alex," Mitchell said, his tone not unkind. "What can I do for you?"

Greg and I had faced each other across the courtroom a few times before. We had a mutual respect—no personal grudges, just business. We understood the rules of the game and had always kept things professional.

"I'm actually calling because I can do something for you, Greg."

He chuckled. "Is that so?"

"Or, for your client, rather. Sorry about the guilty verdict. Tough break."

I could hear Greg's shrug through the phone. Defense attorneys generally cared about one thing and one thing only: getting paid. The only case they considered a loss was the one where they got stiffed. I'd learned that tidbit from Donovan.

"Listen, your client has information that could be useful for a case I'm working. If he agrees to cooperate, I could be persuaded to recommend leniency at sentencing."

"I dunno," Mitchell said, trying to pretend like I wasn't offering his client the only parachute off a plane about to crash.

"Let's save us both some time and dispense with the games. You and I both know that this would be a huge win for Harper. He elected to go to trial rather than plea out. He's lucky to get anything."

That earned another chuckle from Greg. "I know, I know. But what would people say if I just gave in without trying to put up a fight?"

"That you're smart and can recognize a good deal when one's presented."

"I don't know how much he knows, if I'm being honest."

"He's the closest thing I have to a witness, timeframe-wise."

"Careful. If you make him sound too valuable, I'll have to ask for time served."

I barked out a laugh. "Hope you're saying that just to protect your reputation."

"Something like that."

"Thanks, Greg. I'll be in touch." I hung up the phone and Lisa looked at me like she had something to say. "What is it?" I asked.

"Is it really fair for him to get a lighter sentence just because he might know something about Martin?"

The longer I spent with Lisa, the more I realized how idealistic she was. I used to be like her before I'd learned how the system worked. It wasn't a system of checks and balances like they taught you on Schoolhouse Rock. This system was built off of favors and bribes.

There were no guarantees when it came to sentences. Even in the days of mandatory minimums, the prosecuting attorney had the power to choose what to charge the defendant with. The legal system was a never-ending cycle of one person ratting on another. And my profession was the Möbius strip that facilitated this exchange.

I leaned back in my chair, feeling my gaze soften at the younger woman in front of me. "No, Lisa. It's not fair. But fair's got nothing to do with it."

EIGHT

I STEPPED off the elevator and froze. Outside my cubicle, haphazard stacks of cardboard boxes were piled almost to the ceiling.

The discovery from Donovan.

When defense counsel was trying to hide something, they did one of two things: the first was to exclude the evidence entirely. This was dangerous—they risked an appeal and guaranteed themselves disbarment. The second was to hide the evidence in so much irrelevant junk that the other side would have no hope of finding it.

Defense counsel generally liked option two for two reasons: they could bill their client more for the "extra work," and it was a giant middle finger to the DA's office. Of course, Donovan had gone with option two.

I let out an irritated sigh. This was going to take forever to sort through. But there had to be something useful in this legal landfill, some key piece of evidence Donovan wanted to bury.

"Morning," Lisa said, appearing next to me. She let out a whistle. "Is this from Donovan?"

"Yeah."

"What's the plan?"

I clenched my jaw. "I'm getting us a damn office, that's the plan."

I marched toward Tom's door, blowing past Janice's attempt to stop me. Yesterday's extra croissant was worth one free pass, I figured.

"The transfer was finalized yesterday," Tom was on the phone with someone. He looked surprised when I barged in, quickly hanging up the call. "What the hell—?"

"I need an office."

He sighed his telltale sigh. "I honestly have more important things to address right now. Besides, you know only senior assistant district attorneys get offices."

"I honestly do not care about the rules right now, Tom. You want me on this case, I want an office."

Tom scowled but relented. "Fine."

"And an assistant. I've got a mountain of discovery to wade through at my desk and there's no way I'm going to get through it on my own."

"Office only," Tom said, his gaze hard. "No assistant."

I opened my mouth to protest, but Tom put up his hand. "You can have an office *or* an assistant, but I'd think carefully about your choice. An office I can make happen. It's just not in the budget to get an extra assistant."

I crossed my arms. "Let me borrow Janice, then."

He looked at me, and then we both let out a laugh.

"That's a good one," he said. Janice had certain skills. Doing actual work wasn't one of them. "You can take the empty spot where Flanagan used to be."

"Pleasure doing business with you." I tapped his doorframe on the way out. Janice gave me a dirty look as I made my way back to my now-former desk. Her one job was keeping people out of Tom's office, and I had been making that difficult for her lately.

I walked back to my cubicle and grabbed a box. Lisa, having waited for me to finish my debate with Tom, did the same. We trekked over to Flanagan's old office. The faint scent of cheap whiskey caught my nose, stopping me in my tracks. I followed it, tracing the smell to a dark corner near the bookshelf. Hidden behind a stack of forgotten files was an empty bottle, the cap off, the stench lingering even though Flanagan hadn't been in the office for months. The cigar smoke, too, seemed to hang in the air, absorbed into the carpet and walls. He'd gotten a guilty verdict on a big case and walked away without looking back, leaving this mess behind. I could only hope I'd time my own exit so perfectly one day. I moved into the stench-filled room and placed the box on the desk. "It's gonna be a long weekend. We need to go through every box and every page to find whatever Donovan's hidden." I eyed Lisa, not unconcerned. "I hope you didn't have any plans." Attorneys often had to prioritize work over all else, and I wasn't any different. I struggled with that balance more than I cared to admit, but it was just part of the job. That didn't mean I didn't feel a little guilty for pulling Lisa into this mess.

She shook her head.

"Then let's get started."

Lisa took one box, and I took another. We decided to leave the rest at my old cubicle, deciding it would be better to bring in each box one by one. Sifting through documents was a tedious process, but generally mindless. Coming into a case like this, I liked to have everything in front of me before I started to wrap my head around the events. If I dug in too early, I risked forming biases or getting tunnel vision. It was always the one thing that seemed so obvious but was completely overlooked that screwed you over at trial. And you kicked yourself all the way to a "not guilty" when it happened.

The hours ticked by, and outside, the sky bled into a deep indigo, shadows stretching longer as dusk settled in. The room had taken on a softer, muted glow as the last remnants of daylight faded. I glanced over and caught Lisa stifling a yawn.

"Alright, take a break," I told her.

"No, I can keep going," she tried to insist.

"I don't care if you can keep going," I said, stretching myself. "You're tired and you could miss something. Better to start fresh tomorrow."

I had a feeling Lisa had been burning the midnight oil the night before with me throwing the trial on her at the last minute. I could still remember how nervous I'd been before my first trial. Sleep had been the last thing on my mind before I stood in front of twelve people for the first time and tried to convince them that someone deserved to go to jail.

"No use arguing with you," Lisa said, grabbing her bag.

I pulled my lips into a smirk. "Now you're getting it."

I was the only one in the office now. It was Friday evening, and the sentiment "good enough for government work" had most ADAs and staff leaving promptly at 5.

I was fine with being alone in the office. In fact, I preferred it. Working at home was a different beast entirely. I'd made the mistake once of taking a small-time break-in case home with me. Thought it'd be easy to review while half-watching a show. By the time I hit my pillow that night, the case had spiraled in my mind, each detail magnifying, twisting. It was all I could think about, and sleep became a distant thought. No matter how low level the case, bringing work home was like opening a door to never-ending anxiety. At the moment, however, I needed three things: food, caffeine, and Detective Andrews. If I was lucky, I could get him to bring me the first two. I grabbed my desk phone and dialed his number. I knew it by heart.

He picked up on the second ring. "Detective Andrews."

"Still there, huh?" I asked. Andrews had a habit of sticking around longer than anyone, usually well after the cleaning crew had come and gone.

"It's only 5 p.m.," he said. "I'd hardly say that counts as midnight oil."

"We're public servants."

"Good point."

"I want to walk through the Martin case. Can you come by?"

"Alright."

I'd worked with Andrews for a long time. He worked late hours, not because he needed to, but because going home to an empty apartment was a sad reminder of what you don't have, or in his case, what he used to have. The way he tells the story, his wife had gone off with someone who made a lot more money and had a lot more time.

"Did you get a new number?" he asked.

"Nah. A new office, though. They just haven't switched my line to it yet."

"Moving up in the world?"

"Doesn't feel like it," I answered. "Can you bring dinner? I'm starving."

Andrews knew the score, just like I did. In our line of work, there wasn't much room for long lunches or catching up with colleagues outside of necessity. A quick meal between cases was the closest thing to unwinding we allowed ourselves.

Twenty minutes later, he knocked on my office door, a takeout bag in hand.

"Whiskey and tobacco," he muttered, glancing around and wrinkling his nose. "It smells like my granddad's study in here."

I smirked, knowing exactly where the scent came from. "Flannagan's old office. He practically marinated in that stuff."

Andrews paused, trying to place the name. "Flannagan...he retired, right? Not sure if I ever met the guy."

"Probably for the best," I said. He grinned and handed over a container of takeout. We dug into the food, our conversation naturally shifting to the case, both of us knowing this was our version of "downtime." "Let's start at the beginning." I flipped open the chronology he'd prepared. "Can you paint the scene for me? Broad strokes."

Andrews nodded, taking a sip of his coffee before putting his food down and grabbing a second copy of his report. "At 10:17 in the morning on May 19, Harris County dispatch received an emergency call from Edward Martin of 27 Inwood Drive. He reported that he had arrived back to his Royal Oaks home to find his wife, Caroline Martin, dead in their bedroom. Patrol officers responded and arrived on the premises at 10:46. Patrol officers were met in the home's driveway by Mr. Martin who said he had exited the home after it became too difficult to be inside."

I nodded, my fork hovering over the Chinese takeout as he continued.

"Mr. Martin led the patrol officers inside, where they found the body of Caroline Martin in the upstairs bedroom.

"The victim was located lying on the bed with her head hanging off the side. Preliminary assessment indicated signs of manual strangulation. Bruising and petechiae were evident around the neck and upper chest. The victim's face displayed a cyanotic hue, consistent with asphyxiation. There were also clear signs of blunt force trauma."

I pulled three photographs from the folder, dragging them closer as if staring harder at them would reveal the answers I so desperately needed. I poked at my food absentmindedly. The first photo captured the scene in the bedroom where Caroline was found. My eyes darted across the room, piecing together the untouched furniture, the undisturbed bed—like nothing had happened at all. It was too orderly, too clean. The bed hadn't been slept in, confirming what the report said, and everything on the nightstand looked neat, pristine even. No sign of a struggle, no wild disarray that usually screamed murder scene. I bit the inside of my cheek, glancing back at my coffee. It didn't sit right. My gut told me something more had happened here, but the photo painted a different picture. How could so much violence leave such a quiet mark on the room?

I moved to the second photo, and the quiet room in the first image became an eerie contrast to the brutality in this one. A close-up of Caroline's neck, mottled with bruises that told a much different story. The purpling skin, the tiny red dots on her eyes—petechiae—screamed strangulation. The force behind those hands, whoever they belonged to, was chilling. I put my fork down. My stomach knotted. I forced myself to keep looking, to study the pattern of the bruises, to try to get inside the mind of the person capable of this. My thoughts flickered briefly to the size of the assailant's hands—could we match it to Edward's?

Then my gaze snagged on the gash across her forehead, deep and ugly. I swallowed the bile rising in my throat. The raw edges of the wound showed how hard she'd been hit. I pictured her head slamming against the corner of the nightstand, her body going limp. The image haunted me. Blood matted her once-perfect hair, pooling on the bedroom floor—a sharp, shocking contrast to her pale skin. The nightstand, the very one that appeared untouched in the first photo, now bore the truth with that thin smear of blood on its corner. I pressed my lips together and took a long gulp of the now-lukewarm coffee. The room might've stayed pristine, but this was a crime soaked in savagery. Guess we didn't need to go hunting for a missing murder weapon.

"Keep going," I said, my eyes darting from one photo to the other.

"The bedroom showed no immediate signs of struggle. However, a broken necklace was found near the victim's body, suggesting a possible struggle during the attack. The head trauma indicates the victim was likely subdued before being strangled."

I pulled the last of the photos in front of me. It was a detailed close-up of the broken necklace, a gold chain still clasped but broken apart at the center and crumpled on the floor in the pool of blood. I absent-mindedly wiped my hands on a napkin, suddenly feeling queasy again.

"There were no signs of forced entry to the home itself," Andrews continued. "A review of the security system did not show any alarm having sounded, indicating the victim either knew the assailant or let them inside, or the assailant already had access to the home."

I tapped the desk lightly, a nervous habit, as I processed his words. No alarm meant no break-in. Caroline must have known her killer or, worse, they had been inside with her the whole time, waiting. I couldn't help but think of Edward's alibi, shaky as it was, and I was still missing a piece of the puzzle. The security system should have caught something, anything, but here we were—nothing.

A knot formed in my stomach. Something didn't add up. The footage had to exist. I could feel it, buried somewhere, just waiting to be uncovered. I tapped faster. Donovan was slippery, always holding back just enough to throw off a case. Was he stashing the security footage somewhere in this mountain of junk we were wading through? Hiding it because it didn't fit the narrative he was spinning?

The man was notorious for manipulating discovery—only giving what helped his client. If this footage showed anything that could hurt Edward's defense, he'd bury it deep, hoping I'd miss it. "Crime scene investigators documented the scene and collected potential evidence, including fingerprints, DNA samples, and the broken necklace. The body was transported to the county morgue for a detailed autopsy to confirm the cause and approximate time of death, which was calculated to be within an hour of the patrol officers arriving at the scene."

"And Martin stayed in the driveway while the police were examining the crime scene?"

Andrews looked over the report, his fork hovering over a bite of lo mein. "Yes, that's right." He finally took the bite, chewing thoughtfully as I made a note about Edward's whereabouts.

"And the arrest?"

He grabbed his coffee to wash down the food before continuing. "Upon questioning, Mr. Martin's behavior appeared suspicious. He was visibly agitated and provided inconsistent statements regarding his whereabouts at the time of the incident." He paused to spear another piece of his dinner. "Officers requested access to Mr. Martin's clothing and hands, noting what appeared to be recent scratches on his forearms." He took a large bite, chewing slower now as the details unraveled. "He was unable to provide a satisfactory explanation for these injuries. Given this, plus the lack of forced entry and triggered alarms, they decided to take him into custody for further questioning."

Andrews wiped his mouth with a napkin, his food forgotten for the moment. "At approximately 11:45 a.m., Edward Martin was placed under arrest for the suspected murder of his wife. He was read his Miranda rights and transported to the precinct for formal booking and interrogation."

"Who were the arresting officers?"

I'm sure Andrews had already spoken to them, but I wanted to get their firsthand accounts.

He reached for his takeout container again, but hesitated, looking over the report. "Officer Mindy Sanchez and—" Andrews paused. I looked up from my broccoli beef to see what the issue was. His fork hovered above the food, frozen. "Shit."

I shook my head, not understanding. "What is it?"

He looked up at me from the report, finally putting his fork down, his appetite apparently gone. "The second officer at the scene was Louis Ramirez."

NINE

"ARE YOU SURE?"

I really wanted it to be a mistake, but Andrews nodded.

"Yeah."

Both of us pushed aside our nearly empty takeout containers and coffee cups, the remnants of dinner forgotten. Andrews leaned back in his chair, the tension in the room replacing the casualness of our earlier meal.

Andrews already knew about Ramirez's charges—word traveled fast in the precinct. What he likely didn't realize was how deep the connection ran for me. "Do the badge numbers match?" I rolled my chair over to my computer and pulled up the docket report. "7797."

He took a moment to look at the report, then let out a breath. "It's a match."

Shit was right. "We can't put Ramirez on the stand now," I said. "Who signed the report?"

"Officer Sanchez."

"At least there's that," I muttered, glancing at Andrews.

He looked up from his notes, brow furrowed. "What do you mean?"

"Ramirez being brought up on embezzlement charges? It opens the door to character evidence, stuff that would normally stay sealed tight." I leaned back in my chair. "If Ramirez had been the one who authored the report, Donovan could challenge it, argue it's tainted by his personal conduct. That's where it gets tricky for us."

Andrews scratched his head. "That sounds like lawyer stuff."

I smirked. "It is. And it would've been enough for Donovan to get the report thrown out entirely. No report, no case. We'd be toast."

Andrews let out a low whistle. "So, you're saying the fact that Ramirez's name is even in the mix could have blown this whole thing up?"

I nodded. "Exactly. His credibility would've been shot, and that gives Donovan an opening to argue the entire investigation is compromised."

My fingers pressed against my temples, tension building as I stared at the files spread across the table.

"Wait, Ramirez is an assistant chief now. What the hell was he doing as one of the responding officers in the first place?"

My question hung in the air. Andrews leaned back in his chair, rubbing the back of his neck. "That's exactly what I was wondering. He's way too high up the chain for this. Responding to a murder scene isn't his job anymore."

I frowned, scrolling through the report again, searching for anything that would explain why Ramirez would be there. But nothing jumped out.

"So, why was he there?"

Andrews shook his head, his brow furrowing even deeper. "No clue. Doesn't make sense unless...unless he had a reason to be."

I turned to look at him, my stomach twisting as the implications hit me. "You think there's something more going on here?"

"Feels like it," Andrews replied. "Ramirez isn't the type to just 'show up' at random crime scenes. Especially not one like this. He had to be there for a reason. We just don't know what that reason is yet."

The dull throb behind my right eye was starting to sharpen. I glanced at the empty coffee cup beside me, tapping it absently, knowing I'd need caffeine—or sleep—soon, though neither seemed likely.

"Alright, so Ramirez is a question mark. What else do we have?" I asked, ignoring my body for just a few more moments.

He slid a thin folder over to me. "The DNA report just came in."

I flipped it open, skimming through the clinical jargon for the key details. No DNA found at the scene other than the Martins'.

Closing the file, I met Andrews' gaze. "Anything else of note?"

He shook his head. "That's about it for now."

I leaned back in my chair with a sigh, staring up at the flickering lights as I tried to make sense of it all.

"I don't get it," I finally said. "By all accounts, this looks like an open and shut domestic violence case, but Martin is pleading not guilty. And according to Tom, Donovan flat out refused any discussions of a plea agreement early on and they're still not budging on that. What does he know that we don't?"

Andrews frowned. "If Ed Martin didn't kill his wife, then who did?"

"Exactly." I began gathering the files into a neat stack. "That can't be our case. Maybe juries ten years ago would buy it, but not now. We're missing something here."

Andrews slid the crime scene photos back in front of him, scrutinizing each one carefully. "Do you really think Ed Martin is physically capable of this kind of violence?" he asked. "The man's in his late sixties and Caroline was strangled to death. Could he have inflicted that kind of damage with his own bare hands?"

I studied the images again, taking in the extent of Caroline's injuries. Could a man of his age put that much force on her? Then again, she was also older herself. If she were on blood thinners, she might bruise very easily.

"Was there any blood evidence found on Ed or his clothing?" I asked.

Andrews shook his head. "No. He was clean when officers arrived at the scene."

I drummed my fingers on the table, thinking aloud. "Got the autopsy?"

"Right here." Andrews slid it over to me. I took my time reading the entire report.

"It says here that 'clotting factors indicated a therapeutic level of anticoagulation, as would be expected for a patient with atrial fibrillation'" in the toxicology report."

"That would make her more susceptible to bruising."

I nodded. "And more likely that Ed was the killer. It doesn't take much to bruise someone on blood thinners."

"We need to take a hard look at his alibi and confirm it."

I met Andrews' gaze. "Did he claim to be anywhere Saturday night?"

Andrews consulted his notes. "Ed said he was with his mistress, Rachel Adams. Then he went home Sunday morning to have brunch with Caroline like they do every weekend."

I clenched my jaw in disgust. "How thoughtful of him to share a meal with his wife after screwing around. We'll need to verify everything with the mistress."

Andrews nodded in agreement as he jotted down notes.

"What else did he say?" I asked.

"Nothing, but he lawyered up pretty fast. Ever since, Donovan's kept him completely tight-lipped. Not even Henderson was able to get him to crack."

I hesitated, debating how much I could reveal to Andrews. Erin had entrusted me with those photos for a reason. But with Ed not giving up any information about his movements, his whereabouts on the day before the crime were becoming even more valuable.

"There is something else," I said finally. "Ramirez was with Martin the day before the murder."

Andrews' eyes widened. "How do you know that?"

"I can't say much more right now. But it's clear those two have a deeper connection. Then Ramirez shows up at the crime scene? It's too coincidental."

I shook my head, frustration bubbling just beneath the surface. My fingers drummed restlessly on the table as I tried to piece together the missing information. "If Ed's not the killer, then who is? And what does Ramirez have to do with this?"

Andrews leaned back, crossing his arms as he considered. "Any chance we could get him to talk?"

A bitter laugh escaped me before I could stop it. "No." I leaned forward, the tension in my body pulling my shoulders tight. "Ramirez knows the game better than any of us. He's not going to open his mouth, not now, not ever. He wouldn't risk anything backfiring on him."

Andrews rubbed his chin thoughtfully, eyes narrowing. "What if he were offered a deal to cooperate?"

I twisted my lips, tapping my pen against the table in thought. "Shaun Stevens is handling his trial. Ramirez already pled 'not guilty.'"

"You know a defendant can change their mind on that with the right motivation." Andrews' tone was calm, but his raised eyebrow signaled hope.

I rubbed the back of my neck, tension crawling up my spine. "Motivation or not, Ramirez isn't the type to be swayed by a deal. But maybe..." I trailed off, my mind racing with possibilities. "I know, but getting a cop on embezzlement and drug trafficking charges is a pretty big deal. I'm not so sure Tom is going to authorize a plea bargain."

"It's worth the ask, right?"

I shrugged. "I guess. I just think I already know the answer." I made a note to go ask Tom about this Monday, but I had a feeling I'd be wasting my time.

I glanced at my watch, the late hour creeping up on me. The weight of the day settled heavier on my shoulders, knowing that tomorrow would bring another long stretch of sifting through the endless discovery documents with Lisa. "What's your schedule look like tomorrow?" I asked. "We should pay the mistress a visit first thing before I get bogged down in all these boxes."

"I'm free in the morning," Andrews replied.

A smile tugged at my lips, grateful for Andrews' steady presence. I began stacking the case files into organized piles, trying to impose some order on the chaos that surrounded us.

Andrews let out a soft chuckle and moved to help, his hands brushing against the folders as he lifted a few. "Let me take care of these boxes," he offered, his voice light but reassuring. "I know you're planning to bury yourself in them back at your office."

I nodded, appreciating the unspoken understanding between us. We weren't just cleaning up the remnants of the night's work—we were gearing up for another round, another long day. I laughed. "You know me so well."

As Andrews and I lugged the heavy boxes of case files into my office, we nearly collided with Robert Shaw, one of the senior assistant district attorneys. He stepped back quickly, narrowly avoiding a cardboard corner to the chest.

"Whoa there, Alex," he chuckled, steadying himself against the doorframe. "Looks like you're setting up camp."

I smiled apologetically. "Sorry about that, Rob. What's got you here so late?"

"Forgot a file at my desk and decided it was worth coming back for. What's all this?"

"Just bringing in some files for the Martin case. "

His eyebrows raised slightly. "The Martin case? Oh, that's right, you're sitting first on it. That's a big one."

"Yeah," I replied, setting down my box with a grunt. "It's... complicated."

Rob nodded knowingly. "Those are often the most interesting ones." He glanced at the stacks of files. "You know, I've been around the block a few times with cases like these. If you need any guidance or want to bounce ideas off someone, my door's always open."

"Thanks, Rob," I said, genuinely appreciating the offer. "I might just take you up on that."

He gave me a friendly pat on the shoulder. "Good luck, Alex. I'm sure you'll crack it."

TEN

THE FADED RED bricks and overgrown trees loomed into view as we pulled up to the address. I double-checked the house number on the witness list. 418 Willow Street. This was it.

Andrews cut the engine, and the sudden silence felt heavy, like it had weight. We exited the car, the door hinges creaking loudly in the stillness of the neighborhood. As we walked up the front porch, my eyes wandered across the details of the house—or rather, the lack of them. The peeling paint curled at the edges, clinging desperately to the rotting wood. Empty flowerbeds lined the front yard, now little more than patches of dirt and weeds. The once white porch railing had turned a sickly shade of gray, weathered from years of neglect.

The whole place seemed abandoned by life. There was nothing here that suggested warmth, care, or even the hint of wealth I would expect from someone supposedly the favorite mistress of a millionaire. I glanced at the cracked windows, half-expecting them to crumble with a gust of wind.

"This... doesn't quite fit the profile, does it?" I murmured, scanning the hollow shell of a house.

Andrews grunted in agreement, his face twisted in mild disbelief.

"Maybe she has a collection of designer purses somewhere in there, 'cause it's sure not going into house maintenance."

I shook my head, biting back a smile at his joke. "You're terrible."

He smirked, shrugging as we approached the front door. "Just calling it like I see it." Andrews rapped his knuckles against the door. Footsteps shuffled, then stopped. The faint sound of breathing came from the other side.

The door inched open. A petite woman peered out, her eyes darting between us.

"Rachel Adams?" Andrews' voice was steady.

She gave a slight nod.

"Detective Daniel Andrews." He flashed his badge to the woman as confirmation. "We just have a few questions about Caroline Martin's murder."

Her shoulders tensed. She started to close the door. I jumped in.

"It won't take long, ma'am."

She hesitated, then stepped back. "Okay," she murmured, her voice barely even a whisper. The door swung open. My first victory—she was cooperating. For now.

We followed her in. The entryway was dim, cluttered with stacks of old magazines piled high on a small side table. A pair of shoes lay abandoned by the door, as if they'd been kicked off in a hurry. The walls were lined with mismatched picture frames, some tilted as if knocked askew and never straightened. A coat rack, overwhelmed with jackets and scarves, leaned precariously to one side. The narrow hall felt claustrophobic, every inch filled with something, like she had been trying to hold onto too much for too long. She led us to the kitchen and perched on a stool at the counter. I cataloged her appearance—bleached hair pulled back into a tight bun, lounge clothes hanging loosely off her thin frame. Her eyes darted around the room, looking anywhere but at us. It was clear she was ready to flee at any moment. I knew she was in her twenties, but her gauntness made her appear older.

Andrews leaned against the counter opposite her. His tone was calm, conversational. "How long have you known Edward Martin?"

"About a year." Her voice was barely a whisper. "I'm—I was—his assistant."

"And you saw each other regularly?"

"Nearly every day. We worked together."

Andrews nodded, keeping his gaze on her gentle. "What about last weekend? Saturday, Sunday morning?"

Her eyes dropped to the counter. "He was with me. He stayed the night Saturday like he always does. Then he left in the morning."

"What time did he leave?"

"Maybe around ten."

Andrews' eyes flickered to me. If Martin had left here at 10, there's no way he could have made it home to commit a murder and call 911. The timeline didn't fit.

I scribbled a quick note: *Check commute time from Rachel's place to the Martin home.* If the distance was substantial, it could give us a clear alibi or, at the very least, create reasonable doubt. I'd need to pull traffic records for that day, but it could poke a hole in the prosecution's timeline.

Andrews continued after jotting something down, his tone still gentle. "Does he normally stay 'til 10?"

"No. It was later than usual."

Rachel fidgeted with a fraying thread on her shirt sleeve, eyes still downcast. I could tell she was debating how much more to reveal. The longer the silence stretched, the more I wondered what else she knew and wasn't saying. "What time did he arrive on Saturday?" I asked, also keeping my tone soft. This woman looked worn down, her eyes hollow, and the dark circles beneath them told me she hadn't slept well in days—maybe weeks. Life had clearly taken its toll on her.

"Around four in the afternoon."

I scribbled another note. That matched with the timestamp on the photo Erin had given me. Martin's alibi was holding up.

Rachel lifted her gaze to me, her eyes glassy with exhaustion. "Is Ed going to prison?"

I chose my words carefully. "The jury will decide. It's possible he could walk."

Andrews tried to catch my eye, but I didn't look at him. I was focused solely on Rachel, on what else she wanted to say.

The flicker of fear that crossed her face didn't go unnoticed. Her eyes widened and she shrank back against her seat.

I could tell Rachel was on the verge of spilling something, but I also knew that one misstep could have her clamming up completely. Still, I ventured. "Do you want him to go to prison?"

She kept fiddling with the hem of her shirt, her eyes down. "Maybe." It was a whisper, but I heard it.

"Why's that?"

"He's been...different lately."

"Different how?"

"More heated than usual."

I sat down in a kitchen chair so that I would be lower than her, hoping to seem less intimidating. The last thing I wanted to do was scare this woman off. "I want to understand, Rachel. Can you help me understand?"

Rachel let out a big sigh. "He's changed a lot since I met him. When we first got involved, he was calm, collected—charming, even. But now...throwing fits. Sometimes violent. Yelling. Smashing things. Hitting things."

"Has he ever hit you?"

"No." She said the word slowly. "But he's come close."

"Do you want him to go to prison because you are afraid for your life?"

Her head tilted just a fraction of an inch, and then she nodded. "If he walks," she whispered, "I'm not sure I will be safe."

I jotted more notes, and Andrews flipped to a new page. I put my pen down and looked into her eyes, trying to will her to look into mine. "Your testimony could help us."

She curled further into herself and did not look up. "I told you. He was here until 10."

The more times she said it, the less I believed her. I pressed on. "And we can protect you. If you're afraid—"

Rachel's eyes snapped up to meet mine. Her hands dropped the fraying fabric and her voice hardened. "No." Her chest heaved with deep breaths. I'd crossed a line I hadn't known existed. "I don't want to testify. I already told his lawyer that."

"Rachel—"

"Please leave," she said, practically pushing us out the door, then slamming it shut behind us. Andrews and I stood on the porch, staring at each other.

"Well," Andrews said, pocketing his notebook. "That was interesting."

I nodded slowly. Rachel clearly knew more than she was letting on.

"We need to convince her to testify," I said, glancing at Andrews.

He raised an eyebrow. "Why? Her timeline supports Martin."

I paused, feeling my frustration bubble beneath the surface. "She's not being truthful, and you know it."

Andrews tilted his head, considering. "I'll give you that she was jumpy, but her lover just murdered his wife. That's bound to make anyone nervous. Doesn't mean she's lying."

"She was evasive," I countered. "Especially when I pressed her about the timeline. Something's off."

Andrews nodded slowly. "Yeah, she got real cagey the second you applied pressure. But do you think she's hiding something, or just terrified?"

I bit my lip, thinking it through. "Could be both. But either way, I want her on the stand. Donovan's going to think she's a solid witness for Ed, but we can use her contradictions to our advantage."

He looked at me, a little skeptical. "You could just subpoena her. We know where she is."

"A subpoena only gets her to show up," I said. "But if she's not willing to cooperate, she'll be useless to us in court."

"There's gotta be a way," he muttered as we started toward the car. "Did you see how she reacted when you mentioned the jury deciding Ed's fate? She wants him gone."

"Because she's afraid of him," I said, the pieces starting to come together. "She said he's gotten violent lately."

Andrews nodded, his expression thoughtful. "That might be the key." He pulled his phone out of his pocket at the sound of a notification. Grumbling about something, he tapped out a reply and then tucked it back in.

My hand rested on the door handle. "We have to convince her she'll be protected and that her testimony is crucial."

Andrews nodded slowly. "Let's give her some time to process, then come back and lay out her options."

"Worth a shot," I agreed. "I wonder what Donovan said to her."

I glanced back at Rachel's house as we got into the car. Our visit had rattled something loose inside her, I could tell by the look on her face. But fear was a powerful motivator too. We'd have to find the right balance of reassurance and incentive if we hoped to gain her cooperation.

As Andrews pulled away down the tree-lined street, I flipped open my notebook, jotting down impressions rather than just facts. Rachel was Ed's only alibi, and I doubted the jury would believe her if she ever testified—but that was exactly what Donovan was counting on. He'd assume she was a weak witness, his witness.

I tapped my pen against the paper, thinking it through. Donovan would use her to reinforce his narrative: the loyal mistress, too in love or too scared to turn on her lover. He'd paint her as emotional and unreliable, a woman easily manipulated by Ed. My pen scribbled, "Donovan thinks she's his."

But what if I could turn that around? Show the jury that Rachel's fear of Ed was genuine. Use her testimony against him instead of letting Donovan weaponize it for his defense. I paused, staring at the page. It was a risky move. She'd have to walk a fine line—just enough to make the jury believe she was scared for her life, but not so much that she collapsed under cross-examination.

Could I manage that? Could Rachel hold up?

I frowned, noting down, "Donovan will exploit her, but we could flip this." It felt fragile, like the entire case might collapse if the plan backfired. If Rachel faltered, if she seemed too rehearsed or too broken... Donovan would pounce, and all my efforts would come undone.

I underlined "could backfire" twice. My gut told me Rachel had more to reveal, something that could turn the tide, but if I pushed too hard, she might implode on the stand—and I couldn't afford that. "If Martin had anger issues like she hinted," I said, "it may have boiled over that morning. Violent outbursts escalated over time, then came to a head. Would also explain why he would have left later than normal, if that's true."

Andrews nodded. "Plays into the crime of passion angle. But we need more than speculation."

"Rachel's testimony could provide that. Give the jury a clearer picture of Martin's state of mind." I tapped my pen on my notepad. "We'll give her a day or two, then try again."

Andrews frowned, his brow creasing in that familiar way when he sensed trouble. "And if Donovan's gotten to her first?"

I rubbed the back of my neck, tension creeping up my spine. "Then we keep digging," I muttered, leaning back against the car seat. I folded my arms across my chest, feeling the weight of the case settling on my shoulders. "There's got to be a crack in his wall of witness intimidation." My fingers tapped absentmindedly against my arm, my mind racing with possibilities.

Andrews shook his head slightly, eyes narrowing in thought, and I caught him glancing sideways at me, gauging my resolve. "Guy seems untouchable lately," he grumbled.

"Nobody's untouchable. We just have to find his weak spot." I stared out the window, thoughts swirling. "Donovan probably spun all kinds of veiled threats if she cooperates."

Andrews clenched his jaw. "If he's tampering with a witness, that's a felony. He's obstructing justice—manipulating witnesses to control their testimony, maybe even intimidating them to keep quiet or lie on the stand." He shook his head. "If I could get proof of that, we could nail him."

"Defense attorneys are masters at skating the line," I said, rubbing my temple. "Veiled threats, subtle pressure—it's all part of the game." I flipped through my notes, the weariness settling in. "But we still have a timeline forming. And there are clear signs Martin's aggression was escalating."

Andrews frowned. "But it's all circumstantial. We don't have anything concrete placing him at the scene of the crime. You're good, but even with your skills, it's tough to get past reasonable doubt on this one." I rubbed my temples, feeling a headache coming on. He was right. Donovan would twist anything short of an airtight case to suit his narrative. We needed more than what we had to win this case.

"There's got to be something we're missing," I said. "If we can just—"

"Hey!" Andrews slammed the brakes, jolting me forward. A dark sedan zoomed past us, nearly clipping the front bumper.

"What the hell?" I glanced at Andrews. His eyes were fixed on the speeding car.

"I saw that car," Andrews said, his gaze intense on the street in front of him. "Parked outside of Rachel's house. By the curb."

My pulse quickened. "You think someone was watching her?"

Andrews nodded, his brows furrowing. "This just got a lot more complicated."

ELEVEN

"YOU BOTH LOOK A LITTLE SHAKEN." Lisa's soft, almost soothing voice cut through the tension as Andrews and I stumbled into the office. "What happened?"

"Tail," Andrews grunted, thumbing over his shoulder as if the very idea pursued us into the office. His gaze flickered to the windows. "Could've been after us or Rachel."

"Rachel..." Lisa murmured, her brows knitting together. "Rachel Adams? Ed's alibi?"

I nodded. Her brows knotted, mirroring the knot in my gut.

"Why would anyone tail her?" Lisa's question hung heavy.

I shrugged. "Good question. I'd love to know the answer to that, too." My eyes were on the papers littering her desk. "What time did you roll in today?"

"Been here a few hours," she replied, waving vaguely at the clock.

"Find anything good?"

"Just some CDs," she said, holding them up. Then her expression took on a wide grin "Martin's security footage."

"Great work. Get them queued up on my computer," I said.

She moved towards the computer as I turned away. Coffee. Needed coffee to think straight.

I shuffled to the office's coffee machine. Andrews shadowed me, close enough that I could feel his silent question pressing in.

"Did you get a look at the driver?" I asked, thumbing the dispenser button with more force than necessary.

His eyes were distant. "White male. Forties maybe."

"Not much to go on." I grabbed the Styrofoam cup and put another beneath the machine for him. "Do you think Rachel's safe?"

He took too long to answer. My stomach tightened in the silence.

"Hard to know," he finally said, and I caught a flicker of doubt in his eyes.

I watched the dark liquid fill the cup like it could drown all our problems. "Maybe we should station a unit at her place."

Andrews shook his head. "Bad move. She'll clam up for good, thinking she's got a target on her back."

"Better her think that if it's true than become a dead witness."

Andrews opened and closed his mouth a few times. I could tell he was struggling with whether to say his next thought.

I shoved the cup of black caffeine into his chest. "Spit it out."

He took a sip from the steaming cup, wincing as he swallowed. Must have been too hot. "Would that be such a bad thing?"

I looked at him, eyes wide.

"If she disappears, Donovan's alibi goes up in smoke."

"I can't protect a witness who isn't cooperating with us," I said, which was true. Tom would never approve funds to put her into witness protection so she could testify against our case. "Do you really think she's in danger?"

Andrews blew a bit on his coffee. "Depends on who was in that car and who they're answering to."

We turned to go back to my office. "Think this is bigger than just a crime of passion?"

"Ed's got deep pockets and deeper connections," Andrews said. "We shouldn't rule anything out."

I pushed open the door to my office. Lisa was hunched over the desk, staring intently at the computer screen.

"Find anything good?" I asked, taking a sip. The office brew was bitter and always tasted slightly burnt, far from great, but still a welcome comfort after where we'd just been. The familiar taste grounded me, even if it wasn't anything special.

"Donovan gave us two CDs," she said without looking up, motioning to the cases at the edge of my desk. Her voice was edged with frustration. "The first one cuts off Sunday morning at nine a.m. Next one picks up at eleven, same day."

I leaned over her shoulder to look at the paused image of the front of the house. "Please tell me you've got the gap,"

She clicked through the files. "Gap's a ghost."

"Of course," I scoffed, bitterness creeping into my chest, settling around my ribs. "Is there at least anything useful on the tapes?"

"No. The first tape shows Ed leaving the house around 2 p.m. the day before and the second tape shows Ed in the driveway talking to the police after the murder was already discovered."

Lisa scrolled back and forth on the footage. I could see the squad car in the driveway and the two officers speaking with Martin. My eyes focused on Ramirez, the assistant chief who had no business being in a patrol car again—especially at a scene like this. Someone of his rank would typically be behind a desk or coordinating from headquarters, not responding to routine calls. Yet here he was, front and center. I wasn't sure what I expected to see on the tape that would be helpful, but the fact that he was there at all was a red flag I couldn't ignore. Something about it felt off.

"The crime is committed during intermission, and we're left holding the popcorn." I stood up straighter and folded my arms across myself. "God damn Donovan. I'm going to tear him a new one for this."

I reached for the phone, but Andrews' hand clamped down on my wrist, his grip firm. "Think, Alex. There could be a play here."

I paused, breathed out a heavy sigh, and let the red haze clear. Andrews was right. I needed to play this smart, not angry.

I nodded at him, and he let go of my hand. With a cooler head, I dialed Donovan, slipping into a falsely warm tone that I kept reserved for snakes like him.

"Alex," he said, all fake bravado. I could hear his Joker-esque smile through the phone. "What can I do you for?" He could go die in a river, but I didn't say that.

"I was actually calling to thank you for the swift turnover. Saved me the headache of a motion to compel and we were able to get the footage we needed. Thanks for not making this ugly."

There was a pause on the other end of the line before he spoke. "You know me. I like to play fair."

I hung up quickly. I wanted him dangling on the hook.

Lisa looked between me and Andrews. "What am I missing? You bluff Donovan about the footage we don't have? What's the angle?"

I sat down in the chair across from the desk. "I got him to sweat over that missing two-hour gap. He'll be on the phone soon enough, trying to cover his tracks or poke around for mistakes. Whichever he chooses will tell us whether the gap exists and he didn't turn it over or whether he really doesn't have it."

"But—"

"Donovan thinks we have the gap. So, he's going to call and start asking questions. Maybe he thinks his office made a mistake in turning it over. Maybe he thinks we wouldn't find it. But we'll find out just how important to his case it is based on how he behaves in the next few days."

"Smart." She nodded, slowly. "Very smart."

"Sometimes." I shrugged. Who knew in this sort of game.

Her gaze drifted to the mountain of cardboard on the floor. "Any chance we hit pay dirt before we reach the bottom?"

"Probably not," I admitted. "But we gotta look anyway, because you never know."

TWELVE

I BURST through the courtroom doors, my hair askew and my suit jacket half-buttoned, as if I'd thrown it on during a mad dash. My lungs burned with every breath, and the bailiff shot me a stern look as I practically collapsed into my seat, trying to calm my racing pulse. There was no use trying to explain that I slept through my alarm after spending all weekend going through the remainder of the Martin discovery only to find nothing useful in the files. Or that my colleague had only called yesterday evening to ask me to handle this preliminary hearing.

A preliminary hearing was like the first round in a boxing match. No knockout punches, just enough sparring to show the judge there's a reason to keep fighting. The prosecution—me—presented just enough to demonstrate probable cause. Enough evidence to say, yeah, this case has legs. Let's walk it to trial. It was usually straightforward. But since I hadn't actually prepared for this one, I was relying on the evidence to speak for itself.

The judge emerged through the doors, his black robes swishing against the floor as he moved to his seat. I straightened up, trying to look alert despite the yawning pit in my stomach that longed for coffee. I hadn't had enough time to grab any before throwing clothes on and zooming out the door this morning. Can't have the judge thinking I'm unprepared.

"Case number 24756." The bailiff's voice echoed in the hall. "State versus Derrick Rowe."

I glanced at the defendant, a scrawny teenager slouched in an ill-fitting suit. His lawyer, a severe woman in angular glasses, leaned over to whisper something to him. Probably a reminder to look contrite.

"Ms. Hayes," Judge Plimpton said. "Are you prepared to present?"

"Of course, Your Honor." Although that was a little far from the truth.

The truth was that I was covering this hearing for Ryan Chen, another assistant district attorney at the office, in exchange for a promise to return the favor. Conflict of schedule, he said. Couldn't be helped. And who was I to say no? In the DA's office, you traded favors like kids traded baseball cards—hold onto them long enough, and they might turn into something valuable. Well, in today's times, I supposed Pokémon cards were a more apt analogy.

The defense attorney gave me a nod. Her client looked around the room, his gaze traveling anywhere but at me. He knew the dance. Sit still, look innocent, and hope the prosecutor trips up.

Judge Plimpton prompted me to begin. "Proceed when ready, Ms. Hayes." I stood, clearing my throat.

"Thank you, Your Honor." I stood there, a deer in the proverbial headlights, as the judge's gaze settled on me with the expectation of progress.

"Your evidence, Ms. Hayes?"

"Right," I muttered more to myself than anyone else, scrambling for composure. I flipped open the folder Chen had left with his secretary. Supposedly, it had everything I needed inside. There was a note about the clerk having security footage to play.

A quick glance to the clerk—a silent plea—and she was already ahead of me, slipping a disc into the player.

A screen on the side of the courtroom flickered to life. It was a feed from a security camera. The camera had obviously been positioned behind the register given the angle, which gave a clear view of anyone approaching the register and entering or exiting the store.

"Your Honor," I began, my voice growing steadier with each word, "the footage we will view clearly shows the defendant, Mr. Rowe, engaging in the act of theft."

Onscreen, Rowe moved with the jerky confidence of someone who thought they were smarter than the camera lens. He glanced around, reached out, and pocketed an item—small, too small to make out from this angle, but his intentions were clear as day. He didn't buy it. He stole it.

"Here," I said, pointing to the moment his hand contacted the merchandise, "the defendant can be seen concealing store property."

On film, Rowe made for the exit, the stolen item now invisible within his clothing. With a practiced ease, he passed the checkout without pausing, without paying. The clerk hit pause just after Rowe's figure crossed the threshold.

I blinked as I stared at the now-frozen image on the screen. The timestamp in the corner showed this had occurred last Sunday at 8:57 a.m., but that couldn't be right. Because walking into the store was none other than Rachel Adams.

My breath caught in my throat. Rachel had said she'd been home with Ed at that time. Yet here she was, clear as day on the security tape.

I tried to make sense of the discrepancy. It reinforced my suspicion that Rachel hadn't been truthful during our conversation with Andrews. The footage seemed too clear for me to be missing something.

"Counselor?" Judge Plimpton's voice startled me from my thoughts.

"Apologies, Your Honor. Could you repeat the question?"

The judge huffed. "I asked if you had any other evidence to present at this time."

"Yes, Your Honor," I said, hoping I sounded more confident than I felt. "The prosecution would like to submit the sworn affidavit of Linda Johnson, eyewitness to the defendant at the scene."

The clerk handed the affidavit to the judge. He glanced over it briefly.

"Any objections to the affidavit being entered into evidence?" the judge asked, turning to the defense table.

"None, Your—"

"Let it be entered," the judge said, his gavel ready to punctuate the moment. "I find sufficient evidence to bind this matter over for trial. We're adjourned."

I gathered my things, my mind still spinning. I'd have to follow up on this development, but carefully.

Rowe's defense attorney approached me just outside the courtroom. "My client would be grateful for a plea deal," she said.

I gave her a terse smile. "I'm not the one handling this matter, but I'll take the sentiment to Ryan Chen."

She gave me a nod and we parted ways. I moved quickly through the courthouse and then stepped out into the bright courtyard, shielding my eyes from the blazing sun.

I used the walk back to the office to sort through the churn of emotions the footage had stirred up. I wasn't surprised Rachel had lied—I'd never fully trusted her—but seeing the proof, undeniable and right in front of me, still left a sour taste. It wasn't just disappointment, it was frustration. She'd wasted our time, dodging questions and playing games. I clenched my fists, trying to steady myself. What was it about this case that made everything feel so personal? When I arrived, I spotted a missed call from Greg Mitchell, no doubt anxious for an update on his client's sentencing recommendation.

Before returning his call, I needed permission from Tom. While I was there, I could ask about Ramirez, too. I headed straight for Tom's office. Janice, ever the gatekeeper, stood up as I approached.

I kept my tone even, despite the urgency nipping at my heels. "Tom in?"

"Is it important?"

"Need authorization for a sentencing rec and a potential plea."

She gave me a thin smile. "He's just wrapping up a call. I'll let him know you're here."

After a few moments, she waved me in. Tom sat at his desk, rifling through a stack of files.

"Alex," he said, barely sparing me a glance. "What can I do for you?"

I launched right into it. "I wanted to get your approval for a lower sentencing recommendation for Elijah Harper in exchange for his cooperation."

"What did he do?"

"It was a domestic."

"Plea or trial?"

"Trial."

Tom frowned. Generally, if a prosecutor offered the defendant a plea deal and they elected to go to trial instead, we always recommended the maximum sentencing. It was our little way of saying "don't waste our time" and "payback's a bitch." Which is why I knew I needed approval on this, but it was obvious that Tom needed persuading.

"He may have information on the Martin case."

Tom sat back in his chair. "He may or he does?"

"He probably does?" I shrugged, trying not to smirk. Legal speak for "maybe," which lawyers loved to throw around. Tom deadpanned and I resisted the urge to laugh. "It's reasonably likely that he has information that could be useful," I added, using my most professional voice.

Tom rolled his eyes. "Fine, approved. What else?"

"I also wanted to discuss the possibility of a plea deal for Officer Ramirez—"

Tom cut me off with a swift wave of his hand. "Absolutely not. We do not make deals with dirty cops."

"Ramirez was at the scene, and I've got him with Martin the day before the murder. If I can get to him—"

"No way, Alex." Tom's tone took a sharp turn. "There is no plea for Ramirez."

"Tom, he could be valuable," I tried to argue, sensing the door slamming shut even as I reached for it.

"End of discussion." His tone brooked no argument, but I wasn't one to back down that easily.

"Tom—"

He raised his hand, signaling the conversation was over. I bit my tongue in frustration, swallowing the argument that burned at the back of my throat. One battle at a time, I reminded myself, forcing calm.

I left Tom's office, the frustration following me like a shadow, and returned to my own. As soon as I stepped inside, I grabbed a yellow legal pad off the shelf where I'd tossed it earlier and flung it onto my desk with more force than necessary. It landed with a thud, the sound perfectly matching my mood—irritation reverberating in the air. I needed that pad for the conversation I was about to have, and I wanted it at hand to jot down anything useful. But, I didn't mind using it to vent my frustrations, first.

I dialed Lisa's extension, and within a minute, she appeared in the doorway.

"What happened?" she asked, her voice edged with concern.

"Tom's stonewalling on Ramirez," I said, leaning back in my chair. "Because he's a cop, obviously."

Her brows knitted together in a look I recognized all too well—concern mixed with irritation. "Right. Can't show favorites, even if it cracks the case wide open."

"Exactly." I rubbed my temple. "But I need to know what Ramirez knows. It could be the key to everything."

"Need?" Lisa folded her arms, raising an eyebrow. "Maybe. But you want it."

"Badly," I admitted. I picked up the phone again, wasting no time dialing Greg Mitchell's number. I tapped my fingers on the desk impatiently as it rang.

Finally, Mitchell picked up, sounding far too pleased with himself, which was fine, because I was going to fix that in about two seconds. This was the game we attorneys played with one another. Personally, I hated it, but it was sort of like a union. Everyone joined the union.

And everyone played the game. "Counselor, I was just about to call you. Do we have a deal for my client?"

"We do," I said briskly, my voice all business. "And I'd like to speak with him right away. Can you arrange that?"

"Whoa, slow down," Mitchell chuckled, his easy-going tone grating on my nerves. "We still need to discuss the details of the sentencing recommendation. My client will cooperate after you follow through at the sentencing hearing."

"Ha, no way," I shot back, rolling my eyes at the typical defense attorney games. I wasn't in the mood. "We talk to your client now, or the deal's off the table."

A pause. "Fine," he relented after a beat, the edge creeping into his voice.

"Better call your client quick," I added, a small smile forming. "Because I'm heading down to JPC now to talk to him."

I hung up on his protests, shoving my phone away and grabbing my bag from the floor. Lisa was already on her feet, her expression a mixture of amusement and anticipation.

"Shall we?" she asked with a grin.

I shot her a look but couldn't help but crack a smile. "Let's go."

THIRTEEN

I PUSHED OPEN the heavy door to the Harris County Joint Processing Facility, fondly known as JPC. The air reeked of sweat, fear, and regret. JPC was essentially purgatory on Earth. Lives caught in limbo. Here, defendants awaiting trial and inmates awaiting sentencing were jumbled together like mismatched puzzle pieces, all mixed together in the system's grand game of incarceration until their fates were sorted and sealed.

There were three processing facilities like this in the county, but this was the main one. It was positioned just across the Buffalo Bayou. From the courthouse, you could see JPC and vice versa. For those caught by the system, their scenery was a constant reminder of where they'd been and where they might be headed—an unending loop of dread and hope.

"Morning," I said, flashing my badge in routine monotony. Lisa followed my cue and did the same. The dead-eyed guard motioned for us to follow.

We marched down the endless hallway, his keys jangling.

"Feels like a maze designed by someone with a cruel sense of humor," Lisa whispered, her steps cautious, eyes scanning the unfamiliar corridors. Her posture was tight, fingers gripping her bag a little too firmly as we navigated the labyrinth of halls.

"More like a rat trap," I replied, keeping my voice level. This place was designed to extract truth through intimidation. The threat of never seeing sunlight again could make any man talk.

The guard stopped at one of the countless metal doors lining the walls and went through his ritual of unlocking. The locks clicked open, and the door creaked inward to reveal the tiny room within. He waved us in without a word. Lisa hesitated, uncertainty in her eyes.

"You can watch from the viewing room," I said. "This shouldn't take long."

She nodded and hurried off as I stepped inside.

Harper's hands were bound to the cold metal cuffs, but it was his eyes that caught me—the raw contempt in them. I'd seen that look before, the stubborn pride of a man just before this place broke him.

"You better check the attitude," I said coldly. "Your cooperation—or lack thereof—is going to reflect in my sentencing recommendation."

He glared back at me, unblinking. The guard shifted behind me and sighed.

I cleared my throat and asked, "Should we wait for your lawyer?"

"No point." His low growl of a voice dripped with bitterness. "I've bled enough money for that charlatan. Should've just pled guilty from the start."

"Hindsight is twenty-twenty, right?"

"Something like that."

I sat down across from him, unfazed. This wasn't my first rodeo with defendants regretting their choices after the fact. It also wouldn't be my last.

"Let's get on with it then," Harper grumbled, shifting in his seat. I could see the fight draining from him, a begrudging acceptance taking its place.

"Let's talk about the Martin job. I need everything—how you got hired, by whom, when they reached out, what you saw when you were there, and the work you did on the security system."

Harper sniffed. "That's a lot of questions all at once."

"Let's start with who hired you."

"Requests came through my website."

"Ed wasn't the one to call you?"

"No one called me."

I started taking notes. "You never spoke to Ed on the phone?"

"Isn't that what I just said?"

I looked up from my legal pad and leveled him with a glare.

Harper looked down at the table. "No, ma'am."

"So you get a request to go to his house through your website. Did you speak to him when you got there?"

Harper shook his head. "No. No one was ever there. Every time, like clockwork, the place was empty."

"How'd you get in if no one was home?" I asked.

"Work request online always included access codes. Punched them in, did my job, and left."

"What did you see when you were there?" I asked, keeping my voice even, almost disinterested.

"Nothing out of the ordinary," Harper replied with a shrug. "Just a rich person's house."

"Caroline Martin? Did you ever see her around?"

He shook his head. "Like I said, no one was ever home. It was like a ghost house, just me and the silence."

I tapped my pen against the notepad, my thoughts circling back to the footage. It was strange, this picture of a seemingly empty house, yet so much was happening inside it—too much to ignore. My gut twisted at the thought. How could everything look so pristine on the surface, but underneath, something was clearly wrong? If no one was ever home, how was the security system going down so often? Who was tampering with it, and why?

"Tell me about the issues you were called for."

"Security system malfunctions. They claimed it kept going down, without warning. System going down 'unexpectedly,' weird glitches, cameras offline."

"And what did you do to fix it?"

"Nothing," was his reply.

I furrowed my brow. "Nothing?"

"Never found a thing wrong with it." He leaned back. "Every time I checked it top to bottom and found nothing wrong with it. I'd report back, and in another week, they'd send another request. Same story."

"You kept going back?"

"Payment was prompt each time." Harper spread his hands as much as the cuffs would allow. "So, I kept showing up. Customer's always right in my book. Especially if they're paying."

I studied him, searching for any hint of deception. But his nonchalant attitude seemed genuine.

Either the Martins were paranoid and imagined issues that didn't exist, or they were fabricating problems to establish Harper's presence. I wasn't sure which scenario was more troubling.

"You were there July twentieth?"

"Yeah."

"And everything was working?"

"As far as I could tell."

I stood from the seat, trying not to wince at how its legs scraped against the floor. "That will be all for now. I appreciate you clarifying these details."

Harper's smug expression faltered slightly. "So, how's all this work? I cooperated." He said it expectantly and I knew instantly what he was thinking.

"You did, so I'll recommend the lower end to the judge."

A look of confusion washed over his features. He studied me for a moment. "There's going to be a sentencing?"

Now it was my turn to be confused. "That's how this works, Mr. Harper. You were found guilty. There are consequences."

"That's not what I was told would happen."

I paused, my mouth hanging open for just a second, debating on what to say next. "What were you told would happen? And by whom?"

His brow furrowed and then he shook his head, as if he'd made some decision. "Nothing. Got my facts mixed up, that's all."

His shoulders slumped as if some new realization was just hitting him, and not a good one. I left the room without another glance, meeting Lisa just outside the door. She opened her mouth, but I shook my head sharply. Not here. Not with ears all around ready to pick apart our conversation for gossip or leverage.

We walked briskly through the sterile halls, past endless locked doors and expressionless faces, until finally emerging into the late afternoon sun, an alien sensation against my skin after the chill of the jail.

Once settled in my car, I let out a long exhale, allowing the tension to drain from my shoulders. Lisa glanced at me.

"Thoughts?" she asked.

I considered for a moment before responding. "His story could explain the gap in the security footage. But if there were never any actual issues with the system..."

"Yeah, that seems weird," Lisa agreed. "Why make up problems that weren't there?"

"Exactly. It doesn't add up. Either Ed Martin liked wasting money on a repairman who never fixed the problem, or he was calling someone over just to create the illusion that there was a problem in the first place."

"So he could hide the footage showing him kill Caroline?"

I tapped my nose, because that's exactly what I was thinking.

"Did it seem like he thought he was going to walk?"

"It did seem like that, didn't it?"

"Maybe he got bad info from Mitchell?"

I frowned. "No, I don't think so. Mitchell's been playing this beat for far too long. He wouldn't mess something like that up." I closed my eyes, the frustration building behind them. "There's too many things that just feel off lately."

Lisa looked thoughtful. "I mean, maybe it's just one of those things that doesn't have an explanation."

"There's an explanation for Ed and Harper's behavior here. There's always a reason behind people's actions," I said. "Always."

FOURTEEN

THE SMELL of burnt coffee lingered in the hallway as I stepped outside my office. Either that, or it was just how our cheap coffee smelled, brewed perfectly. Ryan Chen nearly collided with me, a sheepish grin spreading across his boyish face.

"Sorry about that, Alex. I was just coming to thank you for covering the Rowe preliminary hearing yesterday."

I waved a hand. "No problem. It was pretty straightforward—judge rubber-stamped it, to be expected."

Chen's eyes lit up. "Hey, we should grab dinner on Friday, and you can fill me in on the details. I'm curious to hear your take."

I hesitated. It's not that I didn't want to grab dinner with Chen. He was one of the more tolerable attorneys at the office. "Sorry, I really can't. Jury selection for the Martin trial starts Monday and I'll be busy prepping all weekend."

"Which is precisely why you should take a break," Ryan countered smoothly. The hint of a smile played at the corners of his mouth. "Get your mind off the case for an hour or two before diving into the deep end. Trust me, it'll help."

"Your offer seems bias-motivated," I pointed out, a smile playing on my own lips.

He shrugged. "Aren't all offers?"

I sighed, sensing I wouldn't shake him. "Fine. But just for an hour. I wasn't kidding about needing to prep. And we leave from the office after work. I can't afford the luxury of leisure these days."

"Perfect," Chen replied, satisfaction evident in his tone. "It's a date then."

I let Ryan stroll away, leaving me in the quiet corridor.

Lisa was handling one of my old cases, a 'disturbing the peace' arraignment. I was confident she could handle something like this alone and had left her to it that morning. In the meantime, I headed over to the precinct to speak with Andrews.

He glanced up as I approached. "What brings you by, Counselor?"

"We should head out to Ed's house before Monday," I replied. "I'm worried we might have missed something that could break this thing open."

He gave me a knowing smirk.

"Don't," I said, frowning and shaking my head. "Don't do that."

"Do what?"

I waved my hand at his face. "That look. That thing that you do."

"You're getting anxious ahead of trial."

"So what if I am? It's the biggest trial of my life, and there's going to be a lot of press. I'd have to be a psychopath not to be anxious."

Andrews considered this. "That's not entirely true. Secondary psychopathy is actually associated with higher degrees of anxiety than—"

"Can we please focus?"

"Can't hurt to take another look," he mumbled.

"Thank you," I said dramatically.

He grabbed his suit jacket and we made our way to the parking lot.

"Alright, what's on your mind?" Andrews asked when I stayed too quiet. "Besides the crippling anxiety."

"Right, besides that," I muttered. "I covered a prelim for Rowe yesterday. Shoplifting from a 7-Eleven. There was video footage and you wanna know who I saw on it?"

"I dunno, do I?"

"Rachel Adams."

His face remained neutral and he blinked at me. "Am I missing something? She's allowed to get a Slurpee, right?"

"Yes, but not at nine in the morning on the day Caroline Martin was murdered."

Realization seemed to dawn on him after that tidbit. "She said she was with Ed right up until he left her place at ten, didn't she?"

I nodded. "Doesn't bode well for her credibility."

"After Ed's house, maybe we should pay her a visit. See if she'll straighten her story out."

"Before that, I want to check with the store. See if they have anything else we could use."

I tugged at the cuff of my sleeve, a habit of mine when pieces weren't falling into place. I was far too close to trial to be tugging at my sleeve.

* * *

WE PULLED up to Ed's sprawling Mediterranean-style mansion. The late afternoon sun was bright against its white stucco walls and terra-cotta roof tiles. A wrought iron gate barred the entrance to the long driveway. It felt more like a fortress than someone's home.

Andrews killed the engine, and we stepped out onto the decorative paver stones, making our way toward the imposing entrance.

"Ed never was granted bail," he said as we made our way up the driveway, more a statement than a question.

"Yeah," I replied. "Wasn't my hearing, but it was a major win for whoever handled it."

"Isn't it a little odd, though?"

His voice carried a hint of skepticism, which matched the uneasy feeling that had settled in my gut since the beginning of this case. "Sure, it's a murder charge, but he had strong ties to the community. First criminal charge ever."

"Judges look at three things," I said. "The nature of the offense, ties to the community, and flight risk."

Andrews pulled out his keys, unlocking the door with a click. Thanks to the standing warrant on the crime scene, we still had full access. I pushed open the heavy oak door, stale air greeting us.

"Exactly, so why no bail?" he pressed, slipping past me into the grand foyer.

"High profile case. Violent crime. Judge probably saw him as a flight risk."

"Still seems odd to me," Andrews said, trailing a hand across an ornate banister as we ascended the staircase.

"Join the club."

Speculating on judicial motives was a waste of time. All that mattered now was scouring the premises for any scrap of evidence I could use to bolster the case against Ed.

The upstairs corridor was lined with doors, but we headed straight for the one at the end, crime scene tape still stretched across the door-way. The master bedroom.

Andrews gestured toward the bedroom, holding the tape up for me. "Shall we?"

"Let's." I ducked under it, stepping into the room.

The bedroom itself was in pristine condition, with no signs of disturbance. The king-sized four poster bed was neatly made, the antique nightstands clear of clutter.

"Nothing out of place," Andrews said, his voice low as he surveyed the room, his eyes scanning.

"Nothing visible," I replied.

I circled the room, scrutinizing every detail. But there was nothing remarkable in plain sight. No stray hairs or fibers, no blood splatters except for the one on the nightstand and the one on the carpet below the bed. No signs of struggle. Just an immaculate, untarnished space.

"Let's check the security system," I suggested, my voice a mask of professional detachment.

Andrews nodded, and we made our way to the garage. The place smelled of stale oil and dust and was filled with tools and sports equipment that seemed out of place in contrast to the pristine interior of the house. In the corner of the space was a locked metal cabinet.

"Control center's gotta be in there," Andrews said, jiggling the handle and confirming its non-movement.

"Seems to be on," I pointed out, noting the small green light glowing steadily through the grate.

"Locked up tight, though."

Andrews crouched down, examining the lock. He reached into his pocket, clearly intending to pick it.

I raised a hand, stopping him mid-movement. "No way. You are not contaminating this crime scene for me and handing Donovan a win on police impropriety." My words came out sharper than I intended, frustration edging into my tone.

He gave me a sheepish grin, retreating from the cabinet. "Fair point."

We left the garage without further comment, the lead feeling more dead-end than promising.

Back at the car, Andrews watched me for a moment before speaking. "You okay? You seem..."

"Upset?" I cut him off, not needing him to state the obvious. "I'm not sure what I expected to find, but it wasn't nothing."

"Pressure's building with the trial so close," he acknowledged, his tone sympathetic but steady.

"It's just...jury selection starts Monday. I've got no motive and no solid forensic evidence. All I've got is speculation and circumstantial bits and pieces." I turned to Andrews, hating the hint of desperation in my own voice. "Right now my whole case rests on 'if he didn't do it, who did?'"

Andrews met my gaze, his expression steadfast. "Then we find something more concrete. We talk to that store clerk, review the footage. There's still time."

I managed a small, grateful smile. Andrews' calm certainty helped temper my rising panic. I nodded, tamping down my doubts.

The security footage. For both our sakes, I prayed he was right.

FIFTEEN

THE 7-ELEVEN LOOKED like it had been slapped together with spit and a prayer, the kind of place where hope came to buy a lottery ticket and left with a pack of cigarettes instead. We pulled into the parking lot, the neon sign flickering like it was on its last leg— "7 ELE_EN," missing the "V" like a hockey player's grin missing a tooth.

"Classy joint," I murmured as Andrews parked the car haphazardly in a front space.

Andrews grunted, his detective face on. It was the same look he'd give a suspect or a particularly tough crossword puzzle.

We walked in, the bell above the door giving off a sad jingle like it knew it wasn't fooling anyone. I noted the security camera behind the clerk. The one that recorded the footage in the Rowe preliminary hearing. It was caked in so much dust it was a wonder it didn't record time in sepia.

"Can I help you?" The clerk looked up, his expression somewhere between bored and dead.

Andrews flashed his badge with all the subtlety of a peacock in mating season. "We need to chat with the manager."

"Sure thing, officers." He popped his gum, leading us through an obstacle course of snack aisles.

"Detective," Andrews corrected him without missing a beat, but the clerk didn't seem to care enough to make a mental note of it.

He knocked on a grimy door marked "Manager." Inside was a small excuse for an office, the air thick with the scent of microwaved meals and lost dreams.

"Mr. Manager, got some company for ya," the clerk announced before vanishing back into retail purgatory.

The manager was an older guy with a comb-over that screamed midlife crisis louder than a red convertible. His shirt, a palette of stains, was buttoned wrong. He was the sort of man who had settled somewhere between "gave up" and "didn't care." He looked up from a cluttered desk that might have been white once upon a time.

"Detectives," he acknowledged with a nod that seemed to take all the energy he had left for the week.

"Got a case that needs cracking," Andrews said, leaning back like he owned the place. The manager's eyes narrowed to slits, probably trying to figure out if this was about to be the most excitement his day would offer.

The man's voice held the enthusiasm of watching paint dry. "Does this have anything to do with that Rowe fiasco?"

"Nope, totally unrelated circus," I chimed in, keeping it light. "We need to see security footage from the same morning, though."

The guy groaned like we'd asked him to run a marathon, but he lumbered over to a relic of a computer that wheezed to life.

"What time frame are you looking for?" he muttered, squinting at the dusty screen.

"July twenty-first. Just before nine," I said.

He clicked around until the grainy footage flickered onto the screen.

There was Rowe, doing his five-finger discount dance. Been there, seen that. But then—Rachel. Right on cue, striding into frame.

I leaned forward, about to say something, but Andrews' hand clamped down on my arm. Subtle as a sledgehammer, that one. I bit my tongue and watched as the plot thickened—the next character in our little drama made his entrance.

Ed Martin, strutting in right behind her.

"Can we get a copy of this?" Andrews asked, thumbing toward the screen.

The manager scratched his stubble. "Sure, gotta burn it onto a disc or something."

"Wait," I said, grabbing Andrews' arm and yanking him out into the hallway. "If we take that footage, it's straight into Donovan's hands, too. Discovery rules are a real pain, you know?"

Andrews' eyebrows knitted together. "Didn't you cough up all the goods already?"

"Technically yes, but there's this charming thing called a continuing obligation. We find new goodies, we share. Like kindergarteners with crayons, only less fun."

He mulled that over, chewing on the inside of his cheek. "What's this footage do for your case? Or Donovan's for that matter?"

I shrugged, feeling the weight of every legal drama cliché on my shoulders. "I honestly don't know yet. It might do nothing, because Ed still could have gotten from here to the house in time to commit the murder. But it does contradict Rachel's statement. It could be the pin we need to pop Ed's alibi balloon."

"Do you still want to confront Rachel about this?"

"Considering it," I said, rolling the thought around. "If she sticks to her 'Ed was with me at the house' story and we whip out this blockbuster hit, it will completely obliterate her credibility. And, if Ed's only alibi is Rachel Adams's testimony, then his case will go up in smoke too."

Andrews nodded. "But?"

"Big but." I chewed my lip, the taste of cheap lipstick and strategy mingling unpleasantly. "There's more here than meets the eye, and I'm not talking Transformers."

"Never pegged you for a Michael Bay fan."

"Everyone loves explosions. Just not in their case."

Andrews squinted at me, the fluorescent lights of the dingy convenience store hallway casting shadows over his earnest face. "So, you might not play that card. Why?"

"I'm worried about chain of custody issues if we get this footage now. We need to do this right." I chewed on my cheek more and tapped my foot against the floor. "I'll have Lisa subpoena the store manager for it. That way, it goes through the proper channels, and we can delay Donovan getting his hands on it. I don't want to be blind-sided by whatever excuse he comes up with next for why Rachel was there."

Andrews considered this, then nodded. "Makes sense. You need to be sure you're solid on this."

"Exactly," I said, crossing my arms. "I want to dig up the truth, not just bury someone with it."

"Could've fooled me," he said, his lips twitching with a smile I'd seen more often in interrogation rooms than out.

"Ha-ha," I shot back dryly. "If I wanted easy wins over justice, I'd defend crooks, not prosecute them."

"Defend?" Andrews chuckled, and I swear the sound bounced off every canned good in the room. "Nah. You'd be terrible as a defense lawyer."

"Ouch," I replied, but couldn't help grinning. "You wound me, sir."

Right on cue, the manager waddled out of his tiny kingdom. "You still need that footage?"

I straightened, slipping back into my professional mask. "No, we're good for now. Thanks for your time."

"Sure thing," he said, shrugging like we'd asked him about the weather instead of evidence in a potential criminal case.

Andrews and I exchanged a glance and turned to leave, the bell above the door jingling its tinny farewell as we stepped back into the real world.

"Rachel's place next?" Andrews asked, his voice low.

"Yep." I stared down the street. Rachel's house was just a short drive away, but it felt like miles.

"Lead the way, Counselor," he said, opening the car door for me with a mock bow.

"Keep it up, and I'll make you wear a wig and robe," I warned him, sliding into the passenger seat.

"Promises, promises." He grinned, and we pulled away from the 7-Eleven, leaving behind a trail of dust and unanswered questions.

SIXTEEN

THE WORLD HAD DECIDED to throw a gray blanket over the sky as we rolled up to Rachel's place for the second time this week. Her brick rancher looked like it had seen better days and was embarrassed about it. Maybe it was the way the unkempt bushes slumped against the house or how the faded curtains hung slightly open, like they were too tired to keep out prying eyes.

"Quiet as a graveyard," Andrews muttered, scanning the street with those piercing blues of his. "Looks clear." He was referring to the car that had tailed either us or Rachel the last time we were here. He kept his gaze moving, though, because Detective Andrews didn't do surprises.

"Let's hope it stays that way," I said, stepping out onto the cracked driveway pavement.

We walked up the path. *Knock, knock.* No answer. Knocked again, because we're persistent—or just plain annoying.

Finally, the door cracked open a sliver. Through the space I could see Rachel. Her eyes were darting everywhere but at us, like she was expecting the boogeyman to jump out from behind the potted plant next to her door.

"Hey, Rachel," I tried, giving her my best 'I'm harmless' smile. "Remember us? We came here to talk about Ed's case a few days back."

Her voice trembled. "What... what do you want?"

"Just a chat," I said, casual-like. I made sure my gaze remained innocent. "Just need to follow-up on some items. Dot the i's, cross the t's."

Her knuckles whitened from her death grip on the edge of the door, and I wondered if she was going to slam it shut or just pass out right then and there. A pause hung between us, heavy enough to make my shoulders itch.

"Go away." Rachel's voice was a hushed hiss, her gaze still down-turned. "No more questions."

"What's got you spooked?" I asked, like I might catch the last word before she slammed the door. "Has someone—"

"Please." That one word was a full stop, and the door followed suit, closing with a finality that echoed down the quiet street.

"Great chat," I muttered, throwing my hands up in mock surrender as we trudged back to our ride. Andrews was a couple of steps ahead, scanning the street like he could sense something was off.

"Real heart-to-heart," he grumbled, reaching for his keys.

"You think she's being threatened?"

"Without a doubt," he said, glancing back at the house. "But figuring out by who—that's the tricky part." I kicked at a loose pebble, sending it skittering across the road. "Donovan pulling strings doesn't add up. He's a very successful defense attorney. I don't care what Martin's paying him. There's no way he'd risk his law license and future income for one case." I rested my hand on the car door handle. "It just feels like we're missing a piece of the puzzle. Someone's playing her."

Andrews tossed a look over his shoulder, still scanning the neighborhood. "Could be Ed."

"Come again?" I squinted at him, trying to follow his logic. "Ed didn't make bail. How could he be the one messing with her head?"

"Just because he didn't make bail doesn't mean he doesn't have people loyal to him on the outside. You never really know with these things."

"You think Ed hired someone to mess with Rachel's head? To scare her into giving a false alibi?"

"Look at the bigger picture," Andrews said, leaning against the hood with his arms crossed. "Rachel claims Ed left around ten. But the footage? It paints a different story."

"Exactly." I raked my fingers through my hair, trying to piece it together. "Her version gives Ed an airtight alibi. But if they were on the road closer to nine, suddenly it's a lot harder for him to explain away his whereabouts."

"Exactly." Andrews nodded, his blue eyes flicking to me before returning to the street.

"You think the tail was keeping tabs on who Rachel met with? Making sure she knew to keep her facts straight?"

I chewed the inside of my lip and nodded slowly. "It's a theory. But everything's a theory. Question is, is it a good one?"

Andrews shrugged. "For all we know, maybe it's someone on our side trying to pull strings."

My face contorted in confusion. "On our side?"

"I'm just saying, you got this case with only two weeks to flush out the information. Seems like someone might want you to fail."

His words hit a little too close to home. The pressure to crack this case was already weighing heavy on my shoulders. Two weeks to solve a murder? It almost felt like a setup. But if I started thinking like that, I'd spiral into a paranoid mess, and that wasn't going to help me win.

"Please don't put thoughts like that in my head," I said.

Before Andrews could retort, a voice laced with sleep and irritation cut through our brainstorming session. "Officer?"

Turning, I saw a woman draped in a fluffy bathrobe, hair like a bird's nest post-storm. She eyed Andrews with the kind of suspicion usually reserved for door-to-door salesmen.

"Detective," Andrews corrected for the second time that day, straightening up.

"Good," she exhaled with a huff, "Glad to know my complaints are finally being addressed."

"Complaints?" Andrews quirked an eyebrow, the universal cop code for "do tell." He jerked a thumb toward Rachel's brick fortress of solitude. "About Rachel Adams?"

She snorted. "Who else?"

"I'm sorry, ma'am, but can you elaborate?"

"Her car." The woman shook her head with a grimace that spoke volumes of lost sleep. "Starts up with a bang every Sunday morning, rattles my windows, scares my cat half to death."

"Bang?" I piped up, intrigued despite myself. "As in a backfire?"

"Yes." She rolled her eyes. "And before you ask, no, it's not because I'm a light sleeper. That thing could wake the dead. I work three jobs during the week. Sundays are my only day off and I want to sleep in!"

"Can you tell us about what time this happens?" Andrews was all business, notebook already in hand.

"Between seven and eight," she said, punctuating each word with a nod. "Like clockwork."

My heart rate ticked up a notch. "Even last Sunday?"

"Of course, last Sunday. *Every* Sunday."

I exchanged a look with Andrews.

"Thanks for bringing this to our attention." I gave her a nod, which only deepened her suspicious squint. "We'll see what we can do to take care of it."

Even as I said it, I knew the odds weren't in her favor. Noise complaints rarely received much attention from the city, no matter how many were filed. Still, she might be someone we'd need to reach out to for a statement down the line, so I kept my tone polite. "Anything to get some peace and quiet," she muttered, retreating to her own personal haven.

"Peace and quiet," I echoed wistfully as we finally got into the car. "A bit of a foreign concept these days, isn't it, Andrews?"

"Seems so," he agreed, putting his notebook in his pocket and gripping the steering wheel as he backed out from Rachel's driveway. "Thoughts?"

"Thoughts are like opinions," I drawled, watching houses blur by. "Everybody's got one, but that doesn't mean they're worth a damn."

"Deep." He arched an eyebrow, skepticism etching his face. "Real deep, Alex."

"Okay, okay," I relented, then shook my head. "I'm stumped, honestly."

Andrews nodded, his eyes never leaving the road, but I could tell the gears were grinding in his head. "Neighbor's timeline doesn't match up with Rachel's story."

I tapped a finger against my temple. "But why? Why lie about something so checkable?"

"Checkable?" Andrews snorted. "Is that even a word?"

"Today it is." I shrugged, exhaustion weighing down my shoulders. "The point is, Rachel's no dummy. She knows cars are loud and neighbors are nosy."

"Like I said, maybe she's not lying because she wants to. Maybe she's lying because she has to."

"Creepy and plausible," I conceded, but my gut churned with doubt. People didn't just lie for the hell of it. They generally needed a reason. In a way, it was sort of an encouraging trait in human beings.

"Maybe Lisa will have a better take on all of this. Get some fresh eyes on it. See if we're missing something that's staring us right in the face."

SEVENTEEN

I SWUNG the door to my office wide open, expecting the usual solitude, but Lisa was perched at my desk, flipping through a stack of papers with that meticulous focus of hers.

Confusion knotted my eyebrows. "Did the preliminary hearing for Campo get continued or something?"

She glanced up, her confused look matching mine. "Preliminary hearing? For Campo?" Lisa shook her head. "I don't have anything about a Campo hearing."

I blinked a few times before I realized the absolute shit situation I'd walked into. This case had been thrown onto my plate at the last minute. When I printed the docket report for Lisa, it hadn't shown up because it wasn't originally assigned to me. The system was a little old school with how it generated its reports. With all my focus on the Martin case, this one had slipped through the cracks, and I hadn't even gone over it with her.

"Shit," I muttered and bolted from the office without another word.

Jacob Campo was a 21 year old kid who was slick with computers. He'd been caught skimming credit card numbers in a sting operation along with several other computer hackers. The only difference for Campo was that he hadn't used those numbers to buy anything. He claimed cold feet had stopped him. Sure, and I'm the Queen of England.

I didn't expect to get much more than probation for him, considering this was his first offense as far as paper was concerned. But I wasn't going to get anything if I didn't make it to the preliminary hearing on time.

I had approximately ten minutes, a measly six hundred seconds, to get to the courthouse. But I wasn't sure what I was going to do when I got there, because I was entirely unprepared.

Turning a corner, I nearly collided with the metal detector. The guards barely glanced up from their stations. They'd seen this drill before. With a flash of my badge, more out of habit than necessity, I hurtled through the security checkpoint.

"Thanks, guys!" I said over my shoulder, not waiting to see if their nods were of approval or concern for my sanity.

I hit the courtroom doors like a wrecking ball, bursting into the solemn chamber with all the grace of a hurricane. Heads turned, papers rustled, and Judge Williams was already on the bench, peering down at me with eyes that had seen this circus act one too many times.

"Nice of you to join us, Ms. Hayes," he deadpanned, voice dripping with so much sarcasm it could've watered the Sahara.

"Apologies, Your Honor." I gasped, trying to catch my breath. "Traffic."

The judge didn't attempt to hide his disdain for my tardiness. "Ready to proceed, Ms. Hayes?"

I tried to keep my heart from pounding and willed my breathing to normalize. "Your Honor, if I may, I'd like to confer with defense counsel."

"Absolutely, counselor. The court has all the time in the world to wait for you to appear late and then to have discussions with opposing counsel that could have been had outside, had you been on time." He exhaled and waved a hand. "By all means, confer."

"Thank you, Your Honor," I muttered under my breath before sidling up to defense counsel to whisper my Hail Mary play.

"How about we make this go away? Nolo contendere, and your guy gets community service instead of probation."

Defense counsel was a man named Jimmy Diamond. It would have been a great last name had his career been a bit more lucrative, but Jimmy was basically a step up from a public defender. He was a regular on what was called the Managed Assigned Counsel Program, or MAC Program, which meant he couldn't get enough work on his own and he volunteered to take overload from the public defender's office.

The justice system paid him a flat fee for each case he took. Whether that case went to trial or pled out at the preliminary hearing stage, his fee was the same. This meant he had negative incentive to take a case to trial.

"Hold on," he said and then turned back to whisper to his client.

I made the mistake of glancing up at the judge, and instantly regretted it. His glare had the kind of weight that made me want to recuse myself from every future case in his courtroom. "Ms. Hayes," he said, "are we having a tea party or can we move forward?"

I offered an apologetic half-smile. "The Court's indulgence," I said, which was lawyer-speak for "Please have patience and don't hold me in contempt."

Diamond turned back to me, his smirk telling me he thought he'd won the lottery. "We have a deal."

The truth of the matter was that had he called my bluff, his client would have gotten off scot-free. Because I had no evidence to present, and given how Judge Williams was looking at me, there's no way the judge would have given me the benefit of the doubt or granted a continuance.

I turned back to the bench. "Your Honor, upon further discussion, we've—"

"Spontaneously reached an agreement?" Judge Williams interjected, arching an eyebrow.

"Exactly. We move to dismiss without prejudice pending a formal plea agreement."

"Marvelous," he deadpanned, scribbling something on the docket.

"Court adjourns. And next time, try not to use my courtroom for your improv exercises."

"Of course, Your Honor. Never again," I said, knowing full well "never" was lawyer-speak for "until next time."

We all shuffled out of the courtroom and Diamond ran off to another hearing without two words to his now-former, client. I started to make my way back to the office, but Campo stopped me.

"Ms. Hayes?"

I turned on the ball of one foot. I didn't think anything good could come of this conversation, but it would be rude to not at least acknowledge him.

"Yes?"

"Why'd you give me a break?" he asked, his head tilted to one side.

I couldn't tell him the actual truth. Because that would mean telling him that I was forced to give Diamond a sweetheart deal because otherwise I'd make a fool out of myself in open court and he would have walked a completely free man. No, I couldn't say that. So, I lied.

"Everybody's entitled to mess up once," I said, shrugging. "Consider it your get-out-of-jail-free card."

His voice was a mix of skepticism and hope. "Really?"

"Cross my heart."

"Thank you." His gratitude seemed genuine. I just hoped it translated into new computer habits. He started fishing something out of his pocket. "If you ever need a favor..."

He handed me a business card.

Jacob Campo: IT Whiz Kid
For all your computer and tech needs

His phone number and email address were at the bottom along with a website.

"Sure, kid." I accepted the business card he offered, tucking it away. I doubted I'd ever use it. "Focus on your business instead of surfing the dark web. Yes?"

He nodded his head and we parted ways.

Back at the office, Lisa was perched on the edge of my desk, her expression a blend of concern and curiosity.

"So?" she prodded, eyebrows arched.

I tossed my leather satchel onto the chair. "Bluffed my way into getting the guy to plead out for community service. Apparently, I can be quite convincing when desperate."

Words tumbled out of Lisa's mouth in a rush, her face creased with guilt. "Alex, I'm so sorry."

"Hey, don't beat yourself up," I interjected, waving off her apology. "It was my fault. I never gave you the information on that case. Just one of those things that fell through the cracks. But it worked out okay."

Lisa nodded.

"Now, let's focus on not getting disbarred, shall we?" I flopped into my chair and swiveled to face her. "What's your take on our case for Monday?"

Her lips curved into an uneasy smile. "We're going to do great."

"Lisa, you're bad at lying," I pointed out, leaning back and studying the ceiling as if it held the secret to winning murder cases. "You've got that 'puppy caught chewing on a slipper' look."

She sighed. "It's just... Ed Martin is slippery. Like an eel in a barrel of lube."

I snorted. "Charming imagery. But we've got some wiggle room. Monday will be jury selection. Opening arguments could start as late as Wednesday. And then, we've got a few of the more boring witnesses to put on first. I get the feeling that our case is going to be won on cross. We'll find a few threads to tug on. Maybe get lucky and unravel the whole sweater in the process."

"Hopefully not while he's wearing it."

"Snarky." I grinned. "I like it."

"Well, your docket is all cleaned up," she said. "So, I've got nothing to get in the way of helping you prepare."

"Good," I said. "We will definitely be here all of Saturday and

Sunday preparing. But take tonight off. Your brain needs a break. And I've got dinner plans."

A silent question mark hung between us before she asked, "really?"

"What?" I leveled her a look; what kind of look was up for debate. "Even attorneys have to eat."

"Fine," she conceded with a chuckle, standing up. "But tomorrow we dive back into the wonderful world of Ed Martin."

"Joy." My voice dripped sarcasm thicker than molasses. "Can't wait."

EIGHTEEN

THE CLINK of glasses and the rhythm of soft jazz filled the air as I sat across from Ryan Chen in a dimly lit corner of Vic & Anthony's Steakhouse. It was a go-to spot downtown for government workers to unwind. The place was all dark wood and fine leather, the kind of place where deals were made over bourbon, not paperwork.

I looked at my watch, and he chuckled. "Relax, Alex."

"I told you," I said with a small smile. "One hour."

He shook his head. "We're government attorneys. One of the perks is we don't have to bill for our time. Which means we don't have to watch the clock."

Ryan was right. We didn't count hours like private sector sharks, but time was still a currency I was cautious to spend. Martin's trial was ever-looming in my mind.

"Decided yet?" he asked, eyes skimming the menu with casual ease.

The waiter, a young man wearing a crisp white apron, approached our table. I always wondered why waiters were made to wear aprons. It's not like they were the ones cooking the meals.

"Good evening, what can I get for both of you?" His voice was smooth and he stood in front of our table without a pad in hand. It was obvious that he'd been working this gig for a while.

"Twelve-ounce steak, medium rare," Ryan ordered without missing a beat, flashing a grin at me. "And your daily sides are fine."

"Make that two," I said, dropping any pretense of salad fantasies. I was firmly past appearances for this dinner. Ryan was attractive, sure, but I knew better than to mix business with...well, anything extra. Besides, I didn't see this going anywhere. If he wanted to foot the bill for a steak dinner, who was I to argue?

"Two steaks, coming right up."

As our waiter stepped away, Ryan reached forward to grab the bottle of wine in the middle of the table. He poured me a glass first, then himself. At least he got points for chivalry.

He swirled his wine and sipped before asking, "How'd the prelim go?" "Ah, you know, same old," I said, waving my hand. "Judge practically used his stamp mid-sentence."

"Thanks for covering," Ryan said, and I nodded.

"Actually, it was sort of a fortuitous request."

He raised an eyebrow. "Oh?"

"The security footage you used as evidence... it ended with the alibi from the Martin case striding into the store."

Ryan's eyebrows knit together, clearly confused. "Said alibi was supposed to be with Ed Martin at her home at the time."

His eyes widened. "Wow. That is lucky."

I took a sip of the wine. It was good enough to get me through this dinner. "Detective Andrews and I went down to the 7-Eleven to speak with the manager there."

Ryan chuckled. "Charming fella, isn't he?"

I let out a genuine laugh. Ryan had likely met him to get the footage against Rowe in the first place. "He definitely wasn't the poster child for 'happily employed.'"

"Did he give you what you needed?"

I nodded. "Should be forthcoming. I had Lisa draft up a subpoena."

"Protect chain of custody. Try and nip any motions to suppress in the bud. Good strategy."

I smiled.

The waiter interrupted our conversation as he returned with our meals. The sight of my plate had my stomach growling. I hadn't realized how hungry I'd been.

"And the Martin case? How is that coming along?" Ryan asked casually while cutting into his own steak.

I faltered, just a breath, a heartbeat. Andrews' words echoed in my ears. Maybe it was someone on our side who was threatening Rachel. I know he said it off the cuff, but it stuck in my head. Could it be Chen? He had the camera footage. Maybe he recognized Rachel and got to her. But, who was he working for, if so?

I shook my head, trying to shake out the negative thoughts. This is how it started—the paranoia. And once it got its claws in you, it dug deep and wouldn't let go. It's what caused some of the best prosecutors to fall victim to tunnel vision on a case. I didn't want that to happen to me.

The rich smell of grilled steak filled the room. I cut into the tender meat, the juices pooling around the edge of the plate. The flavors were perfect, smoky and savory, but somehow, they seemed distant. My mind was elsewhere.

"Going fine," I managed, but my voice lacked conviction. He must have heard it—the subtle strain, the hint of doubt.

"Good," he said softly, but his eyes didn't leave mine. "Ready for trial?"

"Mostly," I deflected. "Just tying up a few loose ends."

"Sounds like you've got it handled." There was reassurance there, or maybe it was an act.

"Always do." My reply came out sharper than intended.

Silence settled between us.

"Anyway," I said, eager to steer away from the Martin trial, "how's your workload shaping up?"

"I've got this white collar crime case I'm working on."

"Oh, yeah? What are the facts?"

"The guy was doing work for the county. Ended up submitting invoices that were a bit too inflated. Turns out he was funneling this extra money to friends of his."

"Classic." I pushed some of the vegetables around on my plate. "What's your endgame on the case?"

"He's already pled guilty," Chen said between bites. "But he reserved the right to litigate the loss amount, or in this case, the amount he stole from the county. Guy's got deep pockets. Throwing everything he can at this sentencing—experts, character testimony, professional videos. It's exhausting going through it all."

"Who's the judge?"

"Greene."

I scoffed and shook my head. "Those antics might backfire." Judge Greene was notoriously pro-prosecutor and hated anything that even hinted at money or private defense attorneys. It was a well-known bias he had.

"Agreed." He nodded, eyes meeting mine for a brief second.

I leaned forward, elbows resting on the cool surface of our secluded table. "What are you doing to counter the expert he's put on?"

"Do you know Cheryl Moultrie?" Ryan asked, a hint of relief coloring his tone.

I shook my head.

He set down his cutlery, giving me his full attention. "She's one of the girls on the transactional side."

I gave Ryan a "really?" look.

He put his hands up in surrender. "My bad, I shouldn't say 'girls.' She's one of the *extraordinary* women who works on the transactional side."

I rolled my eyes. "It's fine. Everyone knows that office is just a whole bunch of estrogen."

He laughed. "You said it, not me."

"Alright, so Cheryl," I said, getting us back on track.

"She used to be an actuary. She's brilliant with numbers. She's helping me make sense of the transaction logs and go through the expert report."

"Is that so?"

He nodded. "She sees patterns where we see chaos. It's her thing—sorting out legitimate from fraudulent."

"Useful skill."

I'd completely overlooked the transactional documents Erin had given me. I'd been so intent on the photographs that I forgot that the bulk of what she'd given me in that envelope were mundane bank statements.

"Could be," he said, oblivious to the gears turning in my head.

I kept my voice casual, betraying none of the urgency I felt. "Think she'd take a look at something... unrelated?"

His brow furrowed slightly. "Unrelated?"

"The Martin trial."

"Ah." He nodded, understanding dawning. "Sure, I'll talk to her. Shouldn't be an issue."

I let out a measured breath, hiding the rush of adrenaline the possibility gave me. "I appreciate it."

"Least I can do." Ryan smiled. "Shall we?" he asked. "After all, I promised to get you home before curfew."

I laughed, and he signaled to the waiter for the check.

* * *

WE STEPPED into the crisp evening air.

"Thanks for dinner, Ryan."

"You're welcome. I know you wanted to get back to the office, but would you consider having a cup of coffee at my place?"

I knew he was hoping we'd share more than a cup of coffee. Had I not had the biggest trial of my life nipping at my heels, I might have agreed.

"Raincheck?" I asked. "I don't think I'd be very good company with everything on my mind."

He was unfazed, nodding as if he expected nothing less. "Raincheck, then."

We parted ways, and I strode toward the office. I couldn't believe that I'd overlooked those additional documents from Erin. The weight of it settled in my chest, tightening with each thought. I could feel the heat rising in my cheeks, and I swallowed hard, biting the inside of my cheek. Foolish. That's how I felt—like a rookie who'd overlooked something so obvious. I clenched my jaw, my mind replaying the moment, chastising myself. Those documents might've been the key, the missing piece I needed to understand what was really going on.

I was so lost in thought that as I opened the glass door to the office, I basically barreled into someone leaving. I looked up to see Shaun Stevens.

"Sorry," I stammered as I tried to regain my balance.

"Not a problem. Have a nice night."

"Wait!" I said, the urgency in my voice cutting through the silence. There was no time like the present. "Officer Ramirez. That's your case, right?"

He nodded, giving me a cautious look.

"I need to talk to him."

"Ramirez?" He frowned, a deep crease forming between his brows, as if trying to decipher what I could possibly want with him. "Now's not a good time."

I shifted my stance, leaning forward just a little, hoping to convey the seriousness of the situation. "I'm not trying to step on your negotiations with him, but he might have something crucial to one of my cases."

He didn't flinch. "Can't be done." Shaun's refusal came fast, with a finality that hit me like a wall.

"Shaun—" I tried again, frustration creeping into my voice. His tone left no space for argument. "Drop it."

NINETEEN

"I CAN'T DO THAT," I said, my tone firm and measured, despite the internal turmoil I was feeling.

Stevens turned and gave me a death glare. "Ramirez is a special case, Alex. Please tell me you can see that." His voice was low and firm, but his tone wasn't nasty. "He's an assistant chief of police, for God's sake. It's not that I don't want to help you. It's just, there are bigger things at stake here."

"And a high-profile capital case isn't special? What exactly does special mean to you?"

"It means that I'm not in control of how this case plays out. I haven't been authorized to make a plea, and I sure as hell am not going to put my career on the line to support yours or anyone else's, for that matter."

I clenched my jaw. "We could at least ask, couldn't we? Tom gave me the Martin case—"

"Tom?" Stevens barked out a bitter laugh. "You think he's the one calling the shots here? He's got no say over this, either. This came from the top."

My heart thudded in my chest. "The top?"

Stevens paused, weighing his words. "The mayor's office. They provided the evidence against Ramirez in the first place. The mayor is clearly going to use Ramirez as a sacrificial lamb to support his re-election bid in November. Tough on crime and all that. No way he's going to agree to let him plea out. He wants this to be a spectacle."

I hated it when politicians used elections to motivate their actions. Tom had been using the upcoming election to fuel his every move, from the press conferences to all the media attention on the Martin case. He wanted to look tough on crime in front of the cameras, playing into the public's expectations. Every decision felt less about actual justice and more about keeping his name in the headlines. It wasn't just frustrating—it made our jobs ten times harder.

"Son of a bitch," I muttered. "So that's it? We're just supposed to roll over and let Martin walk because we don't want to hurt the mayor's reelection campaign?"

Stevens leveled a steely gaze at me. "Whether Martin walks or doesn't walk is on you. That's *your* case, and Ramirez is mine. As far as I'm concerned, he's a dirty cop." His eyes narrowed as he spat out the words. "No deals. You, of all people, should understand—given your family's history."

A pang of hurt hit my chest, and my vision blurred with tears that I fought to contain. Until now, I didn't know who at the DA's office knew of my family's history. To be reminded of and judged for it felt like an old wound being ripped open, raw and exposed He turned on his heel, and I didn't try to stop him.

I fumbled for my phone, fingers trembling slightly as I dialed Ryan's number. It only rang once before he picked up.

"Ryan, I've reconsidered," I said, my voice wavering a bit. I cleared my throat before continuing. "That coffee? I could use it."

His tone was light, but concern laced his words. "Change of heart?"

"Something like that. I need a different perspective."

"Where are you?"

"In front of the office."

"Stay put," he said. "I'll be there shortly."

"Thanks," I murmured, then ended the call. I leaned against the cool stone building and took measured breaths as I waited for Ryan to arrive.

The hum of a worn-out streetlamp faded into the background as I waited, my gaze fixed on the road. I blinked back the tears, thankful none of them fell. It had been a long time since I'd cried over my father. I didn't intend to start again today.

It wasn't long before a sleek Mercedes SUV pulled up, its glossy black finish reflecting the faulty lamp light. Ryan rolled down the tinted window and flashed a grin.

"Need a ride?"

I smiled back and stepped away from my perch to open the door and slide into the passenger seat. The leather, soft and ultra-modern, felt inviting. "This is quite the car for a public servant."

Ryan chuckled, a sound that seemed almost too carefree. "I've always been good at saving."

I traced the fine stitching of the seats with my eyes and a whisper of doubt crept into my mind. Could Ryan's wallet be padded with more than just careful savings? If he were taking a bribe from someone to intimidate Rachel, then—

I didn't finish the thought, instead pushing it out of my head completely. I had already decided I was too close to crossing into paranoia territory. I wasn't going to let myself fall off that ledge.

The engine purred as we merged into traffic. Ryan's calm, relaxed posture behind the wheel made the tension in my shoulders feel even more pronounced, like the way quiet can make a headache throb harder.

"You look like you've had better days," he said, glancing at me out of his peripheral. "What happened between dinner and now?"

"Ran into Stevens outside the office."

"What happened? He's usually pretty laid back"

I hesitated, the encounter still too raw to talk about right away. "I wanted to discuss a plea deal for one of his cases. A trade for information. He could've given me leverage in mine. He shut it down. Wouldn't even consider it."

Ryan nodded, his eyes back on the road. "Some cases are set in stone. No wiggle room."

I leaned back into the leather. It wasn't like Ryan had all the answers I was looking for. Not only was I running out of options on the Martin case, but also time. If someone put a gun to my head, I couldn't even tell them whether Martin was guilty or not. Not how I expected to feel about this the weekend before trial.

Defense attorneys aren't in the business of determining guilt or innocence. Donovan once told me that, in some ways, they preferred defending guilty clients. The stakes were lower—it took the pressure off. If you lost? Well, no one was shocked. But when you lose a case for someone you believe is innocent? That's the kind of failure that keeps you up at night. I'd asked Donovan how many innocent clients he'd ever represented. He told me he didn't know, and he never wanted to.

That wasn't the case for prosecutors. At least, not for me. I didn't want to put someone behind bars if they hadn't committed the crime. I also didn't need to. It was up to the detectives to figure out who was the perpetrator given the evidence. All I was there to do was to make sure people faced the consequences they deserved.

But with the Martin case, the evidence wasn't clear. There was too much left to be explained, and the people who *could* explain refused to. While Rachel's alibi wasn't solid, he still was with her the morning of the crime. There was no blood on him. Yet, there was no DNA from anyone else in the house. Every piece of evidence could play to both sides.

Chen looked at me briefly. "It's the Ramirez case, isn't it?"

I remained silent, my jaw set, knowing full well that any acknowledgment was as good as confirmation.

"But this could crack the Martin case open. You know how important that is to Tom—he's practically riding it straight into his re-election campaign."

Chen glanced over at me, shaking his head. "Yeah, but you're forgetting one thing—mayor trumps the DA. Tom's important, sure, but you mess with the mayor's priorities, you're playing a whole different game."

I huffed, frustration bubbling to the surface. "It shouldn't have to be a game." Chen softened and shook his head. "Try not to let it get to you."

Stevens' cutting remarks slammed back into my mind. I sighed as if I could exhale the memory. "Do you think there's any chance Ramirez would talk without Stevens' cooperation?"

Chen laughed, the sound hollow to my ears. "Unlikely. Why would he talk if it doesn't help his case?"

"Maybe hint at a possibility..."

"Would you really play that card?"

I sighed, heavy with the weight of ethical boundaries. "No."

"Besides, Tom would tear you a new one if you went over his head on this." Chen continued before I could reply. "And, I don't think you having the Martin case is going to change that fact. The two cases are on the same level."

I clenched my jaw, my fingers tightening around the armrest. Every word out of his mouth made the tension in my chest tighten. He was right, and it irritated me to no end. We pulled into his apartment complex. Ryan shifted into park and killed the engine. The quiet hum of the city filled the silence between us.

He turned to me, his expression filled with kindness. "Let's try to forget about work for a night, yeah?"

I sighed and said, "I'll try." But the echo of my own words seemed doubtful in the enclosed space of the fancy SUV.

No promises indeed.

TWENTY

I ROUNDED THE CORNER TO ANDREWS' desk and found him sitting amidst the usual clutter—papers strewn everywhere, half a cup of cold coffee abandoned to the side. The faint hum of office chatter filtered through the precinct, punctuated by the occasional ring of a phone. The fluorescent lights overhead buzzed, casting a sterile glow that made the room feel as clinical as the mood it set. "Got your voicemail."

He looked up, a smirk playing on his lips. "Unusual for you to miss a call."

"I had dinner plans."

"By yourself?"

"No."

He nodded, his eyebrows doing something stupid. "Who's the lucky guy?"

"Let's not wander off-topic."

"Fair enough." His smile didn't wane. "So, did you sleep well?"

I deadpanned and folded my arms in front of my chest. He wasn't helping my already fragile mood. Last night was supposed to have been relaxing, but even spending the night with Ryan didn't do the trick. My brain was still whirling over the case, and Andrews knew exactly what I wanted from him.

"Alright, alright." He held up his hands in mock surrender. "Heard you're trying to get to Ramirez."

"Word travels fast. Who told you?"

"Heard it at the watercooler."

"On a Saturday?"

"The precinct never sleeps."

I scoffed. Gossip spread like a wildfire through the precinct. "I'm onto Ramirez, but I'm hitting walls."

"Those walls are there for a reason." Andrews leaned back and folded his arms. "Ramirez was brought in with evidence from the mayor's office. It's under seal."

"Under seal," I echoed, then let out a frustrated breath. Documents under seal were essentially locked away, kept from public view to protect the integrity of the information or privacy of individuals involved. It was a common practice in sensitive cases, often involving high-profile figures or delicate investigations. It also meant a dead end for me unless I could find another way around it.

I went for the blunt route. "They aren't something you'd have access to by chance?"

Andrews sat up straight, a firm line setting in his jaw. "No, Alex, I don't have access. And even if I did, you know I play by the book. "

"Sorry I asked."

"I'm honestly surprised you did."

I rubbed at the tension knotting my neck. "It's this Martin case— it's like a splinter I can't get out."

"What do you mean?" Andrews leaned forward, elbows on his desk. "Martin doesn't have a good alibi anymore. That's your case right there."

"I need to get to 'beyond reasonable doubt.' I'm not sure the alibi situation gets us there." I started to pace, despite the small space. "We're missing something major here. I don't have a clear picture of how the crime was even committed, let alone how Martin did it, if he was the one to commit it."

"Let's walk through the day again."

I nodded in agreement, and he gestured for me to follow him to one of the conference rooms with a white board. Andrews picked up a marker and started writing times down on the board while I paced again, too anxious to sit.

Andrews looked over his shoulder and asked, "Where do you want to start?"

"Saturday. Martin's at Rachel's. Standard evening affair."

Andrews jotted it down on the board. "And, as far as we know, he doesn't leave her house until sometime the next morning."

"Correct."

"And we're assuming that he didn't leave sometime during the night and come back?"

Catching onto his thinking, I fished the coroner's report out of my files. "Estimated time of death based on the decomposition of the body was 9:46 a.m. Even if he did leave and come back in the night, it couldn't have been to commit a murder."

"Good point."

"So, at 8:57 a.m., they are caught on camera at the 7-Eleven, entirely across town from where Martin lives."

Andrews jotted the time down on the board, the sharp, chemical scent of the marker lingering in the air, mixing with the stale coffee smell from earlier.

"Then 10:17, Martin's call comes into 911—'My wife's dead.'" I stopped pacing and chewed my thumbnail for a moment, scanning the current timeline on the whiteboard. "That leaves 8:57 to 10:17 unaccounted for."

Andrews nodded his head.

I stared at the board, trying to make sense of the times, and what might or might not have happened in between them.

"If Martin bolted from that 7-Eleven straight home," I said, "how long would that drive take? It's early enough on a Sunday morning to assume no traffic."

"Let's see." Andrews grabbed his phone and tapped the screen a few times. He whistled low. "Thirty-four minutes if he hit every green light."

I looked back up at the board and tilted my head. "Estimated time of death is 9:46 a.m. Which means if he left the store and went straight home with the intent to commit a murder, he'd have—" I grabbed another marker and did the math in a corner of the white-board. "Twenty-six minutes to do it."

"That's more than enough time."

"Sure," I said, "but is it enough time to commit a murder, hide any evidence that you committed said murder, and then call it in?"

"Pretty damn tight schedule when you put it that way," Andrews responded. He sat down at one of the conference table chairs and leaned back. He always leaned just far enough that one of these days I was waiting for him to tip over. "Would've had to have been planned. Go in, get to it, and then clean up. Any evidence easily disposed of too."

"Yeah, well, he just strangled her—allegedly." I stared at the wall, picturing the lifeless bedroom in the crime scene photos. "No gunshot residue to shower off, no weapon to ditch."

Andrews laced his fingers behind his head. "The timeline doesn't work for a crime of passion. People usually have fights beforehand. But, that helps us, right? You need to prove"—he squinted his eyes at me, hesitating—"what is it you lawyers call it?"

"Malice aforethought."

"Yeah. That."

"Yes, except I still have no motive other than a relationship gone bad. And that points more to crime of passion than it does first degree murder." I still couldn't believe Tom allowed Gerry to charge Martin with first degree if we were this far away from a clear motive.

I let out an exasperated sigh. People generally lied when they were trying to hide something. I hadn't had the good fortune of coming across a psychopath yet who did it just for the pleasure of it. "Why the hell did Rachel feed us that bogus alibi?"

"Was it really a false alibi?" Andrews countered. "She only said they were together at that time, and footage showed they were."

"Yes, but she said they were together at her place, and then he left at ten. That footage completely contradicts her story."

"Are you going to try and use the footage to impeach her?"

I chewed on the inside of my cheek. "Impeaching a witness means showing the jury their testimony is unreliable and therefore so is their credibility. If I bring out that security footage, it casts doubt on Rachel's whole story. But I'm not even sure that helps our case, right? He had time to commit the crime based on her timelines. Honestly, her testimony makes it even easier to prove he had time, because she's closer to his house."

"But?" Andrews lifted an eyebrow, as if he knew what I was about to say.

"But, the minute I decide to play that card, Donovan gets a peek. I'll have to turn over the footage to him. He'll pull her off the witness list so fast, we won't know what hit us. Or worse, she'll have a different story for the jury. One I don't have a way to disprove."

"Right now, we've got enough to make a case," Andrews said, his voice steady. "We can show he had the time to do it and get back. You don't need to use the footage. You can attack her credibility on the stand through questioning. Maybe bring witnesses from the store who could place her there."

"I don't dispute that," I replied, the edges of frustration creeping into my voice. "But I'm not here just to rack up convictions. I need to know we're nailing the right guy, beyond a shadow of a doubt."

"You're holding yourself to too high a standard there, counselor," he said with a shit-eating grin. "Pretty sure all you need to prove is 'beyond a reasonable doubt.'"

"Beyond *all* reasonable doubt is my standard."

"Aren't they the same thing?"

I shrugged. "If you look inside a law book, yes. But not to me."

"What's the difference for you, then?"

I sat down and put my head in my heads. "If I'm trying to argue that someone committed a crime, then I should believe that they did."

"A lot of people don't see it that way."

"You're right. A lot of people think their job is just to find or argue the evidence and it's for the judge and jury to pass judgment."

"Well, aren't they right?"

I shook my head. "When it comes to the very real possibility of taking someone's freedom away, I want to make sure they deserve that. Then I'll trust the system to validate that knowledge."

"We're waxing a little philosophical here, don't you think?"

"You asked."

His smile never faltered when he said, "I did indeed. And I'll ask you one more thing: what are you going to do if you haven't convinced yourself? Jury selection is Monday and the trial starts Wednesday, right?"

I closed my eyes. " I don't know. Keep searching for that missing piece? It's got to be out there."

Unfortunately for me, the missing piece in this case was Ramirez. Based on what Erin was trying to tell me, Ramirez had been with Ed the day before the crime was committed. Even if he were a dirty cop, he'd probably be willing to sell the true story at a chance to buy a bit more of his freedom. If I could get him to cooperate, it could change everything.

"Let me ask you something," I said, still not opening my eyes. "You're the detective on this case. Why'd you push it over to the prosecutors when the evidence was so thin?"

"Wasn't my decision," Andrews shot back.

"What do you mean?"

"I was assigned this mess the same time you were."

I sat up and opened my eyes to look at Andrews, my brows furrowing. "Who dropped it in your lap, then?" I asked.

"Tom."

"Tom," I repeated. "As in my boss Tom?"

"The one and only."

"You really don't think it wasn't a coincidence that we're working together on this one? That it only dropped in our laps when there wasn't enough time to do anything about it?"

He stared at me blankly. "You've got so many double negatives in there I don't even know what you said."

I shook my head. "What I'm saying is, don't you think it's strange that you and I are on this case together, and it only dropped in our laps when there wasn't enough time to do anything about it?"

He shrugged. "I think you're paranoid."

I sighed. "I hope you're right."

TWENTY-ONE

I SQUINTED at the morning sun as Andrews' voice reverberated through my car speakers over the din of my tires rumbling over the road.

"Alex, are you sure going to see Ramirez is a smart idea?"

"Smart?" I repeated. "No. But it's an idea, and it's about the only one I've got right now."

"What do you even hope to accomplish by going down there? You can't offer him anything."

I glanced at the passenger seat. The photos Erin had given me were safely tucked inside a small white envelope. This might stir up some backlash from Stevens—or even Tom—but if it helped crack the Martin case open, it'd be worth the risk. I wasn't about to let their politics keep me from pushing for the truth.

"No, but I might have something to get him talking."

I didn't know what had been discussed during those meetings in the photographs, but Ramirez did. If I could make him believe I knew too, maybe it'd crack something open.

A repetitive beep jolted me from my thoughts, and I tightened my grip on the steering wheel. Glancing at the screen, I realized my phone was buzzing again. Another call—another distraction I couldn't afford.

I debated letting it go, but curiosity got the better of me as I reached for the phone, tension creeping into my chest. "I gotta jump to another call. I'll catch up with you later."

"Don't do anything stupid," were Andrews' last words before hanging up.

I rolled my eyes and switched over to the new call.

"Alex Hayes."

"Alex?" The voice on the other end of the phone was sweet. "This is Cheryl Moultrie."

Even if Ryan hadn't mentioned that Cheryl worked in transactions, I would have figured it out. She didn't have the jaded tone of someone who'd lost their soul to the grind of criminal law. That side of the profession had a way of wearing you down. "Ryan Chen mentioned you had some documents for me to look at?"

"Hi, Cheryl," I said, cursing under my breath. "I do, but I'm not at my desk right now."

"Look, I'll be out of town all next week. I know your trial is starting soon, and I want to help. So, if you can find a way to get them to me, I can look at them today before I leave."

Transactional people always seem to have vacations lined up. The thought of their relative freedom nagged at me. Although, I did appreciate her willingness to help. That was something I would never get from a litigator.

"Alright," I agreed, trying to focus on the road as well. "I'll figure something out. Give me thirty minutes or so."

Cheryl thanked me and then hung up.

Her schedule was a luxury I could never afford on the criminal side. Taking a vacation meant less to a court when someone else's freedom was on the line. A continuance might have meant an innocent man stayed in JPC longer. And then there was that pesky thing called the "Speedy Trial Act" that just about assured a prosecutor no life. Defense attorneys also loved to play the speedy trial game. Refuse to waive it and make the prosecution scramble, only to waive it last minute. Every move in the legal world had a motive. And if someone said there was no motive, that too, was a motive.

I reached a stoplight and picked my phone out of my lap to find Lisa's number.

She answered after two rings. "Hey, Alex! Are you on your way to the office?"

"Actually, I've got a quick detour to run first." It wasn't technically a lie but I didn't want to reveal my plan until I was sure it would work. "But I need you to do something for me."

"Sure, what's up?"

"In my desk drawer, there's a blank envelope with some papers inside. They look like bank statements. Can you scan them into my computer and send them to Cheryl Moultrie? You can find her in the directory."

"Of course, no problem. Anything else you need?"

"That should be it. Thanks, Lisa. I'll be in soon and we can prep." I hung up, testing the leather of the steering wheel under my fingers as I drove across the bridge.

My last hope seemed to hinge on a game of cat-and-mouse with Ramirez. But the evidence just wasn't there the way I needed it to be. Come to think of it, whack-a-mole might have been a better analogy.

I parked the car and cut off the engine, then grabbed the photographs from my passenger seat and carefully tucked them into my jacket pocket. I didn't want anyone seeing them, and I wasn't even sure I'd need them yet. At the moment, they were an insurance policy.

"Badge, please," the guard at the door demanded. I flashed my prosecutor's badge, the lamination glinting under the harsh fluorescent lights. He eyed it before nodding. "Who are you here to see?"

"Louis Ramirez."

He looked down a list and then told me to wait a moment. I'd never been here on a Sunday before. I thought it would be dead, but it was way busier than during the workweek. People trying to visit incarcerated family on their days off, I supposed.

"This way." The guard gestured for me to follow him. He buzzed me through heavy doors and then led me down a hallway I was far too familiar with. Every time I walked down this corridor, I wondered what it would be like to be on the other side of the law. To know I might never have the freedom to walk out again.

And as much as I tried not to think about him, I couldn't help but wonder what my father thought as he was led down these halls.

We stopped in front of a white steel door and the guard flashed his badge. The door buzzed open.

"Counselor," former Officer Louis Ramirez said, a smirk pulling at the corner of his mouth, eyes narrowing like a cat who'd spotted easy prey. "To what do I owe the pleasure?"

TWENTY-TWO

RAMIREZ WAS a middle-aged man with a weathered face, dark eyes—his orange jumpsuit accentuating the bags underneath even more so—and a smug expression that didn't match his circumstances. A person could hide their true feelings through expressions, but it was the eyes that always told the entire truth. And Ramirez's truth, right now, was fear. Fear was in the eyes of every criminal defendant I'd ever met. What caused the fear was different for everyone. Maybe the fear of not seeing their family, fear of prison itself, or fear that they'd never walk outside of these walls without shackles around their feet. Whatever the cause, it was always there. None of them were immune to it.

"Louis." I took my place across from him. His wrists were shackled to the metal table. It was always an odd thing to see someone handcuffed to a table. I'd stepped into countless interrogation rooms, but I'd never quite gotten over the sight.

He shifted and his hands tugged at the restraints. The sense of powerlessness in his demeanor was hard to miss.

"I see we're on a first name basis." He breathed a lifeless chuckle. "This should be good. Wha'dya got for me, sweetheart?"

I leaned back and folded my arms against my chest. "Questions."

Ramirez barked out a laugh. "Unless you got something worth my while to trade, say an acquittal on my current charges, then you'll probably have better luck asking your questions around town."

"I appreciate the big boy act, Officer. But that's not going to work on me."

"Oh yeah?" His false amusement morphed into a sneer. "Could have fooled me. Word is you're the weakest prosecutor in the city. Always losing cases. Why do you think you're working Martin?"

His nasty comments about me losing cases rolled off my back easily enough. But that last point gave me pause.

I tried to keep the edge out of my voice when I asked, "What do you mean by that?"

"I told you. Unless you have something to trade, I think you should go ask your questions to someone else." He leaned back smugly and raised an eyebrow. "Shaun Stevens. He's the one on my case, yeah? Maybe you could ask him. See what he can do."

I didn't move from my spot or say a word, and instead pulled the photographs out of my jacket pocket. I laid the first in front of him, the one of Ramirez and Martin in an obviously heated conversation. On the back, in Erin's handwriting, it said "May 18, 2024."

Ramirez's eyes flicked with curiosity and leaned in, his smug expression faltering just for a moment. I waited for his eyes to tell me just how valuable this photo might be. They didn't disappoint.

I kept my voice low and asked, "Familiar?"

He leaned back, feigning nonchalance, his mask slipping back into place. "So? What's this supposed to be?"

"You know damn well. And unless you want your situation in here to get a whole lot worse, I suggest you answer my questions."

Ramirez held my gaze for a moment before leaning in again and staring into my eyes, lowering his voice. "If I were you, I'd be careful how much you dig into things. Go handle the Martin trial the way you normally would. Use the evidence that's been gifted to you and stop asking questions about it. You wouldn't want to find yourself on the wrong side of this table. Just like your dad."

"You can spare the whole 'like your dad' talk with me. I haven't spoken to him since he moved to your side of the table."

"And why's that?"

"Because he's a dirty cop, just like you."

"And what if I told you he wasn't?" Ramirez gave me a shit eating grin. I couldn't help the way my jaw dropped. "What if I told you he was framed?"

Every ounce of confidence I had was gone, and I shook my head. "How could I possibly trust you?"

"How does anybody trust anybody?"

I didn't give him an answer.

"You're no fun, counselor. You're supposed to say 'evidence!' and bang your hand on the table dramatically." He tried and failed to bang his own hand on the table.

I hated that I was taking his bait, but how could I not? Curiosity was getting the better of me, which was likely what Alice said before she fell down the rabbit hole. "You have evidence to prove my father was framed?"

His dark eyes glimmered in the harsh fluorescent light. "I don't just have evidence, Ms. Hayes. I can give you direct testimony. Testimony that will get him out of prison complete with an apology and grounds for a civil lawsuit. The man would never have to work again."

"Sounds great." My voice dripped with sarcasm. "And just whose testimony can do all this?"

"Mine."

TWENTY-THREE

I SHOT up from my chair, my fists clenched at my sides, anger coursing through me like wildfire. Ramirez's smirk grew wider, each word twisting deeper like a knife, and I found myself gripping the edge of the desk so hard my knuckles turned white. It wasn't just anger—I felt a pull, a weight pressing down on me, like I couldn't move fast enough or say the right thing to stop him from getting into my head. My chest tightened as his words slithered into my thoughts, wrapping around memories I'd buried, reminding me just how deep my father's mistakes still cut. My fist hammered the door, each thud echoing my rage. The sound of Ramirez's laughter filled the room, grating against my nerves, igniting a desperate urge within me to silence it. The guard appeared on the other side, confused concern etched on his face. He opened the door.

"Are we done here?" he asked, one hand resting on the open door.

"No," I said, barely growling the word. "But I need those cameras off."

"You serious?"

"Now. Or it's your head when this blows up." My threat hung heavy between us.

He muttered something about lawyers and regulations but

retreated. Within seconds, the red light of the camera flickered and died. Silence reclaimed the space, save for Ramirez's stifled chuckles.

I marched back to the table, my hands clenched into fists. Ramirez watched me, his eyebrow arching as if he found my fury amusing. "Let's hear it then."

"Quid pro quo," he said. "What's in it for me?"

"How should I know? You haven't given me anything yet."

He shook his head, almost pitying. "You have leverage, believe it or not."

"And what's that?"

"Martin's conviction."

Exasperation filled me to my core. "That's the entire reason I'm here. How is that a bargaining chip?"

He leaned forward. "What I've got might make you want to drop the entire case."

"Doubtful." My response was automatic, but his assurance unnerved me.

"Then commit. Right now. You won't walk away from the case."

My gut was telling me I was way in over my head. That I shouldn't agree to this.

"Fine," I said anyway. Down the rabbit hole to Wonderland I went. "I'll see the case through to the end. Now talk."

Ramirez settled back in his chair, a smug smile playing on his lips. "Martin didn't kill his wife."

I stared at him, disbelief and anger swirling inside me. "That's absurd. The alibi from Rachel Adams is false, and the timeline fits. He had the opportunity to commit the murder."

"Did he? If they were together at the store across town, in the same car, does he really have time to make it home, murder his wife, dispose of the evidence, and call it in?"

I paused. "How do you know he was at the store across town?"

"I guess I just remember. When I interviewed him at the scene."

Why would Ed have told Ramirez or Mindy Sanchez, the officer he was with, that he was at the store across town if he was threatening Rachel for the alibi she gave? Their stories would have been inconsistent. Besides, I would have remembered reading that in Sanchez's report.

"Let's stay on topic," he said. "Do you remember where Ed's car was found?"

"At his house."

"Right! If they were together at the store across town, in the same car, does he still have time to commit the crime?"

I closed my eyes as the realization sank in. Rachel's neighbor told us she'd been woken up by her car starting that morning. They'd had to have taken her car to the store, which wouldn't have left enough time for Ed to drive back to Rachel's house, pick up his own car, drive home, and commit the crime. But I'd seen Martin pull out of his driveway on Saturday afternoon with his own car.

A cold sensation washed over me as the implications began to dawn. If Donovan had made the connection about the vehicles, there was no way I'd be able to secure a conviction.

There had to be some other explanation.

"What about the DNA evidence?" I asked. "Ed's was the only DNA found at the scene. You're telling me someone else committed the crime and wiped every single trace?"

He scoffed. His arrogance made my blood boil. "A lack of something is not proof that it didn't happen. You're not examining this critically. Forensics has a protocol—they exclude known DNA from their reports. Think about that."

His words were a punch to my gut, and I recoiled as if struck. The forensics report had found DNA from Ramirez at the scene, but it was standard procedure to exclude a reporting officer's DNA from the report.

I looked at him incredulously. "I need you to help me understand. Are you about to admit to—"

"I'll spare you the mental exercise." He rolled his eyes. "Yes, I killed Caroline Martin."

The world dropped from beneath me. I shook my head, unable to take my eyes off him. "Why? Were you threatened? Promised something in return?"

Ramirez was too at ease throughout this discussion. "Now you're catching on. Not threatened but promised certain things if I did. I was assured if I did this thing, everything would be taken care of." He laughed, almost as if to himself. "But I'm starting to worry I shouldn't have trusted the bastards. They've strung me along for years and I've been in here way too long." The chill in his dark eyes gave me goose-bumps. "You ever get so invested in something and know you should turn away from it, but you're so far down that path that you want to see it through?"

I only nodded, feeling uneasy about being able to relate to a murderer.

He sat back in his chair. "See? We're more alike than you think."

"So, that's your reason for killing someone innocent? 'Everything would be taken care of?'"

Ramirez shook his head. "Caroline Martin was far from innocent."

"Guilty enough to deserve to have her head smashed in by a nightstand?"

"You're the lawyer. You tell me." The edges of his lips quirked up. "How many people have you sent to live behind bars for lesser crimes?"

"Don't try and turn this on me. I'm not on trial here."

"You're right. But Ed is. And you're going to see it through. If you don't, I'll come clean about this conversation, and you'll never work as a lawyer again."

"Is that a threat?"

"Think of it more as a guarantee."

"Why tell me this? Why admit to a murder?"

Ramirez looked thoughtful for a moment before I realized I could answer that myself. "You think the people you're working for will protect you. You'll never be brought up on charges for her murder, but you want to make sure—"

"That some girl too focused on ideals doesn't figure out the truth and start digging in where she doesn't belong. Sort of runs in her family. "

"And you're not worried that my ideals would take me into the DA's office right now to tell him what I just found out?"

"They might, but then you wouldn't get what you came for."

I stared at him.

"It's less fun when you don't play the game."

"This isn't a game to me," I yelled. I shot up from my chair, unable to sit any longer. "This is real. People's lives and freedoms are on the line."

"Your father's specifically."

It was the first time I'd felt it. I wanted to hurt Ramirez. It would be so easy. The cameras were off. No one was watching. He was cuffed to a table. I wasn't a huge woman, but I didn't need to be. My chair wasn't bolted down, after all.

But I pushed the violent thoughts aside. This is what he wanted. He wanted me riled up And I was falling right into his trap. I needed to stay calm, get whatever information I could out of him, and get out with my sanity still intact.

I took a breath and sat back down. "Tell me what you know about my father."

"You going to back out on our deal about Ed?"

"No."

"Good."

TWENTY-FOUR

THE PHOTOGRAPH of the two of them stared up at us. Ramirez's fingers grazed the glossy surface, dragging it across the table toward him. I watched, heart thumping, as he scrutinized the image. I hesitated for only a second before my hand dipped into my jacket pocket, retrieving the other photo from the envelope. With a decisive movement, I placed it beside the first.

Ramirez tapped on the first photo. "Day before Caroline was killed. Good shot. Caught the moment where I was given my marching orders."

"Which were?"

"Kill Caroline and then be one of the first responders at the scene. That way, my DNA at the crime scene would be easily explained and ruled out during the investigation. So, I set up a reason to partner with Sanchez that day under the pretense of training her."

It hit me then—why Ramirez, an assistant chief, had been a responding officer that day. It wasn't protocol for someone of his rank to be on the scene for routine calls. He'd orchestrated the whole thing to cover his tracks.

"Why would Ed want his wife killed?"

"He didn't really have a choice. Besides, as far as I understood it, things weren't happy at home."

"Didn't have a choice? "

Ramirez shrugged. "Why do you think Ed's construction company does so well?"

I shrugged. "The bidding process? He wins the bids."

Ramirez scoffed. "Please don't be so naive. Dear old Henry makes sure he wins those bids."

"As in Henry Thompson? The mayor?"

"The one and only."

My eyes narrowed. "Are you trying to tell me that all those contracts Ed's company wins, are really just being handed to him?"

"What I'm saying is that if you follow the paper trail, you'll see a lot of money coming in from the local government and going back out to the mayor. Chief among them, campaign donations."

"So, the mayor awards Ed the contracts, and Ed funds the mayor's campaign. All at the taxpayers' expense." I scoffed. "You realize how far-fetched this sounds, right?"

"I'm only here to tell the story. It's up to you if you want to believe it."

"Okay, but why kill Caroline? What did she have to do with any of this?"

"Imagine you come home, and your wife tells you that her old friend from college is running for mayor, and she no longer wants to support the incumbent. The one you're involved in an embezzlement scheme with?"

"So?"

Ramirez shook his head. "These are the elite of the city. She's played a very active and public role in her support of the current mayor."

I considered what he said. "Okay, I guess that would be a problem.".

"Now imagine she dug through your office and found bank statements with wire transfer confirmations used in this scheme. Except, she doesn't know these amounts are going to the mayor's office. She thinks they're going to her husband's mistress."

I leaned back slightly, pressing my lips together, waiting for the pieces to click into place, though a part of me doubted they ever would. "What do you think Ed would do when she threatens to make these statements public if he doesn't back her friend?"

"It's a bit of a jump to conspiracy to commit murder, isn't it? How about, you know, having a discussion first?"

Ramirez laughed. "The way Ed saw it, it was his life or hers. And he chose himself."

"Charming husband."

"As I said, he didn't have much of a choice."

"We all have choices. It's just whether you can stand the consequences." I leveled him a look. "Why do his dirty work? What's in it for you? First-degree murder isn't a light crime. You know we're one of the few states that still has the death penalty, right?"

Ramirez's expression hardened. "You're getting ahead of yourself."

He slid the second photograph across the metal table, his finger tapping the glossy surface. It was the photo of him with the mayor, dated February 17, 2018. "Because right here is where it all started. I cut a deal with the mayor. Cooperate and be rewarded."

My jaw hurt from clenching so hard. "And what deal was that?"

"Fabricate evidence against my partner in exchange for a promotion."

"Against my father, you mean?"

He shrugged.

"Why would the mayor want my father put away?"

He grinned. "It's not my job to ask why. It's my job to do and try."

I gritted my teeth and resisted the urge to curse at him. "So, you did what you were supposed to do way back then. What does that have to do with now?"

"I can tell you've always been on the right side of the law, counselor. So you probably don't know this, but there's no such thing as a one-night stand when it comes to these types of favors. Once you go there, you're in a committed relationship for life."

"So, you couldn't say no because they'd expose you."

"Bingo." His gaze locked onto mine. "Now you're getting it."

Anger welled in my chest. I didn't know how to process what he was saying. I didn't know whether to believe him or if he was just stringing me along.

I laid the third photo on the table. The one showing Ed, the mayor, and the man I couldn't quite place. Ramirez pulled it towards him. I could tell he didn't like what he saw. He turned the photo over to look at the date and shook his head. A sad smile washed over his features.

"Who is that with Ed and the mayor?" I asked.

Ramirez's next words held a mocking lilt. "Can't place him?"

"Should I?"

"Never met your co-counsel's father, huh?" He chuckled as if sharing an inside joke. He pushed the photo away from him as if it disgusted him. "Guess your relationship wasn't as serious as you thought."

A jolt of surprise shot through me, and I realized where I'd seen this man before. My expression hardened like turning into stone. "Lisa's father?"

"Angry because her dad's not behind bars?"

"Stay on topic."

"Hit a nerve, did I?"

I bristled. "What's Lisa's father got to do with all of this?"

"Hell if I should know. Did he get a promotion recently?"

I recalled Lisa saying that he'd been promoted to Major last year. The date lined up with this photograph.

Ramirez chuckled. "Too bad for him. He'll learn. Most carrots that are dangled in front of you are attached to sticks."

I looked up from the photo. "Are you saying Lisa's father is tied up in all of this, too?"

Ramirez spread his hands as wide as his cuffs would let him. "I'm not saying anything. I'm just pointing out what it looks like."

I sat back in my chair. "Alright, let's say you're telling the truth. What's stopping me from blowing this whole thing wide open? "

He leaned back, mimicking my posture. "Not that easy, counselor.

My testimony is what put him there in the first place. Along with evidence I planted. All of that's got to be revoked. That's my insurance."

"Insurance?"

"Cooperation," he said. "On the Martin case. You secure Ed's conviction, then we talk. About your dad, my sentence, what can be done for the both of us."

I spat out my next words like venom. "Blackmail."

"Call it leverage."

"You're cocky for a man chained to a table. Doesn't seem like Thompson is looking out for you." I leaned forward. "In fact, it actually looks like you're being thrown under the bus."

Ramirez tried to play off what I'd just said, but the fear in his eyes was ever-present, especially after he responded with only, "Whatever."

"What sort of job is going to be left for you when you get out of here?" I asked.

"I'm not worried. They'll come up with something to show that I've been framed. I'll be a hero and the mayor will pardon me."

"You must have a lot of free time to fantasize in here."

"Let Martin walk, and I'll get you disbarred. And your father will never go free. "

I leaned in and lowered my voice. "I'm not going to let Martin walk. I don't believe anything you're saying. I think this whole thing has been the ramblings of a desperate man trying to get out of a no-win situation. And I don't cut deals with criminals."

Ramirez chuckled. "Like hell you don't. Does the name Harper ring a bell?"

I had heard enough. My chair scraped loudly against the concrete floor as I stood from it. I walked to the metal door and knocked, once, twice—a dull echo in the sterile room.

The guard appeared, his face a blank slate. "We're done here."

TWENTY-FIVE

I STEPPED OUT OF JPC, my lungs tight. The humid Houston air was somehow less stifling than the AC inside that building. I walked to my car with measured steps, but I wished I could have run to it. I reached the door handle and hopped inside, closing it behind me. The door clicked shut and I leaned my head back against the headrest.

My heart still pounded through my chest. I reached inside my jacket pocket and retrieved the recording device. Ramirez might have asked me to turn the cameras off, but it was his mistake not to check that I wasn't wearing something. Since Texas was a one-party consent state, it was easy enough for someone to record a conversation they're a part of.

I held my breath, plugged the device into my phone, and hit play. The thing was tucked up against my jacket. It was possible all it had recorded was garbled noise. Ramirez's voice spilled into the confines of my vehicle. Relief washed over me. It wasn't Dolby Digital clear, but it was good enough. I tapped my phone and sent the audio file in an email to myself. Something this important needed a backup imme-diately.

I pulled the device out of my phone. "Drive was removed without ejecting" flashed on my screen, and I swiped it away.

I started up the car and dialed Andrews.

"Well? Was it everything you thought it would be?" Andrews tried and failed to use humor to cover up his concern.

I had no time for pleasantries. "Who handled the forensics?"

"Alex, what's going on?"

Right now I needed answers. Jury selection started in less than 24 hours, and I wasn't even close to figuring out what path to take. "On the Martin case. Who did forensics?"

"Palmer. Why?"

" I'll fill you in later."

I ended the call. My fingers drummed on the steering wheel as I drove back to the office. Could I fill Andrews in? And what about Lisa, when her father was potentially implicated in all of this? If I pursued Martin with shaky evidence, I risked a malicious prosecution charge. No one took kindly to a prosecutor breaking the very laws they were meant to uphold.

People said law was the great equalizer, but I never thought so. The scales always tipped towards those who had more money, influence, and power. Justice played favorites with those rich enough to flirt with her, and never her civil servants. She had an uncanny ability to hear the rustle of dollar bills, to sense the shadow of power. Her scales tipped accordingly.

I didn't want to risk ruining Andrews' or Lisa's careers. I exhaled slowly, realizing I had nothing concrete in my hands. Just words. Ramirez's words against a wall of other evidence. Until I had proof, tangible evidence, everything remained an allegation. To act prematurely could wreck everything. I needed to verify the truth first.

The road blurred past as I dialed Brian Palmer's number. He was, in my opinion, the best forensics expert there was. Palmer specialized in DNA analysis, trace evidence, and ballistics. He also specialized in blowing cases wide open.

I'd met him a few years back when I had a minor drug case. The alleged dealer had an air-tight alibi. Everyone had tried to tell me to drop the charges. Then Palmer found a microscopic fiber on the packaging of one of the dime bags in evidence. The fibers were of a rare fabric used in custom jackets, which the defendant had happened to own. Combine that with the skin cell DNA on tape sealing some of the larger packages, and I'd gotten my guilty verdict. Palmer and I had been friends ever since.

"Palmer," he answered, his voice steady and professional.

"It's Alex. Sorry to call you on a weekend but-"

"You got the Martin case coming up, yeah? What do you need?"

Direct and to the point. It was no wonder we got along. "Can you talk me through how you handle fingerprint and DNA evidence? What's the standard procedure?"

"I catalog, run it through the system-"

"Sorry, what I'm actually after is whether you exclude any fingerprints or DNA from the evidence."

There was a pause on the line. "Yes, anything that matches personnel working the scene is excluded. It's protocol—contamination from handling. Why?"

My stomach dropped as my grip tightened on the wheel.

"Thanks," was all I replied with. "I gotta run. I'll catch up with you later." I ended the call.

The main office was deserted as I walked inside, but so was my own. I walked back out into the hallway and called Lisa's name, but no one responded. I shook my head. Maybe she stepped out after sending things off to Cheryl.

I wasn't upset to be alone It gave me time and space to listen to the Ramirez recording again.

I booted up my computer, drumming my fingers on the wooden desk as it whirred to life. Once booted, I logged on and clicked into my Outlook, but the email with the recording wasn't there. I refreshed the thing a few times, frustration gnawing at the edge of my consciousness, but still nothing appeared.

Fishing out the recorder from my pocket, I connected it to my computer this time, resentful of the precious seconds ticking away. The device was recognized and I moved the file onto the desktop. I double-clicked it to open it.

"The file is corrupt and cannot be played."

The words stared back at me. A deep frown creased my forehead as I clicked the recording again.

"The file is corrupt and cannot be played."

I tried connecting it to my phone instead and emailing it back to myself. This time it came through, but the file still would not play.

I pulled the device out of my phone and a notification popped up. "Drive was removed without ejecting."

My heart hammered against my ribcage. The one solid lead, potentially ruined by haste.

I turned back to my computer, desperate. I opened the main menu and did a frantic search for the first email.

Nothing in Sent. Nothing in Outbox.

"Dammit!" My fist hit the desk, the jolt shooting up my arm. My office phone rang. I snatched up the phone. "Alex Hayes."

"Alex, it's Cheryl." Her tone was urgent, almost nervous. "I've gotten through the documents and I think you should come by. I don't think we should discuss this on the phone."

" I'll be right there." I hung up and grabbed my keys to head back to my car.

As I pushed open my office door, that's when it hit me. Someone had been here, in my office, on my computer when I'd sent the file. Lisa.

She must've heard the real recording, the one that implicated her father. Now she had to be scrambling to bury the truth. And I was left holding fragments of a shattered case.

TWENTY-SIX

THE DOORS of the elevator slid open, and I stepped out onto the fifteenth floor. The lobby seemed a lot more polished and bright. This was where the civil and transactional teams spun their gold, while we —the criminal litigators—lurked below like underdogs in a den. I'd once said litigators were the lowest on the totem pole. Someone had informed me that, traditionally, being a litigator was a position of honor. Here it felt more like a hierarchy.

I navigated the labyrinth of offices, all glass and steel, the quiet hum of privilege thick in the air. Cheryl's office was somewhere in the middle.

As I passed each door, my gaze flickered for signs of Lisa. I wondered if she was still in the building. I was having trouble believing that she was the one to tamper with my recording. Maybe there was some other explanation. I made a mental note to check if Paul, the security guard, had seen her. Maybe someone else had been in my office today and I'd left my computer unlocked.

I finally found Cheryl's office and knocked before walking inside. The air was overly perfumed, thanks to the five incense sticks in each corner of the room. Cheryl looked up from her desk. She was a middle-aged woman, heavier set, with slightly graying hair and a warm demeanor.

Her office was a vibrant collage of personal quirks. A mug emblazoned with "Objection, Your Honor" housed a lush fern. On the walls hung framed cross-stitches of various feline-inspired witticisms: "The more I meet people, the more I like my cat" and "Paws for justice". Each corner seemed to purr with a silent chuckle, an ironic testament to the gravity of our work.

Cheryl gestured toward a chair opposite her cluttered desk. "Take a seat, Alex."

I clicked the door shut behind me and cleared a few files off the chair before sitting down. The weight in her eyes told me this wasn't going to be an ordinary conversation. The room seemed to grow heavier with anticipation, and I braced myself for whatever was coming. "Thanks for meeting with me," I said.

She raised a hand before I could say more, her fingers stained with highlighter ink. She pulled out the folder Erin had given to me. "Look at this."

I leaned in as she opened it. Inside were the pages of financial statements I couldn't make heads or tails of, each annotated meticulously with purple pen.

"Bad news?" I asked.

"I suppose it depends on whose team you're on," she said with a chuckle. She had no idea.

I settled into the chair, my spine a bit too rigid. Cheryl's fingers skimmed over the documents with a slow, practiced precision, as if weighing the significance of each page before turning it. I kept my voice steady, despite the churning in my gut. "So what exactly am I looking at?"

She drew a breath. "These here are bank statements, invoices, and corporate ledgers." She tapped each type of document as she spoke. "Your notes were crucial."

I realized she must have meant Erin's notes.

"They highlighted connections, made it easier to trace the trail.

Every invoice paid out matched the first set of bank statements." Her index finger glided across the rows of figures. "See here, invoice 1427 for the amount of $124,900. It's an installment payment on a building renovation. It matches an outgoing wire on the first set of bank statements. But the corporate records... they don't add up. On the ledger, they only reported receiving one hundred grand, even. And this was the pattern across all of the records."

A furrow creased my brow. "Meaning?"

"Meaning," Cheryl leaned in, her voice lowering to a conspiratorial whisper, "what was reported as income was always *less* than what actually hit the bank."

My pulse quickened. "How much less?"

"It's variable, but substantial." Her eyes never left the papers as she flipped to another page. "To make sense of it, I checked the second set of bank statements." Her finger swiped to another page then stopped, pointing at a specific line. "See?"

I leaned in, trying to make sense of the line she was pointing to. It looked like any other ledger line to me.

"It's the missing $24,900," she clarified.

I squinted my eyes at the line she was pointing at. "It's a $9,000 deposit for a consulting fee?" I wasn't following. This is why I didn't end up on the transactional side. Math and I were never friends.

"Sometimes it was added back in multiple transactions, like for this one, they didn't just wire back $24,900. They did it in three payments, done over the course of roughly a month. This was the first. But they all add up to the deficit."

What she was saying finally clicked. "Can we identify the account holder?"

"The first set's holder is easy," she said, tapping one manicured nail on a crumpled sheet. "These invoices come from Martin Corp, billed to the City of Houston."

"What about the bank account receiving the siphoned money?"

Cheryl's voice was steady, but her hand hovered over the second stack. " It's a dead end. No names. Just numbers."

"Could be anyone," I muttered, frustration knotting in my throat.

Cheryl's eyes locked onto mine in a silent challenge. "Subpoena the bank. It's the next best move if this is part of your investigation."

Cheryl was referring to what was known as a *subpoena duces tecum*, which was a formal discovery request. In Latin—which lawyers were fond of using because it made them feel superior—it meant "you shall bring with you." In practice, it was a court—sanctioned order for documentation.

Cheryl tapped the line again, her finger lingering as if to emphasize the gravity of the situation. "These kickbacks contradict the campaign contribution narrative," she said, her voice hushed yet firm. "Campaign donations are a front, a clean way to funnel money legally. But this," she gestured toward the documents, "this is deliberate embezzlement, plain and simple. Money moving back and forth monthly—personal accounts, private funds. It's not the mayor's campaign; it's someone's slush fund."

I leaned in, scanning the records again, feeling a knot tighten in my stomach. "So, who's pocketing this?"

Cheryl's lips thinned. "Ed's overbilling, kicking back large sums, but it's not just him. Someone high up is protecting him—using him as a shield. We just don't know how far it goes."

It was all becoming clearer, but simultaneously, the edges of doubt sharpened in my mind. Could this all be a setup to make Ed the fall guy? Cheryl's analysis confirmed what I'd already suspected—embezzlement. The proof was finally in front of me, but now I needed to unravel who the setup was for and why they were pulling the strings so carefully. She nodded and tapped the ledger with a finger. "You should think about talking to our department, maybe bringing charges against Ed Martin's company."

My mind was already racing ahead. "The murder trial is our priority right now. Jury selection starts tomorrow." I glanced at the documents, my pulse quickening. "But we're digging into every aspect of his dealings. Trying to shake any dirt loose."

Cheryl's brow creased, confusion etching lines into her forehead. "You're still looking for evidence on the trial?"

I didn't have time for this.

"Thank you, Cheryl," I said sharply, scooping up the papers and stuffing them into my bag. Her question hung unanswered as I strode from the office.

TWENTY-SEVEN

I STEPPED into the courtroom and made my way up to the prosecutor's table. There was some press here, but I suspected the judge had already had a discussion with court security and limited how many journalists were let in.

I looked around at the courtroom, the light bouncing off the wood paneling on the walls. It seemed to be a requirement for any courtroom anywhere. Ironically, this sort of paneling was actually referred to as "lawyers' paneling." Probably because it was used to cover something up.

Lisa was absent. I'd called her last night, but she hadn't answered. Paul had said he hadn't seen anyone in my office, but also hadn't been paying close attention.

It wasn't like Lisa to be late for anything, much less disappear.

Donovan was to my left with some young hotshot in an ill-fitting suit. I stifled an eye roll and rifled through my bag, stacking files on the table with a thud. This was a nightmare. It was hard enough picking a jury when you had co-counsel. Doing it alone guaranteed I'd miss things. I needed a partner to take notes, signal strikes.

In jury selection, signal strikes were subtle but crucial. As the lead attorney questioned potential jurors, their second chair would watch the panel closely for reactions, mannerisms, or any biases that might not be immediately apparent from answers alone. A subtle nod or shake of the head, a scribbled note on a legal pad, all conveyed who to strike without causing a scene. These signals were invaluable— knowing when to dismiss a juror could make or break a case. Without a second chair, I was flying blind. I'd be doing the questioning, watching for tells, and keeping track of answers all at once. It felt like trying to juggle knives while walking a tightrope, and all without the safety net of a trusted partner.

Donovan leaned back in his chair, regarding me with that smug grin. "Seems you're missing someone, counselor."

"Seems that way," I replied curtly, fighting the urge to match his smugness with venom.

"Must be tough, handling voir dire all by yourself."

"Thank you for your concern." I was about to add a choice suggestion for where he could put said concern, but the judge's entrance cut me off.

I bit my tongue as the bailiff called us to rise. The Honorable Judge Beasley strode in, black robe billowing behind him. We sat after being instructed. The room was deadly silent.

Before the judge could start the proceeding, the courtroom door swung open, and Lisa rushed to my side, panting slightly.

"Thank you for joining us, Ms. Cooper," the judge said wryly. Lisa opened her mouth to respond, but my heel found her foot under the table, and she sat without a single word. Message received.

"Let's begin." Judge Beasley leaned forward, hands clasped before him as he surveyed the pool of potential jurors. "This case involves a man accused of murdering his wife." His words were measured, deliberate. As he laid out the charges, I could feel the weight of each syllable pressing down on the room.

I shuffled papers, trying to appear composed, but my focus was fractured. Lisa's hushed apology brushed against my ear. "I'm sorry I'm late."

"Not now," I murmured back, barely moving my lips. "Focus."

The judge started first, asking some basic questions of the jury pool. When the judge began his questioning, the first potential juror hesitated for a moment, then admitted her cousin worked for a law firm that often handled defense cases. The judge exchanged a glance with Donovan and me before dismissing her. Another juror—an older man—blurted out that his brother was a police officer, and that he "didn't believe a word any defense attorney said." Gone. The third? A woman who, when asked about her feelings on law enforcement, went on a rant about how corrupt the system was. The judge swiftly dismissed her as well. Bias was dangerous. If a juror had a pre-existing grudge or allegiance, they wouldn't listen fairly to the evidence, and that was the last thing either of us wanted.

His gaze turned to find mine. "Prosecution, your turn for voir dire."

I stood, feeling every pair of eyes looking at me expectantly.

While this case was undoubtedly my biggest, I'd handled several jury trials in my career. Some attorneys used these as opportunities to showboat in front of the jury, but that wasn't my style. This wasn't about flair. It was about filtering truths from half-truths, finding the impartial among the prejudiced. And this could only be done through simple, measured questions.

"Juror number eight," I called out, my voice steady. "Can you follow the court's instructions without reservation?"

"Yes," came the reply, clipped and clean.

"Juror fifteen, any biases that might affect your judgment in this case?"

"None that I'm aware of." This response was tentative, unsure. I made a signal to Lisa, the smallest finger wag behind my back.

"Juror twenty-two, have you formed any preconceived notions about this case based on media coverage?"

"No," the man said, shifting in his seat. "I don't watch the news much."

"Juror thirty-one, ever been a victim or witness of a crime?"

"Victim, yes. A burglary."

Another signal to Lisa.

"Juror forty-four, any personal connections to anyone involved with this trial?"

"None."

The mundane process of elimination was crucial, laying the groundwork for what was to come. Every decision made now could impact the entire trial. Jurors who seemed indifferent or easily swayed could become wildcards, and any bias—however small—had the potential to unravel weeks of preparation. With each dismissal, the stakes climbed, and I felt the weight of needing a fair, impartial jury.

"Juror fifty-seven. I see you've got a degree in psychology. Do you believe this could influence your perception of evidence?"

"Potentially."

No time for second guessing; psychology degrees could be a wild card—a risk we couldn't afford. Jurors with that kind of background might overanalyze, dig deeper into motive or character beyond the evidence presented. They could challenge facts in ways we couldn't anticipate, turning the trial into a psychological puzzle rather than a straightforward case.

"Your Honor, I move to strike juror fifty-seven for cause."

Judge Beasley nodded and replied, "Motion granted."

"Juror sixty-two, any strong opinions on the criminal justice system?"

" No, ma'am. Just faith that it works as intended," he answered confidently.

"Thank you." A thumbs up to Lisa behind my back.

I finished my first round of questions and took a seat.

Donovan rose, smoothing his expensive suit jacket with a smug smile. I couldn't wait to see what sort of show he put on today. He was a showboater if there ever was one.

"Ladies and gentlemen," he began, his tone too casual. "Let's lighten the mood. Who here has a bumper sticker on their car? What does it say?"

A few chuckles rippled through the room as hands went up. Donovan's charm offensive was in full swing, but it was a calculated distraction. Donovan played the game well. Even still, he didn't have an original idea in his head. Pretty sure he stole the bumper sticker skit from a television show.

"Juror seventy-nine, you have a 'Coexist' sticker. Does that mean you're particularly open-minded?"

The juror shrugged. "Suppose so."

"Interesting." Donovan tapped his index finger twice against his wrist, a subtle but deliberate signal. His co-counsel immediately caught on, scribbling a note down furiously.

He followed up on a few more bumper stickers. It felt odd to have laughter in the courtroom during a capital crime jury selection, but that was Donovan. He was frustratingly charming. He then switched to questions about reading preferences, social media, and problem-solving approaches, before moving to strike four jurors for cause and using five of his peremptories.

"Ms. Hayes." The judge gestured toward me. "Any follow-up questions?"

I stood and rounded the table. I didn't have any further objections to the twelve jurors in front of us, but no one ever passed an opportunity to ask the jury further questions.

"Juror forty-nine, you're a librarian. Does your profession give you a unique perspective on researching facts?"

"Absolutely," she said. "It's all about finding the truth in the details." A thumbs up to Lisa.

"Juror eighty-three, you're a software engineer. Do you value logic over emotion when making decisions?"

"Logic, mostly. But there's a human element in everything."

"Thank you." Educated, logical jurors were gold in a case like this—people who'd see through Donovan's theatrics.

The dance continued, back and forth, until our peremptory strikes ran dry.

Judge Beasley spoke once more. "Okay. The jury is set. Opening arguments will begin tomorrow at 10 a.m. sharp. Jurors, you are excused. " Chairs scraped back and feet shuffled on the raised jury box.

Judge Beasley addressed the prosecution and defense tables. "Any other matters to discuss ahead of trial?"

Donovan stood. "Your Honor, I have a motion in limine."

My heart stopped. Donovan was filing a motion to limit what evidence I could present at trial. I turned back to watch him approach the bench, his young associate trailing behind him.

Judge Beasley raised an eyebrow. "Go ahead, Mr. Donovan."

"We move to disallow the release of any security camera footage from the Martin residence. There's no actual footage of the time of the crime, only before and after. It's more prejudicial than probative."

My heart rate was shocked back to life, immediately spiking. I stepped forward. "Your Honor, I haven't had time to prepare an argument against this motion. Frankly, I haven't even seen this motion." I shot Donovan a glare. "The footage could be probative. We don't know what the defense might claim about the timeline or other activities at the residence."

The judge looked between us, weighing the arguments. "I'll take the motion under advisement. I'll decide at trial if the evidence should be admitted. Court is adjourned for the day."

Donovan's voice slid into my ear as he gathered his things. "Better sharpen up, counselor. Did you hear the judge? Court starts at 10 a.m." He smirked, his young clone chuckling like a parrot at his side.

I bit back a retort. Donovan and his co-counsel strutted down the aisle, their heads held high, shoulders back, each step deliberate, as if they expected everyone around them to take notice. The younger one adjusted his suit jacket, smoothing it down like feathers preening after a rainstorm. They didn't just walk out of the courtroom—they made an exit, puffed-up and polished, like peacocks parading for attention.

I pretended to fumble with my papers, delaying my exit. Lisa stood next to me, her apology quick and hushed. "I'm so sorry, Alex—"

"Save it," I snapped once the last of the spectators had left, turning to face her. "Where were you?"

"I got sick. After I sent the documents to Cheryl, I stepped out to get something to eat. It upset my stomach so terribly." She stumbled over her words. "I ended up going back home and after I threw up, I fell asleep. I completely slept through my alarm. I'm so sorry."

I studied her. There was always a tell when people lied, and the biggest tell of all was giving too much information. Why? Because they ran through the whole story in their head beforehand, making sure they had all their bases covered. No room for questions. A dead giveaway.

I had half a mind to dismiss her from this case right now.

But I didn't know what she'd do if I pulled that card. The better thing to do was to keep her close and act like everything was fine. "And tomorrow? Will you be ready?"

"Of course," she said.

"Good."

"What was that about?" Lisa whispered in a hushed voice. "His motion?"

"I'm not sure. But I'm definitely wondering why Donovan doesn't want us introducing the security footage."

"I'm available the rest of the day to prep."

"I've got an errand to run," I said, grabbing my bag. "I'll see you tomorrow morning. Be on time."

TWENTY-EIGHT

I LOOKED at the address on the card in my hand and then at the number on the door. It was a match. I couldn't believe that I was here, but desperate times and all that. I knocked a few times. There was a bit of a shuffle behind the door before it finally opened.

"Uhh, prosecutor," Jacob Campo stammered, having obviously forgotten my name.

"Alex Hayes," I replied. "Can I come in?"

He hesitated, clearly trying to decide whether it was a good idea to let the prosecutor who had just reduced charges against him into his home. He was smarter than most.

"I'm not here for evidence," I said. "I actually need your help on something."

He squeezed his eyes shut and let out a big breath. Then he swung the door wider. "Okay."

His apartment was about what I expected for a computer hacker. Wires ran across the floor, the place had a continuous hum from all the machines. More of the light came from the blinking lights on electronics than actual lamps.

Jacob led me into a kitchen that looked like it was barely cooked in.

Not because it was sparkling clean, but just because there weren't any pots, pans, or metal utensils anywhere.

"Drink?" he offered half-heartedly.

"No, thanks. I'm in a bit of a rush, actually." I pulled the listening device from my pocket and handed it to him. "It says the file on it is corrupt. Can you fix it?"

He turned the device over in his hand and then gestured for me to follow him into the living room. While there was a sofa in this room, the majority of the space was taken up by computer towers and large monitors. He sat down at one of the desks and plugged the device in.

He pulled a keyboard in front of him and began to type faster than I'd ever seen. He frowned, paused, and then started typing again. He repeated this cycle a few more times before he finally unplugged the device from his computer and turned to give it back to me.

"Sorry," he said. "Nothing I can do. The disk itself got fried somehow."

"Shit. I really needed what was on there."

"Any chance you can get them to admit to the crime again?"

I gave him a confused look. How could he know what was on the file?

He put his hands up in mock surrender. "You're a prosecutor. I'm just assuming this is a confession."

"Sorry," I said. "I'm just a little jumpy lately."

He exhaled. "I can see that."

I reached into my bag and pulled out the security footage CDs. I handed them over and he popped them into his computer.

"What are these supposed to be?"

I leaned a little closer so I could see the screen. "Security footage feed from a defendant's house." I watched as the recording showed Ed's driveway and then Ed pulling his Mercedes out of the garage and driving off.

Then the footage turned off.

"The time of the crime is conveniently missing. Any way to see whether the footage has been cut purposefully?"

He turned to his computer and dragged the video cursor backward and forward. Ed's car moved back and forth across the screen a few times.

"Yeah, it's definitely been altered."

"What do you mean?"

"You don't need computer skills to see it. If you look closely, you can see that the video's been spliced."

"How so?"

"See where he drives the car out of the garage? That's not from the same day. Someone took that footage and edited it in." He pointed to a bush next to the driveway. "See how the leaves change position ever so slightly. Plus the lighting has been played with."

"You can tell all of this just from looking at it?"

He shrugged. "I guess if you stare at this stuff long enough, it's easier to spot."

"Any way to recover the original footage?"

He shook his head. " It doesn't really work that way. Someone spliced it and then exported the edited video. There's no history to go back to." He ejected the CD and handed it back to me.

"Well, thanks for trying. I'd appreciate it if you kept this just between us."

"Who'd believe me anyway?" A smirk flickered across his lips, then vanished.

"Stay out of trouble, Campo."

I slid into the car and slammed the door behind me. My phone rang, and I almost jumped out of my seat. Luckily, it was just Andrews. I contemplated rejecting the call, but he'd just call again if I did.

"What's up?" I asked, starting the car.

"You tell me. I haven't heard from you since you spoke to Ramirez."

"Sorry," I said. "I've been busy." It wasn't a total lie, but I could have made time to call him.

"Cut the crap, Alex." His tone hit me hard, laced with anger that sent a prickle of discomfort crawling up my spine. "What'd he say?"

"Fine," I relented, a bit softer. "My place. Bring coffee, though. And the good stuff, please. I'm going to be up all night prepping for my opening tomorrow and I need quality caffeine."

"Will do." The line went dead.

* * *

WE ENDED up pulling into my driveway at the same time.

We exited our cars and moved, him after me, to the front door. My keys jingled as I unlocked the door. I pressed it open and we stepped inside. I threw my stuff down in the living room as we made our way to the sofa

"You're still alive, at least," Andrews joked.

"Thanks for your concern."

"Don't give me that, Hayes. We're supposed to be a team on this case, and you went off and did something I advised against."

I tried and failed to keep the frustration out of my voice. "I didn't have a choice. All paths led to him."

"And? Was he the soothsayer of this case?"

I grabbed one of the coffees Andrews had placed on the counter and took a long sip. He knew exactly what my order was.

I moved back to the couch and settled in while he sat in the chair across from me. "This all stays between us, okay?"

Andrews leveled me a concerned look. "Alex."

"Just listen before you judge me."

Andrews sighed, but didn't say anything.

"Ramirez admitted to killing Caroline."

"Shit."

I nodded, relishing the warmth of the paper coffee cup between my palms. "Claims Ed and Thompson have been embezzling government funds to line their own pockets."

Andrews rubbed between his eyebrows. "So, why kill Ed's wife?"

"Ramirez says he was ordered to do it."

"I still don't see what one has to do with the other." He took a drink from his own cup.

I shrugged. "Ramirez says that Caroline was going to go public and expose the embezzlement scheme."

"You're saying Ramirez is innocent of the drug trafficking and embezzlement charges?"

"He claims his current charges were a front to cover up his whereabouts. He acted like he was going to be let out of lockup any day. That his charges would be dropped. But, he wants to make sure he's not being played."

"Please tell me you don't believe this."

I took another swig of coffee, wishing it contained something stronger. "I don't know what to believe. But why admit to a murder if you didn't actually do it?"

"Because maybe he's friendly with Ed, and once you drop the charges, he'll deny ever admitting to killing Caroline, especially since you don't have any proof that he did."

"I got the confession."

Andrews' eyes widened. "You got it on tape?"

"Sort of." I definitely needed something stronger than coffee. I took the listening device out of my pocket and tossed it over to him. "File corrupted."

He looked down at it in his palm. "Any chance there's a backup?"

I debated whether to tell him my suspicions about Lisa, but without definitive evidence, I decided against it. "Tried to email it to myself but it didn't go through," was all I said.

I tried to take another sip of coffee, but I'd already finished the entire cup. I set it down on the coffee table with a disappointed stare. Andrews caught on and jerked his thumb over to the counter. "Take mine."

"You're the best," I said with a smile, suddenly having lots of energy to get up for the second cup.

"So, what are you going to do?" he asked. "The trial starts tomorrow?"

I deadpanned. "Thanks for reminding me. I wasn't aware."

"This is serious, Alex." I sat down while he got up to pace. "What about all the evidence against Martin? What did Ramirez tell you?"

"I didn't want to believe it either. Still not sure I do," I said. "Ramirez claimed that forensics routinely eliminates personnel from their report—any trace of them found at the scene. Sort of an 'I know how the system works, so I know how to manipulate it,' idea. Any DNA or evidence of him being there could've been wiped clean because, as a cop, his presence would've been considered routine."

"And you called Palmer?"

Another sip. Another nod of my head. "Yep."

"Shit." Andrews plopped down on the couch. "So, what are you going to do?"

"Right now?" I rubbed my temples. "I've got nothing. Ramirez confessed, but without the recording, it's air. And we've got Ed about to stand trial, with all arrows pointing to him as the killer."

Andrews' eyes narrowed. "But do they really point to him?"

"Dig deep enough, and things blur. The evidence is...convenient."

The defendant's house. The street. How Campo said the security footage had been tampered with. I thought about the placement, the timing, and the angles. The more I thought about it, the more I wondered how deep this went. Who was covering for whom?

"Too convenient." His agreement was quiet, almost to himself.

I stood up to pace the room, trading spots with Andrews. "I can't verify anything Ramirez said. And I can't ask for a continuance. Martin refused to waive the Speedy Trial Act."

"Back against the wall," Andrews muttered.

"All I can do is proceed with opening tomorrow. It's a capital case. Trial should take at least a week. That gives us time to dig into what Ramirez said before things get handed over to the jury. I can dismiss the charges at any time if we come up with concrete evidence that Martin wasn't the killer."

"Tell me what you need from me, and I'll work on it in the background."

I made my way over to my bag and pulled out a few pages from Cheryl. "Here," I said, handing the documents to Andrews. "There's money being moved between accounts, but I don't know who owns this account,. Is this something you can figure out?"

Andrews rubbed his chin. "I'm not really a financial services investigator, but I'll give it a go. Maybe I can shake something loose."

"Thanks," I said with a smile. "Now leave, because I need to prep for tomorrow."

Andrews chuckled. "Just try and get some rest, too."

"Will do, Dad."

TWENTY-NINE

I SHUFFLED the papers in front of me, trying to remind myself that this trial was just like any other. The only difference was in the alleged crime.

Lisa was seated to my right. She'd been on time this morning, earlier than me in fact. We hadn't exchanged much more than a "hello" since I'd arrived. The tension between us was palpable, and I wasn't sure if I was the one creating it.

Across the divide, Donovan sat with his co-counsel. His usual grandstanding was notably absent today. His lips were pressed into a tight line, fingers drumming against the wood of the defense table in a slow, nervous rhythm. He hadn't even come over to my table to make his usual snide remarks. There was an odd emptiness in the air, like a key piece of the usual courtroom theatrics was missing. But his restraint was telling. It was an obvious display that even Donovan, ever the showman, was feeling the pressure of what was to come.

Ed Martin sat to the far left of the room. He was dressed in a well-tailored suit and his thick white hair was combed back. He looked far too calm for a man who was facing first-degree murder charges. Almost as if he already knew what his fate would be.

The judge's clerk, a mousy looking girl with thick-rimmed glasses, came out from the door behind the bench to check in with both me and Donovan. No doubt fresh out of law school. Probably fed the lie that clerking would be a great opportunity for her career. I'd believed it, too. In reality, it was a way for the system to pay you less than fifty grand while making you work for a judge.

I told her I was ready to proceed, as did Donovan, and she disappeared back behind the bench. Within a few minutes, the bailiff's voice cut through the low hum from the audience behind us.

"All rise for the Honorable Judge Beasley." The scrape of wooden benches and shuffle of feet echoed as everyone stood in unison. I knew there was a good deal of press behind me, something I had specifically avoided up until this point, but I knew I'd have to face them after opening today. Tom had scheduled press conferences. This was, after all, an election year. We had to consistently remind people that we were tough on crime.

Judge Beasley took the bench and then called in the jury. Once they were seated, the rest of us sat.

"Ladies and gentlemen of the jury," he began. "I am going to read you some instructions. You will receive a second set of instructions following the close of all the evidence. I want you to pay careful attention to what I say and if you have any questions, you may write them on the provided paper and hand them to the bailiff before any recess."

Judge Beasley began to read the standard jury instructions. How the lawyers present evidence according to rules, and how he, the judge, enforced those rules. That they, the jury, needed to consider all the evidence as a whole, rather than focus on one specific fact. That the trial followed a specific procedure: lawyers outlined their evidence, then the State presented their case, followed by the defendant. The State could then rebut evidence, and the trial would conclude with closing arguments.

Judge Beasley liked to take the "I'm your Daddy" approach with the jury. I guess that made us lawyers their older siblings, because according to the judge, the jury shouldn't listen to anything *we* say, only what he and the witnesses say.

Since this was a criminal trial, the judge also informed the jury that

Mr. Martin did not plead guilty and was presumed innocent as there was no evidence already against him. This also meant that Mr. Martin had no obligation to testify, present evidence, or prove his innocence.

In short, if I didn't do my job, then he walked free.

Some judges took the time to learn the attorneys' names and refer to them as "Mr. or Mrs. So-and-so" during a trial. Some judges even took the time to learn the defendant's name. Those judges who did and referred to the defendants as a person rather than just "defendant" usually had one of two backgrounds: they'd been transactional attorneys lucky enough to buy their way into their much cushier seat on the bench, or they'd been defense attorneys.

Judge Beasley fell into the second category. He'd been a public defender for many years before finally earning his spot on the bench. I had a lot of respect for the man, even if I wished I'd pulled a different card in the judge's pool for this trial. Your background always gave you biases. Always.

"If there aren't any questions, then we'll start." Judge Beasley surveyed the jury and then looked over at me. "Counselor, your opening statement, please."

Different judges had different rules in their courtroom. Some allowed attorneys to approach the witness box, whereas others did not. Judge Beasley, having been a litigator himself, knew the value in speaking to the jury as if they were old friends. Thus, he allowed his attorneys to approach without needing to ask permission.

I thanked Judge Beasley and made my way before the jury, tightening my blazer and wearing my warmest neutral expression. "I was out with a friend the other day and they said something interesting. You see, they'd accused me of stealing a french fry while they weren't looking, and I proceeded to do what lawyers do best. I argued with them." I smiled to lighten the atmosphere, and a few members of the jury smiled along with me. I made note of who they were, because those were the people I didn't need to worry about. They were with me from the start.

But Donovan only needed to sway one juror. One out of twelve. Less than ten percent. I, on the other hand, had to persuade all twelve.

"My friend said, 'the truth is like a lion; you don't have to defend it. Let it loose, and it will defend itself.' Now, I know what you're thinking. That's a pretty intense conversation for two friends at lunch. Well, my friend is a lawyer also." Another few chuckles. Good.

"We're here to talk about a very different story today. We don't care about whether I ate my friend's fries—which in all honesty, I did." More chuckling. Just the way I'd planned. "We care about whether the defendant violently strangled and beat his wife of over forty years, Caroline Martin, to death.

"Now, the defense is going to try and tell you the defendant is innocent. That we have no evidence to prove he's guilty. That we're just playing at, 'if not him, then who?' But that's not true. We do have evidence in the form of witness testimony, financial records, and forensic reports, all of which point to a calculated plan to kill Caroline Martin on the morning of May 19th.

"As we proceed, I ask you to keep an open mind and focus on the evidence. The truth, like that lion, will emerge. It will defend itself and reveal the guilt of Edward Martin. At the end of this trial, when all the evidence has been presented, you will see that there is only one verdict supported by the truth: guilty."

"Thank you, Ms. Hayes," Judge Beasley said as I took my seat. "Mr. Donovan?"

Donovan stood and buttoned his jacket. One look at the man, and he may as well have been about to pull a rabbit out of his hat. "Your Honor, the defense would like to reserve their opening."

There were a few murmurs among the crowd. Even the judge seemed taken aback, but he recovered quickly.

Lisa tapped my shoulder, and I leaned over. "What's he doing?"

I wasn't surprised Lisa didn't know. It wasn't something taught in law school. Most litigation skills weren't. They were something most attorneys picked up through either mentorship or many, many difficult "teaching moments."

I shook my head at Lisa. "Just wait," I said, knowing the judge would explain it.

THIRTY

JUDGE BEASLEY REELED in the crowd and took control of the courtroom. "Alright then." He turned to the jury. "Ladies and gentlemen, Mr. Donovan has elected to present his opening statement once the State has finished presenting its case. With that in mind, we'll adjourn for the day." We all stood as the jury filed out, followed by the judge. Lisa opened her mouth, but I cut her off with a sharp look. Donovan and his team swept past us, out of the courtroom.

Once they were gone, I turned to Lisa. "Anything you say in front of defense counsel can be used against us, you get that right? Like when you showed up late for voir dire, and he mocked me for it?" I raised my eyebrows at her. It was a pretty shitty thing to say, but I was on edge. I kept my tone firm. "What did you want to ask me?"

Lisa looked like I'd just slapped her in the face. She tried to stammer out an apology but I supposed the look in my eye had her reconsidering. Instead, she cleared her throat and asked, "Donovan's strategy... reserving his opening. Will it affect our position?"

"Potentially."

"Are we going back to your office to prep for tomorrow?"

I had to hand it to her—she really sold the confusion about why I was keeping her at arm's length. But she was the only one who could've messed with that recording. And she had motive.

"No," I said. "Got an errand to run."

It was only half a lie. I needed to meet Erin and brief her on the embezzlement scheme. I also wanted her insight on the whole Lisa situation.

I snapped my briefcase shut and began walking out, briefly turning to Lisa before going through the double doors. "Don't talk to the press."

Of course, cameras swarmed me the moment I stepped outside. Questions flew from all directions. I waited, knowing Tom would've planted a prosecution-friendly reporter in the mix.

"How confident are you in your case and evidence?"

I gave my rehearsed answer. "We believe the evidence will prove beyond a reasonable doubt that Mr. Martin viciously attacked and strangled his wife in their marital home after returning from a night with his mistress." Then I pushed past the rest to my car.

I drove straight to Erin's hotel and rode the elevator up to the same room as before. She opened at my knock and ushered me inside.

"How'd the first day go?" she asked.

"You weren't there?"

"What I'm after isn't really in opening statements."

I plopped down in the fabric armchair and raised an eyebrow. "Still not going to tell me what you are after?"

"You know that I can't," was her practiced reply.

I nodded and decided not to keep grilling her. "Donovan reserved his opening," I said. "I'm on edge because of it. I've never had this happen before, and it's not common. I'm not sure how it's going to play out, and that makes me uneasy." A recent Law360 article wrote about a high-powered (probably an alignment error, but it extended the hyphen far more than it should have) litigator out of Washington reserving his opening in a big case involving a poultry farmer. I guessed Donovan didn't want to appear chicken.

Erin laughed. "Defense lawyers and their tricks."

"This common on the federal side?"

"A bit. Federal judges can be stricter about rules. Lawyers play nicer."

I scoffed. "What a dream."

I leaned forward and balanced my elbows on my knees, thinking for a moment. "Can I run something by you?"

She nodded. "Okay."

"Your photos led me to Ramirez. You may have already figured that." I took a deep breath, feeling my palms press against one another. "Well, I got him talking, and he confessed to killing Caroline Martin."

Erin didn't flinch. Federal prosecutor through and through. I doubted even proof of a flat Earth would make her jump. In a moment of silence, she gestured for me to continue.

"Got it all on tape, even. But the recording got corrupted. And I think my co-counsel did it."

That got a slight head tilt. "Why do you think so?"

"For starters, Lisa was the only one with access to my laptop while I was out. " I went on to explain how Ramirez had revealed involvement of Lisa's father, how she may have listened to the recording and heard that information, deciding to delete the file and cover his tracks.

Erin kept her head tilted, her expression thoughtful. "Who's her father?"

"He's a major in the police department. The man in the gala photo."

"What are you going to do?"

"That's why I'm here." I huffed out a breath and slouched into the seat. "What do you think I should do?"

"That's simple," she replied. "You need to figure out if Lisa really did delete that recording."

"How?"

"If she did it to protect her father, she wants it hidden. Mention the recording exists, where it's located, with her in earshot. No one else knows about it. So, if she shows up there, you'll know it was her."

I thought about it before nodding my head in agreement. It would work. "Perfect."

"Now," Erin said, stretching her legs out on the bed and folding her arms behind her head. "Anything that might help me out?"

"I still don't know what your investigation—"

She waved me off. "Just tell me what you found."

"Alright," I said, leaning forward in my chair again. "Remember those bank and corporate records you gave me?"

Erin nodded.

"Ed's company has been invoicing the city regularly."

"That's not unusual for a contractor."

"No, but this is where it gets interesting. After each payment from the city, a portion of that money gets skimmed off the top. Then deposited into a separate bank account."

Erin's eyebrows raised slightly. "Kickbacks?"

"Looks that way." I confirmed what Cheryl had shown me about the remaining balances deposited into separate accounts.

"And you're sure about this?"

I nodded.

"What about the account receiving the skimmed funds? Whose name is it under?"

"That's what I couldn't figure out. It's some third party. My detective is working on tracking down the account holder."

Erin sat up and said, "I don't want you issuing a subpoena for the name of the account holder."

"Why not?"

She shook her head. "Just don't. It could make things difficult on my end."

"Must be nice to be a fed," I said, feeling a smirk cross over my face. "Just give people vague answers to get them to do what you want."

She shrugged. "It has its advantages."

I chuckled, relieved that even with embezzlement and murder swirling around us, humor still had its place. Erin leaned back. "So we've got Ed, the mayor's office, Ramirez and Lisa's father, and an unknown player." She tapped a finger against her chin. "Any theories on who it might be?"

"Nothing concrete yet," I admitted. "But given who we know is involved and the amount of money, it's got to be someone with significant influence. Someone who can make things happen in this city."

"Or someone who protects those who make things happen."

"Exactly." I paused for a minute. "You don't think it could be Lisa's father, do you?"

Erin stayed quiet.

"Because, why else would he be at this gala talking to Ed and the mayor? Maybe he's the one the kickbacks are going to."

"If Lisa shows up to try and destroy what she thinks is another copy of the recording, then you can follow that lead. Until then, I wouldn't speculate."

"Good point." I shook my head. "Whatever this is, it goes deep."

"Stay on it," Erin said, rising from her seat. "We'll see what witness testimony brings tomorrow."

* * *

LISA WAS in my small office, hovering near my desk and flipping through some files. Before entering the open doorway, I quickly pulled out my phone and fired off a text to Andrews. "*Play along. Urgent.*"

I dialed Andrews' number. He picked up on the second ring and then I entered my office, aware of Lisa's eyes on me.

"Andrews, it's about that recording from Ramirez," I said, keeping my voice casual. "I accidentally left it at the storage locker when I was dropping off some files earlier."

I rattled off the address and lockbox code, loud enough for Lisa to hear clearly. She shifted in her seat, seeming disinterested.

Andrews played along perfectly. "You're lucky I didn't file this away under 'Oops' for you," he quipped, adding a dramatic sigh for good measure. "I'll make sure no one gets there before you do. Just, you know, try not to lose any more evidence, alright?"

I fought back a grin at his cheeky tone. "Yeah, I know," I continued. "Rookie mistake. I'll grab it from you first thing tomorrow."

I hung up and turned to Lisa, studying her. If she took the bait, I'd know soon enough. "Sorry about that. What are you up to?"

She hesitated, shifting again. "I was wondering if you wanted to go over anything for tomorrow's witnesses."

"Actually, yeah," I said. "That'd be great. Let's start with the medical examiner."

THIRTY-ONE

THE JURY FILED IN. Judge Beasley's gavel echoed around the room like a clap of thunder, announcing that court was in session.

He looked me in the eye and said, "The prosecution may call its first witness."

I scanned the jury. Five women and seven men. Not ideal, but workable. Voir dire had been a battle over gender. I'd wanted women for sympathy. Donovan had fought to keep them off. A woman murdered by her cheating husband doesn't play well with female jurors. The women were inclined my way, but the men would be tougher to crack.

I stood and smoothed my suit jacket. "Thank you, Your Honor."

I'd chosen to go chronologically, starting with the 911 call and building up to the big reveal: photos of Caroline Martin murdered in her bedroom. Some prosecutors come out swinging with that, but I prefer to let the jury thirst for it. Talk about it, tease it, then, only when they're desperate enough, give them what they want. The sad thing was that all of us have a morbid curiosity.

I looked down at my notes one final time and said, "The State calls John Reynolds to the stand."

John Reynolds approached the stand. He was in his mid-forties, balding, with a paunch that spoke of too many late-night shifts. His uniform was crisp, and the bags under his eyes were heavy. He moved with the deliberate pace of someone used to long hours in a chair, answering calls that could mean life or death. As he raised his right hand to be sworn in, a bit of a faded Navy tattoo showed on his wrist. He settled into the witness chair, folded his hands in his lap, and waited for my questions. This wasn't his first time testifying, and it showed.

"Mr. Reynolds, can you tell the jury a little bit about your job?"

Direct examination was slower, because an attorney was forced to ask open-ended questions, unlike on cross examination where you could lead a witness where you wanted him to go. This meant the jury was often bored by longer narratives of witnesses talking about themselves. I tried to keep the pace brisk, using transitions that subtly guided the witness without overstepping, hoping to keep the jury's attention from drifting entirely.

"Sure," Reynolds began. "I'm a 911 dispatcher."

"And what do you do in that role?"

"We take emergency calls, assess the situation, and dispatch appropriate responders: police, fire, ambulance."

"What sorts of skills are required for a job like yours?"

"The job's about staying calm, getting information fast, and making quick decisions. Lives can depend on it."

"Would you say that this sort of work has made you good at reading people and situations?"

"I'd say it gives me a certain perspective. You learn to pick up on things, because people can't always communicate honestly in every situation. Tone of voice, choice of words. I'm not a mind reader, but I am trained to listen carefully."

I nodded. Reynolds had laid the groundwork well. "Tell us about the morning of May nineteenth."

Reynolds leaned forward slightly, adjusting himself in his chair. "At approximately 10:17 a.m., I received a call from a man who identified himself as Edward Martin. He stated he had just arrived home and found his wife, Caroline Martin, unresponsive in their bedroom. Said he believed she was dead. He provided the address. I dispatched police and emergency services immediately."

"Your Honor, the State would like to introduce Exhibit A, the 911 recording made by the defendant on the morning in question."

I was already turning around to watch Donovan stand. We were only five minutes into today's session. It was going to be one of *those* trials. "Objection, Your Honor." There it was. "The recording is highly prejudicial to my client and unnecessary when a transcript is available."

There was an overwhelming amount of case law supporting the State's right to introduce the 911 call during trial. Most judges didn't need to hear the lawyers argue in order to rule on an objection. In fact, most judges didn't want to hear the lawyers argue at all. However, Judge Beasley's experience as a litigator contributed to his bias toward the defense. So, Judge Beasley wanted me to make the argument.

"Your Honor, a transcript cannot convey the nuances of tone and emotion present in the actual recording. The jury deserves to hear the defendant's own words and demeanor in this crucial moment and come to their own conclusions."

Beasley's gaze moved from me to Donovan, and then back to me. Just because other judges allowed the recording didn't mean Judge Beasley would. Some cared about their appeal record. Beasley was definitely not one of those judges. "Objection overruled. Let's hear the recording."

The clerk pressed a button, and Ed Martin's voice came through the courtroom for all to hear. His voice was calm, almost unaffected as he spoke. It was definitely not the panic you'd expect from a man who had just discovered his wife was murdered.

As the 911 call played in court, I listened intently, my eyes on the jury. Ed's voice came through, calm but strained as he reported finding his wife unresponsive. He claimed he had just returned home, found her not breathing, and immediately called for help. The operator asked all the usual questions—was he safe, was anyone else there —and Ed's responses were flat, almost rehearsed. I could sense the jurors shifting in their seats. They were listening closely, just like I was, waiting for something—anything—that might give them more than just the facts. When the police arrived, he cut the call short, hanging up without hesitation, despite the operator's attempt to keep him on the line. That abrupt ending left an odd feeling hanging in the air. The courtroom was dead silent. Ed Martin showed no sign of emotion, remorse, or conviction. Meanwhile, Donovan skimmed over his notes, his eyes darting across the page, acting completely unbothered by the audio.

"Was this an accurate recording of the 911 call you received that morning?" I asked Reynolds.

"Yes."

"Did you note anything unusual about this call?"

Donovan jumped out of his seat. "Objection, Your Honor. Calls for speculation."

Beasley turned to me. "Ms. Hayes?"

"The witness isn't speculating here, Your Honor. I'm asking him what he noticed when he took the call."

"Overruled. Continue."

I turned back to Reynolds. "Did you note anything unusual about this call, Mr. Reynolds?"

Reynolds shifted in his seat, leaning slightly forward as he responded. "Ed Martin's voice was unusually calm given the circumstances."

"Can you elaborate for us?"

"There were no signs of distress or panic that I typically hear in such situations."

"Now, only because we know defense counsel will ask you anyway, how long have you been in this job and how many of these situations have you encountered?"

"In my five years as a dispatcher, I've had about ten such calls."

"And those other calls, how would you say they compared to the defendant's call?"

Donovan jumped up again, his tone indignant. "Objection, Your Honor! Relevance?"

"Ms. Hayes?"

"This goes to the defendant's state of mind, which is a critical element of the case, Your Honor."

"I'll allow it, but tread carefully, Ms. Hayes. The murder was already complete at this point."

I nodded, indicating my understanding and motioned for Mr. Reynolds to continue.

"Most other calls seemed more distraught than this one."

"The circumstances being that he had just discovered his wife of forty years strangled to death in their bedroom?"

I could almost feel Donovan roll his eyes behind me at that follow up question. If he could have objected to it, he would have, but even he knew that doing so would only highlight the point for the jury.

"Yes."

"No further questions, Your Honor."

I sat, waiting for Donovan to take his turn.

He approached with flair, smiling at the jury like they were best friends with an inside joke.

"Mr. Reynolds, can you list those ten other calls in detail?"

Reynolds frowned. "Not specifically, no."

"You can't?" Donovan's voice dripped with sarcasm. "Then how can you know for sure they were more agitated than Mr. Martin's call?"

"I remember the general tone, even if not specifics. They happened some time ago."

"Ah. So you remember that convenient detail, but not others."

I stood. "Objection, Your Honor. Asked and answered. He's badgering the witness."

Beasley looked at Donovan, who raised his hands. "No further questions."

"Redirect?" Judge Beasley asked me.

I didn't always take the opportunity for a redirect, but if the judge asked for one in front of the jury, saying "no" often did more harm than good.

"Mr. Reynolds, why can you remember the specifics of this call as compared to the others?"

"In my experience, people finding loved ones in that state are typically frantic, emotional. They often struggle to give clear information. Mr. Martin's call was different. He seemed almost detached. Gave details clearly, didn't ask for help beyond police. No urgency in his voice. It was like he was reporting a minor inconvenience instead of a tragedy. Of course that would stand out to me."

"Thank you, Mr. Reynolds," I said, turning back to my seat. "No further questions, Your Honor." I tried to hide the smirk from Donovan as I sat back down. I wasn't successful.

Judge Beasley thanked Reynolds for his testimony and he stepped down.

"We'll take a brief recess before continuing," Judge Beasley said. Everyone rose as the judge and jury exited the courtroom. I turned around and scanned the audience.

Beyond the press, Erin was sitting toward the back. I watched her slip out the courtroom doors. It was obvious she didn't want to be seen here. What did she hope to learn here that she couldn't ask me for directly? And just beyond her, was Tom, but he wasn't looking at me. He was looking at Erin leaving the courtroom.

THIRTY-TWO

I STEPPED out of the courtroom during recess. Lisa headed for the restroom, leaving me alone in the hallway. A few eager reporters approached, fishing for statements. I kept my expression neutral and stayed silent as they harassed me for answers, and soon the rest got the message that I wasn't talking.

Tom appeared beside me as if out of thin air.

"Surprised to see you in the audience," I said.

He raised an eyebrow. "Why's that?"

"You're a busy man. Figured you had other priorities."

Tom glanced around, then jerked his head towards a nearby door. "Let's talk privately."

We slipped into an empty witness room. These spaces, scattered near courtrooms, were designed for waiting witnesses who had been sequestered from the trial. Even during big trials, you could usually find one unoccupied.

Once inside, Tom turned to face me. "This is a high-profile case in an election year. Of course I'm here."

"That makes sense," I said, keeping my eyes trained on him. "What's on your mind?"

Tom's eyes narrowed. "What's your strategy on this case?"

I leaned against the wall, crossing my arms. "Going chronological. Walk the jury through the crime, get them invested. By the time we show Caroline's photos, they'll be convinced it was Ed."

He nodded. "That's good."

I started to relax, but Tom wasn't finished.

His voice dropped to a near-whisper. "We absolutely have to get a guilty verdict on this one."

"I told you when I took the case that I'll do my best, but—"

Tom cut me off, his face hardening. "That's not good enough. Everything should be lined up. I need you to get the jury there."

I nodded slowly, choosing my next words carefully. "I understand the importance, Tom. We're solid on this."

He held my gaze for a moment longer, then turned and left the room without another word.

I wasn't sure if it was my paranoia or nerves, but something about this didn't sit right. Tom should understand that a guilty verdict is never guaranteed, even in an election year—so why was he treating this like it was do or die? In the back of my mind, Ramirez's confession still gnawed at me, unresolved and adding another layer to the mess. Shaking off the unease, I checked my watch. Five minutes until recess was over. I pulled out my phone and dialed Andrews.

"Andrews."

"Anything on the account holder?" I asked, referring to the bank records.

"No," Andrews said, frustration coming through loud and clear. It wasn't like him not to figure something out.

"You'll find it," I said. "Hey, I'm also gonna need you to stake out that location I mentioned tonight. See who shows up."

"Who do you think—"

Lisa appeared in the doorway. "Lisa," I said, answering Andrews and greeting her in one go.

"Gotta run. Trial's starting." I hung up.

Lisa eyed me. "Who was that?"

I pocketed my phone. "Andrews. Following up on a potential lead for me."

"Don't we have all our evidence lined up already?"

I nodded. "We do. But it's always good to be on the lookout for anything else we could use."

We headed back to the courtroom and took our seats. The judge came back on the bench before the jury.

"State's witness?" asked Judge Beasley.

I called Officer Mindy Sanchez to the stand. She was in her late thirties, had brown hair cut short, and her expression was matter-of-fact. She approached, was sworn in, and took her seat.

"Officer Sanchez," I said, "please introduce yourself to the jury."

After she did so, I continued. "Were you present at the crime scene on May 19th?"

"I was," Sanchez confirmed, her voice steady.

I retrieved a document from my table and approached the witness stand. "I'm showing you a report. Did you author this?"

Sanchez examined it. "Yes, that's my incident report."

"Your Honor, I'd like to submit this as State's Exhibit B," I said, then turned back to Sanchez. "Officer, could you please read your description of the scene and the defendant upon arrival?"

Donovan was on his feet. "Objection, Your Honor. The jury can read this report for themselves."

I kept my voice calm as I responded. "Your Honor, it's common practice for witnesses to authenticate their reports in this manner."

Judge Beasley considered for a moment, then nodded. "Overruled. The officer may read from the report."

Donovan sat down, a flicker of frustration crossing his face. I caught Lisa's eye as Sanchez began to read, her expression unreadable.

Officer Sanchez cleared her throat and began to read from her report.

"Upon arrival at the scene, I observed the residence appeared clean and orderly. There were no signs of forced entry or struggle on the main floor. Proceeding upstairs, we discovered the body of Caroline Martin in the master bedroom. The victim was lying on the bed, deceased. Notable was the significant bruising around her neck and signs of blunt force trauma to the head."

I watched the jury as Sanchez read. The jurors' faces tightened at the mention of the bruising. Good. They needed to feel the weight of this crime.

Once she finished, I asked, "Anything else stand out to you, Officer?"

Sanchez looked up from the report. "The lack of disruption in the house was unusual for a violent crime scene. Everything was in its place, except for the victim herself and the blood around her."

I nodded, letting her words sink in. The immaculate house, the brutalized victim. Just the picture I wanted to paint for the jury.

"Can you tell us how the victim died?"

"Objection!" Donovan called. "Officer Sanchez is not a medical examiner. She cannot opine on cause of death."

I rolled my eyes and noticed two jurors did the same. Donovan was coming off as whiny and given that he'd reserved his opening, they didn't even know him yet. I was surprised he was making these sorts of errors. It was odd for someone like him.

"Your Honor, I am not asking the witness to give us technical information," I said. "I am asking for her opinion as to cause of death based on her observations at the scene."

"Overruled."

I prompted Sanchez to go on.

"Given the intense bruising around the victim's neck, I concluded the victim had been strangled to death."

"Strangled?" I asked. "With hands?" I took my own hands and wrapped them around my neck to illustrate the point.

"Yes."

"And the gash on her forehead?"

"Likely a result of the struggle at the outset."

"After you visited the scene, what did you do?"

"I returned to the driveway where the defendant was waiting and asked the defendant some questions."

"What was your impression of the defendant when you spoke to him?"

"He seemed completely calm, almost unbothered by the fact that his wife was dead."

"Thank you, Officer. No further questions, Your Honor."

Donovan was jumping up before the judge even had a chance to say "cross."

"Officer Sanchez," Donovan said, "are you an expert in psychology?"

Sanchez cocked her head to the side, as if considering the question. "I would say that my job requires me to be able to read people and situations."

"But are you an expert?"

"Do I have a degree in psychology? No."

"Then, can you definitively say Mr. Martin's demeanor when you questioned him was not the result of shock at seeing his wife dead upon arriving home?"

This time I objected. "Calls for speculation."

"Sustained," Beasley replied. "Tread carefully, Mr. Donovan."

Donovan put his hands up in mock surrender and sat back down. The judge didn't ask if I wanted a redirect, and I didn't move for one. He then adjourned court until 10 am tomorrow.

As I gathered my things, I looked out at the audience. Tom and Erin were now missing.

Lisa garnered my attention. "Heading back to the office?"

I nodded.

The two of us made our way back and grabbed a coffee on the way. Once settled behind my office door, Lisa asked who I intended to call on tomorrow.

"Palmer," I told her.

"Anything we need to do to prepare?"

I shook my head and plastered on a smile. " Why don't you head home? I'm gonna call it quits early, too."

Lisa gave me a small smile, said, "See you tomorrow," and left. As soon as she was out the door, I called Andrews back.

"She's loose for the evening," I said. "Let's see where she shows up."

THIRTY-THREE

I DROPPED my briefcase onto the coffee table, the remnants of dinner scattered nearby. The dim light of my house felt too quiet after the tension of the courtroom. Just as I reached for my laptop to half-heartedly prepare for the next day, my phone buzzed on the couch.

Andrews called me back within the hour. "I'm at the lookout," he said.

"Anything yet?" I asked.

"Quiet as a graveyard."

"Want some company?"

"You don't want to prep for tomorrow?"

I considered his question. "Not really. I'll just spin myself up if I try and work on things anymore." I grabbed my jacket from the chair, shoving my arms into it as I balanced the phone between my ear and shoulder. The cool night air would do me good. "Where are you parked?"

"Corner of Helberg and West 34th. You'll see why it's a good spot when you get here."

"I'll be there in fifteen."

"Make sure you park far enough off and walk over to me. I don't want you scaring anyone off."

We hung up, and I made two thermoses of coffee. Chances were it would be a long night. I grabbed a jacket and headed out. The streets were quiet, the city settled into its late-night rhythm. I made my way over to where Andrews was parked, leaving my car about two blocks back from his location. I grabbed a pair of sunglasses and a baseball cap and threw them on. It was dark enough out, so I doubted anyone would recognize me, but it was still a good precaution.

The streets were deserted in this part of town. We'd decided to scout out the same storage locker that our office used to park old files. The office manager had looked into hiring some people to scan everything in, but too many people grumbled about the tediousness of the task, so an offsite storage locker was the best alternative.

If Lisa did come here looking for the recording device, we'd be able to catch her opening the locker, and there would be no doubt that she'd been the one to alter my recording.

I approached Andrews' beat-up Camry that blended with the surroundings. I quickly slid into the passenger seat and handed him the thermos, asking, "Any movement?"

"Still nothing," he said, grabbing the hot mug and taking a sip. A rather expensive looking camera was in his lap.

We watched the outside of the facility, able to see anyone driving up to the units. The building had cameras that would catch anyone opening the locker, which Andrews could gain access to later if we really needed to.

"How do you feel about the trial?" he asked, breaking the silence.

I kept my gaze trained on the rows of storage lockers. "I'm not sure. Donovan hasn't even given his opening yet, so I don't know what his theory of the case will be. Even if I think the jury is going my way right now, all that could change."

"Still trying to get a guilty verdict?"

"Are you any closer to figuring out if Ramirez was telling the truth?"

"Nope."

"Then yes to the guilty verdict," I said. "There are still too many pieces of information floating around. I can't figure out whether they go to our puzzle, or whether we should throw them off the table."

He chuckled. "You and your metaphors."

I rolled my eyes at him.

Andrews shifted in his seat, eyes still on the storage facility. "So, what's Erin in town for?"

I played dumb. "Erin?"

He snorted. "Cut the crap. We know she's here, watching the trial."

"How'd you—"

"Everyone at the precinct knows when feds are around. It's like our spidey senses or something."

I sighed. "Honestly? I don't know what she's looking for."

"Bullshit."

"No, really," I said. "She refuses to tell me."

Andrews laughed, a short, sharp sound. "No special treatment for old friends?"

"No way," I said, shaking my head. "Erin's all business."

Andrews was silent for a moment before turning to look at me. "You think she's onto something big?"

I shrugged. "Could be. With Erin, you never know."

"Great," Andrews muttered. "Just what we need. "

I took a swig of coffee. "Tell me about it."

Andrews tensed beside me. "Heads up."

Headlights pierced the darkness. A car pulled into the storage facility lot.

We both fell silent, barely breathing. Andrews raised his camera, zooming in on the license plate. I could hear the rapid-fire click of the shutter as he started taking photos.

The car parked, and the driver turned off the engine. Then, whoever was inside just sat there for several moments. Andrews and I looked at one another.

"Come on," Andrews muttered under his breath, as if he could will the stranger to get a move on.

The driver's door opened. We leaned forward, straining to see.

They didn't step out of the car.

I whispered, "What's taking so long?"

Andrews shook his head, camera poised.

More seconds passed.

"Maybe they spotted us," I said.

"Impossible," Andrews hissed back. "We're too far."

Finally, a foot emerged. Then a leg.

Janice hoisted herself out of the car. Andrews and I looked at each other with wide eyes. He blinked a few times, then started snapping a bunch of photos.

Without warning, he got out of the car.

"What are you doing?"

"Stay put," he told me. He moved quickly, following Janice as she headed into the facility.

I sat in the dark car. Minutes dragged by. I kept my eyes glued to the entrance, watching for any sign of movement. Finally, I saw Andrews walking briskly toward me.

He got in, and before I could ask him what he found, my phone rang. I nearly jumped out of my seat at the shrill tone before pulling the damn thing out of my pocket. I glanced at the screen and then showed it to Andrews.

"Janice."

"Answer it."

I took a deep breath and strove to keep my voice steady, then pressed the answer button and put the call on speaker. "Hello?"

"Where's the thing you put in the storage locker?" Janice demanded, her tone impatient.

Andrews and I exchanged a glance. "What thing?"

She huffed in frustration. "Tom said you left something here and that I should go and get it. But I don't even know what I'm looking for."

"Oh, uh, it's actually in my office." I looked at Andrews, but he seemed just as confused as I was.

"Seriously?" she grumbled. "Fine. Leave it on my desk tomorrow morning."

"Okay, will do," I agreed, and then the call ended.

I pulled the phone down from my ear and stared at it. Five minutes later, Janice walked back to her car, looking flustered. She got in and drove off without a second glance.

Andrews and I stared at each other, bewildered.

Finally, he broke the silence. "What the hell just happened?"

I shook my head, still processing what we had just seen. "I...honestly have no idea. I thought Lisa would be the one to show up, not Janice. But this...this doesn't make sense." My mind raced, trying to piece together how Janice could be connected to everything. "Something's off here." Andrews dropped me off at my car. As soon as I was alone, I pulled out my phone and dialed Erin's number. It rang once, twice, three times. No answer.

Voicemail. I took a deep breath.

"Erin, it's me. Something's happened. The person who showed up was Janice. At Tom's request. Call me back. Soon."

I hung up and stared down at my phone. The cryptic message felt insufficient, but it was all I dared to say over an unsecured line.

I started my car and began the drive home. Poor Lisa probably had no idea why I was being so cross with her. I owed her an apology.

I tried to make sense of Tom deleting the Ramirez confession. Is that why he pulled me aside to tell me that I *needed* to get a guilty verdict? Had he listened to the conversation with Ramirez?

But, why? Was he that worried about securing a conviction on this case during an election year that he would put a man on death row just to secure votes? And if he had heard Ramirez confess, why not turn that information over to Stevens? Was Tom really prioritizing politics over making sure the right men were put away for the right crimes?

And what did this mean for me? I had potentially exculpatory information? What would he do if I didn't come forward with it?

I had a lot of questions, very few answers, and the coffee was already wearing off. I was pretty sure I wasn't going to get much sleep tonight.

THIRTY-FOUR

AS I'D ANTICIPATED, I couldn't sleep the entire night. The image of Janice showing up at that locker haunted my thoughts, twisting every possible explanation into knots. Why was she there? Did Tom know something I didn't? And why was he acting so desperate for a guilty verdict in this case?

The restless hours blurred together until finally, I gave up on sleep entirely. I ended up getting to court earlier than usual, bypassing the standard morning rush hour traffic. It was strange pulling into the nearly empty lot, my mind still spinning over Janice's involvement and Tom's erratic behavior. Stepping into the courthouse, I half-expected to see Tom, like he had somehow beaten me here and was waiting with more cryptic pressure about the trial.

It was unusual to see a courtroom so empty. The silence amplified the weight of my thoughts. I took a deep breath, feeling the cool, stale air of the empty room settle over me. The benches were bare, the hum of fluorescent lights buzzing faintly overhead. My steps echoed off the tile floor as I approached the prosecution table, the questions in my mind louder than the emptiness around me.

I sat at my table and took in the silence. "How many innocent men and women have been convicted in this room?" I wondered aloud.

"How many guilty people have walked free?" I shook my head, questioning whether the system worked at all.

The door opened, and I looked behind me to see Palmer stride in. I stood to greet him. "What are you doing here so early?"

"Looking for you," he said. "I've been trying to find you since you called. Thought you might get here early."

"Something wrong?"

"I'm afraid you might have run off with a bad assumption based on our call."

My stomach dropped. "Can you clarify?"

"You asked if I printed the CSIs at the scene, and I said yes. But I worried that maybe you got the wrong idea based on what I said."

I stayed silent, letting Palmer continue.

"We know asphyxiation from strangulation was the cause of death, but Ed's fingerprints were all over Caroline's neck and matched the bruise pattern. There's no way that wasn't Ed's handiwork." He paused, his expression a grim smile. "No pun intended."

I shook my head and tried to stifle a laugh. Forensic guys usually had a pretty morbid sense of humor.

But even as he laid it all out, I couldn't shake the dissonance in my mind. This didn't line up with what Ramirez had told me. I felt a knot forming in my stomach. If what Palmer said was true, then Ramirez had to be lying—or at the very least, misleading me. But why? What was he hiding? I looked him in the eye and nodded. "Thanks, Palmer. That does help clear some things up."

People started coming into the courtroom, so he excused himself. "I'll see you in a bit."

As people filed in, a tall, thin woman slid into the back row. She was older with graying hair pulled back tight into a bun. Her eyes darted around the room, never settling, while she clutched the strap of her bag as if it were a lifeline. There was a heaviness in her posture, as though the weight of whatever had brought her here was more than she could bear.

She looked my way and made eye contact. I'd been staring too long, trying to figure out where I'd seen her before.

Just then, Lisa walked up and said, "Hello."

"Hey." I turned to her and put a hand on her shoulder, leaning in close. "I'm sorry for the last few days. I've been really anxious before the trial and took it out on you."

I wasn't sure she would buy it, but it was worth a shot.

Her shoulders relaxed, and she seemed to breathe easier now. "It's okay. I understand."

"There's an older woman in blue in the back row. Do you recognize her?"

Lisa glanced over and nodded. "That's a friend of Caroline's, Sarah Hodgkin."

"How do you know?"

"I remember seeing her post something on Caroline's Facebook."

"You looked at Caroline's Facebook?"

Lisa shrugged. "Thought it couldn't hurt."

The woman looked at us again.

"I feel like she wants to tell me something," I whispered.

"You think?"

I nodded. "She keeps looking at me."

"Well, you are the prosecutor on her friend's murder trial."

I shook my head. "No, that's not it. It's a different type of look. " I signaled Lisa to come with me. "Let's go find out about it."

We approached the woman and she looked up at us.

"Sarah?"

She nodded.

"You were Caroline's friend, right?"

Another nod.

"My name is Alex Hayes. This is my associate, Lisa Cooper."

"I know who you are," Sarah replied softly, looking down at her hands.

"This must be difficult for you to watch," I said gently.

She nodded, her eyes darting all over the room. "It is."

"Would you like to step into a waiting room with us for a bit?"

She agreed, and we walked into one of the empty witness rooms outside the courtroom.

"How did you and Caroline meet?" I asked, once inside.

"Caroline and I were real estate agents together before she and Ed got married. We've been close ever since."

"How long were you friends?"

Sarah let out a long sigh. "At least twenty years. Maybe more. Ed wasn't her first husband, you know."

I blinked, surprised. How had I missed that? Why hadn't that come up before? "I didn't know."

"She left her first husband for Ed. It was a pretty big deal. A lot of gossip surrounded it, but she claimed it was for love. And then after all she went through to be with him, the bastard started cheating on her."

"I was under the impression everyone knew about Ed's affair. That Caroline had accepted it."

Sarah scoffed. "What was she supposed to do? Leave him? He made her sign an ironclad prenup. She gave up her career when she married him. He told her she didn't need to work anymore. Sure, she may have known, but she was never okay with it."

"That's terrible," I said.

Sarah nodded. "No one ever came to speak to me."

I sat down in front of her. "You mean from her family?"

"I mean during the investigation."

Lisa and I shared a look.

"Is there something you would have shared with an investigator?"

"Absolutely. I came here today because I didn't know what else to do. I want you to be able to use this. To make him pay for what he did."

My heart began beating out of my chest. "What is it you have?"

She pulled out her phone and swiped a few screens before setting it down on the conference table. I looked at the screen as she had pulled up a voicemail from Caroline. She pressed play and Caroline's voice started to play.

"Hey, sorry I couldn't make it this morning. I'm just not feeling up to it." There was a pause and then Caroline continued. "Here he is. Coming home from his night with that stupid assistant of his. I know you told me to leave well enough alone, that he's old and he'll be dead soon, but I just can't take it anymore, honestly. Call me back later."

There was a rustling on the line, as if she'd put the phone down, but the call didn't end. Then, as if from further away, I could hear Caroline's voice again. "Don't just walk by me. I know you were with her."

Ed's voice sounded from further away, harsh and uncaring. "I'm with her every Saturday evening, Carrie, you know the deal."

"Don't call me that. I'm not your Carrie anymore. The moment you started up with her, that was over for us."

"Are you done with your bitching?"

"How dare you swear at me!" Caroline's voice was enraged now. "I'm done. Done with you, done with this stupid, lonely house." Something clattered, as if she'd thrown it down onto the floor. "I'm going to ruin everything you built, just like you ruined me. I know all about the money. I'm going to bring it all out in the open and then you'll know what it feels like to lose everything you love."

There was a scuffle, and then a good deal of screaming. Caroline's voice started to fade, as if Ed was moving her further away from the phone. Another minute or so of silence went by, broken by loud bangs. Then footsteps passed by the phone followed by a door closing. Then the line went dead.

The recording ended with a sickening silence, leaving us all in stunned horror. Sarah's hands were trembling as she put the phone away.

I looked at her, blinking several times, trying to make sense of what I'd just heard. "Sarah, has anyone else heard this voicemail?"

She shook her head and her voice wobbled when she spoke. "No. Like I told you, no one came to talk to me. I was afraid to come forward with it. But I don't want him to get away with killing her. Even if it means something bad happens to me."

I put a hand on the table. "Nothing bad is going to happen to you. I'll make sure of it."

She gave me a small smile and a nod.

"Do you know what Caroline meant about the money?"

"Not really. We didn't really get into details like that."

"Did she mention him meeting with anyone in particular a lot?"

Sarah shrugged. "He had a very close relationship with the mayor. That's why he always got all of those contracts."

"Right." I nodded, trying to think of my next move. This all but confirmed that Ramirez was lying when he said he'd been the perpetrator. Between this and what Palmer told me this morning, I was having a hard time seeing how Ed wasn't guilty. But I couldn't make sense of admitting to a crime you didn't commit, especially murder. Although, his theory on Caroline knowing something about dirty money was spot on.

"Can you text me that recording?"

Sarah nodded and pulled up a text message, attaching the recording. I put my number into her phone, and then she sent it off. I confirmed I received it.

"What are you going to do with it?" she asked.

"I don't know yet. I want to make sure I do it right so that the judge doesn't try and exclude it."

"He could do that?"

"He could," I said. "Generally speaking, lawyers have to have all their evidence in before the start of trial and the other side has to be given an opportunity to review it. He could strike this as prejudicial."

"But it proves he did it!" Sarah all but shouted, clearly starting to get upset.

Lisa placed a gentle hand on the woman's shoulder and I put my hands up to try and calm her down. "Don't worry. I'm not going to let him get away with this."

She studied my face for a moment before nodding. "Okay. I trust you."

I glanced at my watch. Court was about to reconvene in exactly two minutes. "We've got to get back inside the courtroom," I said to Sarah. We all walked back in and took our seats.

"All rise!" the bailiff shouted the moment we sat down. Judge Beasley entered and then the jury.

Once they were settled, Beasley turned to me. "State's next witness?"

"Your Honor. I'd like to request a brief recess to discuss something in chambers."

He cocked an eyebrow and said, "That is highly unusual, Ms. Hayes."

I cocked an eyebrow back. "Yes, Your Honor. I agree."

THIRTY-FIVE

DONOVAN and I walked to the judge's chambers, and the bailiff closed the door behind us.

Judge Beasley folded his arms. "This better be good, Ms. Hayes."

Judge Beasley's chambers felt cramped, with dark wood paneling and a desk cluttered with stacks of papers and files. A single reading lamp, gold with a green shade, sat on his desk and served as the only light source for the entire room. I hated those lamps. Any attorney who had one was always a certified asshole, in my experience.

"I apologize for the request, Your Honor, but I just received a new piece of evidence this morning before court began. I felt it best to bring it up privately, as I anticipate there will be some discussion surrounding it."

"Go on, what is it?" Judge Beasley seemed more annoyed than curious.

"It's a recording," I said, pulling it up on my phone and putting it down on a small empty space on his desk. "I'd like to introduce it into evidence and let the jury listen to it."

The judge looked between Donovan and me. With a heavy sigh, he said, "Let's hear it," his tone clipped, signaling this better be worth the interruption.

I pressed play. Caroline's voice filled the small space. Her call to Sarah, her complaining about Ed, Ed coming home, and then the faint sounds of a struggle. The judge and Donovan's faces paled as the recording played. Halfway through, the judge waved his hand. "Turn it off."

Donovan started arguing. "Judge, this can't be allowed. It's highly prejudicial to my client. Not to mention that this was never turned over to me during discovery and I haven't had time to prepare any cross."

"I understand," I said. "As I said, I only got this this morning. I would have turned this over earlier had I had it."

The judge wore a sour expression for a moment, then asked, "Who gave it to you?"

"A friend of Caroline's," I replied. "She is in the courtroom this morning."

Beasley rubbed his temples as if this entire thing was giving him a headache. "How do you plan to authenticate the recording, Ms. Hayes?"

Under the rules of evidence, a recording needed to be proven to be original—authenticated in lawyer speak. This could be done through expert testimony or the caller themselves admitting that it was their voice.

"The owner of the recording will testify," I said.

"That's not good enough," Donovan argued.

"It's my opinion that it is. Judge, the owner of the recording has been friends with Caroline for decades. She's far more qualified to opine on whether this recording was actually her friend versus an expert witness who has never met Caroline Martin before."

"There's no consent for this recording, then," Donovan said. "State law requires that at least one party consent to a recording in order for it to be used as evidence."

"Caroline left this message," I countered. "She knew she was being recorded. So, there was consent."

"Calm down," Judge Beasley said, using his hands to gesture for us to stop. "We're not in front of the jury. There's no need for either of you to put on a show." He sighed. "I'm going to allow the recording."

Donovan sputtered, "But, Your Honor—"

Beasley cut him off. "I'm aware of your objection, Mr. Donovan, and it will be so noted in the record. Court will recess for the day so that you have time to prepare for a cross. Ms. Hayes, please be sure to give Mr. Donovan the name of the witness you intend to call."

"Yes, your Honor—"

"*Before* you leave court for the day. I don't want any squabbles over whether enough time was given."

"Of course, your Honor."

The bailiff led me and Donovan out. Before we stepped back into the courtroom, Donovan turned to me. "If I find out that you were holding this back from me in discovery—"

I put my hand up. "Again, if I'd had this any sooner than this morning, I would have slapped it on your desk so fast. Your client would have been an idiot to plead not guilty with this as evidence. Why would I risk it not being admitted?"

"You might be getting this into evidence now, but I'm going to argue on appeal that this should never have been allowed."

"I'd expect nothing less from a desperate man," I said. "And don't even get me started on missing discovery. You don't think I put two and two together about the security footage? You don't want the footage admitted, why?"

He gave me a confused look. "It's completely irrelevant. There's no footage of the crime, so why would I let you try and confuse the jury?"

I paused. "You don't have the gap."

"Of course I don't. Do you?"

Donovan bristled, but I didn't have the energy to engage in another back and forth with him. I walked into the courtroom and took my seat.

Court was reconvened and then promptly recessed. I scanned the crowd, looking for Sarah, but she must have left while we were in chambers. That was not ideal. I wrote her name down on a sticky note and handed it to Donovan. "Here," I said. "This woman gave me the recording."

"And I'm entitled to the recording itself," he said.

I bit my tongue, clenched my jaw, and texted the recording to him.

He smirked at me. "I see you still have my number."

"Don't flatter yourself. I've still got my grandmother's number in here and she's been dead for six years."

I turned back to Lisa. "Come on. Let's try and get out of here before the press gets wind."

We'd almost made it down the courthouse steps before a reporter accosted us.

"Can you comment on what you discussed with the judge in chambers?"

Reporters were getting bolder. Or stupider.

"Obviously not," I said, pushing past the rest of the reporters. Lisa was right on my heels, pushing through the crowd herself.

"I need to stop by the cafe," I said to Lisa.

We hit the place between the breakfast and lunch rushes. The lull was enough to walk right up to the counter.

"Caramel frap and a croissant," I said. Lisa shot me a surprised look, eyebrows raised slightly as if questioning the indulgence of such an order. "Not for me. For Janice."

"Why?"

"I need information from her. Why else?"

We grabbed the order and made our way back to the office. As soon as my office door clicked closed, I turned to Lisa.

"We need to get a subpoena issued on Sarah Hodgkin ASAP, otherwise we won't be able to call her to the stand tomorrow."

"I'll get to work on it," Lisa replied.

"Good. I'll be back in a minute." I grabbed Janice's order and left my office.

Janice frowned at me as I approached. The foul expression softened when I held up the treats

"Got something for you," I said, handing her the coffee and croissant.

She snatched them from me. "It is the least you can do after sending me out so late."

"Speaking of that, did Tom say what you were supposed to pick up? I'm having a hard time remembering."

"How should I know?" Janice took a long pull from the drink. "Tom just said you put something in the storage locker."

"That's just the thing. I put a few things in the locker, so I'm not sure what he's after."

Janice rolled her eyes. "Maybe I wrote it down on a note." She shuffled papers on her desk, and I happened to glance down.

FIRST HOUSTON BANK stared back up at me in its signature red ink on one of the papers. I recognized it this time since studying Erin's documents a bit closer. "Is this it?" I said, moving a piece of paper aside so I could see the account number.

"Don't touch anything!" Janice exclaimed. "I have a system."

I put my hands up in surrender and then started repeating the last four digits of the bank account number from the statement to myself. Four - eight - nine - three.

"I can't find any note," Janice said.

So much for the system.

"No problem, I'll talk to Tom." I ran back to my office, repeating the numbers over and over on the way.

Four - eight - nine - three.

As soon as I opened the door Lisa tried to ask me something, but I shook my head.

Four - eight - nine - three.

I pulled over the folder I'd gotten back from Cheryl and looked at the mystery account.

Four - eight - nine - three.

The numbers were a match.

Ed was funneling extra money back to Tom.

THIRTY-SIX

"CAN YOU HANDLE THAT SUBPOENA?" I asked Lisa, stopping briefly at her desk.

She glanced up. "Sure, I've got it covered."

"Good. I may or may not be back later."

Lisa furrowed her brow, swiveling in her chair to face me. "Where are you going?"

"Don't worry about it. I've just got to take care of something." I turned and strode away before she could ask anything else.

I made my way toward my car and fished through my bag with one hand. Waves of heat rose off the dark asphalt, and I was already sweating through my suit. I found my phone, dialed Andrews, and placed it to my ear.

"Meet me at JPC," I told him. "I've got information, but I don't want to relay it over the phone."

"Why are we going there?"

"I need to talk to Ramirez."

I got into my car and started it, keeping the door open and cranking the AC as cold as it would go.

"I'm not sure that's a good idea."

"I've got to get to the bottom of this, and you're the only one who can help me piece it together." Desperation seeped into my voice. "Please, just trust me on this."

A heavy sigh came through the line. "Alright. I'll head over there now."

By the time I got there, Andrews was already waiting for me. He leaned casually against his car's bumper, despite the oppressive temperature. I pulled up next to him, and he climbed into the passenger's side.

"What's this about?" he asked. "What's got you so rattled?"

"I talked to Janice."

"She rattles me too."

I shook my head, unable to appreciate his joke. "I saw a statement on her desk. A *bank* statement."

Andrews knit his brows together.

"The corporate records. The bank account we couldn't figure out who owned it."

"It's Janice's?"

I closed my eyes and leaned my head back, taking a deep breath. I needed to slow down, because I was obviously losing Andrews on this.

"No," I said. "It's Tom's."

Then I waited for realization to make its way across his face. "You mean Tom Matthews?"

I nodded.

"How does that make any sense?"

"I don't know yet. But, there's more." I took my phone out of my pocket and put it between us. I pressed play on Caroline's voicemail to Sarah and watched Andrews listen to Ed Martin strangle his wife to death.

When it finished, he let out a slow breath.

I blinked at him. "Now do you see why I need to talk to Ramirez?"

Andrews nodded slowly. "Why would he admit to killing someone he didn't kill?"

"That's what I'd love to find out."

"Do you want me to go in with you?"

"Yes, but I don't want him to know you're there. Hang back in the viewing area?"

Andrews nodded, and we exited the car. He went in ahead of me. His badge expedited our entrance more than mine did. By the time I made it through the labyrinth of metal detectors and locked doors, Ramirez was once again cuffed to the table, and I could only assume Andrews was behind the tinted viewing glass.

Ramirez smirked as he saw me walk in. "Well, if it isn't my favorite lawyer. You here to tell me Martin's been convicted?"

I stayed silent as I pulled out my phone, pressed play on the voice-mail, and set it on the table. Ramirez's smug expression melted away as Caroline's terrified cries and Edward's enraged shouts filled the small room. His face paled, eyes widening in disbelief.

I stopped the recording. "Why did you lie about killing Caroline? It *was* Edward all along."

Ramirez didn't say anything. He just stared at me.

"You should also know that Edward Martin has been sending money to Tom Matthews." I set my jaw and glared back at the man. "Wanna tell me what's going on?"

The color drained from his face at that. He slumped back in his chair, defeated. "I've been double-crossed, is what's going on."

"Explain how. Maybe I can help."

He scoffed. "There's nothing you can do. I'm as good as gone, just like your father."

"Would you cut the crap?" I raised my voice and banged a hand against the table. "Why are you lying to protect them?"

Ramirez leaned forward, dropping his voice. "I wasn't lying about anything. The mayor told me to kill Caroline." He paused, glancing around even though we were alone. "He also told me that Ed would take the fall. That he and his wife knew too much and needed to be dealt with."

My stomach churned. Why couldn't this just be a homicide case?

"Who was in charge of making Ed take the fall?"

Ramirez shrugged. "I never asked."

"Was it Tom?"

"If Tom's getting money from Ed..."

I finished the thought. "Then Tom's in on it. There's no way the mayor doesn't know his DA is getting kickbacks."

"Which means Tom's the one who was supposed to plant the evidence against Martin."

I thought for a moment. "Tom told Thompson he'll have Ed convicted, but they both told Ed they'd get him off." I looked at Ramirez. "Sound about right?"

We sat in tense silence for a moment before Ramirez spoke again.

"The evidence that Tom set up," he said, "can you prove Martin did it, beyond a doubt? Or are there...gaps?"

I thought about Rachel's alibi and the footage I'd found. How the two couldn't possibly line up.

Ramirez continued. "Gaps that Tom created. To introduce doubt at trial. He's playing both sides."

"Tom wants Ed to think he's going to get him off," I said slowly. "But Tom's gotta make sure Ed gets a guilty verdict."

Ramirez nodded. "Otherwise Thompson will come after him. I'm sure of it."

"Lovely little den of snakes you all belong to." I rubbed my forehead with a knuckle. "Why'd you lie? Why'd you say you killed Caroline?"

Ramirez didn't answer. He kept his head down, but the fear in his eyes was ever-present.

He finally leaned forward against his chains. "If you tell anyone about this, you'll never get your father out of prison. You need me as much as I need you."

His lip curled derisively on the last words. I opened my mouth to respond when a sharp voice cut through the room.

"I wouldn't be so sure about that."

Andrews walked out from behind the one-way glass.

Ramirez nearly jumped from his seat, then spat on the floor once he saw his new guest. "And why's that?"

Andrews moved to the side, allowing Erin to emerge from the viewing area.

"Because you're going to cooperate," she said, "or else your current charges will be the least of your concern."

THIRTY-SEVEN

"AM I SUPPOSED to know who you are?" Ramirez's words dripped with disdain as he sized up Erin. His shackles against the table lessened the intimidation.

I shot Andrews a sidelong glance, trying to convey both "what the hell?" and "when did she get here?" but I didn't think he got all of that.

Erin adjusted her blazer, unfazed. "I'm a federal prosecutor, and you're just the kind of easy win I need to hit my quota." Her lips curved into a predatory smile. "Conspiracy to commit murder, embezzlement, wire fraud—shall I go on?"

The crack in Ramirez's facade betrayed his unease. He was smart enough to know that federal prosecutors were experts at stacking felonies like Russian nesting dolls. He squirmed in his seat a bit, and I looked at Erin to see a twisted satisfaction in her eyes.

"What do you want?" Ramirez growled, leaning back with feigned nonchalance.

Erin's gaze didn't waver. "Everything. Every conversation with Ed Martin, Tom Matthews, Mayor Thompson—anyone involved. You'll testify, or we'll make sure you never see daylight again."

Ramirez scoffed, but I caught the flicker of doubt in his eyes. "And what do I get in return?"

"Immunity from federal prosecution on the attempted murder charge."

"No deal." Ramirez's nostrils flared. "I want immunity across the board."

"You're in no position to negotiate. Your testimony would be helpful, but not strictly necessary. So please don't pretend you're holding a better hand than you are. I'll call your bluff and let you rot in here."

He didn't respond and Erin shrugged. A terse chuckle escaped her lips. "Alright, let's give Mr. Ramirez a moment to consider his predicament." She began moving to leave the room.

"Fine." Ramirez spat the word like venom, his jaw clenched. "But I want it in writing first."

Erin stopped and turned back around. "Of course." She motioned for Andrews and me to follow as we all walked back into the viewing room.

"Well done shaking him loose, Alex." The faintest glimmer of approval flickered in her eyes. "I knew you had it in you."

I bristled at the backhanded compliment. "If you'd told me what you were after from the start—"

"And risk biasing the investigation?" Erin arched an eyebrow. "We might never have uncovered the full truth."

"You played me just as much as you played him."

"I did what I had to do."

Andrews shook his head. "This is why we don't like the feds."

Erin shot him a death glare and he put his hands up, then attempted to get the conversation back on track. "We still need to get Matthews to crack. Ramirez clearly doesn't have the whole picture. We need to figure out what Tom's agreement was with Ed and the mayor."

I nodded, gnawing my inner cheek, mulling over the limited threads of leverage at our disposal. "Tomorrow I can call Ramirez as a witness."

"How would that help?" Erin asked.

"If what Ramirez says is true, then Tom is the one in charge of planting evidence. He put Ramirez in jail on false charges to eliminate any chance of him spilling the beans against him or the mayor."

"I'm still not following."

I swallowed the urge to make a jab at Erin. If she were litigating as much as I was, she would know this.

"Evidence Rule 609. Prior crimes cannot be used to attack a witness's character—"

"—unless the crime is one involving dishonesty or a false act," Erin finished.

"In Texas, the rule is a crime involving moral turpitude. But same thing."

"Moral what?" We'd lost Andrews with attorney-speak.

"It just means that normally you cannot show the jury proof that a witness committed previous crimes. However, if the witness committed a crime that involved something like fraud or dishonesty, then it can be admitted."

Andrews' brows knit together. "So, Tom brought Ramirez up on these false charges—specifically the embezzlement—just so that he couldn't testify in Ed's trial? Why?"

"More like Tom didn't want me talking to Ramirez in the first place," I said. "He planted fake evidence to indict Ramirez on other crimes to give him an alibi for committing the murder. Crimes that would make it very unlikely for me to consider him a witness despite the fact he was an officer at the scene. According to Ramirez, he was supposed to be the one to kill Caroline. Somehow Ed got to her first."

"So, if things had gone according to plan," Andrews mused, "Ramirez would have committed the murder, had an alibi, and a more reasonable attorney wouldn't have wasted their time trying to talk to him."

I gave him a look. "I'm not sure what you're implying by that last part, but yes."

"Why would Ramirez agree to being arrested?" Andrews asked.

"He didn't," Erin said. "It came as a shock to him. But, based on Alex's last conversation, it seems like he may have been in touch with Tom and given reassurances."

I continued the train of thought. "Which is why when he found out that Tom was taking money from Ed, he realized he'd been double-crossed."

"Which is why he's going to cooperate with us." Erin looked at him through the window. His fingers drummed nervously on the table, his leg bouncing under the chair. Tension lined his jaw, and he kept glancing toward the door, like he was calculating an escape. I couldn't blame him.

"So, how does this help us get to Tom?" Andrews asked.

A dull throb was forming behind my eyes. Sometimes I wished people could just behave and tell the truth. Sure, I might be out of a job, but life would be a lot easier.

"When Ramirez is named as a witness, he'll be brought to the courthouse," I said. "Tom will undoubtedly try and talk to me first about not calling him, but I'll refuse in a naive way. When that happens, he'll pay Ramirez a visit. Likely threaten him into giving the 'right' testimony about Caroline's murder. Remember, he's under pressure from Thompson to secure a guilty verdict, and he thinks Ramirez was the one to pull the trigger," I paused, remembering the woman was strangled to death. "So to speak."

Andrews nodded, finally understanding. "If we get Ramirez wired and coax Matthews into talking..."

"We might just get him to incriminate himself," I finished.

Erin nodded slowly, her expression contemplative. "It could work."

"What about the mayor?" Andrews asked. "Even if we nail Matthews, there's still the matter of his involvement."

"In any normal situation, Ramirez's statement would give us enough to arrest someone for conspiracy to commit murder. But this is the mayor." Erin's lips pursed into a thin line. "I hate to say it, but the burden of proof is going to have to be higher for me to get a magistrate to sign off on a warrant."

Her gaze met mine. "If we can get to Matthews tomorrow, then we can use him to get to the mayor. I'm not going to put a request before a mag unless I have him dead to rights."

"I'll do my best," I said, because what else was I supposed to say?

"Good." Erin looked between me and Andrews. "Give us a

moment?" she asked him and he nodded, stepping outside into the service hallway.

Her voice was hushed, as if she worried that someone might over-hear us. "What did Ramirez mean about your father?"

For a beat, I could only stare back in silence. My mouth had run dry. Did she know Ramirez had tried to blackmail me?

I was silent for too long. She lifted her hands in surrender. "Okay, I get it. You don't want to talk," she said. "But I want you to know Ramirez won't be able to get your father out of prison. He was convicted on federal charges, and the evidence against him was solid. You have to know that."

I swallowed hard. "Ramirez claimed the evidence was planted. He was trying to convince me that the whole case was set up."

Erin shook her head, her brows furrowing. "I reviewed the file myself. There was no sign of anything being planted. The case was airtight."

I swallowed hard and gave her a small nod. "Okay."

Her features softened and she placed a reassuring hand on my shoulder, giving it a firm squeeze. "Try and put it behind you."

That's all I'd ever done concerning my father. I gave her another nod.

"Go grab Andrews," she said. "I need to make a call."

She left the room and I ducked my head out to tell Andrews he could come back in.

"What was that about?" he asked. "Or are you not allowed to tell me?"

I didn't see any harm in sharing it with him. "Just that whatever Ramirez said about my father was a lie, according to Erin."

Andrews nodded. "Sorry about that."

"It's fine."

"Is it?"

"Always knew he was guilty," I said. "I guess I just wanted to be wrong."

The lie tasted bitter, but the alternative—voicing the fact I'd actu-ally thought what Ramirez said held a grain of truth—was even worse.

Erin's return to the interrogation room pulled me from my reverie. Andrews and I watched from behind the glass as she handed Ramirez a folded sheet of paper and a pen. His eyes raked over the page as Erin outlined the terms of his immunity deal.

Andrews leaned in, his brow furrowed. "You sure you're good with this? What if he really did lie? He signs that and you've got nothing else to bargain with."

I clenched my jaw, forcing another nod as Ramirez's pen scratched across the paper, extinguishing the last flicker of hope.

"Yeah," I said. "I'm good."

THIRTY-EIGHT

I SHIFTED in the hotel recliner as Erin clipped the wire to my bra strap. The room was dim, the curtains drawn tight to block out the neon lights from the city street below. The hum of the air conditioner filled the silence, its cold draft brushing against my skin. I glanced at the small mirror across from me, the reflection of scattered case files on the bed catching my eye—a vivid reminder of what was at stake. Erin worked with steady hands, focused. The quiet tension between us made the space feel even smaller.

I was preparing to confront Tom, to see if I could lure him into speaking with Ramirez. The plan was risky—Tom wasn't stupid, and I didn't know how much he already suspected. But Erin insisted this was our best shot. The wire felt heavy against my chest, a physical reminder of the stakes. She chuckled. "Never worn a wire before, huh?"

I gave her a look full of derision. "No. Never needed to."

"Aww, you're missing out on so much fun."

She was a complete sadist, apparently. "I wouldn't consider conspiracy, murder, and political conniving particularly fun."

"Looks like you're not living up to your full potential then." She stood back up and assessed her work.

Beside us, Andrews stood with his brow furrowed. "And you're sure this is safe?"

"No one has shown any indication of being violent," was Erin's reply.

"That's not generally how that works," Andrews said. "No one's had their back up against a wall yet. Once they do, that's when the violence starts. Caged mouse and all that."

"Thanks for making me feel better," I muttered. I glanced down at the floor, my foot tapping against the worn carpet. The tension buzzed in my chest like a growing storm, and the small hotel room felt tighter by the second.

Andrews' frown deepened. "I still don't understand why we can't just get Ramirez to do the talking. Why do we have to put Alex in harm's way?"

Erin's expression turned serious. "Because we can't trust what either of them says. They're both playing a game. A classic prisoner's dilemma. The only way to pin this down is to hear what they say to each other."

"How is that any different from Alex speaking with Tom?"

I gave Andrews a confused look, unsure why he wasn't catching on. "Because I'm not playing a game."

Andrews shook his head. "No, I mean Tom may not be fully truthful with you."

"That's the point."

He threw his hands up in frustration. "Well, I don't see the point of all this."

"Because between what he says to Alex and Ramirez might be the truth," Erin said. "It's often what people don't say that speaks volumes."

"Waxing philosophical over here," Andrews muttered with a roll of his eyes.

Erin finished adjusting the wire and gave my shoulder a gentle pat. "You'll do great."

I shifted my weight, the wire's presence against my skin a constant distraction. "Gee, thanks."

As Erin moved to the other side of the hotel room, Andrews pulled me aside. "I'm worried about you doing this. I don't want you to get hurt."

"I don't have a choice. But I'm grateful you'll be around to watch my back."

His expression softened. "Of course."

Erin returned, her expression bright and optimistic. "Alright, everything's ready to go. We should head out, get to the courthouse early."

I glanced down at my watch. 7 a.m. Definitely an early start for a day like this, though I'd barely slept, so it didn't make much difference.

The air outside felt cooler than expected for summer, but that did little to calm my nerves. The streets were still quiet, save for a few early commuters, and the distant hum of the city slowly waking up. Andrews and I made the drive to the courthouse in tense silence. Every stoplight, every turn, I could feel the weight of what was about to unfold.

As we approached the building, he turned to me. "Don't try and look for me, okay? I'll be around, watching to make sure you're okay. Just focus on what you need to do." I nodded, gripping the steering wheel a little too tightly. The last thing I needed was the distraction of knowing he was there, but his words had the opposite effect— comforting and unsettling at the same time.

"Thank you," I said. With a deep breath, I exited the car. My heels clicked against the pavement, a familiar but hollow sound that seemed to echo louder in the stillness. I adjusted my bag on my shoulder, the weight of its contents pulling me back into reality. Ahead, the courthouse loomed larger than usual, its stone facade stark and uninviting. I took another deep breath, squared my shoulders, and headed toward the entrance, bracing for whatever came next.

The courtroom was still empty when I arrived, save for the staff members opening the blinds and preparing the space. Just as I began organizing my notes, the door burst open and Tom strode in.

"Where have you been?" he demanded, his voice sharp and his face contorted. "I've been calling nonstop, trying to find you at the office."

My heart was beating out of my chest now, but I forced myself to remain calm, offering a placating tone. "Sorry, I've had my phone off and then I came in early to prepare. What's wrong?"

One of the staff came closer to us to adjust the blinds, oblivious to our pending argument.

His jaw tightened, and he glanced around the room before gritting out, "Let's talk in one of the witness rooms."

I followed him out of the courtroom, trying to breathe slow and keep my heartbeat steady. I idly wondered if Erin could hear it through the wire. The moment the door closed behind us, Tom's volume rose.

"You named Ramirez as a witness?"

I feigned naivete. Given the state of my nerves, it wasn't hard. "What's the issue with that?"

"The problem is that he's been arrested on grounds of fraud and embezzlement." Tom gawked at me. "Donovan's going to have a field day with him."

I could practically hear the unspoken "you should've known better" in his voice. That familiar patronizing tone. It was something I'd come to expect in this line of work, especially as a female in the profession. Whether it was from opposing counsel or even colleagues, men like Tom always seemed eager to point out what they thought was my naivete, my supposed inexperience. It was frustrating, infuriating even, but I wasn't going to let it show. "He has information that I think will be useful."

Tom pinched the bridge of his nose. "What information could he possibly have that is worth risking the entire case?"

"For starters," I said, my voice firm, "he was at the scene."

"So was Sanchez. Next."

I huffed. "I don't really have time to get into it. I want to prep before court starts."

"You've got almost three hours before the trial resumes." His gaze was hard and I tried not to shrink under it. "Talk."

I glanced at the door as if making sure no one would come in, then dropped my voice low. "I went to visit him in JPC. He claims he's had conversations with the mayor. Thompson tipped him off that Ed planned to kill Caroline."

A flicker of something crossed Tom's features, but he schooled his expression. "Anything Ramirez says about that will be hearsay and inadmissible."

"But the jury will still hear it before Donovan objects. And that's worth it, in my mind."

Tom's frustration was evident, his voice turning into a low growl now. "The mayor's office got Ramirez arrested in the first place. How could he have had these supposed conversations?"

"Maybe they're trying to stop him from talking. Ya know, framed him for crimes that would make it difficult for me to call him as a witness?"

"And yet, here you are, calling him for testimony."

"It's not my job to poke holes in his testimony. That's for Donovan to do."

"I know for a fact Thompson didn't tell Ramirez any of that."

"And how could you possibly know that?" I spat.

The muscles in Tom's jaw tightened as he regarded me in silence for a long moment, likely trying to figure out his next play.

Finally, he spoke in a calmer, quieter tone. "Because the mayor and I are friends. We talk a lot. And we spoke about Ramirez. I reviewed the evidence against him when it was first received. Conversations he had with Thompson would have come up."

"Maybe Thompson hasn't shown you everything."

This was delicate. I needed him to bite, to question things for himself, but I had to be careful not to push too hard. One wrong word and he could dig his heels in, shut down, and I'd be no closer to answers. My pulse quickened as I kept my expression neutral, hoping he'd be more curious than defensive. Tom's gaze hardened. "I found out you went to visit Ramirez in lock up. You should have asked me before you went down there. I told you that the witnesses and evidence I wanted you using on this case were already lined up." He gritted his teeth, merely biting out the next words. "You're way out of line here."

"He was at the scene!" I raised my voice. "Excuse me for not wanting to be blindsided at trial. You don't think Donovan went to go interview him?"

Tom scoffed. "No, I don't. Because no lawyer in their right mind would ever even consider calling him as a witness."

"You told me that I needed to get a guilty verdict." I pointed my finger at him. "And that's what I'm trying to do."

"You're being an idiot, is what you're doing."

I crossed my arms. "You're stressed. So, I'll let that one go."

"Stressed? That's an understatement of what you're doing to my mental health. Because of your little act, I had to go have Janice scout for anything you might use at trial from Ramirez. She said she over-heard you speaking to Lisa about a recording and I told her to retrieve it. But I never anticipated you would add him to the witness list."

"Wait." I shook my head, my forehead scrunching. "That's why you sent Janice to the storage locker?"

"Completely useless secretary. Didn't even tell me that she came up empty-handed until today." He turned his attention back to me. "Had I known I would have counseled you a lot sooner on not trusting Ramirez."

Could I have pegged Tom wrong in all of this? His explanation for why Janice was at the storage locker was plausible. But then, what was the explanation for the bank statement on Janice's desk? I quickly recovered my composure.

"Ramirez gave me records between Ed and the mayor's office. I can't make complete sense of them, but it seems to corroborate some kind of relationship there. And makes me think Ed may have mentioned something to Thompson about killing his wife."

"I won't allow you to let Ramirez testify." Tom's expression dark-ened. "And you better hand those records over to me."

I couldn't help but laugh, the sound sharp and humorless. "And how exactly do you plan to stop me? Threaten my job? Good luck with that. I'm the lead prosecutor on this case, and the judge isn't going to let you waltz in and change the witness list."

"Do you have any idea how much Donovan's going to destroy his credibility on cross-examination?" He paced the small space. "All that work to get a guilty verdict and you're going to risk it just to have him testify."

"Ramirez can corroborate Ed's involvement in Caroline's murder. Combined with the recording from her friend, the jury won't have any choice but to convict. In my eyes that benefit outweighs the risk."

Tom's eyes narrowed. "You're going to regret this," he growled, before storming out of the room.

I watched him go, my heart pounding in my chest. Two minutes later, the door to the witness room opened. I startled, but it was just Andrews. He jerked his head and I followed him out of the room. We walked through the halls of the courthouse to a back service hallway, and then into a back room.

Andrews opened the door and Erin was sitting inside next to someone with headphones on in front of a computer screen.

"Nice work," she said.

I shrugged. "I'm not sure it was really anything useful."

"It's useful that he's running to go talk to Ramirez in lockup now. Just like we'd hoped. Got enough time to watch the show?"

I looked at my watch. ""I think I can spare a few."

As I sat down, I turned to Erin. "Did you hear what Tom said about sending Janice after the recording? Does that change anything?"

Erin shrugged off the question. "Let's wait and see what we get from him with Ramirez."

THIRTY-NINE

THE SCREEN CAST an eerie glow across our faces as we huddled in the cramped observation room. My gaze was fixed on the monitor, watching intently as the door to the holding cell swung open and a guard stepped in. He exchanged a few words with Ramirez and left again.

Seconds ticked by, and I was beginning to lose hope that our plan would work. Then, Tom strode into the room. Before saying anything, he began scanning the walls and ceilings, obviously looking for hidden surveillance. Seemingly satisfied, his shoulders relaxed as he turned his attention to Ramirez. I made a note to ask Erin how she hid a camera so well.

"Officer Ramirez," Tom greeted, his tone cordial. "Or, I suppose I should say Mister now, since you've lost your badge." A practiced smile tugged at the corners of his mouth, but his eyes remained cold.

Ramirez offered a tight-lipped smile in return, forcing politeness. Neither of these two were winning any Oscars anytime soon. "District Attorney Matthews," he acknowledged, his voice laced with thinly veiled contempt.

"I understand you've been called as a witness in the Martin trial."

"Sort of why I'm here." Ramirez was copping an attitude, and we weren't even sixty seconds in.

Tom ignored him. "I hear you've been talking a lot lately. Trying to save your own skin. I get it, but you need to be careful about what you say. I'm not against adding perjury to your list of offenses."

Ramirez's jaw tightened. "I'm just telling the truth. As you said, I've got my own neck to worry about here."

"Truth can be a tricky thing. Sometimes it can come back to bite you. Especially if the truth you're telling isn't, well, entirely accurate."

"What are you getting at?"

Tom lowered his voice, his tone hardening with every word. "Let me be clear. I know you're under pressure. But if you go in there and start spinning tales, things might not go the way you expect."

I leaned forward, my breath catching in my throat as the weight of Tom's warning sank in. Everything he was saying was above board, despite the implied threat behind his words.

Fucking lawyers.

Beside me, Andrews shifted in his seat. My gaze flicked to Erin, her brow furrowed in concentration as she kept her gaze transfixed on the screen. A muscle twitched in her jaw, a silent sign that she was just as irritated.

Ramirez tilted his head, feigning confusion. "You worried I'm going to say something about you? Or the mayor?"

"Remember who your friends are," Tom said. "Remember who helped you get where you are today."

Ramirez grabbed at his orange jumpsuit. "In jail?"

Tom stiffened. "The mayor is a man of integrity. Any insinuation otherwise is baseless and irresponsible."

A derisive snort escaped Ramirez.

Tom's irritation was visible as he pressed his lips into a thin line. I found myself leaning forward.

At last, Tom exhaled slowly and squared his shoulders. "We're not here to discuss the mayor. We're here to discuss Ed Martin's murder trial." His tone brooked no argument. "Mr. Martin's actions will be judged by the courts, as is proper. It would be unwise to complicate matters further."

Tom's words hung heavy in the air. I found my fists clenching beneath the table. We were so close, and yet Tom hadn't once said something incriminating. If anything, he seemed to be the one leading the conversation, when Ramirez was supposed to be drawing him out.

"I'm not a lawyer but I'm pretty sure it's not slander if it's true." Ramirez leaned back in his chair. "Ed was definitely making contributions to the mayor. Some may see those transactions as too beneficial."

"I'm not sure what the implication is, Mr. Ramirez. Ed was a big supporter of the mayor. They did a lot of business together. It would only be natural for him to contribute to his campaign."

I watched as the two men stared one another down. The air felt stifling, the walls closing in around us. My throat constricted and I struggled to breathe. Andrews turned to me and wrapped his hand around my wrist, squeezing. I looked up at him and he took a deep breath, then another, and I followed. My heartbeat slowed, and my attention returned to the scene in front of us.

"I'm sorry, but what exactly is the purpose of this visit?" Ramirez asked, trying to force Tom's hand.

"I'll be blunt. I'm concerned that in an effort to save yourself, you may commit perjury. As the district attorney, I'm here to ensure that this trial doesn't end up in a mistrial."

Ramirez's gaze sharpened. "We both know there were conversations about how to... handle her."

My breath caught. But Tom didn't even flinch. "Maybe I wasn't direct enough. The consequences of you opening your mouth will be severe. Catastrophic, even."

Ramirez's bravado seemed to waver before he regained his composure. "Or what? You gonna make me disappear like Caroline?"

My heart skipped a beat. I exchanged a loaded glance with Erin, silently urging her to stay calm. This was the moment—the one where Tom might let something slip, something incriminating. The air felt charged with anticipation, and I could feel the adrenaline surge in my veins as we both waited for what would come next. Tom's composure finally cracked, his nostrils flaring with fury. Just as quickly, the mask slipped back into place.

"I have no idea what you mean. I suggest you consider your future very carefully, Mr. Ramirez." With that, he strode out of the cell, slamming the door behind him.

A heavy silence descended upon the room. I could feel the adrenaline coursing through my veins, my heart still pounding from the charged confrontation.

Finally, Erin broke the tense quiet, offering a soft, "Thank you" to the tech, dismissing him. He slipped out of the room and we all sat in silence for a minute.

"He didn't outright confess to anything," I said, rubbing my forehead in a desperate attempt to stave off my impending migraine. "Legally speaking."

Andrews gave me an incredulous look. "Are you kidding me? That was a clear case of witness tampering and intimidation." The words tumbled out, laced with frustration. "He all but admitted to a coverup."

Erin sighed, pinching the bridge of her nose. "Alex is right. It's not enough for the conviction we want on Tom."

"What about the mayor?" I asked. "Do you still have what you need for a warrant?"

"Probably not. Plus, I wanted both of them."

I looked between her and Andrews. Their expressions were pained and weary, likely mirroring my own. "There's got to be something we can do."

"Just finish the trial," Erin said, rising from her seat. "Maybe we can convince Ed to talk in exchange for a sentencing recommendation."

I nodded. The idea that someone like Tom or even Ramirez was able to pull one over on me made my insides churn. This was the exact reason I gave up a cushy office job to become a prosecutor. It was time to drag the truth into the light, kicking and screaming.

FORTY

I REENTERED THE COURTROOM, and despite the AC on full blast, the air was heavy with tension.

Lisa's concerned gaze met mine when I took my post at the table. "Where were you?" she mouthed, her voice drowned out by the sudden call for order.

"Don't worry about it," I muttered, and squared my shoulders.

"Welcome back, all," Judge Beasley said, greeting us as if this were a classroom and not a murder trial. "Ms. Hayes, would you like to call your first witness for the day?"

"Thank you, Your Honor," I said. "The State calls Officer Louis Ramirez to the stand."

The crowd murmured behind me as Ramirez was brought to the stand. He was still wearing his orange jumpsuit. The Supreme Court had ruled that defendants had the right to appear in civilian clothes, but that didn't extend to witnesses. Generally, the judge would instruct the jury that they should not speculate as to why someone was in prison garb. As if that would eliminate any bias toward the witness.

I glanced over my shoulder, catching Tom in the back of the court-room. His face was a mask of barely contained irritation, his jaw tight and eyes narrowed. His gaze locked onto me for a second, and I could practically feel the heat of his anger. I turned back around, forcing myself to focus.

Ramirez was sworn in, his eyes briefly meeting mine as he took his seat. There was a glint of something in his expression—confidence, maybe. He leaned back, settling into the chair, his gaze never leaving me. My stomach twisted, a knot forming tighter with each passing second. A sinking realization hit me: calling him as a witness might have been a bigger gamble than I'd anticipated. Doubts clawed at my confidence, gnawing at the edges of my carefully laid plans. I cleared my throat and began. "Officer Ramirez, can you tell the jury who you are and what you do for a living?"

"My name is Louis Ramirez, and I am a City of Houston police officer."

"Did you visit the Martin residence after Mr. Martin called 911 after the death of his wife?"

"Yes."

"Can you tell us a bit about what you saw there?"

"Along with Officer Sanchez, I was dispatched to the scene after receiving word of a reported homicide. When we arrived, Mr. Martin was in the driveway. He took us inside and up to the master bedroom where we found the body of Caroline Martin."

"Could you describe the emotional state of the defendant?"

Donovan leaped out of his seat. "Objection! The witness is not a psychologist."

I did very little to hide my exasperation. "Your Honor, I'm not asking the witness to make a clinical diagnosis of the defendant. Just asking him for his common sense assessment of the defendant."

"All these trials tend to blur together," Beasley said, "but I believe we've addressed this sort of thing with a previous witness." He turned over a few pages of notes. "Let's not rehash old history. Objection overruled."

"Officer Ramirez, could you describe the emotional state of the defendant?"

"No."

I blinked. "No?"

Ramirez shook his head. "No, I can't do that."

"I'm sorry, is it that you can't or you don't want to?"

"Is there a difference?"

I could tell I was losing the jury. Not only them, but also Ramirez.

But something told me I'd already lost him long before he took the stand.

"Let's switch gears. Officer Ramirez, can you tell me about the conversations you had with the defendant and the mayor?"

"I don't recall any such conversations."

I blinked at him and he stared back at me.

"You're saying, under oath, that you don't recall any conversation between the defendant, Ed Martin, and Mayor Thompson?"

"Objection," Donovan said. "Asked and answered."

"Move it along, Ms. Hayes," the judge scolded.

I could see Ramirez stifle a chuckle, as if he thought this entire thing was hilarious. He was trying to make me appear weak.

I chanced a glance at the jury. Their expressions ranged from confusion to disbelief. Their skepticism radiated into the courtroom. This direct examination could easily unravel my entire case.

With a final, feeble attempt, I asked, "Mr. Ramirez, are you certain you have no recollection of those conversations?" The damage had already been done. Ramirez shook his head, his features a mask of false sincerity.

He offered an apologetic shrug. "I'm afraid I cannot recall anything of the sort."

This was the first time I'd ever lost control of a witness. As I sat down, I vowed it would be my last.

"Cross," Judge Beasley said.

Donovan stood and began, his voice smooth. "Mr. Ramirez, I couldn't help but notice that you're currently under arrest for fraud and embezzlement. Is that correct?"

I was on my feet in an instant. "Objection. Mr. Ramirez has not been tried or found guilty of those charges. He is innocent until proven otherwise."

The judge nodded, his gaze stern. "Sustained. The jury will disregard the line of questioning."

"Nothing further," Donovan said, but doubt crept into the jurors' expressions. I'd put an unsound witness on the stand, shaking the entire foundation of my case.

I sank back into my chair, the heavy weight of my failure settling upon me. What the hell had I been thinking? Ramirez had played me, turning my own questions against me. I'd given Donovan exactly what he needed to poke a giant hole in my case. Now, the jury's confidence in me was as shaky as my own. Each stolen glance at their faces sent a wave of regret crashing over me—this wasn't just a stumble; it felt like the beginning of a collapse.

The judge's voice cut through the swirling turmoil of my thoughts. "The court will take a brief recess. We will reconvene in fifteen minutes."

I gathered my notes, and Lisa's gaze settled on me. "Are you okay?"

I forced a tight-lipped smile. "I'm fine. I just need a moment to clear my head before the next witness."

I made my way out of the courthouse, drawing in a deep breath of the humid air, somehow less stifling than the air-conditioned courtroom. I all but collapsed on a nearby park bench.

Closing my eyes, I focused on the sounds around me—the distant hum of traffic, the chirping of birds, the murmurings of passersby—and willed my mind to stillness.

"You look like you're contemplating the mysteries of the universe."

I cracked one eye open to find Andrews regarding me with a wry smile, thumbs tucked into his belt loops. At my mute stare, he jerked his chin toward the vacant spot beside me. "Mind if I join you?"

"Be my guest." I sighed and scooted over to make room. For a moment, we sat in companionable silence before he spoke again.

"Want to talk about it?"

I barked a mirthless laugh. "About how this whole case is rapidly circling the drain? How every time I think I'm making progress, something pulls the rug out from under me?" My hands opened and closed helplessly. "At this point, I don't know what's real anymore."

Andrews nodded. "I get it. It's easy to start questioning everything when the pieces don't seem to fit. But you're a damn good lawyer, and you're too stubborn to let this case go. Whatever's going on, you'll figure it out. Stay focused on what you know to be true."

The sun filtered through the trees, casting shifting shadows over the pavement, and a warm breeze played with my hair. Despite the pleasant day, a knot of tension sat heavy in my chest, refusing to ease. Even the calming sounds of the world around me couldn't drown out the chaos in my head. I allowed his words to sink in. "Thanks."

Andrews nodded, rising from the bench. "Let's get back inside."

I stood and started to follow Andrews. I paused as my phone buzzed in my pocket. I pulled it out and Andrews looked back at me. "You go on ahead," I said.

I fished it out. The screen displayed an unlisted number. Against my better judgment, I swiped to answer.

A recorded voice was on the other end. "You have a call from an inmate at USP Beaumont. To accept the charges, press one."

In any other situation, I would have declined the call. But I started to think about what Ramirez told me. About revoking his testimony. About my father being set up, just like how the Martin case was shaping up to be an elaborate smokescreen.

For a fraction of a second, my thumb hovered over the keypad as indecision gripped me. Part of me was desperate for clarity. I had so many questions for my father, wondering if his story lined up with what Ramirez told me. But a larger part recoiled at the thought of allowing myself to be manipulated yet again.

Glancing at the time, I realized the recess was nearly over. With a frustrated exhale, I stabbed the reject button.

Andrews had been walking slow on purpose and turned back around to look at me. "Everything okay?"

"Just a wrong number," I lied, tucking the phone away as we reentered the courthouse. Andrews took a seat at the back of the courtroom. I scanned the audience to see Tom was no longer here.

As I moved to take my seat behind the counsel table, Donovan leaned over just enough for me to hear him. "Debated whether to come back?"

I refused the bait and took my seat next to Lisa. "Just needed some air."

Donovan chuckled, the sound grating on my nerves. "Maybe I should move for a directed verdict right now. After all, this case seems to be slipping through your fingers faster than you can catch it."

Before I could retort, the bailiff's voice rang out, calling the court to order. As the jury filed in, I carefully observed their faces, looking for any subtle cues—raised eyebrows, tight lips, or nervous glances—that might give away their thoughts or leanings.

An elderly woman in the front row maintained a frown as she sat down. Beside her, the burly mechanic kept picking at a hangnail, his attention seemingly anywhere but on the courtroom.

The young accountant in the third row met my gaze, an intelligence behind her eyes. She looked away, and my mind's gears began churning with a new strategy. Instead of trying to convince twelve people, I could convince one who could convince the rest.

The judge's gavel pulled my attention back to the bench. "Ms. Hayes, your next witness please."

I stood. "The State calls Sarah Hodgkin to the stand."

FORTY-ONE

I KEPT my tone measured and professional. "Please state your name for the record."

Her voice quivered as she responded, "Sarah Hodgkin."

"And how do you know the victim, Caroline Martin?"

"We were friends back when we worked together as real estate agents." She kept her gaze down as she spoke. "We've known—knew each other for years."

I nodded. "Can you tell the court about any conversations you've had with Caroline regarding her husband?"

She wrung her hands in her lap as she spoke. "Caroline had confided in me that she left her previous husband to be with Edward. It was a pretty well-known scandal, and she suffered a loss of reputation for it. She said Ed was worth it."

"Did anything change?" I asked.

"Yes. A year after they got married, she discovered Edward was having an affair with his assistant at the time." Her lips pursed into a thin line." Since then, he's had several new assistants and had affairs with many of them. She wasn't happy about it but felt powerless to do anything."

I could see a flicker of recognition among the jurors—cheating, betrayal, the kind of real-life drama that pulled them in. I could almost feel the jury's attention piquing. Everyone loved a good cheating story. This was the opening I needed to get things back on track. "And did Caroline ever mention planning to confront her husband about the affair?"

Sarah hesitated, her eyes flickering with uncertainty. "She said she was going to talk to him about it. She was tired of looking the other way."

I hated that my case was turning into a scorned lover's tale. Sure, it might sway the jury, but it felt like a cheap tactic. I wanted to be above that—to win on the merits of the evidence, not by playing into their thirst for drama. Yet, without Ramirez's testimony, this was all I had at the moment. I pressed on. "And what happened after that conversation?"

"She called me the next morning. I... I actually missed her call that day. It went to voicemail."

"And did Caroline Martin leave a voicemail on your phone?"

"Yes."

"What time was that voicemail recorded?"

"At about 9:45 a.m."

"The State would like to submit Exhibit C into evidence, Your Honor, and requests that it be played for the jury."

"Admitted." Judge Beasley put a hand up to Donovan, who was already on his feet. "Your standing objection has already been noted, Mr. Donovan. You may sit down."

Beasley nodded at the clerk, who pressed a button on her computer screen. Caroline's voice could be heard throughout the courtroom. The familiar cadence of her voice made my skin crawl. It was eerie, knowing she was gone, and this was the precise moment in which it happened.

I could feel the weight of the moment pressing down on me, my pulse quickening as I glanced at the jury. I knew the damn thing by heart at this point—Caroline complaining about the affair, saying she was going to confront him. Ed coming home, the scuffle, the screams, and then the call ending. Every single member of the jury was paying attention now.

The recording ended and the courtroom was deathly silent. I took a moment to compose myself before continuing, the stillness of the room heavy, almost suffocating.

I kept my tone neutral. "Can you tell us what we just heard?"

Sarah's eyes glistened with unshed tears. "That was the voicemail Caroline left for me."

"Do you recognize the other voice on the recording?"

"Yes."

"Can you tell us who that was?"

"It was her husband, Edward Martin."

"Is that man here today?"

"Yes."

"Can you point him out for the jury?"

Sarah pointed at Ed, sitting ramrod straight in his overpriced suit. For the first time, a flicker of nervousness crossed his face, his jaw tightening as his eyes darted briefly toward the jury. I took note of the shift—was he finally feeling the weight of the accusations?

"Let the record show that the witness is pointing at the defendant," Judge Beasley said and the court reporter typed away.

"Thank you for your testimony, Sarah," I said. "No further questions, Your Honor."

As I returned to my seat, I scanned the jury again, gauging their reactions. Some were still processing the weight of the recording, others sat more rigidly, their faces harder to read. But I could feel it—there was a shift. If I could bring it home with Palmer's testimony, I might be able to win this thing.

"Cross?"

Donovan rose, his gaze fixed on Sarah. "Ms. Hodgkin, you mentioned that you heard Caroline's voice on the recording, along with Mr. Martin's. Is that correct?"

"Yes, that's right," Sarah replied, her voice wavering.

"But you weren't actually present at the scene, were you? You couldn't see what was happening between Caroline and Mr. Martin in that moment."

Sarah frowned. "Well, no, I couldn't see what was happening, but the tone of Caroline's voice was clearly—"

"Yes or no, Ms. Hodgkin?" Donovan snapped. "Could you actually observe what was taking place between the two of them?"

Sarah hesitated, her lips pressed into a thin line. "No, I couldn't see what was happening."

"Then you can't say for certain that Mr. Martin harmed Caroline in any way during that interaction, can you?"

Sarah's eyes narrowed. "It's pretty obvious from the recording that—"

"Yes or no, Ms. Hodgkin?" Donovan asked again, his voice smooth and calculated. "Can you know for sure what was happening in that moment?"

Sarah let out a resigned sigh. "No."

"No further questions."

I felt the familiar surge of frustration rise within me. I watched the jury, their expressions shifting from rapt attention to uncertainty. I had worked hard to paint a clear picture, and now Donovan had managed to fray its edges. He'd managed to undermine the impact of the recording. I could almost hear my heartbeat as I clenched my fists under the table. The moment I won ground, I'd lost it again immediately.

"Does the prosecution have any further witnesses?"

I rose from my seat. "Yes, Your Honor. The State calls Dr. Brian Palmer to the stand."

As Palmer took the oath, I caught Donovan shifting in his seat, his usually confident posture faltering as he leaned forward, elbows resting on the defense table. His jaw clenched, fingers drumming the surface in a nervous rhythm. Concern etched his features, a subtle crack in the facade he wore so well. This was the witness he had been dreading—the one where the gruesome photos of the victim would be shown, an assault on the jury's senses that no amount of cross-examination could undo. They were a defense attorney's worst nightmare, and Donovan knew it.

I moved to the center of the room. "Dr. Palmer, can you state your name and occupation for the court?"

Palmer kept his voice calm and authoritative. "My name is Dr. Brian Palmer and I am a forensic pathologist with additional qualifications in fingerprint comparison and analysis."

"And how long have you been working in this field?" I asked.

"Over fifteen years. I've conducted thousands of autopsies and have testified in numerous court cases."

"Dr. Palmer, were you the forensic pathologist assigned to Caroline Martin's case?"

"Yes, I was."

"Can you describe the condition of Caroline Martin's body when you first examined her?"

Palmer nodded. "Caroline Martin's body showed multiple signs of trauma. The most significant were the bruises on her neck, which were consistent with manual strangulation. She also had petechial hemorrhages in her eyes, a common sign of asphyxiation, and a laceration to the front of her forehead."

"Your Honor, the State offers Exhibits D, E, and F into evidence." I passed printed copies of the photos to the bailiff, who handed them to the judge and another copy to Donovan.

"Your Honor, I must object," Donovan said, standing. "These photos are overly graphic and prejudicial. They will unduly influence the jury."

"Your Honor," I responded, "this evidence is critical to understanding the nature of the crime and the manner in which it was committed. The jury has a right to see the injuries that led to Caroline Martin's death and to understand the forensic analysis tying these injuries to the defendant."

Judge Beasley considered both arguments before deciding. "Objection overruled. The jury will see the evidence."

Donovan sat down, his posture deflated, disappointment etched across his face. His shoulders sagged as if the weight of the decision pressed down on him.

I walked over to the screen and projected the first image: a close-up of Caroline's neck, showing the deep purple bruising from where her life had been choked out. The jury collectively tensed, eyes widening. One of the jurors looked away, her hand instinctively covering her mouth. Another leaned forward, trying to scrutinize every detail with a mixture of morbid curiosity and horror. The tension in the room thickened, the reality of the crime settling over them like a heavy blanket.

"Dr. Palmer, can you tell us what we're looking at?"

"These bruises," Palmer continued, "indicate a significant amount of pressure applied to the neck, cutting off both blood flow and air supply to the brain. This would cause the victim to lose consciousness within seconds, and death could follow within minutes if the pressure is maintained."

I displayed another image, the pattern of the bruising in greater detail. "Can you tell us about the pattern of these bruises?"

Palmer leaned forward. "The bruising pattern is consistent with fingers pressing into the skin. We took fingerprints from Ed Martin and compared them to the bruising marks on Caroline's neck. The prints matched, indicating that Ed Martin's hands were likely the ones that inflicted these injuries."

I continued, showing a final image of Caroline's body, highlighting the various bruises and injuries. My pulse quickened as I glanced at the jury, my stomach knotting with the importance of this moment. The expressions on their faces varied—some jurors were horrified, their eyes fixed on the images, while others looked down, seemingly unable to take in the violence of the scene. This was it—the undeniable link. If this didn't convince them, I didn't know what would. Dr. Palmer, in your professional opinion, what was the cause of Caroline Martin's death?"

"The cause of death was asphyxiation due to manual strangulation."

"And can you speak to us a bit about the time of death?"

"According to my findings, Caroline Martin was killed at approximately 9:46 a.m. on the morning in question."

Donovan rose, his chair scraping against the floor. "Objection, Your Honor. The doctor's testimony is speculative and lacks sufficient evidence to determine the precise time of death."

Judge Beasley's gaze narrowed. "Overruled. The witness may continue."

I glanced over at Donovan, noting the slight twitch in his jaw. "Dr. Palmer, can you elaborate on the significance of the time of death in relation to the evidence we've heard?"

Palmer's expression hardened. "The time of death corresponds with the timeline presented in the audio recording. It places the victim alive and in the presence of the defendant, Ed Martin, shortly before her murder."

I nodded. "Thank you, Dr. Palmer. No further questions." I moved back to my seat and exhaled a slow breath, my fingers gripping the edge of the table. I tried to keep my face neutral, but my heart was racing—this was a pivotal moment.

"Mr. Donovan," Judge Beasley prompted. "Your cross?"

Donovan stood, his face carefully composed, though there was an intensity in his eyes. His suit jacket stretched as he adjusted his stance, his movements deliberate, like a predator closing in on its prey. He approached the stand with a measured pace. "Dr. Palmer, in your experience, can bruising patterns always definitively match a suspect's fingerprints?"

Palmer remained composed. "Not always definitively, but in this case, the match was very strong."

"Is it possible that someone else could have inflicted these injuries?"

"Possible, but unlikely given the evidence."

"Could the bruising pattern have been caused by some other means?"

Palmer shook his head. "The bruising and other signs of trauma are consistent with manual strangulation, not with any other cause."

Donovan shifted his strategy. "And the petechial hemorrhages you mentioned—could those be caused by something other than asphyxiation?"

"Petechial hemorrhages are most commonly caused by asphyxiation. They can occur in other circumstances, but the presence of neck bruising and other factors make asphyxiation the most likely cause."

Donovan nodded, but his expression showed frustration. "No further questions, Your Honor."

FORTY-TWO

RELIEF SURGED through me as Palmer stepped down from the stand. Despite Donovan's attempts to discredit the evidence, the testimony had been powerful. The jury now had everything they needed to make a decision.

"Given the length and gravity of today's testimony, we will recess for the rest of the day. Court will reconvene at 10 a.m. Monday." Judge Beasley struck his gavel and we all stood as the judge and jury left the courtroom.

"Are we heading back to the office?" Lisa asked as we made our way out of the courthouse.

I shook my head, fishing my keys out of my purse. "No, you take the rest of the day off. I'll call if I need you."

Her shoulders relaxed. "Sounds good. Enjoy the quiet while it lasts." She gave my arm a gentle squeeze before heading off toward her car.

I broke off to walk to my own car. My pocket buzzed with an incoming call for the entire walk, but I ignored it, opting to wait until I got to my vehicle. Once inside, I pulled my phone out. Three missed calls. One from Erin, one from Andrews, and the one I'd rejected earlier from my father.

I stared at the screen. A voicemail notification from my father floated at the top of my inbox. My phone lit up again with another incoming call from Erin. A twinge of guilt tugged at my conscience, but I silenced the call and tossed the device onto the passenger seat. They were probably anxious to talk about what happened today, needing answers as much as I did. But after everything, I just couldn't handle it. My mind was maxed out, stretched thin from hours of testimony and back-and-forth arguments in court.

The drive home was a blur. The day's events replayed in fragmented flashes—Ramirez's testimony, the shaky ground of my case, the lingering stares of the jury, each moment gnawing at my thoughts. It felt like I was trying to piece together a puzzle, but the more I focused, the blurrier the edges became. I dragged myself inside and poured myself the largest glass of red wine possible. Sitting down heavily on the sofa, I took a moment to just sit in the silence, the kind of silence that feels thick and hollow at the same time. The house, still and untouched, had a way of reminding me how disconnected I felt from everything, like the empty spaces on the walls where family photos should've been.

My phone lit up again, buzzing loudly against the coffee table. I leaned forward to check it, seeing this time the caller was Andrews. I knew they were all just looking out for me, but I wasn't ready to talk. I silenced his call too. Right now, I didn't want to be attached to any more wires, or try to convince someone to talk, or to explain myself over and over again. I needed the quiet.

The ringing ended, and my phone went back to its normal screen, with my father's voicemail icon sitting right at the top. It was hard to shake the sense that there were too many things left unsaid between us—too many loose threads I wasn't sure how to untangle, or if I even wanted to. I stared at it, drinking my wine and waiting for the sun to set. The dim lavender-scented air slowly thickened into the kind of twilight that makes everything look softer, but the weight of the day didn't lift. It settled in deeper. When I was finally in the dark and my glass was empty, I picked up the device. The silence of the house pressed in on me, but I knew eventually, I'd have to face the messages.

I pressed play, and for the first time since the day he'd been led away in handcuffs, I heard his voice.

"Hey, honey, it's me." Stinging immediately pricked my eyes and nose, but I wouldn't let it release. "I hope you get this call. I know I'm a little late to the game, but things make their way here a little slower.

" I heard you're working on a homicide case, and I just wanted to congratulate you." His clear pride in me made my chest ache. "I know you're going to do a great job."

I closed my eyes, the image of him behind bars flooding my mind —the man I had once idolized, reduced to a shadow of his former self by the very system he had sworn to uphold.

"I hope this doesn't come off in the wrong way, but I may be able to help." He paused, a hint of uncertainty creeping into his voice. "Not that you can't do it all on your own, but... I just want to be a part of your life, Alex."

The use of my name struck, the weight of our estrangement crystallizing in that single word. As the voicemail came to an end, I sat in silence. Tears burned down my cheeks, and I closed my eyes, willing them to stop.

What if all this time I'd been wrong about my father? The guilt gnawed at me, clawing at the edges of my mind. All this time he'd been in prison and I'd refused to see him when he was truly innocent. Erin had told me Ramirez was just bluffing. But Ramirez had been his partner and had testified against him. His words had put my father behind bars, and I had believed him. And judging by his performance in court today, he is just as dirty as he'd claimed my father to be. I could feel the anger rising in my chest, a tightness I couldn't shake. What if Erin was wrong?

Wiping the tears from my eyes, I took a deep, steadying breath and stared down at the phone in my hand. Hearing my father's voice had stirred up a tumultuous mix of emotions I had suppressed for years. Regret. Sadness. Rage. But most of all, confusion. How had I let it get this far? How had I cut him off so completely without ever giving him the chance to explain?

With a sigh, I rose from the couch, the empty wine glass clinking against the coffee table as I set it down. As I stood there, my mind blank, the sudden ring of my phone startled me. Chen's name flashed onto the screen. I cleared my throat and answered, trying to make my voice sound even.

"Ryan," I greeted.

"Hey, you," he said. "I heard the case is going well and you're in recess until Monday."

"That's right," I replied, my tone somewhat cold. It was the best I could manage at the moment. Better that than breaking down in tears.

"I just wanted to check in and see if you'd be up for grabbing dinner tomorrow night?"

I hesitated. "I wish I could, but I've got other plans."

"I see." A note of disappointment crept into his voice, but he recovered. "Maybe another time then."

"Actually, Chen," I said, cutting him off before he could continue. "I was wondering if you could tell me why you couldn't make it to the Campo hearing the other day?"

There was a brief pause. "That's the one you covered for me, right? Tom scheduled a mandatory meeting for me at that time."

"Do you mind me asking what it was about?"

I so desperately wanted Ryan to tell me that it was something important—something serious. If it was, then maybe Ramirez was wrong. Maybe Tom wasn't involved in planting evidence, like Ramirez claimed. If Tom had pulled Ryan off the case for a legitimate reason, I could dismiss what Ramirez said, not only about Tom but also about my father. But the fact that Tom had pulled Ryan off the case for no apparent reason made everything Ramirez said seem far more plausible. It made it harder to ignore the gnawing possibility that Tom was orchestrating something far worse. "Funny you should ask. When I went to go see him, Janice said he got pulled away for something else and he'd catch back up with me. But by that time it was too late to make it to the hearing. I followed up with him, but he still hasn't gotten back to me." He paused. "Why? Did he mention something to you?"

My heart sank. "No, nothing like that. I was just curious, that's all. I appreciate you taking the time to talk."

"Anytime, Alex." The sincerity in his voice was real. "Maybe after the trial is over we can grab that dinner. Take care of yourself until then, okay?"

"I will," I assured him. I put the phone down and stared back out the window. Ryan's answer made the decision for me. Maybe Ramirez was bluffing, but I had to be sure.

FORTY-THREE

I STARED at the looming concrete walls of the federal prison, a far cry from the county jail I'd grown accustomed to visiting. The air was thick with a sense of despair that seeped into my bones. Gone were the revolving doors of JPC, where hope still flickered in the eyes of short timers. This place reeked of lost dreams and abandoned futures.

I joined the queue of visitors, my usual shortcut stripped away. No badge to flash, no preferential treatment. Just another face in a sea of the desperate and dutiful. The guard's voice was a monotone when I gave him my father's name. "Wait in the room. We'll call you."

The waiting area was a study in contrasts. Excited chatter from some corners, muffled sobs from others. A young woman bounced a toddler on her knee, her forced smile a thin veneer over obvious strain. An older man sat ramrod straight, eyes fixed on the wall, as if willing himself to be anywhere else. The room hummed with a nervous energy that had my teeth chattering.

"Hayes, Alex," a voice finally called. I stood, following a different guard through a maze of corridors and security checkpoints.

He led me to a row of booths, thick glass separating visitors from inmates. I sat and stared at my distorted reflection, wondering if I'd recognize the man I'd come to see. Minutes ticked by, each one an eternity.

Then he was there.

If I'd passed him on the street, I would've kept walking. This gaunt specter bore little resemblance to the man I remembered. Gone was the full head of hair, replaced by a patchy, graying stubble. The jovial smile that once seemed a permanent fixture had vanished, leaving behind deep lines etched by worry and regret. But his eyes... when I looked into his eyes, I saw my father.

We stared at one another for a long moment. My breaths were shallow but I broke from my trance when we both reached for the phones. I opened my mouth, but no words came out. Thank God he spoke first.

"Hello, dear," he said, his voice rougher than I remembered. "How've you been?" he asked, as if this was just another Sunday dinner.

"Okay," I lied. "You?"

"Same," he replied. The falsehoods hung heavy between us.

He didn't ask why I'd come after all this time. Didn't mention my absence. He just smiled that ghost of a smile and acted like this was routine.

"Heard about your case," he said.

"Yeah, you mentioned it in your voicemail."

"Trial over yet?"

I shook my head. "Resumes Monday. I'll probably rest my case in the morning, then it's the defense's turn."

"I'm sure you're doing great." His eyes crinkled at the corners. "I'm so proud of you."

His words hit me harder than I expected. I swallowed, forcing myself back to the reason for my visit. "Dad, on the phone... you said you might be able to help."

He nodded slowly. "Recognized the defendant's name. Don't know if it'll help, but... before I was arrested, I remember finding some documents. In a suspect's car. They mentioned Edward Martin."

"Where are these documents now?"

He sighed, suddenly looking even older. "I hid them."

"Why?"

My father shifted on the hard plastic chair, his hands resting tensely in his lap. He glanced down at them for a moment, his fingers tapping against his knee, as if trying to find the right words. "It's important, Dad. If you think they could help, I need to see them."

Another sigh. "They're in a storage locker. I still make the payments so it should still be there. Key's in the kitchen junk drawer back home. If you can't get in, ask Phyllis next door. She's keeping an eye on the place."

I studied his face. Something in the set of his jaw, the way his eyes wouldn't quite meet mine, told me there was more. "Who did you hide them from, Dad? And when?"

He was quiet for a long moment. When he spoke, his voice was barely above a whisper. "I hid it before my trial. When I knew I'd been framed."

I closed my eyes, took a deep breath. When I opened them again, I leaned closer to the glass, as if we weren't speaking over connected phones. "Tell me your side, Dad. All of it."

He ran a hand over his stubbled head, a nervous gesture so familiar it made my chest ache. "It was supposed to be a routine stop," he said. "Broken taillight but the driver matched the description of a B&E suspect. I asked for license and registration. When he opened the glovebox, I saw it. A folder, stuffed full of papers."

He paused, his eyes distant. "He got taken in and we searched the car. I don't know why I looked. Call it a hunch. But what I saw... Alex, it was bad. Names, dates, amounts. Looked like payoffs. And not just street-level stuff. I'm talking judges, city officials."

"Ramirez was there with you." I said. "He had to have seen the folder too."

He nodded. "I couldn't take it in. Not right away. So I hid it. Planned to dig deeper, build a case. But Ramirez must've gotten wind of it. Next thing I know, I'm being investigated on bogus charges. Evidence appearing out of thin air. You know the rest."

I did. The trial, the conviction, the sentencing. My father, the dirty cop. Except...

"Why didn't you say anything?" I asked. "Told them you found the documents in a suspect's car? Used them as leverage?"

He smiled, but there was no humor in it. "And put you in danger? Alex, these people don't play by the rules. I figured if I went down quietly, took my lumps, you'd be safe. That's all that mattered to me. That's all that still matters to me."

I recoiled like I'd been punched in the gut. All this time, I'd believed he was guilty. That he'd betrayed everything he'd taught me about right and wrong.

"Dad, I—"

He held up a hand. "No apologies. I made my choice. But now, with this case of yours... maybe there's a chance to set things right."

"Dad, there's something else you should know." I leaned forward, my hands gripping the phone tighter. "Ramirez was arrested."

His eyebrows shot up. "Was he now?" My father's eyes clouded over, a mix of emotions I couldn't quite read. He was quiet for a long moment, his free hand rubbing his chin.

I wished I could reach through the glass and grab his hand. "Dad, Ramirez told me his testimony against you was fraudulent. All of it."

I expected anger, maybe even a burst of the old fire I remembered. Instead, he just smiled. A sad, tired smile that made him look older than his years.

"Yeah," he said softly. "Yeah, it was."

"But this means—"

"Honestly, Alex? I've given up hoping to get out of this place. I'm halfway through my sentence. There'll be a life for me after all this is over."

My throat tightened, tears welling in my eyes. "But it's not right. We can fight this, we can—"

"Alex." His voice was firmer now, reminding me of when I was a kid and he'd wanted to stop an argument in its tracks. "I don't care about any of that right now. You're here. That's what matters."

I blinked hard, fighting back the tears that threatened to spill. "Dad, I—"

"Listen to me." His eyes bore into mine through the thick glass. "The only thing I care about is you staying safe. These people, the ones behind all this? They're dangerous. More dangerous than you know."

I wanted to argue, to tell him I could handle it. But the look in his eyes stopped me cold. This wasn't just fatherly concern. This was fear. Real, bone-deep fear.

"Promise me," he said, his voice barely above a whisper. "Promise me you'll be careful. That you won't do anything reckless."

I swallowed hard and nodded. "I promise, Dad."

"Good." His shoulders relaxed down his spine. "Now, tell me about this case of yours. I want to hear every detail."

As I started talking, filling him in on the twists and turns of the trial, I couldn't shake the feeling that there was more he wasn't telling me. That beneath his resignation and his concern for my safety, there was something else. Something that scared him more than prison ever could.

But for now, I pushed those thoughts aside. My father wanted to hear about my life, about my work. And after all this time, after all the silences and missed visits, I owed him that much.

So I talked, and he listened, and for a little while, it felt almost normal. Almost like the old days, before everything went to hell.

The guard's voice cut through our conversation. "Five minutes, Hayes."

I nodded, then turned back to my father. "I'll be back soon, Dad. I swear."

He smiled, a real smile this time. "I know you will, kiddo."

As I walked away, his words echoed in my head. I had a lead now, but that lead might also have put a target on my back. The case had just gotten a lot bigger. And a lot more personal.

I stepped out of the prison, the weight of everything I'd learned pressing down on me. The sun was setting, casting long shadows across the parking lot. My hands were shaking as I got into my car.

This wasn't just about winning a case anymore. I started the engine, pulled out of the parking lot, and headed to my childhood home. I promised my father I'd be careful, but I wasn't going to be steamrolled any longer.

Let them come. Whoever it was, I was ready for a fight.

FORTY-FOUR

THE GRAVEL CRUNCHED under my tires as I pulled up the long driveway. My childhood home came into view through the trees, their leaves gently rustling with the wind. A floodlight flickered on, illuminating the familiar facade. It was like stepping into a time warp, the house unchanged since I'd last seen it over five years ago.

The place screamed 1970s, all brown stone on the bottom half giving way to wood paneling that climbed up to the angled rooflines. I knew without looking that the interior would match—a sea of wood paneling and shag carpeting frozen in time.

As a kid, I remembered how peaceful and quiet things were with just me and my father at home. We lived out in Dayton, about an hour's drive from the city. He did the commute everyday into work without complaint. Said he didn't want me growing up in the city. It was a sacrifice he'd made so that my younger years were surrounded by nature instead of buildings and asphalt. It was my safe haven.

But now, in the fading daylight, the place felt haunted, like some ghost of my past I was trying so hard to escape. I walked up to the front door and tried the handle. I wasn't sure why—obviously, it was locked. I looked under the mat, but the spare key was gone.

Out here in Dayton, houses were islands unto themselves, separated by stretches of overgrown land. I picked my way through the dense, unkempt path to Phyllis's house, feeling like an intruder to my past. The late afternoon sun was sinking fast as I rang her doorbell, willing her to be there.

The door swung open and there she was. She was shorter than I remembered, her steel-gray hair cut in a sensible bob. Laugh lines crinkled around her eyes as she broke into a wide smile.

"Alex!" She squeezed me into a hug before I could say anything, then looked me up and down with wide eyes. "My word, I haven't seen you in ages. Come in, come in!"

I tried to refuse, but Phyllis was having none of it. She ushered me inside with the practiced ease of a woman who'd spent decades corralling reluctant guests.

She led me to a well-worn sofa. "Please, have a seat. I'll go grab some refreshments!"

Nothing had changed in Phyllis's house. The same faded photographs adorned the walls and a musty scent of aged wood lingered in the air. It was as if time had stood still in this little pocket of the world.

"I can't believe it's been five years since you've been home," she said on her way back in. She placed a tray of cookies and iced tea on the coffee table in front of me. "Feels like yesterday you were out on the front lawn running around." She took a seat in the plush chair across from me, clearly seeing this as a time to catch up. "How have you been? What are you up to these days?"

"I, uh, went to law school," I said, perching on the edge of the intensely floral sofa cushion. "I'm working at the DA's office now."

Phyllis beamed. "That's wonderful! Your father must be so proud."

The mention of my dad brought me back to the reason for my visit. "Thanks for looking after his house, by the way. I really appreciate it."

"It's no trouble at all. How is he doing?"

"I think he's okay." I swallowed hard. "I mean, given the circumstances..."

Phyllis's face darkened. "I still can't believe what they did to him. Such a good man. It was obvious those charges were fake."

Guilt twisted in my gut like a knife. Had everyone believed in my father's innocence except for me?

"I went to see him just last month," Phyllis continued. "He seemed in good enough spirits then, considering."

The knife twisted deeper. Phyllis had been visiting my father while I'd stayed away for five years.

"I actually just came from there," I said, desperate to change the subject. "I need to get something for him from the house. Do you have the spare key?"

"Of course," Phyllis said, then rose to retrieve it from a nearby drawer. "Just return it when you can. I check on the place weekly, make sure no one's trying to move in or steal anything."

I thanked her and took the key. As we said our goodbyes, Phyllis mentioned she was heading to the store. "Just drop the key under the mat when you're done, dear. I'll grab it when I get back." She gave me one final hug. "It's good to see you. Please don't be a stranger."

I nodded and thanked her, then made my way back through the overgrown path to my childhood home. I stood before the front door, key in hand for several moments before I willed myself to move. The lock turned with a soft click, and I stepped inside.

The interior was a time capsule. Wood paneling everywhere, just as I'd predicted. Dad wasn't one to worry about renovations or having the next best thing. The furniture was all the same, down to the ugly blue couch he had loved so much. I'd expected the place to smell musty and abandoned, but it was clear Phyllis had been taking good care of it. The air was fresh, with just a hint of lemon cleaner.

I made my way to the kitchen, my footsteps echoing in the empty house. The junk drawer was where it had always been. I yanked it open, pawing through the accumulated detritus of years. At first, I saw nothing resembling a storage unit key. Frustrated, I all but emptied the drawer onto the counter.

Then, buried beneath a tangle of rubber bands and a pile of expired coupons, was a small Masterlock key. A scrap of paper with an address was taped to it. I scooped everything else back into the drawer, shoving it closed with more force than necessary.

I turned to leave, but before I knew it, I was walking down the hallway, toward my old room. The door was closed, just as I'd left it all those years ago. I hesitated, my hand on the knob. Did I really want to open this Pandora's box?

Curiosity ached in me, and I pushed the door open.

My room was a shrine to my teenage self. Posters of bands I'd forgotten I liked plastered the walls. Trophies from high school debate tournaments lined a shelf. My old computer sat on the desk, the tube monitor looking far too large for the space.

I walked over to the dresser, pulling open the top drawer. My journal was still there, exactly where I'd left it. I reached for it, then jerked my hand back as if burned.

Its contents included pages and pages of notes and letters to my mother. Words I'd had nowhere to send, no hope of a response. The pain of her absence surged up with surprising force, like a long-dormant volcano erupting from my core.

I slammed the drawer shut. Without a backward glance, I strode out of the room, pulling the door closed behind me. I walked straight out to my car, forcing thoughts of my mother back into the box where I'd kept them locked away for years.

FORTY-FIVE

MY PHONE BUZZED as I sped down the highway. Andrews' name flashed on the screen. I'd been dodging his calls all weekend, and I could practically feel his frustration radiating through the phone. With a sigh, I answered.

His voice came through as a mix of anger and relief. "Where the hell have you been?"

"I had to do something," I said, keeping my eyes on the road. "Needed a break from talking about this case for a moment."

"You couldn't have answered a call? Sent a text?" I could practically see him shaking his head through the phone. "I've been thinking the worst."

I felt a twinge of guilt. "I went to see my father."

The line went quiet for a moment. When Andrews spoke again, his tone had softened. "How'd that go?"

"It went," I said, not ready to unpack that emotional landmine. "Now I'm driving to some storage locker. He left some documents in there that might help clear his name and blow my case wide open."

Andrews was silent for a moment. "Are you sure about this, Hayes? Sounds like you might be heading down a rabbit hole."

"What choice do I have? If I don't look, and what he said is true... I can't take that chance. I feel like everyone's been lying to me. I need to figure out the truth for myself."

There was a long pause on the other end of the line. Then, "I'm coming with you."

I kept my tone firm when I said, "No."

"It's not up for discussion. Either you tell me where you're going, or I'm using the GPS tracker I put on your car to find out myself."

Anger flared through me, and I gripped the steering wheel tighter. "You put a tracker on my car?"

"Just tell me where you're going, Hayes."

After scolding him, I relented and gave him the address of the storage facility. As I pulled into the lot thirty minutes later, I took in the rundown appearance of the place. Rows of rusted metal doors stretched out before me, the paint peeling and faded. The air of neglect crawled against my skin.

Andrews' car pulled up beside mine, and he got out, a smirk on his face.

I didn't return his amusement. "Show me where you put the tracker."

He laughed. "There isn't one. I was bluffing to get you to tell me where you were going."

I gawked at him. "I can't believe you."

We walked to the locker number indicated on the slip of paper attached to the key. An old, rusted Masterlock kept the door shut. I inserted the key and tried twisting, but it wouldn't budge. I took it out and tried again but to no avail.

"Let me try," Andrews said. He took the key from my hand, inserted it, and tried twisting. It wouldn't budge at first, but with a grunt of effort and a sturdier grip, he managed to force it open.

The door rolled up with a screech of protest, revealing a jumble of old furniture. I recognized a broken dining table from my childhood, along with other odds and ends—boxes of Christmas decorations, a moth-eaten armchair, and stacks of yellowing newspapers. In the corner, partially obscured by a dusty sheet, stood a filing cabinet. Its metal surface was rusted, a relic of another time, just like everything else in this storage unit.

We stepped inside, and my lungs protested against the dusty air, compelling me to cough. I made my way to the corner of the locker stepping over old board games and covered boxes. I tugged at the filing cabinet drawers, but they were all locked.

"Was there another key?" Andrews asked.

I shook my head. "My father didn't mention one."

Andrews eyed the cabinet, then glanced back at me. "You care about keeping this thing intact?"

"Not really, why?"

"Stand outside the locker."

"What? Why?"

"Just do it."

Huffing in annoyance, I complied. A moment later, a gunshot rang out. The bullet pounded against a metal surface and echoed through the unit, making me jump and let out a startled yelp. I whirled around to see Andrews grinning. The cabinet was now open.

I strode back to the cabinet and smacked his shoulder. "Are you insane?"

He shrugged. "Got the job done, didn't it?" Although, he rubbed his ears from the noise.

Carefully avoiding the jagged metal edges from Andrews' impromptu lockpicking, I began rifling through the cabinet's contents. Old utility invoices, tax documents—nothing relevant. Frustration began to build as I realized this might have all been for nothing.

Then Andrews pulled something from the bottom drawer. "This what you're looking for?"

We moved to the battered dining table, positioning ourselves so that the tiny bit of light filtering in from the doorway illuminated the contents. Slowly, Andrews opened the folder.

"This is..." I began, my voice a whisper.

Andrews nodded. "Exactly what you need."

We spread out the contents of the folder across the top of the broken dining table. The more we read, the quieter we became.

There were handwritten notes from the mayor, detailing specific "tasks" to be completed. These weren't vague allusions or coded messages, but explicit instructions for intimidating a rival businessman of Ed Martin. Locations, times, even methods of intimidation were spelled out in black and white.

"Look at this one," I said, passing one of the notes to Andrews. It looked like notes from a phone call.

Clearwater Construction - CEO, Doug Delgado

Call Monday at 0800, untraceable. Mention family (wife Linda daughter Jessica son Mitchell)

Arrange meeting Tuesday 2200. Warehouse 5th & Maple

Drop out of bid for new town center

Contact DA after

"Holy shit," Andrews muttered.

"DA?" I stared at the page. "You think it could be Tom?"

Andrews shook his head, as if to say he didn't know. I put the page down and turned to the next pile.

Printed copies of email exchanges between Mayor Thompson and Ed Martin painted an even clearer picture of corruption. They discussed payments, coordination of illegal activities, and specific instances where they had worked together to eliminate threats or secure business advantages. The language was coded but with context, it was easy to decipher. References to "projects" and "events" were clearly criminal activities.

Subject: Town Center Bid

From: Ed Martin (ed.martin@martincorp.com)

To: Henry Thompson (mayor@houstoncity.gov)

Henry,

Regarding our upcoming construction project, I wanted to ensure that everything is on track. I've noticed some unexpected competition from Clearview Construction. It would be beneficial if our usual precautions were taken to ensure smooth progress.

Best,

Ed

From: Henry Thompson (mayor@houstoncity.gov)
To: Ed Martin (ed.martin@martincorp.com)
Ed,
I understand your concerns. Rest assured we will handle the situation as per
our established protocols. I've confirmed with DA that everything is in place.
Regards,
Henry

Then there were photographs. A few snapshots of a middle-aged man standing outside an office building. Above his head, the sign read, "Clearwater Construction." Ed's competition and the target of this job. There were also photographs of this man with his family— likely the wife and kids mentioned in the handwritten note, and what they planned to use for intimidation.

Andrews and I looked at each other.

"We need to get these to Erin," Andrews said.

I shook my head. "Not yet. The moment we hand these over, Erin's going to do whatever she wants with them. She'll cut us out of any leverage, just like she did with Ramirez."

"Okay," Andrews said slowly. "So what's the plan?"

"We need to find out what happened to the owner of these documents. And fast."

FORTY-SIX

I SAT across from Andrews at his desk. It was late Saturday afternoon, so the precinct wasn't that busy. The last thing we wanted was some overeager rookie catching wind of what we were digging into.

Andrews sifted through arrest records, trying to find the arrest my father made that started this downward spiral. I had my laptop open and was reading up on Doug Delgado and Clearview Construction.

"Got something," I said. Andrews looked up from his screen. "Article about Clearview Construction. Says they were on the verge of bankruptcy after trying to switch to commercial projects. Shocked everyone since they'd been doing so well. But they weren't able to get any new projects. They ended up going back to residential. Still in operation today, but obviously not as big as Martin Corp." I rested my chin in my hand. "Maybe we should pay Doug a visit, see if he knows anything.

Andrews frowned. "Is that smart? He might not even know he was a target. We could end up scaring him for no reason."

"We can be careful about what we say. Feel him out first."

He nodded slowly. "Alright."

"He's got a showroom downtown," I said, scrolling through his company website. "Looks like it's open today. Maybe he'll be there."

Andrews' attention returned to his computer. "I found the arrest record. Your dad was on patrol with Ramirez when they pulled someone over. Routine traffic stop." He squinted at the screen. "Guy's name was Christopher Lopez."

"What happened to him?"

Andrews' brow furrowed as he pulled up inmate records. "Says here he died while being transferred from JPC to another jail awaiting trial."

I blinked. "That doesn't make sense. Why transfer him? JPC's where they hold people for preliminary hearings and arraignment. Did he even have those?"

"Doesn't look like it," Andrews said, scanning the file. "Says he was having some kind of medical issue. They had to transport him to Huntsville State Penitentiary."

I shook my head. "No, that's not right. I dealt with a case where an inmate in JPC sued the county for failure to provide medical care. Guy was having epileptic seizures, and JPC's medical facility couldn't handle it. They didn't transfer him somewhere else, they just took him to the local hospital."

Andrews shrugged, looking as confused as I felt.

"Is there a coroner's report?" I asked.

He clicked a few times, then nodded. He got up and grabbed the document from the printer.

We both leaned in, scanning the report. "Cause of death: acute myocardial infarction," I read aloud. "What did the records say he was having an issue with originally?"

"Severe abdominal pain," Andrews said, double-checking his screen.

"That doesn't add up," I said, the pieces refusing to fit together. "Why transfer him for abdominal pain and then have him die of a heart attack? Whose name is on this report?"

Andrews squinted at the bottom of the page. "Dr. Elena Vasquez."

A chill ran down my spine. "I know that name."

He glanced at me. "Is there a problem with her?"

"She's in charge of the coroner's office. I'm gonna have to talk to Palmer about this. See what he thinks." I paused. "What did it say he was arrested for?"

"Your father noted that he matched the description of a B&E suspect."

"Right. He mentioned that to me this morning."

Andrews shut his computer, his expression shifting. "Alex, what if this wasn't just some medical situation gone wrong? What if Lopez was actually killed for what he knew?"

The question hung in the air, heavy with implications. I realized I hadn't let myself think that far ahead. "I... I don't know."

Andrews leaned in, lowering his voice. "We need to think this through. I know you don't want to hand this over to Erin yet, but we need to be careful about keeping things from the feds."

I ran a hand through my hair, frustration bubbling up. "I want to be sure I can clear my father's name first. If I can't... then yeah, we turn everything over to Erin. But if we do that now, she'll cut a deal and cut me out completely."

"You really think she'd do that?"

"Absolutely. She already tried once with Ramirez."

"Aren't you two supposed to be friends?"

"We're lawyers first."

Andrews shook his head. "Glad I'm not a lawyer."

"Wish I could say the same," I grumbled as we gathered our things.

Andrews rolled his eyes at me. "Oh, stop. You're having fun."

I scoffed. "What's fun about trying a man for his wife's murder, who's possibly tied to high-ranking officials in a conspiracy involving blackmail, embezzlement, and maybe even framing my father for something he uncovered during a routine traffic stop?"

He blinked at me. "All of it?"

Now it was my turn to roll my eyes. "You're driving."

"Where to first?"

"Clearview Construction. Let's see if we can catch Doug before he leaves."

"Are we going in as ourselves or are we posing as a couple who want to buy a house together?"

I gave him a look. "You? Me? A couple?"

He shrugged.

"No. Let's just go as ourselves."

"Suit yourself, counselor."

"What's with the tone?"

He laughed. "What tone?"

I waved my hand as we walked out the door toward the car. "The tone you just used."

"I just think it's funny that you get a chance to pretend to be something else and you still choose to be a lawyer. Like I said, you love it."

"Don't test your luck, Andrews," I said, climbing into the passenger seat.

"Against you?" he asked. "I wouldn't dream of it."

FORTY-SEVEN

WE PULLED up to the showroom just as the sun was sinking below the horizon, hues of deep orange and red filling the sky. The place sat on the north side of the I-610 Loop, a collection of miniature model homes dotting the front lawn like a suburban dollhouse display. With only ten minutes until closing, the parking lot was nearly empty, save for two cars out front.

Inside, we found Doug Delgado talking to a young couple. He looked just like the photos, albeit with a touch more gray at the temples. As the couple passed us on their way out, Doug approached us, all smiles and salesman charm.

"Interested in looking at some models?" he asked.

Andrews and I flashed our badges. "Actually, Mr. Delgado, we'd like to speak with you if you have a moment."

The smile faltered. "Am I in trouble? Should I call my lawyer?"

"We're investigating someone else," I said. "We just have some questions about what happened to your business a few years back."

Doug hesitated, then went to flip the sign in the window from "Open" to "Closed" before leading us to a nearby table. We all sat down, Andrews and I side by side with Doug taking the chair on the opposite side.

Wariness etched every line of the man's face. "What do you want to know?"

I dove right in. "Five years ago, you made the switch to building and selling commercial real estate. It almost bankrupted you. What happened?"

Pain flickered across Doug's features. He likely hadn't expected to talk about his business's past tonight, if ever. "Business was booming. We had investors encouraging us to move into commercial. But when we started bidding on projects... nothing. We'd slowed down our residential side to focus on what we thought was a sure thing. We were burning through cash fast."

"Why do you think you weren't getting any projects?"

Doug's jaw tightened. "One of our lenders tried calling in a loan that wasn't due for a decade. The few residential projects we had left suddenly couldn't get permits. When we did get permits, inspectors swarmed the place. For the sake of my business—my sanity—I let that dream die and went back to what I knew was safe."

"So, you think someone was out to get you?" I asked.

"I don't see any other explanation."

"Any idea who might've been behind it?"

"Never found out for sure. But Martin Corp was getting most of the commercial business. I always assumed it had something to do with them." A bitter laugh escaped him. "Can't say I'm surprised the man's on trial for murder."

My ears perked up. "What do you mean?"

Doug sighed. "I was getting voicemails. Threatening ones. Not overt, but... I could read between the lines."

"Do you still have those voicemails?" I asked, trying to keep the eagerness out of my voice.

Doug's eyes darted between Andrews and me. "Look, I don't want any trouble. I've got a wife, kids. I'm happy with my life now. I don't want to stir things up again."

I leaned forward. "I understand. But those recordings could be crucial. I promise, we'll keep your name out of it."

After a long moment, Doug nodded. "Wait here."

As he disappeared into a back office, Andrews and I exchanged glances. "Think the calls will be enough?" Andrews asked. "It's just a voice, and Doug doesn't want to get involved."

"Anything extra is worth getting at this point," I replied.

Doug returned with a USB drive. "The voicemails and everything I investigated are on here. But this is it. I don't want to be contacted about this again."

We thanked him and left. In Andrews' car, I suggested we pull into a nearby gas station to check out the contents of the drive.

I popped the USB into my laptop and quickly scanned the files. "There's more than just voicemails. Copies of Clearview's bids, and Martin Corp's bids for the same projects."

"What do you make of them?"

I frowned. "I'm no expert in construction, but it looks like Clearview should've won the work. Their bids were better priced."

Andrews shrugged. "A lot can go into those decisions."

"Yeah, but on its face, it doesn't look right."

I clicked on one of the audio files, and a man's voice filled the car.

"Hey Doug, it's Henry. Listen, I've been hearing some things around town, you know how it is. Word gets out. There's a lot of interest in that town center bid you put in. A lot of interest. Now, I respect your ambition, I really do, but sometimes it's best to step back from certain... opportunities. You never know what kind of trouble might come knocking if you keep pushing forward on this one. People get protective about their investments, Doug. It's a small community, and we all look out for each other. Just a friendly piece of advice: reconsider your position. You wouldn't want to find yourself tangled up in something unpleasant. Take care now."

Andrews and I stared at each other, his expression of shock likely resembling my own.

"You think that's Henry as in Henry Thompson?" Andrews asked, his voice barely above a whisper.

"Who else could it be?"

The implications were staggering. Henry Thompson, the mayor of our city, caught on tape making thinly veiled threats. This wasn't just corruption anymore. This was organized crime masked with a smile and a handshake.

I took a deep breath, trying to steady my nerves. "We need to go through everything on this drive. Every recording, every document. There might be more in here."

Andrews nodded. "What about Erin? We're sitting on evidence that implicates the mayor. That's way above our pay grade."

I hesitated. He had a point, but something held me back. "Not yet. We need to connect a few more dots first. If we can tie this directly to my father's case, to Ed Martin, to Tom... then we'll have something solid to take to her."

"And if we can't?"

"Then we hand it all over and hope she doesn't cut us out completely."

The trial resumed on Monday, and the clock was ticking. We had two nights to unravel years of corruption, clear my father's name, and stay alive in the process.

Piece of cake.

FORTY-EIGHT

AS I STUMBLED into the coffee shop, the smell of freshly brewed espresso hit me, but it did little to shake the heavy fog clouding my mind. The wooden door creaked behind me, the sound jarring in the quiet morning hum. I shuffled over to the counter, my feet dragging across the tile floor, and then slumped into a chair near the window. Outside, people passed by, completely unaware of the chaos swirling in my head. I'd been up all night, unable to sleep. Most of the night I lay awake, staring at the slow, hypnotic spin of my ceiling fan, trying to piece together the tangled web of lies everyone had fed me. The bitter taste of betrayal lingered in my throat.

I couldn't stop seeing my father—his once vibrant, warm smile contrasted with the broken man I'd visited in prison. The system had crushed him, and for what? A crime he may not have even committed? I looked around the café, spotting Palmer at the back. He was sitting in the corner in a wingback chair, sipping a steaming cup of coffee. In the middle of summer. I found it strange, but then again, the man spent his days in a freezer with dead bodies. Maybe his internal temperature was skewed by all the time he spent in the morgue. Drinking hot coffee in the heat was probably the least odd thing about him.

Palmer's eyebrows shot up as he saw me. "You look like hell."

"You always did know how to charm women," I said, collapsing into the velvet sofa across from him.

I'd called him last night, but he'd insisted on meeting here instead of the office. "Need a day away from dead bodies for my sanity," he'd said. "Andrews joining us?"

"Should be along soon." I mumbled.

The café was your typical Starbucks knock-off—all faux-artisanal décor and overpriced pastries. Palmer leaned in, his voice low. "So what's up? Sounded urgent on the phone."

I didn't waste any time. "What can you tell me about Elena Vasquez?"

Palmer shrugged. "My boss. I don't interact with her much, to be honest. Everyone pretty much does their own work."

Andrews arrived then and exchanged greetings with Palmer. I continued, figuring Andrews would catch on. "Is she still solid at exams? Or has she maybe been in leadership too long, lost her edge?"

Palmer's brow furrowed. "What do you mean? She doesn't do exams."

"Clarify that for me?"

"In her position, she never does exams. She's not even qualified. She's just the office manager—hands out assignments and such. Business degree, not medical."

Andrews and I exchanged a look. I pulled out the coroner's report and slid it across the table. Palmer's eyes widened as he read it.

"This doesn't make sense," he said. "She can't do exams. Where did you find this? Who's it for?" We hesitated, and Palmer's frustration grew. "Come on, you've got to tell me something."

I sighed. "It's a long story, but we think it might be part of a cover up. Someone who was silenced for knowing too much. You know the cliché."

Palmer blinked. "Why are you focusing on this now? Aren't you tied up with the Martin trial?"

"It's possible it could relate."

"What proof do you have?"

"I know it sounds far-fetched, but things like this keep popping up. " I hesitated before asking, "Think Vasquez would talk to us?"

Palmer snorted. "Highly unlikely she'll answer her phone on the weekend. Not everyone's as amazing as me."

I forced a smile. "Yes, yes, you're a paragon of virtue."

Palmer took a sip of his coffee. "What's your next move?"

"We're at a dead end," I said. "It sounds outrageous, but it looks like Ed and the mayor are neck-deep in a corruption scandal. Intimidating rivals, embezzling city funds. The works."

Palmer whistled low. "That's a hell of an accusation."

"Which is why we're trying to figure it all out before going public."

"I wish I could be more help, but that's about all I know."

"Thanks," I said.

As Andrews and I left the café, he turned to me. "Why didn't you mention Tom?"

"I'm not sure about him yet. Can we really trust Ramirez? Besides, Palmer seems skeptical."

"Wouldn't you be if this was the first time someone suggested the mayor was having people assassinated?"

"Touché."

He shook his head. "I still think you should have mentioned Tom. Maybe he would have known something that connected the dots."

We got into the car. "What's a medical examiner going to know?"

"I don't know," Andrews said, starting the engine. "What about Janice showing up at the storage locker looking for that recording? You still can't answer how it got deleted."

"Tom said that was because he heard I'd talked to Ramirez."

Andrews frowned. "And the things Tom said to Ramirez before he took the stand?"

I sighed. "Did you actually hear anything concrete? Or are we just hearing what we want to hear?"

Andrews conceded the point. "So what now?"

"Let's go back to Ramirez," I said. "See what we can shake loose with this new info. Maybe drop the name Chris Lopez."

The drive to JPC was mostly silent. Both of us were in our own heads, trying to figure out whether we were chasing ghosts.

Once parked and inside the jail, Andrews flashed his badge at the guard at the check-in desk. "Here to see Louis Ramirez."

The guard typed something into his computer and then shook his head.

"Ramirez had a medical emergency. He's been transferred."

Andrews and I exchanged alarmed glances. "Where?" I demanded.

"Huntsville."

Andrews pulled me aside. "That's the same place they took Chris."

"Shit," I cursed. "I hate to say this, but we need to tell Erin."

"What about her cutting you out of a deal?"

I shook my head. "There won't be any deal if Ramirez ends up dead."

We sped toward Erin's hotel, the car weaving through traffic. My heart thundered in my chest, each second stretching longer than the last. I gripped the edge of my seat, glancing at the clock and mentally calculating how long it would take to get there. Too long. Every red light felt like an eternity, the tension building as dread gnawed at the back of my mind.

By the time we screeched into the hotel parking lot, I could barely contain my panic. I ran up to her door, hammering on it with my fist. The door opened quickly, Erin standing on the other side with wide eyes, her expression a mix of confusion and alarm at the sight of me.

"What's going on?" she asked, breathless, as if sensing the urgency.

"I think Ramirez is about to be killed."

The words hung in the air, heavy with implication. Erin's eyes widened, and for a moment, the fa[]ade of the tough federal prosecutor cracked. She ushered us inside, closing the door with a soft click.

"Start from the beginning," she said, her voice low and intense. "And don't leave anything out."

As Andrews and I laid out everything we'd uncovered—the documents from my father's storage unit, Doug Delgado's story, the suspicious death of Chris Lopez, and now Ramirez's convenient "transfer"—I could see the gravity of the situation sinking in for Erin.

"Jesus Christ," she muttered, running a hand through her hair. "This goes way deeper than we thought."

"And now Ramirez is in danger. We need to move fast."

Erin was already on her phone, barking orders to someone on the other end. "I want a protection detail on Ramirez now. I don't care about jurisdiction. Make it happen."

She turned back to us, her eyes blazing with a mix of anger and determination. "You two have been sitting on a powder keg. Do you have any idea how dangerous this is?"

"We do now," Andrews said.

Erin paced the room. "Okay, here's what we're going to do. I'm calling in every favor I have to get Ramirez secured. You two are going to give me every scrap of evidence you've collected. And then you're going to stay put while I figure out how to keep you both alive."

I started to protest, but Erin cut me off. "This isn't a negotiation. You've stumbled into something much bigger than you realize. The kind of thing that gets people killed."

FORTY-NINE

"YOU'RE BEING PARANOID, ERIN." I grabbed my bag, casting a sidelong glance at the darkened windows. "This whole case has been a publicity circus. No one is going to try and attack me while the whole city is watching."

"That's precisely why I'm concerned," she said, worry etched in her features. "High stakes breed desperation."

I moved toward the hotel door, my hand resting on the knob. "What do you honestly think is going to happen?"

She stayed quiet and kept her eyes trained on me.

"If you can give me a solid reason, I'll stay."

"Isn't the Lopez murder enough? And Ramirez being transferred?"

"They're actual hitmen. I'm just a lawyer working the case."

"You're a high-profile target," Erin said.

I narrowed my eyes at her. "I think you know something. I think you know something and you're not telling me, which is exactly what this entire trial has been. You holding information back from me, and letting me do your dirty work for your own investigation."

Erin stepped in front of me. "Alex, please. I'm asking you to stay—"

"Just tell me," I said, my voice softer. "What are you not telling me?"

She averted her gaze.

"Then I'm leaving."

Before Erin could respond, Andrews' voice broke the tension. "I'll go with you." I turned to find him leaning against the doorframe, hands tucked into his pockets. His jaw was set and a familiar stubbornness glinted in his eyes.

"That's really not necessary—"

"Wasn't a question." He straightened and gave me a glare that said, *Don't argue.*

I shot one last skeptical glance at Erin. "Fine."

Andrews grabbed his keys, and we stormed out of the hotel room, letting the door slam behind us. Andrews' footsteps echoed behind me.

"She's using you," Andrews said as the elevator doors closed on us.

"Tell me something I don't know," I said. "She's been the catalyst for this entire ordeal. She shows up when I'm assigned the case and drops me documents and photos with no explanation, tells me I can't introduce them as evidence, and leads me down a rabbit hole of secrets and lies." I ran a hand through my hair, my frustration mounting. "I'm tired of following the breadcrumb trail she's set out for me."

The elevator doors opened, and we walked through the lobby and out to Andrews' car. I slid into the passenger seat.

"Cryptic evidence, wild conspiracies." I shook my head. "She's always had an angle. Even in law school. I remember one time she pretended to lose an important study guide just to watch the rest of us scramble to make sense of the exam prep on our own. She turned up with the guide an hour before the test, of course, claiming she 'found' it." I sighed at the memory. "I'm tired of being a pawn in whatever game she's playing."

Andrews started the car and drove off, putting Erin's hotel in the rearview. I stared out the window and took a moment to catch my breath. The city lights flickered by, casting a muted glow on the passing streets. The hum of the engine and the occasional honk of distant traffic filled the silence between us. Storefronts whizzed past, their signs glowing brightly in the early evening. Pedestrians moved along the sidewalks, heads down and focused, while buildings loomed above, their windows reflecting the soft amber of streetlights.

"Maybe it really is as simple as an angry man killing his wife," I said. "And she's got me thinking it's some sort of grassy knoll situation in the making."

Andrews was quiet for a long time. When he finally spoke, his words were measured. "I've learned to trust my instincts over the years. And it feels like someone is trying to cover their tracks. Since the start, nothing has fallen into line like a normal investigation should." He trailed off, leaving the unspoken to hang between us.

"Is it that? Or, have you been tricked into seeing what isn't really there?"

"Then how do you explain the bank records? The notes in the filing cabinet? Your father's arrest?"

"Think about it. At trial, there is only one truth. Either a defendant did commit the crime, or they did not. But one side is trying to trick twelve people into believing their story. I bet you they get it wrong more than they get it right, and we just never know."

Andrews made a noncommittal grunt and silence filled the rest of the drive. He pulled the car up to my neighborhood and arched an eyebrow at me. "You think Ed did it? Because his wife was going to leave him and he didn't want to give her the chance?"

I placed my palm on the door handle. "That's what I'm arguing."

"Maybe it's 13 people, then."

I gave him a confused look.

"Twelve jurors and one lawyer can be tricked into thinking the wrong thing."

"You think Ed's innocent?" I asked incredulously.

"I honestly couldn't tell you."

"Then let's hope I'm a convincing liar." I got out of the car, letting the door slam shut behind me.

"You've never been a convincing liar," Andrews murmured, as he closed his door.

I marched up the steps to my door. Andrews followed behind me, his gaze darting around as if he thought someone would jump out of the bushes and shoot us.

"You're making me anxious." I said, putting my key in the door.

"Even if she's using you, I don't think you should completely discount what Erin said just because you're angry with her," Andrews said. "She's calling a security detail out for Ramirez. Someone's likely to trace that back to us."

He looked down at our feet and bent down to retrieve the small package. "Did you order something from Amazon?"

I pushed the door open, grabbed the package, and led him inside. "Honestly, I can't even remember." I tossed the thing on the counter and turned to him. "Thanks for the escort, but I'll be fine from here."

"That's great," he said. "I'm still staying."

I opened my mouth to argue and Andrews' mouth curved in a wry smile. "You're always trying to argue with me. How's that work out for you?"

With a martyred sigh, I conceded defeat. "Fine. Hope you like the couch."

"Love it."

"I'm ordering us something to eat. I'm starving." I stood in the kitchen on my phone. "You like sushi?" I asked.

"Can you get me a spicy tuna roll?"

I nodded and placed the order, then tossed my phone on the counter, wincing at the way it clattered.

I grabbed the package and sliced through the white vinyl wrap with a pair of scissors. Inside was a cheap thumb drive and a torn scrap of paper. Four scrawled words leered up at me.

Caroline knew too much.

"Alex?" He turned, and upon seeing me, got up and rushed over. I handed him the note without a word.

I watched him read it, and the color drained from his face.

Without a word, we made our way to my computer. I slotted the drive home and tried to push down the nausea threatening to move up my throat. The drive lit up and a folder appeared on my desktop labeled "Caroline Martin."

I double-clicked it.

Inside were two more folders. One labeled "Video" and one labeled "Photos."

I clicked into the video folder. Inside was just one file, named May 19th. It was the estimated time of death for Caroline.

My hand shook. I double clicked the icon. The video started to play.

The video was from the perspective of Ed Martin's driveway. It was obviously from the camera attached to the floodlight on the house. A minute went by, and nothing happened. Then, at 9:35 a.m., Ed's white Mercedes G350 pulled into the driveway.

He didn't get out of the vehicle right away. Instead, he waited. "What is he—" I began to say, but then a second car approached. An unmarked black Suburban. Ed got out of his car, and two men got out of the Suburban.

The two men in the Suburban were wearing black hats and leather gloves. One of them was wearing a ski mask, completely obscuring their identity. The other hadn't been so smart.

"Holy shit," I said. "That's Elijah Harper."

"Who?" Andrews asked.

"The electrician," I said. "The one in jail for hitting his wife."

Andrews whistled and we continued to watch.

Ed walked into the home using the front door. He left it open. The masked man followed him in after about two minutes. Harper made his way over to the garage, disappearing through the side door.

Nothing happened for about ten minutes. After that, the masked man walked back out to the car and got in. Harper followed. The driver backed the Suburban out of the driveway and drove off.

A few minutes later, Ed exited the house and put his phone to his ear. Eleven minutes later, police cars arrived, and Ramirez stepped out of one in his uniform.

The video ended at 10:46 a.m.

"Do you think Ramirez..." Andrews' thought trailed off, but I knew what he was asking. Did Ramirez actually kill Caroline? Had he been telling the truth after all?

"I don't know," I said. I clicked on the photos folder.

Inside were three files.

I clicked the first and gasped. It was a close-up shot through the window. Ed was dragging Caroline up to the bedroom, one hand on her neck and the other gripped under her arm.

"The bruising on her neck," I muttered under my breath.

The second photo was now of the masked man standing over her, pressing down on her neck, wearing leather gloves. She was reaching up to try and stop him. Ed stood in the background with a calm expression, his arms crossed.

The third photo was through the side window of the garage. Only Harper's back was visible, but it was unmistakably him, fiddling with wires in the security system cabinet.

I closed all the files, copied the drive's contents onto my computer, and properly ejected the disk before placing the USB on the table in front of us. We both stared at it for a beat, not saying a word.

Andrews' voice finally broke the silence. "Do you think these are real?"

I stared at the thumb drive resting on the desk in front of me. "I don't know," I admitted. "But we need to find out."

"How are we going to do that?" Andrews asked.

I grabbed the device and then my keys. "I'm driving. You coming?"

He sighed. "I guess this means no spicy tuna roll."

FIFTY

"WHERE ARE WE GOING?" Andrews asked for the third time.

I sighed for the third time. "I told you, I know someone who's good with computers. We need to make sure this footage is legitimate."

"And how do you know this person?"

"That's not important right now." I kept my eyes fixed on the road ahead, the streetlights casting fleeting shadows across the dashboard. My grip tightened on the steering wheel, trying to ignore the weight of Andrews' questions. I didn't think it was worth sharing that this kid owed me a favor because I'd been unprepared and let him off at his preliminary hearing.

"And, we're supposed to trust them with this information, why?"

"Can I just vouch for him and we leave it at that?" My voice was firm, but inside, I could feel the unease creeping in.

Andrews' face contorted. I could tell it hurt for him to give in on this. The man excelled at interrogation. We shared that in common. "Fine," he huffed, settling into the passenger seat.

My headlights switched on, and I weaved my way through the back streets, going mostly by memory. I finally pulled the car up to Campo's apartment. I stepped out and approached the front door. Andrews followed.

I knocked. "Open up. It's Hayes."

The door swung open on the second knock. Campo's brow furrowed in confusion. "What're you doing here?"

"I need your help."

He gave me a skeptical look.

"You know, the more you act like you've got something to hide, the more I think you're hiding something."

He just looked at me, blinking. I huffed. "This isn't about you. It's something else. Can we come in?"

He studied me for a moment. Then, with a slight nod, he stepped aside. We walked in and Andrews looked around at the cluttered wires and computers. He gave me a look but I ignored him.

"What is it you need?" Campo asked, leading us into the living room. His tone was guarded, but I could understand his apprehension.

I reached into my pocket, pulled out the USB drive, and held it out to him. "I need you to take a look at this."

He took the drive and turned it over in his hand.

"This was dropped on my doorstep, and I need to know if the footage and photographs on it have been altered in any way."

Without a word, he moved to the computer in the corner of the room and plugged the drive into the port. I followed closely, Andrews hovering just behind me.

As Campo began sifting through the contents, his expression remained neutral, betraying none of his thoughts. The only sound in the room was the soft hum of the computer and the rhythmic tapping of his fingers on the keyboard.

After what felt like an eternity, he turned to face me, the USB drive in his outstretched hand. "It's all legitimate," he said, his voice low and measured. "As far as I can tell, the footage and photos haven't been tampered with or generated by AI for that matter."

I let out a breath, relief and trepidation warring within me. "And the contents? Can you tell who it belongs to or anything about the source?"

Campo shook his head slowly. "No, it's all been wiped clean on that end. There's no identifying information that I can find."

Nodding, I reached out and took the drive from him. "Thank you."

"Next time call me before you show up in the middle of the evening," Campo said in a lighthearted tone. "Every time you knock on the door it gets my heart thumping."

"Our relationship is strictly platonic," I said and he laughed.

Andrews and I left the apartment. As I started my car, I caught a shift in Andrews' expression.

"What are you going to do with that information?" he asked.

I backed the car out of the driveway and started to drive back to my house. I stared straight ahead at the road. "I'm going to do the right thing."

"Is that so?"

I nodded. "And I'm probably going to get fired for it."

"Guess I gotta start looking for another assistant district attorney to work with." I caught Andrews' smirk out of the corner of my eye. "I wonder if Coop will team up with me."

"Replacing me so fast?"

"No one can replace you, Hayes."

I couldn't help the way my face warmed. "Don't go all sentimental on me now."

"I'm not. I'm just saying that your brand of crazy will be hard to replace."

I let out a laugh and allowed the last few weeks' tension to melt.

We entered my driveway and promptly hopped out after I turned the engine off. Andrews saw the white takeout bag in front of my door after we trudged up the stairs. "Hope this is sushi and not the severed hand from a cold case or something."

I wrinkled my nose at him. "Gross."

He opened the bag as soon as we got inside, mock-sighing with relief. "It's just raw fish."

"Thank goodness," I replied, kicking off my shoes.

He handed me my plastic containers and a pair of chopsticks and we sank into the couch.

After more than a minute of him staring at me while he ate his spicy tuna roll, I finally couldn't take it anymore. I met him with a glare. "What?"

He shrugged. "What's the plan now, counselor?"

"I told you, I'm going to do the right thing."

"Which is?"

I took another bite, hoping I could figure out an answer in the time it took to chew. I couldn't. "I'm still trying to figure that out, but obviously Martin wasn't the one to kill his wife."

"Aiding and abetting, though. Carries the same sentence."

I nodded. Most people didn't realize that whether you murdered someone or helped someone murder someone, it often carried the same sentence. For that matter, conspiring to murder someone was also punishable to the same degree.

"He should be charged with the right crime," I said. "If he goes down for her murder, then Ramirez walks for it."

"Sounds like someone is trying to make sure Ramirez lies down for the rest of his life."

I gave him a look.

"You know, like in the dirt."

"Yeah, I got it. I'm just not sure this is a situation for jokes."

"That's because your humor isn't dark enough yet," Andrews said between bites. "I've been trying to work on that with you."

"Sorry if I'm not in a joking mood after watching someone murder a woman."

Andrews shrugged. "You're forgiven."

I gave him another look.

"Oh, come on," he said. "Lighten up. Everything is gonna be fine."

"How can you say that?"

He put his food down and reached across the table. He grabbed my hand before I could snatch it away. "I know you're upset. Just know that I'm with you, whatever you decide."

I stared at him for a moment, not hating the way my hand felt in his. The ringing of my phone interrupted the moment and made me jump. I shot Andrews an apologetic look before answering. He went back to his tuna roll. "Hello?"

"Alex, it's Erin." Her voice was laced with urgency. "Ramirez is safe for now. He's been put in solitary for his protection."

"Protection from what?" I asked. "Did you figure out who's after him?"

"I can't say much more right now," Erin replied, her tone cautious. "Just that he's safe. I'll see you at trial tomorrow."

She ended the call before I could ask anything else. Andrews raised a brow. "Didn't tell her about the USB, huh?"

I shook my head, tucking the phone back into my pocket. "It's better if she doesn't know everything right now. Too much is still at stake." I closed my eyes, and the video footage played on my eyelids. "It was him," I mumbled.

"What?" Andrews asked.

"The masked man," I said, my eyes widening. "It was Ramirez. It has to be."

Andrews considered this, then nodded slowly. "I trust your instinct on this one. It's usually right."

I hoped that was true.

FIFTY-ONE

I PULLED into the courthouse parking lot, Andrews silent beside me. I cut the engine, but didn't move to get out of the car.

"You ready for this?" Andrews asked, his voice low.

I tapped my fingers against the leather armrest. " I'm not sure. But it's not like I have a choice."

"You always have a choice."

I turned to look at him and shook my head. "I don't think that's true."

He held my gaze but didn't say anything.

We got out and walked toward the courthouse. Even first thing in the morning, the sun was already suffocating. Or maybe that was my anxiety.

It didn't help that the press was swarming en masse, microphones thrust toward Tom as he stood at a podium. It'd been a minute since I'd seen him agree to a press conference. A heads-up would have been nice.

"We are very confident the jury will return a guilty verdict..." Tom was saying. "With the defense starting their case today, we are prepared to refute any claims they make. Justice will be served."

I climbed the steps, and the reporters turned their attention to me.

I squinted at the harsh light as I tried to look at them. Tom stepped aside, giving me space at the microphone.

"Are you ready for the defense to begin their case?" one reporter called out.

I leaned in, and said, "No comment at this time," then pushed past the crowd into the building. I could hear Tom try and smooth over my "no comment" as the press clamored behind me.

Tom caught up with me in the lobby and pulled me to the side. "What the hell was that? This is our chance to sway public opinion before the defense muddies the waters."

I studied him for a moment. If I told him my plan, he would try to stop me. There was no way I could involve him in this decision. It was obvious he cared more about election politics than he did the truth. I didn't trust him.

"It's nothing, Tom." I hoped my voice sounded steadier than it felt. "I just need to focus on the defense's case now. Can't afford any distractions."

I moved past him into the courtroom.

"You could act like you want to win this case," he called out behind me. I didn't turn around to respond.

Lisa was already at the counsel table. She wore the same smile she always had on. But ever since the recording incident, I still couldn't shake this nagging suspicion that she was involved. I still had no explanation for the photo Erin had given me with her father in it. It hurt to doubt Lisa, but I didn't trust her either.

Paranoia was setting in. The feeling that anyone could be the culprit and everyone was against me.

But when I sat down, her tone was sweet and genuine when she asked, "How was your weekend?"

"Fine," I replied curtly and leaned in close. "I'm going to do something at the start of court that may be surprising. Don't react."

Her eyes widened like a doe's. "What is it? What's going on?"

"We'll talk after."

If this conspiracy involving the mayor was real, the less she knew, the better.

I turned back to my notes, which was just a way to fill time until court started. I wouldn't be using them today.

To my absolute chagrin, Donovan sauntered over, grinning. "Ready to face the music? I hope you brought your A-game today." His tone was light, but the challenge in his eyes was unmistakable.

"I don't have the energy or patience for your ego right now. Please don't talk to me."

His smile faltered. I was rarely so blunt with him. A flicker of disappointment that he was unable to rile me up crossed his features before he smoothed it over with a smile and a shrug. "Suit yourself. May the best lawyer win." He moved back to his table and sat down.

The door to the judge's chambers opened, and the clerk emerged. She walked between counsel tables. "Any preliminary matters to bring to the court's attention before we get started?"

I took a deep breath. "Yes. The State will be making a motion."

Donovan's expression darkened. "What motion?"

My fingers wrapped around the USB drive in my pocket.

"Alex," Donovan said, trying to get my attention as the clerk walked away. "What motion?"

I ignored him and closed my eyes, trying to think of what I was going to say when court started.

"All rise."

The judge and jury entered.

"Court is in session," the bailiff called.

Judge Beasley looked at me. "I understand the State has a motion?"

"Yes, Your honor." I stood and leveled the Judge with a steely gaze. "The State moves to dismiss all charges."

The courtroom erupted. The outburst of energy behind me was palpable, even with my back turned. I knew Tom was in the seats. Possibly Erin. The only person who knew I was going to do this and why had been Andrews. To everyone else, I must have appeared insane.

Judge Beasley banged his gavel repeatedly, like claps of thunder in succession, until the crowd quieted down.

Tom crossed the threshold, approaching the attorneys' podium.

The bailiff moved toward him. "Mr. Matthews, I hope you've simply lost your way, because as far as I recall, you are not listed as counsel of record and the court will not be entertaining any discussion from you."

"But, Your Honor—"

"I have no problem holding you in contempt," the bailiff said. "No one is above the law here."

Tom took his hand off the divider and sat back down in his seat. I could feel his gaze burn a hole through the back of my head, but I didn't turn around.

"Ms. Hayes," Judge Beasley said, turning his attention back to me. "We'll discuss this motion in chambers."

Donovan jumped up, his tone indignant. "Your Honor, I must insist on being present for any discussions regarding my client's case. It would be highly inappropriate for the court to engage in *ex parte* communications with the prosecution."

The judge nodded curtly. "Fine."

Donovan's presence was tangible behind me as we made our way to the judge's chambers, his expensive cologne failing to mask the stench of his smugness.

But he had no idea what was coming. Neither did I.

FIFTY-TWO

I STOOD in Judge Beasley's chambers, my heart pounding. The judge looked at me expectantly, his bushy eyebrows raised. "Care to explain yourself?"

"Your Honor, I've come into possession of exculpatory evidence that proves Mr. Martin's innocence. Given this, I can no longer ethically proceed with the prosecution."

Donovan scoffed. "This is ridiculous, Your Honor. She's only doing this because she knows she's going to lose. If you grant this motion, this 'so-called evidence' is going to disappear and her case is going to look very different the second time around. This is nothing more than a Hail Mary from a prosecutor who knows she lost the game." His eyes locked onto mine, challenging me. "Ms. Hayes is grasping at straws, hoping for a second bite at the apple."

My face flushed with anger. I bit back a scathing retort, forcing myself to maintain my composure. The hypocrisy of his accusation was beyond insulting. I kept my voice steady but clipped. "If I may, Your Honor, the defense's theatrics doesn't change the fact that this evidence is both relevant and exculpatory."

"Where did this evidence come from?" the judge asked.

I hesitated. "I... I don't know, Your Honor. It was left anonymously."

"Why did you not bring it forward sooner?"

"I only received it last night."

"Likely story," Donovan sneered.

Something in me snapped. The weeks of frustration, combing through mountains of useless documents, feeling played—it all came boiling to the surface.

"That's rich coming from you, Counselor. You dumped boxes upon boxes of irrelevant evidence on me, clearly trying to hide the original security footage in the first place." I gripped the drive in my fist. "For all I know, you've had this all along."

Donovan's face turned red. "How dare you!" We were past all composure in front of the judge now. The past and present collided in this moment. "If I had evidence proving my client's innocence, why on earth wouldn't I have turned it over? I would have brought it to you on a silver platter."

"Enough!" Judge Beasley's voice boomed. "This bickering is beneath both of you and not in keeping with our profession."

I held back a snort of derision. I couldn't agree with the judge less on that point.

"We're going to watch this evidence," he said. "Now."

I handed him the USB drive. He fumbled with it, trying to get it into his computer. "Blasted thing," he muttered. "Meghan!"

The mousy law school graduate came running into chambers, almost shaking. "Yes, Your Honor?"

He gestured to the computer and USB. "Can you help with this?"

She took the device from him and plugged it into the computer, pulling up the folders.

Judge Beasley didn't even thank her before she ran off, clearly used to the borderline mistreatment.

I hated judges.

Almost as much as I hated lawyers.

As the video began to play, the room fell silent. We watched, transfixed, as the footage revealed a masked-Ramirez following Ed into the house to commit the crime. The photographs that followed were what removed any doubt.

When it was over, Judge Beasley sighed. "Given this evidence, I'm inclined to grant the State's motion."

Donovan opened his mouth to argue, but the judge held up his hand.

"However," he looked at me as he continued, "I'll only grant it if you move to dismiss with prejudice."

My stomach dropped. Dismissal with prejudice meant the state couldn't refile charges against Martin, even if other evidence came to light later. I was trusting Campo's word that this footage hadn't been altered. That Ramirez really was the killer. Normally, in a case like this, I'd consider reducing the charges from first-degree murder to something lesser. But conspiracy and aiding and abetting—what Ed actually did—weren't lesser-included offenses of first-degree murder. They were entirely separate crimes. To charge him with those would require a new indictment. I'd have to start over from scratch. It'd be political and career suicide.

I took a deep breath. "The State moves to dismiss all charges with prejudice, Your Honor."

The judge nodded solemnly. "Motion granted. We'll reconvene in the courtroom to inform the jury."

As we filed out, I caught Donovan's eye. I tried to walk past him, but he grabbed my arm. His voice was low, with a light wobble. "What's your game, Hayes?"

"No game," I said simply.

"Bullshit. Someone just drops evidence off on your doorstep that exonerates my client the night before you rest your case? How long have you been sitting on this? If I find out you've been holding onto it, I'll have you disbarred."

I turned and glared at him. "Some of us don't lie, Donovan. Some of us don't have clients who are footing the bill to send twenty-five boxes of bullshit documents to opposing counsel to try and obscure evidence. Some of us really are just trying to do what's right and I'm not going to put a man in prison for the wrong crime. He was obviously a party to it, but this trial is to prove he did it, and I can't in good conscience continue." I looked to where he was still holding my arm. "Now, if you could please let go of me, I'd like to get this over with."

Donovan had told me once he prided himself on never being taken by surprise. In fact, he'd said that he didn't like Christmas for that reason. On any other day, I would have relished in his look of pure shellshock. Today, I couldn't have cared less.

We filed back into the courtroom. As I made my way to the counsel table, I caught Tom's eye in the audience. His gaze was filled with fury, and his chest heaved with shallow breaths. Next to him sat the mayor, his face a mask of controlled neutrality. A few rows back I spotted Erin, her expression unreadable.

In the corner, Andrews caught my gaze and gave me a subtle nod of encouragement. It wasn't much, but it steadied me. At least someone was in my corner.

I took my seat next to Lisa. She was doing her best to hide her surprise, but I could see the questions burning in her eyes. Donovan slumped into his chair, still looking stunned. I guess there was a limit to the bastard's ego.

The courtroom fell silent as Judge Beasley took the bench. His voice boomed in the silence. "For the record, I'd like the State to renew its motion."

I stood, my legs jelly underneath me. "Your Honor, the State moves to dismiss all charges against Edward Martin with prejudice."

"Motion granted." He turned to Donovan's client. "Mr. Martin, you are free to go. The jury is thanked for their service and is dismissed."

The courtroom erupted into chaos. Voices raised in shock, confusion, and anger. I could see Tom pushing his way through the crowd, Thompson hot on his heels. Their faces were thunderous. Panic rose in my throat.

I didn't wait before grabbing my bag, sidestepping the approaching storm, and hurrying down the side aisle. Lisa tried to catch up with me but I was already in the wind. Andrews was moving to meet me.

"Let's go," I muttered as we fell into step together, pushing through the doors into the hallway.

Behind us, I could hear Tom calling my name, his voice sharp with anger. But I didn't look back. I couldn't. Not yet.

Andrews and I picked up our pace, heading for the exit. The courthouse had shrunk and was now too small, too confining. I needed air, space to think about what I'd just done and what it meant for my career, for justice, for everything.

As we neared the doors, I could hear Tom's footsteps getting closer. "Hayes! Where the hell do you think you're going?" His voice echoed off the marble walls.

Andrews and I were just about to push through the courthouse doors when a figure stepped into our path. Erin.

"We need to talk," she said, her voice laced with urgency.

"Later," I replied, trying to move past her. "I need to go."

But Erin didn't budge, silent and immovable, blocking our exit. Through the open doors, I could see the press gathered outside, their cameras and microphones at the ready.

Before I could say anything else, I heard an angry voice behind us. "Andrews, you son of a bitch!"

I turned in confusion to see Tom approaching rapidly, Thompson close behind him. Behind them were Donovan and Martin. But before any of them could unleash whatever tirade they had prepared, Erin spoke up.

Her voice rang out clear and authoritative. "Henry Thompson, Ed Martin, you have the right to remain silent. Anything you say can and will be used against you in a court of law. You have the right to an attorney. If you cannot afford an attorney, one will be provided for you."

The hallway fell silent for a split second. The weight of her words hung in the air, thick and suffocating. Every breath felt heavy, like the calm before a storm, as if everyone was bracing for the impact. Then everything erupted into chaos.

"This is outrageous!" Mayor Thompson spat back. "On what grounds?"

Erin continued, her voice steady as she recited, "You are both being charged with multiple federal offenses, including racketeering, bribery, wire fraud, mail fraud, money laundering, obstruction of justice, conspiracy, extortion, witness tampering, and violations of the Hobbs Act, among others."

The world was tilting on its axis. I watched, stunned, as agents materialized from the shadows of the hallway. They converged on Thompson and Martin, securing their hands behind their backs with handcuffs. The sound of the metal clicking closed was unmistakable, even above the roar of the crowd.

Tom's face went from angry to shocked to pale in the span of seconds. Without a word, he turned and disappeared into the crowd.

Erin's eyes met mine for a moment. Then she was gone, pushing past me without a word, her attention focused solely on the two felons.

The press, likely sensing a bigger story than they had anticipated, surged forward. They pushed past Andrews and me, their cameras flashing, microphones extended, all clamoring for a shot of the hand-cuffed Mayor Thompson and Ed Martin.

Questions rang out around us.

"Mr. Mayor! Do you have any comment on these charges?"

"Ed Martin, what do you have to say about your arrest?"

"Do you plan to fight these charges in court?"

"What evidence do you have linking the mayor and Ed Martin to these crimes?"

"Is anyone else expected to be charged in connection with this case?"

Guards rushed to control the situation, trying to keep the press from flooding into the courthouse. Erin didn't say a word. She didn't even look at the press or acknowledge their presence. Thompson and Martin were shoved and locked into squad cars, as they each shouted, "I'm innocent!" to the crowd and then they were gone.

In the ensuing mayhem, Andrews caught my eye. With a slight nod, we slipped away, unnoticed in the frenzy.

FIFTY-THREE

ANDREWS and I sped away from the courthouse, the chaos still visible in the rearview mirror.

Andrews' eyes flicked between me and the next intersection. "Where to?"

"Just drive," I replied, turning to look out the window as we pulled away from the courthouse.

"You can't avoid this forever, you know. Sooner or later, you're going to have to face the music."

I let out a mirthless laugh. "Face the music? That's a nice way of putting it. I'm pretty sure my career just went up in flames back there."

Andrews drove onto the 610 Loop, the flow of traffic helping to calm my nerves, and steady my breathing.

"Let's go to my place," I finally said.

He nodded, and within twenty minutes, we were pulling into my neighborhood. Two news vans were parked outside my house.

"Looks like they beat us here," he commented dryly.

"Of course they did," I muttered, sinking lower in my seat. "Just drive past. I don't want to deal with them right now."

Andrews nodded, accelerating past my home.

"Never seen Tom that angry before," he said lightheartedly. "He may have burst a blood vessel."

"Guaranteed I'll get to see it again whenever I decide to show up in the office." I rubbed my temples. "Maybe I just won't go. I think it's called soft quitting. Yeah, that's what I'll do." But Andrews was right. I'd have to face the music at some point. For now, I just wanted to get away from it all.

"He can't fire you for doing what you thought was right. You had exculpatory evidence. It would have been an ethical violation to continue prosecuting the man for murder."

I laughed bitterly. "No, but he can fire me for not coming to him first with the evidence. He's my supervisor, remember? Lawyers are experts at getting around things like this."

He was silent for a moment. His voice was quieter when he said, "Maybe you should give up on being an attorney. Doesn't seem like you like the job that much."

I gaped at him. "And do what with my life instead?"

"Ever think about the police academy?"

"No."

"Why not?"

"Because I can't do a push up?"

"Have you seen most officers? They're not doing any push-ups either."

I gave him the best smile I could manage. "I appreciate it, but I just don't think that's me."

He nodded. "Alright, well, if we can't go to your place, or the office, where to?"

Without thinking, I started giving him directions to my childhood home. I'd forgotten to return the key to Phyllis anyway. We drove in silence, except for my occasional, "Turn left here."

As we pulled into the driveway, Andrews looked around curiously. "What is this place?"

"Where I grew up," I told him. He unbuckled his seatbelt and followed me up the front steps. I fumbled with the key, my hands shaking despite my attempts to steady them.

"Here, let me." Andrews took the key from my hands and opened the door.

"Thanks."

We walked inside, and I collapsed onto the couch while Andrews wandered around, taking in the faded wallpaper and dated furniture. Finally, he sat across from me.

"What happened in the judge's chambers?" he asked.

I rubbed my temples again. "Beasley said he'd only grant the motion if I dismissed with prejudice."

"But that shouldn't matter. We're sure Ramirez is the killer, right?"

I shrugged. "I don't know what to believe anymore."

Andrews leaned forward. "Don't do that to yourself. You did the right thing. Sometimes the law doesn't align with the truth, but that doesn't make what you did any less important. Put it out of your mind. It's done now."

I slumped back into the decades-old cushions. "How long do you think the media will camp out at my place?"

"Probably not long," he said. "We could head back in an hour or so."

I hesitated before asking, "Actually, would you be willing to take me somewhere else?"

He quirked an eyebrow. "Where to?"

"I want to visit my father."

Andrews studied me for a moment, then gave a small nod. "Okay," he said, and soon we were on our way to USP Beaumont.

As we arrived, he turned to me. "Want me to come in?"

I shook my head. "No, I'll be okay. Won't be long."

I exited the car, entered the building, and hurried to the back of the line. The processing felt painfully routine as I checked in and waited to be escorted back. When the guard finally called my name, I rose and followed him, each step carrying me closer to the man I both loved and resented.

As they brought him out, I was struck again by how gaunt he looked, so different from the jovial man in the family photos I'd seen just an hour earlier.

The visiting area was bleak, filled with harsh fluorescent lighting and concrete walls that seemed to absorb any warmth. Guards stood by the doors, their expressions impassive, watching the interactions with quiet detachment. My father sat down, offering a wan smile. "How are you?"

I struggled to find the right words. "I'm...managing. I actually have some news to share with you."

His smile faded, replaced by concern. "What is it?"

"After I visited you, some evidence showed up on my doorstep. It exonerated Ed Martin of his wife's murder, but it implicated Ramirez." I paused, gauging his reaction. "Did you have anything to do with that?"

His eyes widened, and he shook his head. "No, I didn't. What happened from there?"

I explained how I'd dismissed the charges against Martin, potentially at the cost of my job. He tried to reassure me, but when I mentioned the mayor's arrest, his demeanor changed.

"You gave those papers to the feds?" he asked, probing.

"Yes," I said slowly. He wiped a hand across his jaw. "I wish you hadn't. If it ever got traced back to you, you could be in serious danger. I thought it might help crack things open for you on the Martin case. But I didn't think you'd turn the documents over."

"They were going to kill Ramirez, Dad. The same way they killed the guy you arrested." My temper flared. "What was I supposed to do? He's the only chance we have of getting you out of here."

My father looked sad. "I don't care about getting out of here at the expense of your safety."

"I'll be fine. Besides, I'm usually with Andrews."

"Who?"

"A detective. Works with me on most of my cases."

"Can he be trusted?"

"I've never questioned him, not even once."

"That's what I thought about my partner," he said. "And look where I am."

"No way, Dad," I said, shaking my head. "Not Daniel. He's not like that."

He eyed me for a moment. "Okay. I trust your judgment."

But did I trust my own judgment?

"Just, please be careful," he said.

I sighed. "I don't understand your concern. The mayor was the one pulling the strings. The papers you hid made that clear."

He shook his head. "I don't think he's the only one in charge."

My father had been in prison for years. If I could become paranoid working on a case for a few weeks, he most certainly could be influenced by his own setting.

"Speaking of Ramirez," I said, "I'm not sure if I can get him to revoke his testimony. He's going to be charged by the feds for the murder. I don't have any leverage against him now."

I saw a flicker of disappointment in my father's eyes, quickly masked.

"You did the right thing," he said softly. "I only have a few years left. What matters is that we can see each other now and then."

My eyes stung with unshed tears. I placed my palm against the cold glass, desperate for connection. But nothing was going to make up for the fact that I'd failed to see him for the past five years. My next words caught in my throat. "I'll try to come and see you again next week."

He nodded, a flicker of hope and sadness in his tired eyes. "I'll be here," he whispered, though we both knew the weight behind those simple words. I hurried out of the prison, desperate to escape the haunting disappointment in my father's eyes. As I stepped into the bright sunlight, I stopped in my tracks and took a shaky breath before making my way back to the car where Andrews waited.

"You okay?" he asked.

"I'm fine," I lied, settling into the passenger seat. "Can you take me home now?"

He nodded, and we drove back to my house in silence.

FIFTY-FOUR

ANDREWS' car coasted to a stop in front of my driveway. We both looked around, but neither of us spotted a media van.

Andrews turned to me as he shut the car off. "You sure you'll be alright? I can come up with you."

"I'll be fine." I offered him a weary smile. "You should get some sleep yourself."

Before I got out of the car, I paused. "Hey, Andrews?"

"Yeah?"

"How did Erin have agents ready to make arrests? Outside of us, no one but the judge and Donovan saw what was on that drive."

Andrews looked guilty. "I called her. Sent her a copy of the evidence."

I was so exhausted that I didn't even have the energy to be mad or feel betrayed. "Why?"

He shook his head. "I guess I just thought it was the right thing to do."

I let out a tired sigh, rubbing my temples. "Maybe it was."

Andrews drove off, and I headed inside. The sushi containers were still laying around on the coffee table. I sighed, switched on the TV, and went about cleaning up the mess.

"In a shocking turn of events, Assistant District Attorney Alex Hayes dismissed all charges against defendant Edward Martin in the Caroline Martin murder trial, only for Mr. Martin to be arrested, alongside Mayor Thompson, for multiple charges including the conspiracy to commit Caroline's murder. When asked for comment, District Attorney Tom Matthews had this to say."

The television cut to Tom standing on the steps of the courthouse. "This is a day of reckoning for those who believe they can operate above the law. The dismissal of charges against Edward Martin was based on newly uncovered exculpatory evidence. This evidence revealed that Mr. Martin was not the killer, and we could not ethically proceed with this trial as a result. However, this same evidence has brought to light a much broader conspiracy, implicating both Mr. Martin and Mayor Thompson in a series of crimes, including the conspiracy to commit Caroline Martin's murder. Today's arrests serve as a clear message: no one is untouchable, and everyone is accountable to the law."

I watched him speak for a few moments before gritting my teeth and jabbing at the power button. The television switched off, and I sat alone in the darkness. The more I thought about it, the more I surmised that Tom was the one who orchestrated all of this. How easy would it have been for him to plant evidence? Plus, Janice at the storage locker, the bank statement, "DA" on the documents I found in my father's storage locker. It all pointed to him.

The fact that Erin didn't think she had enough to bring him in was bullshit.

Sinking into the sofa, I stared blankly at the now-dark screen. I wondered whether anyone would hire a washed-up prosecutor who'd only been on the job for four years and threw away the biggest case of her life.

Probably no one.

Maybe I should have taken that job offer from Erin. Maybe I wouldn't be in this mess now.

I expected her to call me. Say something after that look she gave me in the hallway of the courthouse. But so far, my phone had remained ghostly silent.

A sharp knock at the door jolted me from my thoughts about Erin. I froze. My heart pounded. I approached the door cautiously. My hand hovered over the doorknob as I peered through the peephole. The tension in my shoulders eased, and I opened the door.

"Andrews," I said, relief evident in my voice.

He pushed his way inside, giving me a quick glance. "I got two blocks down the road and then realized that until Erin brings Tom in, I don't think it's safe for you to be alone."

"You really think he would try and hurt me?"

"I'd rather not take the chance."

"Make yourself comfortable," I said. "I gotta catch up on laundry; otherwise, I won't have anything to wear tomorrow."

Andrews flipped the television back on. I made my way over to the alcove where my double-decker machine was and started to sort lights and darks.

I emptied the pockets of a few coins from a pair of jeans and tossed them into the washer. As I grabbed a jacket and turned its pockets inside out, a piece of paper fluttered to the floor. I bent down to pick it up, recognizing the "autographed" photo of Andrews I'd swiped off his desk when we first started working on the case. Back then, it had been a joke—something to laugh about in the middle of this mess. He had written on the bottom in permanent marker: *Best of the Best. You're in good hands, rookie.*

I smiled at the memory but then looked at the picture closer, feeling the joy drain from me. Andrews was standing with a few other officers at a barbecue, smiling broadly. But my attention narrowed as my gaze drifted to the chain around Andrews' neck—thick, gold, gleaming in the sunlight. It looked familiar, too familiar.

I stared at the words Andrews had scrawled on the bottom of the photo. *You're in good hands, rookie.* The words seemed to mock me now, taking on a different meaning. My pulse quickened, and a surge of nausea hit me.

Clutching the photo, I rushed over to my computer, my heart thudding painfully in my chest. Andrews, still lounging on the couch, glanced up, sensing something was off. "What are you doing?" he asked, his voice laced with confusion.

I didn't answer. My hands were shaking as I opened the files on the USB drive from the masked man. I pulled up the image of Caroline clawing desperately at her attacker's neck. My breath caught in my throat as I zoomed in. There it was—a gold chain. My mind raced.

Then, I flipped through the evidence files, stopping when I reached the photo of the gold chain found on the bedroom floor. I stared at it, bile rising in my throat. The same chain. It was undeniable now.

I GLANCED down at the photo from the barbecue, my eyes locking onto the gold chain Andrews wore. The nausea twisted inside me like a knife. There wasn't a shred of doubt in my mind anymore. My breath caught in my throat. This entire time, it had been staring me in the face.

I turned to look at him, my blood running cold.

"Don't move, Alex," he said, his voice eerily calm. His gun was pointed at me.

I stared at him, the weight of the betrayal crushing me.

His eyes were almost sad as he said, "I can't let you go any further with this."

FIFTY-FIVE

THE WALLS of my living room felt like they were closing in, the dim light casting long shadows that seemed to creep closer with every second. My heart pounded, but I forced myself to stay calm.

He gestured to my sofa with the gun but didn't take it off me. "Sit down, Alex."

"Put the gun away," I demanded, as the reality of what was happening started to seep in.

He shook his head. "I can't do that."

I sat down on the sofa. Andrews kept the gun trained on me, his eyes cold and unflinching.

That's when it finally hit me. The realization crashed over me like a tidal wave. It wasn't Tom that Erin was after. It was Andrews. He was the puppet master behind everything.

"I always knew you were smart." A small smile played at the corners of Andrews' mouth." But you get easily distracted by the details."

His statement sent my skin prickling. "So what? It was all fake? The evidence? The murder? How far does this go?"

He leaned back slightly, eyes distant as he started the story, though the gun remained steady in his grip.

"I remember the first time I knew I wanted to be a cop. I was just a kid—maybe eight or nine. Some punk had stolen my bike, and I was furious. That thing was everything to me. I figured it was gone for good, but then, out of nowhere, this cop shows up, dragging the guy who took it by the collar. I just stood there on the sidewalk, watching as this officer put the cuffs on him, calm and in control, like he had all the power in the world.

"He didn't know me, didn't have any reason to care about my stupid bike. But that cop looked me dead in the eye as he handed it back and said, 'Justice served, kid.' There was something about the way he said it, like it was more than just a job to him. He was the hero in that moment. Untouchable."

He paused, shaking his head slightly, a bitter laugh escaping.

"That night, I told myself, 'That's what I want to do. I want to be the guy who gets the bad guys. I want to work for the good guys.' It all seemed so simple back then."

His voice grew harder, more cynical.

"That's the thing, though—when you're a kid, you don't see all the shades of gray. You just see good guys and bad guys, and you pick a side." I swallowed, trying to keep my voice steady as I asked, "So what happened?"

My mind was racing. Andrews—this man I'd worked with, trusted, who had been there through so much of this case—was now sitting across from me, a gun in his hand. It felt surreal, like a bad dream I couldn't wake up from. How had I not seen this coming? Or was this something I'd willfully ignored, hoping my instincts were wrong?

His eyes darkened, and for a moment, I wondered if he even heard me. My pulse quickened, fear gnawing at me, but I tried to keep calm.

Andrews sighed, his grip tightening on the gun before he leaned forward, elbows on his knees, like we were just having a normal conversation. Like the weapon wasn't still aimed in my direction.

"What happened?" He echoed my words with a bitter laugh. "I started working for the good guys, just like I wanted. Got my badge, wore the uniform. But you know how it is, right, Alex? The system... it grinds you down. All the cases you lose, the ones that fall apart because of a technicality, because some rich bastard can afford a better lawyer, or because the good guys don't always play by the rules either. After a while, you start seeing the cracks."

I could feel my breath catch in my throat. His words felt like an indictment—of him, of me, of the entire justice system. Was this where I was headed too? Would I become as disillusioned as he was, crossing lines, losing sight of everything I believed in?

Andrews leaned back in his chair, his gaze cold and calculating. "You know what the bad guys figured out?" he said, his voice low. "They exploit those cracks in the system. They don't care about rules, justice, or any of the crap we believe in. They do it with something the good guys can never match—money."

He laughed bitterly, shaking his head. "You see it, Alex. I know you do. The bad guys? They've got endless resources. They buy their way out of trouble, grease palms, make problems disappear. All while we're stuck trying to do everything by the book, on a shoestring budget, chasing dead ends because some bureaucrat won't approve the right warrant."

I stared at him, my stomach twisting. His words were too close to the truth. I'd seen it. The powerful slipping through the cracks, walking away while victims were left with nothing. I knew the system wasn't perfect, but what he was saying—what he was doing—it went against everything I still believed in. Everything I thought he had stood for too.

"But you took the easy way out," I said, my voice barely above a whisper. "You let them pull you in."

His eyes met mine, unflinching. "No, Alex. I let them pay me. And trust me, the price was right."

"How could any amount be enough to make you turn your back on everything you believed in?" I silently pleaded for him to offer some kind of explanation—something that would make sense, that could somehow lessen the weight of this betrayal. The thought of it was unbearable.

Andrews looked distant, his gaze drifting to some far-off memory. A sad smile tugged at the corner of his mouth. "Love makes you do crazy things. Things you never thought you were capable of. Some-times, it's not about the money... it's about what you're willing to lose, and what you're not."

"That's just an excuse," I snapped, my hands curling into fists in my lap. I could feel the tension in my shoulders as I tried to keep my voice steady, but the hurt bled through.

Andrews sighed deeply, shaking his head. "Maybe to you. But, to me, a man who was about to lose the woman he loved, it was the only thing that made sense." He looked down, rubbing the back of his neck as if trying to ease a weight that had been there for too long. "My wife started seeing someone else. A richer man, who worked less and made more. I was devastated, but I loved her... and I wanted to keep her." His voice trailed off, and for a moment, he just stared at the floor, the sadness in his posture more palpable than his words. "In the course of this goal, I met a man named Henry Thompson, who had his sights set on getting into politics. He knew a man named Ed Martin, who just wanted to get rich. They had an idea. They just needed someone on the inside to make it all work."

He shifted in his seat, his gaze drifting across the room as if searching for something that wasn't there. "I work with criminals, so I was the perfect fit. I needed money, and they needed someone to do some dirty work. So I did it just one time. Hired someone to intimi-date a business owner. It seemed to work. Ed was the only one bidding on the project, I got paid, and so did Thompson. He used that to fund his first campaign. I went back to being a good guy and they did whatever they wanted."

"Then he got elected, and four years later they wanted to do it again. I told them no. My wife had already left me by that point, so what was really in it for me? But they didn't care. If I didn't play ball, they would throw me under the bus." His voice hardened. "I didn't like that idea at all. So, I decided that I would play along for a while, but I was going to do what I needed to get them out of my life for good.

"So I planted evidence. That was what I was supposed to do, after all. Financials so that Ed's wife would find them, knowing Ed would go to Thompson on what to do, and that Thompson would ask me. And then I could tell them I'd get it taken care of and assure them we'd clean up like last time and no one would be any wiser.

"I used an officer who was okay with taking bribes. Ramirez. Told Thompson he'd be the one to do the deed, he'd take the fall. He'd done it once before, he would do it again."

Andrews paused and gave me an annoyed look. "Don't look sad for him. Thompson told him to go kill a woman and he agreed, no questions asked. The only reason he didn't is because when he got there, she was already dead."

My body shook as the pieces clicked into place. "What about Tom? Is he involved?"

Andrews shook his head. "He's not, but I'm glad the feds are on his tail. The guy's been a problem since the start, and I'd just as soon get rid of him." He gave me a sly smile. "Although, I did enjoy making you think he was the one pulling the strings. Lined up perfectly with his re-election bid. Sometimes, manipulating people like that is the only fun in this mess. Makes it easier to handle when you know exactly where the pieces are going to fall."

I took a deep breath, trying to process everything. "How do you account for the bank statements and Janice showing up at the storage locker?"

He chuckled. "That was my perfect opportunity to try and get Tom implicated. You and Erin were talking a lot. I figured I could lead her to Tom through you. It was almost too easy to use Janice to tip Tom off that you had a conversation with Ramirez. He knew Louis would screw up the case for you and didn't want you anywhere near him. Tom immediately jumped and tried to send Janice after the tape. As for the bank statement, it was the same thing. I left it on Janice's desk knowing you'd see it." He grinned. "The account belonged to me."

I shook my head, unable to take my eyes off the man in front of me. The man I didn't know so well after all. "You were the one to delete that recording?"

"No, that was a little twist of fate. Lisa was the one to do it after all. Thought it could implicate her father. You were right to suspect her, but she didn't mean any true harm. Just a young girl in over her head."

My mind was a whirlwind, and my breaths were shaky and quick. "What part does her father play in all of this?"

"The man's just doing his job," Andrews said. "He was clued in to the planted evidence against Ramirez and was the one to bring him in." He smiled. "I'll use that to my benefit, though. Tell him about his mistake in the future, use it as leverage if I need him again."

I felt a cold chill run down my spine. "And the reason Ed's alibi, Rachel, was so scared? You were threatening her, weren't you? The drive-by. That was you, too?"

Andrews gave a small, satisfied smirk. "Ed told her to say he was with her. I made sure she was given a little scare about lying, and that drive-by? Yeah, that was me. Just enough to make her think someone was watching her, and to throw you off your game. No matter what she did, whether she testified or stayed quiet, I'd win, and Ed would lose."

"And the last USB with the video and the photos?"

"I don't know who dropped that off for you, and I'll admit, I was worried you'd recognize me." He shrugged. "But when you thought it was Ramirez, I let you roll with it."

I leaned back as the enormity of Andrews' confession washed over me in waves of disgust and fury. In the end, it was all about power— the one currency that seemed to matter to men like him.

He sighed. "I wouldn't have said anything, but you had to start poking around." He shook his head. "Why'd you have to go and do that? We had a good thing going. I liked working with you." He shook his head. "Like father like daughter, I suppose. He had a penchant for poking his nose where it didn't belong, too."

Nausea turned my stomach inside out and almost clambered up my throat. And then it hit me. "The 'DA' in the papers my father found. It never stood for 'district attorney,' did it? It stood for—"

"Daniel Andrews."

"My father knew. Five years ago, when Thompson was up for his first election, you bribed Ramirez into testifying against my father when he found those papers in Lopez's car. You followed me to the storage locker because you wanted to see if the evidence against you still existed."

A cold smile spread across Andrews' face. "Guilty."

The word hung between us, the silence in the room deafening.

The bang of the gun shattered the quiet. Pain erupted in my body as I crumpled onto the floor. Darkness edged my vision, threatening to consume me. As I lay gasping for air that wouldn't come, I wondered if the truth had ever mattered at all.

FIFTY-SIX

MY FRONT DOOR exploded inward as federal agents burst inside. Their loud shouts and the commotion that followed jarred me back into hazy consciousness. Through the fog of pain, I saw Andrews being wrestled to the ground, his gun kicked to the side. Handcuffs clicked as an officer dragged him away, and my vision started to fade again. Erin's face and her shouts of my name were the last things I saw before the darkness swallowed me.

Everything after that was a blur. I was lifted onto a stretcher, and the piercing wail of sirens made my head throb. Erin's presence beside me, and the bright fluorescent lights above were all fuzzy.

The darkness became a friend, one I returned to for comfort when things became too intense or painful, only to be wrenched from it time and time again.

Finally, the steady beep of machines slowly pulled me back out of it one last time. I blinked, my eyes adjusting to the bright lights of the hospital room. Erin sat beside the bed in a chair. She was reading something on her phone before she finally realized I was waking up and tossed it to the side.

"Welcome back," she said, leaning forward. "How are you feeling?"

I swallowed against my dry throat. "Like I've been hit by a train." My voice came out raspy. "What happened?"

Erin got up and grabbed a glass of water.

"Andrews shot you," she reminded me. "I don't know if it was on purpose or if he was startled when we came into the room. The bullet grazed your shoulder, and you hit your head on the way down. You'll be sore, but you'll be okay."

She gave me the glass. I reached out with my right hand, but immediately regretted it. Sore was an understatement.

I still took the glass and sipped the water. It soothed my throat. "What happened to Andrews?"

"He's in custody." Erin paused. "I'm sorry, Alex. It wasn't supposed to go down like this."

I searched her face, trying to make sense of her words. "What do you mean?"

"As soon as we realized he was pulling the strings, we put him under close surveillance. The FBI was ready to move in. They'd been tracking his every move, waiting for the right opportunity. But, had I known Andrews would turn on you, I would have tried to pick him up sooner."

My mind felt like it was wading through mud. "I don't understand. You were investigating the mayor, and Tom."

She shook her head. "That was just a cover. I was actually looking into reports of a crooked cop."

I looked down at my hands, still trembling from the rush of everything that had happened. "So, I was the bait."

"You were the key, Alex," Erin said softly. "Andrews had been hiding in plain sight, manipulating everything. We needed him to make a move, and unfortunately, that meant using you to get him to show his hand."

The whole thing crystallized in my mind. I stared at her. "You... used me?" The words were barely above a whisper, laced with hurt and betrayal.

Her shoulders sagged. "I know it sounds bad. I never meant for you to get caught in the crossfire. I had no idea it was Andrews until just yesterday. Until he called me to give me the evidence you used to exonerate Martin."

"I don't understand."

"I planted that evidence on your doorstep. Andrews needed Martin's conviction. With the exculpatory evidence, he knew you'd move to dismiss the charges. He couldn't let Martin walk. The moment Martin walked, Andrews lost all control. So, he called me. Sent me the evidence knowing that I, as a federal agent, would be able to get an arrest warrant on it."

"I don't see why that confirms he was a dirty cop."

"Because it wasn't the proper channel for a detective. He should have taken the information to the district attorney, gone through the normal channels to get another indictment." She shook her head. "He wanted fast action. We knew someone was framing Martin for the murder and that Caroline's murder was an inside job. We just didn't know who."

Erin glanced at me, her tone softer but insistent. "As soon as you had the information in hand, word would travel fast through the precinct. We were counting on it. The person framing Ed? They'd make a move, do something that gave them away. That's what we were waiting for."

"How did you even get those photos? That video?"

Erin shifted, her eyes darting around the room. I could tell she was uncomfortable. "I can't reveal my sources."

I narrowed my eyes, the pieces clicking together, but one still didn't fit. "Then what about Tom? He's been demanding a guilty verdict in this case from day one. Andrews said he mislead me on purpose, but are you sure Tom wasn't part of the conspiracy?"

Erin sighed, rubbing her temples, clearly reluctant to share more. "Because we knew Thompson was involved. We've been monitoring his communications for months." She paused, searching for the right words. "He made it clear to Tom that if he didn't secure a conviction against Ed, he would publicly withdraw his support for Tom's re-election campaign. Tom was under pressure, and his actions reflected that."

I closed my eyes. "So everything—the photos, the bank statements, all of it—was just a ploy to get to Andrews?"

"I'm sorry, Alex. I should have been upfront with you from the start." She reached out but I flinched away.

I was furious. "You had me involve Lisa, Andrews, and Donovan. I put people on this, pulled in favors to figure out those bank statements, and the whole time, you had the answers planted in front of me. You let me spin my wheels when you could've just told me the truth."

Her hand fell to her side. "My job was to find out which cop was dirty. Yes, I used you to do it."

"You lied to me." My words were laden with disappointment. "After everything, how could you do this?"

"I was trying to do the right thing. I was given my marching orders. I never wanted to deceive you. It's just where things landed."

Silence hung between us, the hum of hospital machines the only sound in the room.

"What about Ramirez?" I asked her. "And Harper?"

"Both dead."

"You lied when you said you had Ramirez secured, didn't you?"

"Yes," she admitted. "We were trying to fish out who Andrews was working with on the inside. Ramirez was already dead by the time you found out he was being moved."

"Did you find out who did it?"

"We think so."

"And this person also killed Harper?" I shook my head. Back then, I couldn't understand why Harper had seemed so confident that he would walk away from his charges, as if the whole thing would just go away. Now I realized why—Andrews, or someone working for him, must have told Harper the same thing he told Ramirez: that he'd be "taken care of." Harper had believed he'd be protected, just like Ramirez. But in the end, they were both expendable.

I swallowed hard. "Without Ramirez revoking his testimony, my father's conviction..." My words trailed off.

"I'm so sorry, Alex. I wish there was more we could do. We'd need

someone to testify that the evidence against your father was fraudulent. Without Ramirez, I don't see who can do that."

"What about Andrews' confession?"

"He only alluded to the fact that he bribed Ramirez into testifying
against your father. He never said the evidence was fraudulent. You
know as well as I do that that's just not enough. Especially because
your father pled guilty."

"Can't you cut a deal with him?"

She shook her head. "The feds aren't going to risk their larger
conspiracy case to help your father."

My fingers curled into fists at my sides. "The system always
protects its own, no matter who they hurt in the process."

"I know this isn't the outcome you were hoping for. I wish I could
do more. But the reality is, we're under constraints."

Tears started to roll down my cheeks. I turned my head so she
couldn't see. In that moment, the weight of every disappointment,
every heartbreak, every moment of disillusionment I had experienced
over the years came crashing down on me. The legal system, the very
institution I had dedicated my life to, had taken both my parents
from me.

"Maybe there is something I can do–"

"Don't." My raspy voice was filled with exhaustion. "You know as
well as I do that the system doesn't care about the truth. It cares about
winning. And I lost the moment I started trying to play the game."

"I'm sorry," Erin said softly.

I turned my head away from her. She left the room, and I sat in
silence. In that moment, I felt more lost and alone than I had since the
day my mother disappeared.

FIFTY-SEVEN

"MS. HAYES," Jim, the prison guard, greeted me warmly as I stepped into the familiar gray-walled lobby of the prison. The harsh fluorescent lights overhead buzzed faintly, casting a sterile glow over the cold, linoleum floors. I'd been visiting my father every week for a year since I'd gotten out of the hospital. At this point, most of the staff there knew me.

I returned his smile, feeling a mix of anticipation and nerves. "Morning, Jim."

The faint clang of gates opening and closing echoed in the distance, a reminder of where I was, though the slight smell of bleach and the muted murmur of guards' voices almost made it feel routine.

He leaned forward, lowering his voice. "Today's the big day, huh?"

"Yes, it is," I replied, my voice steady despite the emotions roiling inside me.

The bench I sat on was cold beneath me as I waited, my mind drifting back over the tumultuous events of the past year. It had been exactly twelve months since I'd taken a bullet, a souvenir from my ill-fated encounter with Detective Daniel Andrews. In that time, Andrews had faced justice, been tried and convicted on multiple federal charges, including first-degree murder. He'd lucked out with a federal trial—no death penalty to worry about.

I'd stepped away from the legal world after that, taking an extended leave of absence. With my savings and the decision to move back into my childhood home, I'd bought myself time. Time to heal, to think, and to figure out what the hell I wanted to do with my life now that everything had changed.

The sound of a heavy door opening snapped me back to the present. My father emerged, dressed in civilian clothes, clutching a clear plastic bag containing his meager belongings. His eyes found mine, and a smile spread across his face, crinkling the corners of his eyes.

"Good luck on the other side, Mr. Hayes," Jim called out as we made our way to the exit.

As we stepped into the sunlight, I reflected on the legal battle I'd waged to get to this point. I'd filed a habeas corpus petition, a last-ditch effort to challenge the legality of my father's imprisonment. I'd cited Andrews' confession, Ramirez's confession, anything I could throw in there. It had been a long shot, and like most such petitions, it had been unsuccessful.

But then fate, or karma, or whatever you want to call it, had intervened. Mayor Thompson was given the opportunity to throw his co-conspirators under the bus, and he hadn't looked back. It didn't get him off the hook completely—far from it. But it kept him away from a life sentence. It had taken almost a year, but he'd come clean about how he and Andrews had set my father up. The governor had caught wind of my father's case and, in a surprising turn of events, granted him a pardon.

We walked to my car in silence. I watched my father tilt his face toward the sunlight and survey the surroundings as if he were seeing them for the first time. It must have looked different when not seen through a fence.

"Thank you, Alex," my father said softly as we reached the vehicle. "For getting me out."

I shook my head, unlocking the doors. "I really had nothing to do with it, Dad. My attempts all failed."

He just smiled, a knowing look in his eyes. "I don't believe that."

As my father settled into the passenger seat, my phone rang, and I stepped away to answer.

"Alex," Tom said, his voice warm but tinged with hope. "Are you ready to come back to work yet?"

I glanced at my father, waiting patiently in the car, and sighed. "Tom, you keep trying, and I keep giving you the same answer. Not yet."

He laughed, undeterred. "When you're ready, just give me a call. We want you back, Alex."

"Okay," I replied, then hesitated. "Hey, Tom?"

"Yeah?"

"Something's been bothering me for a while."

"What is it?"

"The Martin case," I said. "Why'd you give it to me and not someone more senior?"

"You want the truth?" he asked.

"Always."

"I really did believe you were the best woman for the job, and I wasn't lying when I said a female prosecutor would resonate better with the jury. That aside, we were up against the wall, and you'd move heaven and earth to get to the bottom of what was going on. Which you did."

I let his words sink in. "Thanks, Tom," I said. "I'll let you know when I'm ready."

We both ended the call.

It was ironic. I'd expected to be fired when I'd gone behind Tom's back and dismissed Martin's case without permission. Instead, I'd been hailed as a hero for doing the right thing.

I was about to get into the car when my phone rang again. Assuming it was Tom calling back, I answered without checking the screen.

"Hello," I said, but instead of Tom's familiar voice, I heard a chilling, distorted sound. The words came through in an unnaturally deep, robotic growl, clearly altered to mask the caller's identity. It sent a shiver down my spine.

"Your mother's disappearance was not an accident," the voice said. "There are answers at the District Attorney's office."

The line went dead before I could respond. I stared at my phone, my heart pounding. The number was unlisted.

I slid into the driver's seat, my mind reeling. My father turned to me, concern etched on his face. "You look like you've seen a ghost. What's wrong?"

"Nothing," I lied, starting the engine. "Let's go home."

* * *

LATER THAT NIGHT, I said goodnight to my father, who was settled in his old chair, the blue glow of the television washing over him. He smiled, looking more at peace than I'd seen him in years.

In my old bedroom, I pulled out the journal from my top drawer. I'd coped with her loss as a child by filling the pages with notes and letters. Her death had been the worst type—a cold case with no answers. I stared at the journal, the mysterious phone call echoing in my mind. *Your mother's disappearance was not an accident.*

With a deep breath, I picked up my phone and dialed Tom's number. "Tom? It's Alex. I'm coming back to work on Monday."

The die was cast. Whatever answers awaited me at the DA's office, I was going to find them.

* * *

The story continues in *11th Hour Witness*. Get your copy now! https://www.amazon.com/dp/B0DTJ7WFRT

Join the LT Ryan reader family & receive a free copy of the Alex Hayes story, *Trial by Fire*. Click the link below to get started: https://ltryan.com/alex-hayes-newsletter-signup-1

ALSO BY L.T. RYAN

Find All of L.T. Ryan's Books on Amazon Today!

The Jack Noble Series

Never Cry Mercy

Deadline

End Game

Noble Ultimatum

Noble Legend

Noble Revenge

Never Look Back (Coming Soon)

Bear Logan Series

Ripple Effect

Blowback

Take Down

Deep State

Bear & Mandy Logan Series

Close to Home

Under the Surface

The Last Stop

Over the Edge

Between the Lies

Caught in the Web (Coming Soon)

Rachel Hatch Series

Drift

Downburst

Fever Burn

Smoke Signal

Firewalk

Whitewater

Aftershock

Whirlwind

Tsunami

Fastrope

Sidewinder

Mitch Tanner Series

The Depth of Darkness

Into The Darkness

Deliver Us From Darkness

Cassie Quinn Series

Path of Bones

Whisper of Bones

Symphony of Bones

Etched in Shadow

Concealed in Shadow

Betrayed in Shadow

Born from Ashes

Return to Ashes (Coming Soon)

Blake Brier Series

Unmasked

Unleashed

Uncharted

Drawpoint

Contrail

Detachment

Clear

Quarry (Coming Soon)

Dalton Savage Series

Savage Grounds

Scorched Earth

Cold Sky

The Frost Killer

Crimson Moon (Coming Soon)

Maddie Castle Series

The Handler

Tracking Justice

Hunting Grounds

Vanished Trails

Smoldering Lies (Coming Soon)

Affliction Z Series

Affliction Z: Patient Zero

Affliction Z: Abandoned Hope

Affliction Z: Descended in Blood

Affliction Z : Fractured Part 1

Affliction Z: Fractured Part 2 (Fall 2021)

ABOUT THE AUTHORS

L.T. RYAN is a *Wall Street Journal* and *USA Today* bestselling author, renowned for crafting pulse-pounding thrillers that keep readers on the edge of their seats. Known for creating gripping, character-driven stories, Ryan is the author of the *Jack Noble* series, the *Rachel Hatch* series, and more. With a knack for blending action, intrigue, and emotional depth, Ryan's books have captivated millions of fans worldwide.

Whether it's the shadowy world of covert operatives or the relentless pursuit of justice, Ryan's stories feature unforgettable characters and high-stakes plots that resonate with fans of Lee Child, Robert Ludlum, and Michael Connelly.

When not writing, Ryan enjoys crafting new ideas with coauthors, running a thriving publishing company, and connecting with readers. Discover the next story that will keep you turning pages late into the night.

Connect with L.T. Ryan
Sign up for his newsletter to hear the latest goings on and receive some free content
➜ https://ltryan.com/jack-noble-newsletter-signup-1

Join the private readers' group
➜ https://www.facebook.com/groups/1727449564174357

Instagram ➜ @ltryanauthor
Visit the website ➜ https://ltryan.com
Send an email ➜ contact@ltryan.com

* * *

LAURA CHASE is a corporate attorney-turned-author who brings her courtroom experience to the page in her gripping legal and psychological thrillers. Chase draws on her real-life experience to draw readers into the high-stakes world of courtroom drama and moral ambiguity.

After earning her JD, Chase clerked for a federal judge and thereafter transitioned to big law, where she honed her skills in high-pressure legal environments. Her passion for exploring the darker side of human nature and the gray areas of justice fuels her writing.

Chase lives with her husband, their two sons, a dog and a cat in Northern Florida. When she's not writing or working, she enjoys spending time with her family, traveling, and bingeing true crime shows.

Connect with Laura:

Sign up for her newsletter: www.laurachaseauthor.com/

Follow her on tiktok: @lawyerlaura

Send an email: info@laurachase.com